Her Every Fear

'A **stylish** story, cleverly told from multiple points of view. **Slick and grisly**.' *Sunday Mirror*

'Once again Peter Swanson delivers a thriller that shoves the recent wave of domestic noirs into the shade.' *Reader's Digest*

'A **masterclass** in psychological insight and intricate plotting . . . beware, those with a nervous disposition!' *Lancashire Evening Post*

'Swanson's follow up to the **gripping and dark** *The Kind Worth Killing* is equally suspenseful . . . Edgy all along it builds to an **explosive climax**.' *Lovereading*

'Swanson, who also wrote *The Girl with a Clock for a Heart* and *The Kind Worth Killing*, has quickly established himself as today's **master of the suspense novel**.' Otto Penzler

'Chapter by chapter, the text peels back layers to reveal a pathological relationship between Kate's cousin and a long-ago acquaintance that's reminiscent of a folie à deux out of Patricia Highsmith.' *Wall Street Journal*

'A **compulsive** thriller.' *St. Louis Post Dispatch*

'Psychological thriller devotees should block time to read Swanson's novel in one sitting, preferably in the daylight.' *Library Journal*, starred review

'Swanson's third thriller cracks to life in the opening pages . . . an excellent whodunit with a magical appeal for the mystery thriller lover.' *Seattle Book Review*

'Most readers won't anticipate the **Hitchcockian twists and turns** in this standout suspense tale.' *Washington Post*

Peter Swanson's debut novel, *The Girl with a Clock for a Heart* (2014), was described by Dennis Lehane as 'a twisty, sexy, electric thrill ride' and was nominated for the *LA Times* book award. His follow-up, *The Kind Worth Killing* (2015), a Richard and Judy pick, and a top ten paperback bestseller, was shortlisted for the Ian Fleming Steel Dagger and named the iBook stores Thriller of the Year. Peter Swanson lives with his wife and cat in Somerville, Massachusetts.

@PeterSwanson3
www.peter-swanson.com

Her Every Fear

PETER SWANSON

FABER & FABER

First published in 2017
by Faber & Faber Limited
Bloomsbury House,
74–77 Great Russell Street
London WC1B 3DA

First published in the United States in 2017
by HarperCollins Publishers,
195 Broadway, New York, NY 10007

This paperback edition first published in 2017

Printed and bound by CPI Group (UK) Ltd, Croydon, CR0 4YY

A CIP record for this book
is available from the British Library

ISBN 978-0-571-32712-6

FSC
www.fsc.org
MIX
Paper from
responsible sources
FSC® C101712

2 4 6 8 10 9 7 5 3

For Susan, Jim, David, and Jeremy

Every fear is a desire. Every desire is fear.
The cigarettes are burning under the trees
Where the Staffordshire murderers wait for their accomplices
And victims. Every victim is an accomplice.
—James Fenton, "A Staffordshire Murderer"

PART I

LONG-LEGGEDY BEASTIES

Chapter 1

The fastest route from Logan Airport to downtown Boston is a mile-long tunnel called the Sumner. Dark, damp, and low ceilinged, the Sumner feels as though it were built a hundred years ago, which it very nearly was. And on Friday, April 24, a warm spring evening, a Boston University freshman ran out of gas halfway through the tunnel, reducing rush-hour traffic to just one slow-moving lane, instead of the usual two. Kate Priddy, who had never been to Boston and had no idea she would wind up in a tunnel under Boston Harbor, sat in the back of a stopped taxicab and began to panic.

It was not her first panic attack, not even of that particular day. She'd had one earlier that morning when she'd stepped outside of her flat in Belsize Park in London into a cold, gray dawn and suddenly felt like the whole idea of the apartment swap had been the worst idea she'd ever agreed to. But she'd done her breathing exercises, and repeated her mantra, and told herself that it was too late to back out now. Her second cousin, whom she'd never met, was on an overnight flight from Boston to London at this very instant. He was taking her flat for six months while she was going to live in his apartment in Beacon Hill.

But this attack, with the taxicab stalled in the dark tunnel, was far worse than anything she'd had for a long while. The glistening walls of the endless tunnel curved at the top. It was like being inside a massive constricting snake, and Kate felt her stomach fold within her, her mouth turn dry.

The taxicab crept forward. The backseat smelled of body odor and the flowery perfume of some car deodorant. Kate wanted to roll down the window, but didn't know what taxicab customs were like in the United States. Her stomach folded again, starting to cramp. *When did I last go to the toilet,* she thought, and her panic ratcheted up a notch. It was such a familiar feeling: heart speeding up, limbs turning cold, the world sharpening before her eyes. But she knew what to do. Her therapist's voice was in her head. *It's just a panic attack, an accidental surge of adrenaline. It can't hurt you, or kill you, and no one will notice it. Just let it happen. Float with it. Ride it out.*

But this one's different, Kate told herself. The danger felt real. And suddenly she was back at the cottage in Windermere, crouched and cowering in the locked closet, her nightgown wet with urine, George Daniels on the other side of the door. She felt almost like she'd felt then, cold hands inside of her, twisting her stomach like it was a damp dish towel. There'd been the shotgun blast, then the terrible silence that lasted for hours and hours. When she'd finally been pulled from the closet, her joints stiff and her vocal cords raw from screaming, she didn't know how she was still alive, how the fear hadn't killed her.

The sound of an echoing horn brought her back inside the cab. She pushed the thoughts of Windermere, of George, away, and breathed in as deeply as she could, even though it felt like something heavy was sitting on her chest.

Face it. Accept it. Float with it. Let time pass.

The words weren't working, and Kate could feel her throat closing, becoming a pinhole, her lungs frantically trying to pull in oxygen. The back of the cab now smelled like that closet had, mustiness and rot, as though something had died many summers ago in the walls. She thought of running, and that thought filled her with even more panic. She thought of her pills, her prescription benzodiazepines, that she rarely took anymore but that she'd brought anyway, the way a child who doesn't need his blankie anymore still keeps it close at hand. But the pills were in her suitcase, which was in the bloody boot of the cab. She opened her dry mouth to say something to the cabdriver, to ask him to pop the boot, but the words didn't come out. And that was the moment—one she'd had many times—when she became convinced that she really was dying. *Panic attacks can't kill you. Of course they can't,* she thought, and squeezed her eyes shut anyway, as though a train were barreling down on her. It was the worst thing to do. The world dissolved into a closet full of blackness, death choking her. Her insides began to liquefy.

Face it. Accept it. Float with it. Let time pass.

The cab jolted forward a whole car length, then stopped again, and that small movement made her feel slightly better, as though saying the mantra had caused the car to move in the first place. She repeated it again, while doing her breathing exercises.

The driver shook a hand, his fingers spread, and muttered something at the dirty windshield in a language Kate didn't understand. For some reason, she'd thought that cabdrivers in America would be stereotypically American—short men with caps and cigar stubs and loud American voices. But this cabdriver was turbaned and heavily bearded; except for the fact that he was sitting on the left side of the car, she might as well have been in London.

"How long is this tunnel?" Kate managed to ask through the partition. Her voice sounded cracked and timid in her own ears.

"There's something up ahead."

"Is it always like this?"

"Sometimes," the driver said, then shrugged.

Kate gave up and moved back from the partition. She rubbed her hands along her thighs. The cab kept jerking forward, a few feet at a time, but after it passed the stalled Chevy, two lanes opened up and the cab was moving again. Kate breathed in through her nose and out through her mouth. She unclenched a hand and one of her knuckles cracked. She began to tap her thumb against

6

her fingertips in ordered succession. The pinhole that was her throat opened up a little.

They cleared the tunnel, and Kate caught a glimpse of swollen clouds dominating the sky just before the cab dipped and swayed into another tunnel, but one in which the traffic was barreling along. The cabdriver made up for lost time before emerging onto another fast-moving road that wound along the Charles River. There was enough light left in the sky for Kate to make out the backsides of brick houses whipping past on her left. On the river, a rower on a scull skimmed along its placid surface.

The driver took a sudden, lurching left, doubling back to get onto a narrow road, square, brick houses on either side, blossoming trees along the sidewalk.

"Bury Street," announced the driver.

"It's 101."

"Got it." The driver sped up, then slowed down and halted suddenly, one wheel riding up onto the sidewalk, in front of a brick archway surmounted by a small stone on which the number 101 was carved. Kate could see into a courtyard with a low fountain. The apartment building, three stories high, ran along three sides of the courtyard. Kate's stomach ached a little, a leftover from her earlier panic attack, and she thought guiltily of her second cousin, Corbin Dell, arriving at her unexceptional flat in North London earlier in the day. But he'd known what he was getting. They'd sent several e-mails back and forth. Her one-bedroom was cozy and conveniently located near a tube station, but Corbin's place—she'd seen the pictures—was like something out of a Henry James novel. Still, she hadn't been prepared for the courtyard entrance, very Italian, that seemed out of place with the small amount of Boston she'd already seen.

She waited on the curb while the driver removed her two bags—a large rollie and an even larger duffel bag. She'd gotten dollars at her bank in London the previous week and she paid the driver with the thin, papery notes, not quite knowing what to tip, so probably giving him too much. After he drove off, she balanced the duffel bag onto the rollie and made her way through the archway.

She was midway across the courtyard, paved half in flagstone and half in brick, when the central door swung open and a doorman shaped like a pear darted out waving his hand.

"Hello, hello," he said. He wore a long brown raincoat over a suit, and a peaked cap. Under the cap he wore dark-framed glasses with thick lenses. He had dark black skin and a very white mustache, one side slightly thicker than the other.

"Hi," Kate said. "I'm Katherine Priddy. I'm here to stay in Corbin Dell's apartment."

"Right. I know all about it. Mr. Dell's moving to London for half a year and you're moving here. London's loss and Boston's gain, I suspect." He winked at her, and some of the tension that was still gripping her chest dissipated.

"I don't know about that," Kate said.

"I'm rarely wrong," he said. Kate had read somewhere that Bostonians were notorious for their lack of warmth, but the doorman was proving otherwise.

"I see you brought everything you own," he said, surveying the two bags. Kate sensed, more than saw, a woman pass by her and into the building. The doorman didn't seem to notice.

"If you can get the suitcase, I can get the duffel," Kate said, and the two of them managed to navigate the three worn marble steps that led to the building's lobby. He left the suitcase on the tiled floor and moved swiftly to the other side of the front desk. He was light on his feet for a heavy man.

"I promised Mrs. Valentine I'd call when you got here. She's the president of the building association, and wanted to give you the tour of your new apartment."

"Oh okay," Kate said, looking around. The lobby was narrow but beautiful. A glass-encased four-lamp chandelier hung from the high ceiling. The walls were painted in a lustrous shade of cream.

"Miss Priddy is down here in the lobby," he said into the telephone, then replaced the receiver. "She'll be right down. Let's get your luggage onto the elevator. You're on the third floor of the north wing. You have a nice view of the Charles. Have you been to Boston before?"

While Kate told him that she had actually never been to the States before, a tall, painfully thin woman somewhere in her seventies came down one of the side stairs, her shoes clacking percussively on the tiled steps. She wore a long black dress and a floral scarf around her neck. Her hair was silver and pinned up into an elaborate bun. Kate wondered if she always dressed like this or if she was going out later. The woman introduced herself as Carol and shook Kate's hand. Her hand was like a bundle of chopsticks covered in a layer of tissue paper.

"I'm sure you could have figured out Corbin's apartment all by yourself, Kate, but I thought it wouldn't hurt to have a welcoming committee." After the doorman had loaded Kate's luggage into the elevator, Carol got the key from him, then took Kate up the winding stairway. "Do you mind walking? It's my daily exercise."

Kate told her she was happy to walk, relieved that she didn't have to ride the elevator.

At the third floor, Carol turned left and Kate followed her down a dark, carpeted hall, with a doorway on the left, one on the right, and one at the end. A woman about Kate's age was rapping on the door on the left. Kate thought she was the woman who had flitted by earlier in the courtyard.

"Can I help you?" Carol asked loudly.

The woman turned. She wore jeans and a scoop-neck sweater. Her dark hair was cut in a bob, and she was almost pretty, except for the lack of a chin. It was so noticeable that Kate wondered, for a moment, if she'd been in some kind of terrible chin-obliterating accident.

"Do you work here? Could I get a key for this door?

I'm worried about my friend." Her voice was nasal, pitched high with anxiety.

"Why are you worried?" Carol asked. "Is everything okay?"

"I can't get in touch with her. We were supposed to have lunch, and I called her work and she didn't show up there, either. And now I'm worried."

"Did you talk with our doorman?"

"No, I just came straight up here. It's not like her, you know. I've texted her, like, a thousand times."

"I'm sorry," Carol said. "I don't have a key, myself, but maybe you should speak with our doorman Bob. He'll know something. What's the name of your friend?" Carol had started to walk again, and so did Kate.

"Audrey Marshall. Do you know her?"

"I've met her, dear, but don't know much about her. Go talk with Bob. He'll help you. He *should* have helped you when you first arrived."

Kate found herself walking along the edge of the hall, her shoulder almost rubbing against the paneled wall. The upset friend, with her shrill, panicked voice, had caused Kate's chest to seize up again, the panic inside of her like an expanding balloon. She thought of her pills, in the toiletry bag in the rollie, unreachable for now.

"It's so unusual," Carol was saying, as she slid a key into the lock of the door at the end, "for someone to be in here without having gone through the doorman first. I'm sure there's actually nothing wrong with anybody."

She said this as though nothing bad had ever happened to anyone anywhere. It was the type of ridiculous but well-meaning proclamation that Kate's father might make. Kate, herself, from the moment she saw the worried woman knocking frantically on her new neighbor's door, knew that someone was dead. It was how her mind worked. And knowing that her mind worked that way—constantly stretching logic all the way to its worst possible conclusion—did not lessen her certainty. Already that day, Kate had *known* that the youth with the sweaty forehead and the fuzzy mustache in the departures lounge was carrying a homemade explosive device in his backpack. And she had *known* that the stretch of turbulence over the Atlantic Ocean would grow in ferocity until it ripped one of the jet's wings off as easily as a sadistic child shredding a butterfly. These hadn't happened, but that didn't mean that behind the door down the hall, there wasn't a dead or dying girl. Of course there was.

Kate turned her attention to Carol, who was still fiddling with the key. She wondered if the tumblers of the lock were too much for Carol's birdlike bones to handle, then heard, with immense relief, the oily snap of the door unlocking. Even though she'd never been in Corbin's apartment, she'd already taken possession of it in her mind. She badly wanted to get inside and feel the safety of a home. It felt like years since she'd stepped out of the comfort of her London flat, double-checking the lock of the outside door, a minicab idling at the curb. Carol swung the door inward just as Kate heard voices again in the hall. She turned to see the doorman, Bob, lugging the duffel bag, the chinless woman at his side protesting her case. "Let me take care of this young lady first, then we'll see to your friend," he was saying.

Carol ushered Kate into her new home, and Kate immediately asked for the toilet. "Of course, dear, there's one attached to the bedroom," Carol said, pointing, and Kate walked rapidly, barely taking in the extravagance of her surroundings before shutting herself into an enormous bathroom, tiled in black and white. She sat on the toilet lid, and even though she knew the pills weren't there, she opened her purse anyway. Inside, tucked into the side pocket, was her plastic bottle of benzodiazepines. As soon as she saw them, she remembered moving the bottle from her suitcase to her bag early that morning. How had she forgotten that so soon? With trembling hands she unscrewed the lid and dry-swallowed a pill. A feeling of dread—almost worse than the panic—spread over her.

She should never have come to America.

Chapter 2

Even though the apartment was enormous, it shouldn't have taken Carol Valentine thirty minutes to deliver the tour, but she clearly relished the role. She pointed out the walnut-stained oak floors, the coffered ceilings, the working fireplace, and what she called the Juliet balcony, which was really just a hip-high railing one foot out from the floor-to-ceiling French doors that Kate knew she would never open. The apartment wasn't particularly high up, but it was high enough.

"You like it?" Carol asked, after the tour was complete, even though Kate had expressed her admiration about thirty times already.

"I do. I love it. Cozy."

"It's beautifully furnished, don't you think? You'd think a young man like Corbin . . ." Carol left the thought unfinished and smiled with just her mouth, the papery skin that covered her face shifting in such a way that Kate felt like she could see the exact contours of the woman's skull. "What's your apartment—your flat—like in London?"

"All of it would fit in this living room," Kate said. "I'm feeling a little guilty. I got the better bargain."

"Yes, but London . . ."

Kate yawned, quickly covering her mouth.

"My dear, you must be exhausted. I forgot all about the time change."

"I am tired," Kate said. "It's my bedtime if I were home."

"Well, try to stay up a little later than you usually do so you get used to it here. And as soon as you get settled in, you'll have to come and have a drink. I'm on the other side, exactly opposite. Our place has the same layout as yours. These end apartments are the absolute best in the building. Especially yours, since you have a view toward the city *and* a view toward the river." She lowered her voice, as though the other apartments might hear what she was saying.

"It's beautiful," Kate said.

"The building was modeled after a Venetian palazzo, you know."

"I thought it looked Italian. The courtyard."

"The architect was from Boston, but he visited Italy and came back here. This was *years* ago, of course. My husband would love to tell you all about it when you come for that drink."

Carol left, and Kate shut the door behind her. She stood for a moment, still rattled by what had happened in the bathroom, finding her pills in her purse after forgetting that she'd moved them there. But since then, she'd talked herself through it a little, and she'd calmed down.

15

Or maybe the pill was simply doing its job, spreading its calming fingers over her skin.

She retoured the apartment herself this time, taking in all the details, the built-in bookshelves, the paintings on the wall. Every room was beautifully furnished but somehow impersonal, as though all the items had been picked out by a decorator, which they probably had. In the bedroom, across from a king-sized bed with a cushioned headboard, there was a low bureau, the top of which was covered with about fifteen framed photographs. Family pictures, most in black and white, most taken on holiday. Boats and beaches. Kate studied them. She recognized Corbin's father, her mother's cousin, but only from other photographs she'd seen. He was in most of the pictures, usually with Corbin and Kate's other second cousin, Philip. Kate wondered why Corbin had no pictures of his mother on the bureau, but then it occurred to her that this apartment had been owned by Corbin's divorced father before he died, and these must be the father's pictures, not the son's.

Kate wondered how much of the rest of the apartment was in the style of the father. She guessed most of it. From what she'd gathered from her mother, Richard Dell had moved to Boston sometime in the 1970s to be with his American wife. His work had something to do with finance ("moving lots and lots of money around," Lucy Priddy told her daughter), and during the 1980s, he made a fortune. Richard and Amanda, his wife, had lived on the North Shore, in a seaside mansion in the town of New Essex. When their children were teenagers, they got divorced, Amanda keeping the seaside house and Richard buying the apartment at 101 Bury Street in Boston. The apartment had been left to Corbin after Richard died in a swimming accident while on holiday in Bermuda.

Kate had learned all this information two months earlier, during Sunday dinner with her parents.

"Your second cousin Corbin got in touch with me," Lucy had said. They were in the conservatory, done with dinner, but still drinking wine. Kate's father, Patrick, was taking Alice, their border terrier, for her walk.

"Oh," Kate said.

"I don't think you've ever met him. Have you met him?"

"He's your cousin Richard's son, right? The one who died a few years ago?"

"He drowned, yes. You met Richard, actually, at Charlotte's wedding. I don't know if you remember. I met Corbin for the first time at his father's funeral." Kate's parents had traveled all the way to Massachusetts for the funeral, although they'd tied the trip in with a driving tour up the Maine coast, something they'd both always wanted to do.

"He seemed very sweet. And so handsome. Almost looked like—who's that actor you like from *Spooks*? Rupert something."

"Rupert Penry-Jones. Why are you telling me this? I feel like you're on the verge of telling me you've arranged my marriage to a second cousin. Have we gone back in time?"

Lucy laughed; the spontaneous version, not the contrived ringing bells that sometimes came out in social situations. "Yes, darling. It's all arranged. No, but I'm telling you this for a reason. I haven't slipped into full senility. Corbin Dell is moving to London—a company transfer, or something—for six months, and he sent me an e-mail because he knows you live in London."

"He didn't ask to stay with me, did he?"

"No, no. Of course not. But he did say he wanted to check and see if you were potentially interested in a home swap. He said he'd love to have someone staying at his place in Boston, and then he could stay at your place, and that way he'd save some money, and you'd have the opportunity to spend half a year in America."

Kate took a sip of her wine. It was white, and far too sweet. "What would I do in Boston?"

"I thought that maybe you could take classes, like you've been talking about. They must have graphic design schools. And you'd keep drawing, of course."

"What about my job?" Kate had just gone from part-time to full-time at an art-supply store in Hampstead.

"Well, that's not a career, exactly, is it?"

Kate, who agreed with her mother on that point, was annoyed nonetheless and said nothing. A part of her knew that this was the type of situation she'd be foolish to turn down. Six months in another country. She'd never been to America, and Boston was supposed to be nice. A manageable city, she'd heard, not like New York or Chicago, or London, for that matter. She'd have a place to live. Probably a beautiful place to live. And the more that these reasons popped into her head, the more anxious she got, realizing that she would probably turn it down. It was too soon. She was better, but she wasn't completely well yet.

"I feel like I'm just getting settled in London, and everything is going smoothly, and I just don't know if I should rock the boat."

"Absolutely, Kate. He asked, so I thought I'd ask. I totally understand." As her mother spoke, Kate realized that her mother had never believed that Kate would actually take the opportunity to move to Boston for half a year. It was this thought that pestered Kate for the remainder of the afternoon. Her father returned from walking Alice, and the three decided to go to the White Swan in Braintree center for one more before Kate had to catch a train back to London. Kate was tipsy on the ride home, her mind picturing all the things that could go right in Boston, then all the things that could go wrong. And she kept thinking about the tone of her mother's voice, the way she'd clearly known that Kate was going to say no. It was that, more than anything, that caused Kate to ring up her parents when she got back to her flat in London and tell them that she'd changed her mind.

"Oh," her mother said.

"I think I'd be foolish to not do it. There's nothing keeping me here, right now. Except you and Dad, of course."

"We'd come visit."

"Tell Corbin I'd like to do it. Or better yet, send me his e-mail and I'll tell him myself."

She'd written Corbin that night, before she lost her nerve. He'd been thrilled. They arranged the swap from late April to early October. Kate had given notice at her job, then had found a graphic design school were she could take courses in InDesign and Illustrator. And now she was here, her first class scheduled for Monday afternoon. Kate walked back down the hallway that led to the living room, where Bob the doorman had deposited her bags. She knew she should unpack, but a wave of tiredness spread through her. Also, hunger. She went to the kitchen, with its limestone counters and stainless steel appliances. It looked like it had never been used. She opened the fridge. All alone on the middle shelf was a bottle of champagne, a yellow sticky note attached to it. *Welcome, Kate—Enjoy!* was written in cramped handwriting. A pang of guilt went through Kate that she hadn't left anything for Corbin in her flat, although she'd left him a much longer note, welcoming him and describing the neighborhood.

Except for the champagne and an assortment of condiments, the refrigerator was practically bare. She opened the freezer and found a stack of frozen dinners from someplace called Trader Joe's. She read the directions on the back of a frozen boeuf bourguignon and decided she could handle it. The box was familiar and yet different, the nutritional information using ounces instead of grams and calories instead of energy. She figured out the microwave and began to heat up the dinner, then filled and emptied a water glass from the tap before wondering if the water was okay to drink. It tasted okay, but different than the water she was used to drinking. More minerals. After pouring herself a glass of champagne, she walked to the front door and pressed her eye to the peephole, wondering what had happened with the missing girl down the hall. Would Bob have let the friend in? Probably not, she thought, and wondered what the friend would do next. The police would probably not be helpful. Kate had watched enough American police procedurals to know that you couldn't file a missing persons report if the person had been missing for less than a day. The hallway was empty. Maybe Kate had overreacted and nothing was really wrong. Maybe the girl had grown tired of her pushy, chinless friend.

Kate ate the dinner, surprisingly good, sitting on one of the stools around the L-shaped granite island in the kitchen. She poured a second glass of champagne, took one sip, and was overcome again with exhaustion. Her head was heavy on her neck, her stomach slightly queasy. She had planned on unpacking and setting up her laptop so that she could send e-mails, and she'd hoped to watch some American television, but instead she rolled her suitcase into the bedroom, dug around in it to find her toiletry kit, plus the boxers and T-shirt she liked to sleep in, then managed to brush her teeth and wash her face before climbing between the cool, crisp sheets. Despite being exhausted, she lay awake for a time, listening to the barely discernible sounds of the apartment: the far-off rumble of traffic, the muffled click of a heating system, something else—a soft hissing—she couldn't identify. The bed, she thought, before falling asleep, was the most comfortable bed she had ever lain on. She sank into its grip.

Kate woke once. Intermittent blue lights were flashing along a diagonal stretch of the high ceilings. *Where are the sirens?* Kate thought. Then: *Where am I?* And, finally, after a confused two seconds, she remembered. Her mouth was dry and she was desperately thirsty. She heard what sounded like a distant train. She rolled to either side, looking for the illuminated numbers of a clock to tell her what time it was, but, except for the police lights streaking through the c urtained windows, the room was black.

*

Kate sat up, then lay back down. She was far too tired to even find the bathroom and get a drink of water. What was the name of that neighbor again? The girl who was missing? Audrey Marshall, Kate remembered. She was good with names. It was her superpower, George had said. He'd dubbed her Never-Forgets-a-Name-Girl. Kate closed her eyes, heard someone whispering to her in a dream, and jolted awake again. The voices disappeared, and the room was dark again. Had she dreamed the police lights? *I'll find out about it tomorrow,* she thought, and let herself fall back into a black pool of sleep.

Chapter 3

She did find out about it, but not until late the following day.

She woke early, the room still dark. She knew she should try to sleep in a little later, to adjust herself to Boston time, but she was wide awake and desperate for coffee.

It took a while, but she found the coffeemaker and some coffee and figured out how it all worked. While the coffee brewed, she walked around the enormous apartment again. The thin light of morning was beginning to suffuse the windows. The largest room of the apartment, the central living room, had the view of the Charles River, quiet in the gray dawn, traces of mist above its unruffled surface. There was a footbridge that spanned both the river and the road next to it.

The living room looked ready for a cocktail party. There were scattered chairs, plus two large couches facing one another, and in between them a glass-topped coffee table. Kate hated glass tables. Putting anything on one made her think it would instantly shatter, or at least crack. She always lived in the next moment, the tragic moment. For this reason, she'd always loathed low railings, crossing busy streets, waiters carrying multiple plates. These had always been prickly, annoying phobias, but then, five years earlier, the incident with George had happened and her life had changed forever. She couldn't leave her house for over a year. No, worse than that. She couldn't even imagine leaving her house; fear and grief had immobilized her. Her parents and her therapist had slowly pulled her out of that hole, and life had gotten better. It was inconceivable to her that she had made it all the way to the States, to this enormous apartment with its glass table. She didn't like the glass table, but she could live with it.

There was no television in the living room, and she wondered, with a sense of horror, if the apartment was television free. Then she remembered what Carol Valentine had called "the den," a dark-wood-paneled room with a soft leather couch. For a brief moment, she couldn't remember where the den was located, but it was off the hallway that led toward the two guest bedrooms. She was right; the television was there—a monstrous screen hidden behind wooden doors built into a bookshelf. On the table (thankfully not glass) in front of the couch, there was a universal remote on top of a laminated card listing at least a hundred channels.

There was also a large wooden desk in the den, and Kate noticed a sticky note on its surface. It listed the name of a wireless account ("Angel Face") and a password. It made her realize that she ought to check in with her parents, and also with Corbin, to make sure he'd made it safely to her own flat.

Kate retrieved her laptop and adapter from her suitcase, stopped back in the kitchen for a mug of black coffee, and returned to the den. She marveled once again at the expanse of the apartment. She sat at the desk, the leather chair creaking authentically. She had many e-mails, mostly junk, but one from her mother and one from Corbin. She opened Corbin's first:

Kate,

It only took the driver a few false turns but we finally found your beautiful flat, and I read your incredibly thoughtful note. I'm ashamed I didn't write a similar thing for you, and I have no excuse, but once I'm used to the jet lag I will send you an exhaustive list of good bars and restaurants near my apartment. I promise.

Quick question: I see you have a washer but don't see a dryer. Am I missing something?

More later. I'm looking forward to the next six months.

Corbin

Kate wrote back:

> I am too. When I walked into your place, I thought
> that I must have come to the wrong apartment.
> How gorgeous. I'm truly ashamed of my measly
> flat with a washing machine that also thinks it's
> a dryer. It *is* a dryer, as well, that's why you're so
> confused. There are instructions in the drawer on
> the left of the sink, I think. My advice, however, is
> that if you start a clothes wash don't expect dry
> clothes for at least a day. Please don't hesitate to
> write with any more questions. I really am in love
> with your apartment. Best, Kate
>
> P.S. Thanks for the lovely champagne, which is
> gone, of course.

Next, Kate read her mother's e-mail—"so proud of you, darling"—and responded to that as well. She sipped at her coffee, so much better than the instant coffee she was used to drinking. She could hear a police siren in the distance and suddenly remembered the night before, falling asleep, and how she could see police lights on her ceiling. Had that been real, or part of a dream? For a moment she didn't know, and she was filled with a sense of dread again, the same feeling she'd had when she found her pills in her purse after being sure they weren't there. *Am I losing my mind?* she thought. Then told herself: *No, it wasn't a dream*. It had definitely been real. Maybe something actually had happened with the girl from down the hall.

Kate unpacked her toiletries, then showered in the en suite bathroom. The shower was enormous, the head coming straight out of the ceiling, dumping a deluge of water. Again, Kate thought of her own flat in London, the bathtub that had been converted to a shower with its rubber tube that was always flopping out of its holder. After showering, Kate dressed in dark tights and her favorite Boden dress, and decided that she would brave the outside world. Before coming to Boston, she'd studied Google Maps images of her neighborhood and located the nearest pharmacy and the nearest market. Her plan was to go out and get the basic essentials to get her through the next few days. On Monday, she was starting at the Graphics Institute in Cambridge, about five subway stops away. She was not looking forward to that particular ride, but she knew she could do it—her therapist in London had had her take the tube several times as practice.

"The tube's a choice," Kate had said to Theodora. "I can take taxis everywhere."

"It's all a choice, isn't it," her therapist had said back to her. That placid northern accent had irritated Kate to no end when she had first met Theodora, but she had grown used to it, just as she'd grown used to the halo of curly hair and the purple jumpers.

"Well, I don't choose to skydive, either. You're not going to make me do that, are you?"

"No, I won't make you skydive, but riding the Underground, and taking elevators, and flying I will make you do. That's all part of a life you want, isn't it, Kate?"

She'd been right, of course. Life was full of tight places and sealed exits. She'd learn to deal with them.

Kate left the apartment, locking the door behind her. She slowed as she passed the missing girl's door, listening for any sounds, but there weren't any. She took the stairs down to the lobby, passed the doorman, and walked straight out into the courtyard. The sky was gray and scalloped, the light so much like dusk that Kate had an alarmed moment when she wondered if she'd slept through the entire day. A waft of cigarette smoke reached her nostrils. Kate had quit smoking after university, but she still loved the smell. She looked for the source and saw a man perched on the edge of the courtyard's central fountain. He was rubbing the cigarette out on a flagstone. Kate was walking past him as he began to stand.

"Sorry," he said, indicating the snuffed-out cigarette in his fingers.

"I don't mind," Kate said, stopping and looking at him. He was thin, verging on gaunt, but with wide shoulders. His narrow face was dominated by a large, crooked nose. His eyes were grayish-green and deeply sunken, and his skin was lightly pocked with ancient acne. He should have been ugly, but he wasn't. All his outsized features combined into a sad and handsome face.

"I actually don't smoke. I've quit. But then I found this

one cigarette in my drawer and figured I'd smoke it, just to remind myself how awful it is."

His voice was deep and friendly, and Kate, jet-lagged and still confused about the time of day, felt a ruffle of weakness in her legs. "Was it awful?" she asked.

"No, of course not. It was great."

"Smoking's great," Kate said. Why were they speaking like old friends? Was this how people spoke with strangers in America?

"You smoke?"

"I did. I quit. It wasn't easy."

"How'd you do it?"

"By not smoking."

The man laughed. His teeth were alarmingly white, the top ones straight and the bottom ones slightly overlapping. "I'm Alan Cherney."

"I'm Kate. I'm living here, temporarily." She was shy suddenly, and didn't provide her last name.

"You're English?" he asked.

"I am. I'm staying at my cousin's apartment, here, and he's staying at my flat in London."

"Which apartment is it?" Alan Cherney's eyes scanned the building.

Kate bobbed her head in the direction of her wing. "Uh, Corbin Dell's place. Up there."

"Ah, north wing. I'm on the other side, third floor. I know Corbin. A little."

"You know him better than I know him. We've never met."

"That's funny," Alan said. "How'd that come about?"

Kate told him the story, omitting the fact that the trip for Kate was at least partly inspired by her need to overcome the past traumas of her life.

"Well, you got a good deal," Alan said. "These are pretty nice apartments."

"How long have you lived here?"

"Just over a year. I moved in with a girlfriend—a rich girlfriend—and she moved out, and I can't really afford it anymore, so I need to start thinking about finding a new place."

"Sorry about that."

"Sorry about what?" he said. "Sorry I lost my girlfriend, or sorry I'm going to have to move out?"

Kate laughed. "I don't know. Sorry about both."

He smirked and said: "Sorry you used to have a rich girlfriend and a beautiful apartment, and next month you'll be alone in some hovel."

"Something like that."

A gust of wind peeled a sodden yellow leaf off the brick courtyard and plastered it on Kate's boot. She bent over to pick it off. When she stood, there was a moment of silence, and Kate realized she'd been talking with this stranger for close to fifteen minutes.

"Well," she said, but didn't continue. Her eyes skidded off his, and she felt the prickle of a blush suffusing her cheeks. For one brief, terrifying moment she knew that if he'd asked, she'd have followed him straight up to his apartment and into his bed. He was handsome, yes, even with the large, crooked nose, but she'd have followed him because it felt as though they had known each other for years.

"You need to go," he said, speaking her thought out loud.

"Yes." And then they both laughed.

"I'm in apartment 3L," he said. "I'm not leaving anytime soon. We'll see each other."

"Okay," Kate said.

She started to move away, then stopped. "Do you know a woman named Audrey Marshall? She lives here."

Alan's brow creased. "I do know Audrey. Well, I know *who* she is. I don't actually know her."

"When I got in last night, a friend of hers was at her door, looking for her, saying she'd gone missing."

Kate expected him to dismiss it, but instead he said: "That doesn't sound good. She's not the type to go missing."

"What do you mean?"

"Oh, I don't know. I guess I mean she's always around. I see her around. A lot. I'm sure she'll turn up."

*

Kate had brought a printed map of her neighborhood, but she'd studied it so many times in the previous weeks that she didn't need to remove it from her bag. She navigated down Bury to Charles Street, where she got a breakfast sandwich and another coffee from a packed Starbucks. The second coffee was a mistake. She was jittery and wired while shopping at an upscale grocery store with tight, congested aisles. She had been planning on getting ingredients for a pasta she liked to make with smoked salmon, but a mild panic had set in, and she bought only a loaf of sourdough bread, some cheddar cheese, milk, and two bottles of red wine. Back out on the street, warm, mild rain had mixed in with the gusty air. It felt good against her skin after the overheated store, and she walked slowly back along Charles, noting, for future reference, a bar that looked well lit and friendly, plus a coffeehouse much less crowded than Starbucks had been.

She deliberately walked past the gaslit side street that would take her back up the hill to Bury Street, and continued to the outskirts of the Public Garden. Her groceries were heavy, but she wanted to at least see the famous park. The rain was picking up, and several parents were ushering their kids away from a line of bronze ducks. Willow trees shimmered by the pond. She almost entered the park, but decided against it. She was here for six months and there would be time.

Kate swung through the doors into the lobby. She introduced herself to the doorman, Sanibel, a thin man with high cheekbones and ink-black hair. He offered to help her with her bags. She said, "No, thanks," just as a white cat that had been perched on the lobby desk jumped to the floor and rubbed against Kate's shin.

"That's Sanders," the doorman said.

"Does Sanders belong to you?"

"No, no. He belongs to Mrs. Halperin. Upstairs." He indicated with a fractional move of his head the direction of Kate's own apartment. "He likes to go everywhere, though. All over. Unlike Mrs. Halperin."

Kate walked up the stairs, Sanders following her. Carol Valentine had mentioned Florence Halperin; she had the other apartment on Kate's wing. Passing the door, Kate noticed it was cracked open, presumably for Sanders, but the cat followed Kate down to her own door and managed to slide into the apartment, even with Kate trying to block the way with her foot.

She put away her groceries, then went and found Sanders. He had leapt onto one of the windowsills and was looking out at the rainy day. Kate scooped him up, expecting resistance, but he arranged his back paws on Kate's forearm and his front paws on her shoulder, and purred quietly into her neck. Kate, usually ambivalent toward cats, felt a surge of affection. She carried him to the hallway, saying, "Wrong apartment, Sanders," and dropped him back onto the hall carpet. She quickly shut the door as he padded away.

Kate went to the bedroom and got the sketchbook that she'd brought with her from London. It was brand-new, a way to commemorate the beginning of her time in a new country. She removed a charcoal pencil from a fresh pack, then sat down on the lushly carpeted floor and thought about trying to draw Sanders. Instead, she drew Alan Cherney's face, getting it just about perfect. Something was a little off, the eyes spaced too close together, the hairline a little too low, so she pulled out a kneaded eraser and fixed it. It took her longer to fix the sketch than it had to draw it, but then it was him. She wrote his name, and the date under it, then added BOSTON, MASSACHUSETTS. She almost exclusively drew portraits, and her sketchbooks were comprised of the faces of people she had recently met. She had stacks of these notebooks, the earliest ones from grade school. Flipping through them—something she often did, especially when she'd been housebound—was like reading a diary. She'd find faces of close friends that she'd sketched hours after she'd met them for the first time, and she'd find faces of people she'd forgotten all about. Looking at Alan's likeness, she wondered if, ten years from now, she'd even recognize who he was. Or maybe it would turn out to be the drawing she'd done right after meeting her future husband. Probably the former.

She flipped to a blank page, closed her eyes, and tried to picture Carol Valentine, the older woman who had given her the tour of the apartment. She could remember her eyes, her forehead, her hair, and her neck, but couldn't quite picture her nose and mouth. Instead of drawing her, she drew herself; she could remember the way she'd looked that morning in the mirror of the bathroom. Her hair, recently cut, tucked behind one ear. Her eyes a little puffier than usual from the long, dehydrating flight. But she gave herself a slight smile, a smile that ended up looking like the frightened smile of a nervous bridesmaid about to deliver a speech. It didn't quite capture her mood, but she left it as it was. She almost never erased her self-portraits.

On the next page, she drew Sanibel, the doorman she'd just met. Instead of drawing just his face, she drew him standing next to his desk, and she added Sanders down by his legs. She was not used to drawing cats, and Sanders looked wrong, menacing when he was anything but.

She slid the sketchbook under the bed and stood. She was hungry again, went to the kitchen, and ate some bread and cheese, thought about opening some wine, then decided against it. The rain outside was now slashing against the windows, and she thought, randomly, of a painter whipping a spray of paint across a canvas. She stared at the kitchen windows for a while, deciding that she loved her new apartment, not for its obvious luxury, but for its high ceilings and oversized windows. She could breathe in this place. She decided to make tea, realized she hadn't bought any, but then found a box of Red Rose in one of the high cupboards. She filled a kettle with water, put it on the gas stove, then went into the living room. One wall had built-in bookshelves, and she looked at some of the selections. Hardcover nonfiction, mostly, although there was one complete shelf of John D. MacDonald paperbacks. She plucked one out. *Darker*

Than Amber. A Travis McGee adventure. The cover had a pulpy image of a sexy girl in a crop top. The pages were yellowed with age. These had to have belonged to Corbin's father, Kate thought. Where were Corbin's books? Did he have any? Below the Travis McGee books was a shelf of other paperback mysteries. She pulled out a Dick Francis—*Bonecrack*—that she didn't think she'd read yet, and brought it with her to the long beige sofa under the largest window in the room. She lay down and read the first few paragraphs, then closed her eyes and fell immediately to sleep.

She dreamed of the park, the pond now whipping and rippling in the ferocious rain. She stood under one of the willow trees, its branches yellow. George Daniels was on the other side of the pond. Kate wasn't surprised that he was in Boston—and she wasn't surprised that he was still alive—because in her dreams he was always alive, and he was always coming after her. He spotted her hiding under her willow tree and began to swim across the pond. Kate had a rifle with her, and when George came out of the pond, dripping and smiling, she shot him several times, the bullets pocking his shirt but not doing much else. One of the bullets struck him on the chin, and he brushed it away like it was a horsefly. He kept coming.

She woke, neck and chest filmed in sweat, then smelled something bitter and acrid in the air. She remembered the kettle, leapt from the couch, the Dick Francis falling to the floor, and ran to the kitchen to shut the gas off. The kettle had boiled dry and was beginning to smoke. She opened one of the windows as far as she could and, using a hand towel, put the smoldering kettle on the windowsill. The rain striking it made sharp hissing sounds. Something about the near-disaster made tears spring to her eyes. Then she remembered her dream. George in the park, the bullets barely penetrating his shirt. It almost made her smile that he'd followed her to America in her dreams. Of course he had. If her dreams were a realm, George was king for life.

After the kettle cooled down she took it from the windowsill. Its bottom was completely black; she'd have to buy a replacement. The metal was still warm, so she put it in the deep stainless steel sink and returned to the couch. This time she read half of the book before falling back to sleep.

*

She was woken by a knock on the door. She blinked herself awake, momentarily confused by what time it was. It was daylight outside still, but the inside of the apartment was dark and dusky. There was another knock, louder and longer. She stood, her knees popping. How long had she been asleep?

She went to the door and peered through its peephole. She almost expected to see Alan, but it was a woman's face through the fish-eye lens, a woman with close-cropped hair, coffee-colored skin, and dark brown eyes. The calm disinterest in those eyes made Kate say *policewoman* to herself. *Audrey Marshall's dead,* came a voice. It was George Daniels, whispering in her head. Kate swung the door open.

Chapter 4

The woman introduced herself as Detective James, unclipping a badge from her belt and holding it up for Kate to see. Kate invited her in, noticing before she shut the door that two uniformed officers stood a little ways down the hall, one of their radios crackling.

"Is Audrey Marshall dead?" Kate asked automatically.

"Why do you ask that?" the detective asked, a touch of surprise in her eyes.

"I, uh, heard that she was missing."

"When did you hear she was missing?"

Kate explained about her arrival the evening before, the friend in the hallway who was pounding on the door.

"When was that exactly?" the detective asked, pulling out a small notebook from the inside of her dark gray suit jacket.

Kate gave her best guess at the approximate time and the detective wrote it down. Kate studied her while she wrote. She had a long face, with high cheekbones, and Kate didn't think she was wearing any makeup. The detective raised her eyes from her notebook, and Kate watched her nostrils minutely flare.

"I left the kettle on," Kate said.

"I'm sorry. I don't—"

"I left the kettle on the stove earlier and I burnt it. That's the smell."

"Oh. I did notice that."

"Do you want to sit down?"

The detective's eyes scanned the room briefly before she said, "No, thanks. I'm just collecting statements right now. And I'd like to get a little more information from you regarding timelines."

"She is dead, right?" Kate asked.

"We are investigating a suspicious death in the apartment next to yours. We don't have a proper identification yet on the body."

"Okay."

"You said you just came over here from London, right? You didn't know her?"

"No, I don't know anyone here. It was a murder, then?"

"We're treating it as a suspicious death, yes. What can you tell me about the owner of this apartment?"

"He's a second cousin. Corbin Dell. I don't actually know him, either. We've never met, but we arranged this house swap because he's been transferred to London for his work."

The detective wrote something else down on her pad, while asking: "I don't suppose you know whether Corbin Dell had any kind of relationship with Audrey Marshall?"

"No, I have no idea."

"Can you give me the phone number for your apartment in London?"

"It doesn't have one, actually. I just use my mobile. But I have Corbin's e-mail. I can get it for you, if you'd like?"

"That'd be great," the detective said.

Kate went to the computer in the study and brought up her e-mail page. There were several unread messages, in bold, at the top, including a response from Corbin. She opened it:

> Thanks for recommending the Beef and Pudding. Can't say I'd have tried that one if left to my own devices. It reminded me a little of a place called St. Stephen's Tavern near where you are. Check it out. Also, met a neighbor of yours named Martha something. She seemed to recognize me, or else she heard my loud American accent and just guessed. Hope all's well. C

Kate found a piece of scrap paper and jotted down Corbin's e-mail address. She'd worry about the Martha situation later.

She brought the scrap of paper to Detective James, who was now looking at the screen of her cell phone. "Thanks. I'll write him," she said, folding the piece of paper and sliding it into her jacket pocket.

"Should I let him know before you do? He just e-mailed me, and if I wrote him back . . ."

"You can tell him the police were here and that we'll be in touch. I don't want to make any pronouncements about Audrey Marshall till we have an identification, okay?"

"Yes, of course."

"You've been very helpful." She was turning back toward the door. Kate went around her and opened it. There was now a small crowd in the hall, including an older man in a suit who immediately spotted Detective James and said, "Jesus. There you are."

Before leaving, Detective James said: "We might need to search your apartment. Would you agree to that?"

"Why?" Kate asked.

The detective pressed her lips together before saying, "If we find anything that might connect the death next door with your cousin, then we'll need to take a look around. That's all."

"It's okay with me, I guess," Kate said.

"Thank you very much. We'll be in touch." The detective handed Kate her card before leaving. Kate studied it after shutting the door. ROBERTA JAMES, DETECTIVE. Under the name were the Boston Police Department shield, a phone number, and an e-mail.

Kate pressed her ear to the door to see if she could hear anything from the hallway. There were noises—the squawk of radios and the muddy tones of indiscernible voices. She looked through the peephole and saw the same detective knocking on the door of the third apartment on her hall. The door swung open, and the detective held up her badge to its resident; Kate couldn't see into the apartment. While the other neighbor was being questioned, two more plainclothes officers entered the hall from the stairwell, both heavyset men in dark suits. One was clean-shaven and the other sported a gray goatee.

A ripple of panic swept over Kate, not so much because of the murdered neighbor, but because her exit was blocked by all those police officers. Something about walking down a hallway filled with police and crime scene investigators seemed impossible. Kate backed her way into the apartment, breathing through her nostrils and blowing out through her mouth. She calmed herself and picked over the brief conversation with the detective. Was it standard practice after a murder to search the nearby residences? Kate didn't think so. There must be a reason. She went to the computer and searched for Audrey Marshall. It was a common name, bringing up many genealogy sites and several Facebook profiles. She added Boston to the search and found a blocked LinkedIn profile but with an image attached. She clicked on it. It wasn't a large image, and it was in black and white, but showed a woman with intensely large eyes and a boy's short haircut, almost like Jean Seberg's hair in that movie *Breathless*. She worked for a publishing house in Boston, and all her previous employment had been in New York City. Kate knew she'd found the right Audrey Marshall. She stared into the pixelated eyes on the computer screen and they stared back at her. *I'm dead now,* those eyes said, *but this is what I looked like when I was alive.* Audrey Marshall had been pretty, and Kate wondered if Corbin Dell and she had been involved in any way. They must have known each other, or seen each other frequently when they were coming and going.

Kate stood, knowing what she needed to do. Well, knowing what she *wanted* to do. She'd search the apartment herself. If the police were going to look around, maybe she'd look around first, and be able to find what they were looking for. It would give her something to do, a purpose. She started her search in the bedroom, going through every drawer, looking for hiding places, lifting the mattress. She was struck, as she had been when she first looked around the place, by the lack of personal items. She did find an old battered bureau in the corner of the walk-in closet that was filled with photographs, most still in their envelopes from the developing place. She quickly flipped through several of them; they were obviously photographs that had belonged to Corbin's father. Old family vacations. Christmas Day celebrations. A whole roll dedicated to what looked like a vintage Porsche speedster. Where were Corbin's photographs? On his computer, and his phone, of course, like Kate's own pictures.

She searched the bathroom, then the main living area, and then the kitchen. It was in the kitchen that she found something that might be relevant. In one of the drawers, behind the cutlery tray, there were several loose keys. Some were unmarked, but a few were affixed with a white circular tag, block letters saying what they were for. One said STORAGE, and one said N.E. HOUSE, and one had the initials AM. Did Corbin have a key to Audrey Marshall's apartment? If so, why? It could mean so many things. Maybe they had been in a romantic relationship, close enough that they'd exchanged keys. Or it could simply be a key he kept so that he could water her plants when she was away.

She continued to search the rest of the apartment. She found more remnants from Corbin's father's life than she found from Corbin's. In the den, in a closet, she found a cardboard box of videotapes with labels like CLARISSA'S WEDDING and CHATHAM RENTAL, AUGUST '95. There was an old leather football in the box as well. Kate ran her finger over its dusty surface. This box with the videotapes and football was sitting on a larger plastic container that looked like a recent addition to the closet. Kate moved the box of videotapes and pulled out the container. Inside was a stack of college textbooks, economics related. There were two framed degrees, one for an M.B.A. from Andrus College in New York City and one for a B.A. from Mather College in Connecticut. Both were made out to Corbin Harriman Dell. She pulled the whole container out into the better light of the den. Was it odd that Corbin would bury his own things underneath the boxes that had belonged to his father? She went through the container's contents. In the midst of the textbooks, there were a bundle of papers, a few photographs, and a small notebook all tied up with a piece of kitchen twine. She ruffled the edges of the papers and the photographs to see what they were. Several seemed to be grade sheets from college or business school, but she was able to dislodge one of the photographs, a glossy image of a dark-haired woman, about college age, sitting on a cold, windy-looking beach. She was in jeans and an oversized turtleneck sweater. She was looking away from the camera, her mouth open as though she was speaking. She flipped the photograph over and read the writing on the back: RACHAEL AT ANNIS-QUAM BEACH. There was no date. Kate thought: *Where is Rachael now?* And her mind imagined tragedies and murdered girls. She shivered, tapped her fingertips together. *Just because I think something doesn't make it true,* she told herself. Another one of her internal mantras.

Kate was about to slide the photograph back into its bundle, then decided, on impulse, to also look at the notebook. She unpicked the knotted string and pulled the notebook out. It was leather bound, embossed with the seal from Andrus College. She flipped it open, feeling guilty, but it was just a regular engagement diary, segmented into days. It was from six years ago, and was filled with a spiky, minuscule handwriting. She read a few entries—mostly class times and due dates, but sprinkled throughout were social engagements, such as "drinks with H," or "dinner party at the Esterhouses." She closed

47

the diary, rebundled it, and returned it to its container.

She was walking back across the apartment, wondering whether she should write Corbin back in London, when there was another knock on the door. It was Detective Roberta James again, this time accompanied by two uniformed officers.

"We'd like to look around your place, if you'd give us permission to do so." The detective's jaw seemed tight, her voice controlled.

"Sure, I guess," Kate said. She wondered if she was making a mistake letting them just march into Corbin's apartment. Should she have asked for a warrant?

"It won't take long," the detective said, as the two officers, each wearing light blue latex gloves, made their way into the apartment. Kate watched them turn left toward the bedroom. As was always the case with American police, she found herself fixated on the guns on their belts. She wondered what would happen if she reached out and touched one of them. Would she be thrown to the ground and handcuffed immediately? "I have a couple more questions," Detective James continued. "We could sit."

Kate led the detective to the two couches that faced one another and they both sat. "This is a beautiful apartment," Detective James said.

"I know, isn't it? My place in London isn't like this at all. Just an ordinary flat."

"So, in your conversations leading up to this apartment

swap, did you two talk about neighbors at all? Did Corbin ever mention Audrey Marshall?"

"No, nothing. He didn't talk about anyone. Can I ask you what you're hoping to find by looking in here?"

The detective pressed her lips together, then said: "I'm not *hoping* to find anything, but we need to look. We have no reason to suspect that Corbin was involved in anything, if that's what you're wondering."

"No, no, I know."

"What can you tell me about your cousin's flight from here to London?"

"All I know is that he took a night flight that got into London on Friday morning, so he would have left on Thursday night."

Detective James wrote in her notebook, while one of the police officers came through the living room heading to the other side of the apartment. They seemed to be searching quickly.

"And you didn't meet up with him in London before you left to come here?"

"No. Like I said, I've never actually met him."

"Okay." The detective slid her notebook back into the inside pocket of her jacket. She pressed the palms of her hands against her knees and stood. "I'm going to see how the search is going. Should be almost done. Have you found any locked doors here, or were there any rooms or closets that you were told were off-limits?"

"No."

Kate stayed seated as Detective James slowly walked toward the west side of the apartment, pausing to look out a window. It had stopped raining, and the clouds were breaking up. The detective moved a curtain with a finger, stared outside, then moved on. She was tall, with perfect posture, and Kate automatically hitched back her own shoulders. One of the police officers with the latex gloves came back into the living room. The detective looked questioningly at him, and he said, "Nothing." It sounded as though he had a cold. The other policeman emerged from the kitchen. Kate hadn't heard the sound of drawers being opened. Should she mention the key she'd seen with the initials on it? Was that the type of thing they were looking for?

Before she could decide, all three were headed toward the exit, the detective thanking Kate and asking her to call if anything came up. Kate stood, but they were through the door before she could even respond. She was alone again in the apartment.

Chapter 5

Kate made bread and cheese again for dinner, and opened a bottle of wine. She ate in the den, flipping through cable channels, then settling on an American reality show about crab fishermen in Alaska. When that was through, she found a channel that was showing a thriller called *Midnight Lace,* with Doris Day and Rex Harrison. She started watching; it wasn't very good, but it had just enough of a plot to distract her from thinking exclusively about what was happening down the hallway.

Halfway through the film, Kate discovered a lever on the leather sofa that caused the end seat to recline separately from the rest of the sofa. She maneuvered it all the way back so that she was practically prone and continued to watch the film. She was suddenly exhausted, her limbs like dead appendages. And then, almost instantly, the film was different, something in black and white, although it also starred Rex Harrison. He was bearded and in a black turtleneck. The movie was familiar, and Kate thought she'd seen it before. She'd fallen asleep—she must have—without even knowing it. She felt disoriented and alarmed. The clock on the cable box said it was 5:45 in the morning. Kate's mouth was gluey, and she had a sliver

51

of a headache from the wine she'd drunk. She felt that the past day had been many days, punctuated by naps as deep and troubling as full nights of sleep. It was only Sunday, but it felt like she'd been in Boston for a week.

She flipped the television off, returned the reclining sofa to its normal position, and stood. Her nose was running and she slid a hand in her dress pocket to look for tissues. She didn't find any, but her fingers touched a single key. She pulled it out of her pocket. It was the key she'd seen earlier, in the cutlery drawer, the one with AM written on its label in block letters. Kate didn't remember putting it in her pocket. When had she done it? Earlier, when she first looked in the drawer, or since then? She rapidly shook her head, trying to wake herself, trying to force herself to remember.

She walked to the kitchen, the air around her seeming to part at a slower rate than it normally did. God, she was knackered. It had been years since she'd traveled to a different time zone and experienced jet lag. She placed the key on the counter and began to make coffee. When it started to brew, she picked up the key again, and knew, suddenly, that she needed to find out if this key opened Audrey Marshall's apartment. *I'll just turn it, and find out, and then I can let the police know,* she told herself. It probably wasn't the right key. *AM* could mean many things.

Not even putting shoes on, Kate left her apartment and went to Audrey Marshall's door. Crime scene tape had been plastered in an X pattern from side to side. She slid the key into the lock, turned it, and pushed. The room yawned open before her. Knowing she shouldn't do it, but knowing that she had to, Kate ducked under the tape and entered the apartment. The tiredness and the fear made her feel as though she was watching herself, observing, not doing. She shut the door behind her, using her elbow, then stood still, her arms down by her sides, allowing her eyes to adjust. She was looking from a short foyer into a living room, much smaller than the living room in her end apartment, but just as elegant. Kate scanned the floor for any sign of where the body of Audrey Marshall had been found, but saw nothing. Was she in the right place? She took three careful steps into the interior of the apartment. There was an almost chemical smell in the air. It was dark, but the curtains were open, and the faint glow from the dawn sky allowed her to see the outlines of furniture, a coffee table cluttered with books and wine bottles.

There hasn't been a murder here, she thought. *Where's the blood, the overturned chair, the smell of death?* Was she dreaming now, or had she been dreaming before?

Even with these thoughts, she was strangely calm. One of the paradoxes of her anxious life was that in the midst of doing something slightly reckless, Kate often felt the most normal. It was as though her anxiety, always with her, was given a reason for existing. Standing in a murdered woman's apartment the morning after the body had been found, she thought the quickness of her heart and the coldness of her limbs made sense. She was about to turn back, but instead took a few more steps forward so that she could get a better look out of the large picture window. The window faced the courtyard, and Kate could make out pale orange light over the flat roof of the opposite wing. The windows on the other wing of the building were all dark, but Kate sensed motion in the window directly across from where she was looking. She instinctively took a step backward into the deeper shadows of the apartment.

She watched as a light came on and a figure passed in front of the window, then stopped and looked across. There was just enough light for Kate to know for sure that the figure was Alan Cherney, the man she'd met in the courtyard. The hair was right, and the angularity of the features, the slope of the shoulders. Kate stopped breathing, worried that any movement would mean that he could see her. They stood like that for a long, terrible moment, Kate unable to move. He kept staring across the way. At one point, he raised a hand and rubbed at one of his eyes. Then the dawn light that had been building in the western sky edged over the roof, and Kate suddenly realized that Alan might be able to see her. She moved backward, tracing her steps, like someone trying not to make tracks in the snow.

He kept watching, and Kate pressed her back to the door, frightened of being seen and frightened to take her eyes off him.

Chapter 6

Alan stared through his window into Audrey Marshall's dark apartment. For one moment, he could have sworn there was someone there, staring back at him. He'd barely slept in twenty-four hours, though, and the gray shadows across the way blurred and shimmered in his vision. Still, he watched—legs trembling with exhaustion, queasy with hunger—like a cat that watches the crack between the molding and the floor for the mouse that appeared there once upon a time.

Police cars had clogged the street all afternoon. An ambulance had arrived, and uniformed officers were in and out of the building.

Why was he still watching Audrey's apartment? Out of habit, he supposed. He'd known her intimately, having watched her in the privacy of her home for so long. He knew how she walked across a room, what she wore to bed, how long she brushed her teeth. Everything—almost everything—he'd known about Audrey he learned by watching out his window.

It had begun over a year ago, a few months after Alan and Quinn had moved in together. It had been a Saturday in December, a typical Saturday with Quinn. They'd had brunch with friends, then been shopping, then gone to the gym, then bought a Christmas tree that was almost too big to get up into the apartment and that had shed pine needles along the stairs and down the hall. The plan that night had been to stay in, decorate the tree (their first as a couple), drink eggnog, and watch a movie. But Quinn's best friend Viv had texted that everyone was going over to some new hotel bar that had just opened.

"Let's go," Quinn said, finishing off the eggnog that she'd been sipping at for over half an hour.

"Really?"

"It'll be fun. The bartender there is the same guy who used to bartend over at Beehive. You remember that drink he used to make, with the sherry in it, that you used to go on about . . ."

"The Aston Martin."

"That's right. The Aston Martin. Let's go drink one."

Alan was all set to agree, drank down his own eggnog, then surprised himself by saying, "Maybe I'll just stay here tonight."

"Seriously?" Quinn said. She was standing now, stripping off the Lululemon yoga pants she'd been wearing since they returned home.

"I'm tired," Alan said. It was a lie. He wanted to stay home in order to spend some time alone. His head was pleasantly fuzzy from the brandy in the eggnog, and the idea of a Saturday night alone suddenly felt heavenly. He could keep drinking, find a horror film to watch, something gory that Quinn would never agree to.

"We don't have to go if you don't want to," Quinn said.

"You go. I don't have a problem with it. It's a relationship milestone. You going out and me staying in, and neither of us minding."

"Oh, you're just assuming I don't mind," she said, but she was smiling. In the end, after changing, and having another drink, and putting on makeup, Quinn went out.

Alan had been alone in the apartment before, of course, but it felt different on a Saturday night with Quinn off with friends. Before looking for a film to watch, he put *Chet Baker Sings* on the old record player he had been dragging from apartment to apartment his whole life, made himself another drink, then wandered from lamp to lamp, adjusting the lighting to the way he liked it. It had just begun to snow earlier that evening, when he and Quinn had returned with the tree, so Alan went to the large picture window in the living room, parted the curtains, and looked out to see what the weather was doing. It had stopped coming down, but everything was covered with a thin scrim of pure white snow. He studied the footsteps in the courtyard, trying to identify Quinn's, but there were too many.

There was a light on in the apartment on the other side of the courtyard. Alan looked, his eyes taking a moment to adjust. The woman who lived there—Alan couldn't remember her name, if he'd ever known it—had left her own curtains half parted. She was seated on her couch, her back against one of the arms, a book open in her lap. There was a single tall lamp above her that produced a cone of warm yellow light. On the coffee table in front of the couch was a glass of red wine, an open bottle next to it. It was such an idealized image, almost cliché, that Alan laughed out loud to himself. He took a step to the left so that she was framed more perfectly in the space between the parted curtains.

The woman startled a little and looked up from her book, and Alan took an instinctive step back, sure that he'd somehow been spotted. She stood, though, without looking toward the window at all. She disappeared out of sight, then returned to the couch, that white cat called Sanders walking with her. The cat leapt onto the coffee table. The woman returned to the sofa and the book, idly scratching Sanders under its chin. He belonged to a woman on the other side of the building, but was allowed to roam the place at free will. Alan had seen him frequently in the lobby, sometimes sleeping on top of the reception desk.

Alan snapped the nearest lamp off, so that his own living room was plunged into near darkness, and continued to watch the woman. She looked so at peace, so content within the small sphere of her existence, that Alan felt an almost physical pain in his chest, a sharp desire to be with her. He imagined himself stretched out on the other side of the couch, their bare feet touching. In this fantasy, he only knew that they were completely at ease with one another.

The track on the record was "My Buddy," and Alan realized just how long he had been staring out the window. He pushed the curtains closed and sat back down on the couch. His phone vibrated: a text from Quinn that she was at the bar. He wrote back, telling her to say Hi to everyone. She wrote back a half second later: Mike said to say you are a losah!

The record ended, and Alan sat in the quiet apartment. He thought of playing something else, or looking for a movie to watch, but all he could think about was continuing to watch the woman. He got up, returned to the window, and peered through again. She was still reading on the couch, but Sanders the cat was gone, and she'd pulled her legs up so that her book was propped against her knees. Alan remembered that he had binoculars, a small pair that he'd bought that year he'd split a Celtics season ticket in the nosebleeds with some of his college friends. He couldn't remember exactly where they were, but guessed they were still in the canvas messenger bag he'd been using back then. He went and checked, and he'd guessed right. With the binoculars in his hand, he hesitated, knowing somehow that there was a genuine difference between simply watching your neighbor through a window and watching her with a pair of binoculars. It will be just for a moment, he told himself. A way to get a really good look at her, maybe even see what book she's reading.

He returned to the window, and peered through the binoculars. It made her look as though she was about eight feet away. He could see her features clearly, the texture of her clothes, the way she was absentmindedly touching one of her earlobes with a finger. The book was called *Wolf Hall,* large black-and-white font on a red cover. She licked the tip of a finger with her tongue before turning a page.

Alan felt his breathing slow down and get heavier. Looking at her up close he felt dirtier, aware that what he was doing was wrong, but unable to stop himself. She wore old jeans, the denim splitting at the knees, and a tight crewneck sweater with black and brown stripes. She yawned, arching her back, and he could see a sliver of her pink stomach. Alan felt himself stiffen in his pants, and that reaction caused him to lower the binoculars, pull the curtains shut, and step away. Feverish shame swept over him, as though he had suddenly become ill.

He put the binoculars in his underwear drawer, then undressed, pulled on a pair of boxers and a T-shirt, brushed his teeth, and got into bed. He read for a while. John Le Carré's *Tinker, Tailor, Soldier, Spy*. He'd read it before, but not since middle school. His eyes scanned the words while he thought of the girl in the window. He wondered what her life was like, if she had a boyfriend. Maybe he was out for the night the way Quinn was. He didn't think so, though. There was something about the way she looked in her apartment that made Alan think she lived there alone.

He tried to read some more, then shut the book, turned

out the light, and lay awake, listening to the baseboard heating click on and off. There was no way he was going to be able to fall asleep, he told himself, and then he did.

Quinn slid next to him under the covers. She smelled like red wine and Marlboro Lights. "You smoked?" Alan asked. They'd quit together recently.

"Shhh," she said. She was naked, and she slid one of his hands between her legs, then climbed on top of him. Quinn was gray and featureless in the darkness of the room, and Alan, half awake, imagined it was his neighbor, the girl whose name he didn't even know, moving back and forth on top of him.

*

It didn't take him long to learn her name. The following Monday, after Quinn had left for work, Alan walked through the building's lobby and to the other wing. It was easy to figure out which was her door; she was in apartment 3C. Back down in the lobby, Alan asked the doorman if he could look through the bundle of mail that had just arrived. And there she was on a credit card solicitation: Audrey Marshall, Apartment 3C.

Over the course of that winter he got to know her schedule, when she got out of bed in the morning and when she got home at night. She rarely had anyone over. Once or twice a woman, skinny and with a homely face, came by and they would drink champagne, the other woman talking nonstop while Audrey listened,

61

interjecting occasionally. But she was usually alone, and that was the way Alan liked to watch her.

"What's so interesting out there?" Quinn asked one night, when he thought she was watching the television.

"I thought I heard someone shouting in the courtyard, but it's probably just out on the street."

"Yeah, whatever," she said.

"What does that mean?"

"It means I see you looking out the window all the time. And I can't remember the last time you actually looked at me for more than a second."

"We ate lunch together today, remember? We were looking at each other the whole time. I helped you get that sesame seed out from between your teeth." Alan laughed.

Quinn shrugged from behind her cell phone. This was March, and Alan was pretty sure that Quinn had met someone new, some guy named Brandon who worked at her firm and who was always included in the group of coworkers who were inevitably getting together after work for a drink. It was something about the way she said his name, rushing through the two syllables in sentences such as: "Oh, and of course, Brandon was also there." Alan wasn't upset. He wasn't even jealous, really. He had Audrey.

As winter turned to spring, and spring turned to summer, she cracked her windows, and so did Alan. On quiet summer evenings, when the breeze blew in the right direction, he occasionally could hear music coming from across the courtyard. Audrey listened to classical when she was reading, and she read a lot, usually in the same position on her living room couch as the first time he'd spied on her. Sometimes she read in the bedroom, especially when the weather was hot, since her bedroom, like Alan's, had a ceiling fan in it. He never saw her fully naked, but he'd seen her in various stages of undress many times, usually as she got ready in the morning for work, or just after she came home, always around six in the evening. One hot night, Audrey left her curtains cracked, and Alan, chair pulled up to his own window in his unlit bedroom, watched through his binoculars as she read a paperback called *The Little Stranger*. She was naked except for a pair of black briefs. Alan imagined, for a moment, that if he opened his window all the way he could float across the courtyard and into her bedroom.

By late summer, Quinn had moved out—citing Alan's distance, although Alan had heard through the grapevine that she was now dating Brandon from work—leaving him with less than half the furniture and a monthly rent he couldn't afford. She'd also left him with more time to focus on Audrey. He'd formed a plan, a way to meet her that would seem natural and that would throw them together for a lengthy period of time. Alan had begun to occasionally follow Audrey when she left the apartment. He now knew where she worked—a small publishing house just over the river in Cambridge—and he knew that on weekends she liked to go and read at a low-ceilinged coffee shop in Harvard Square called Café Pamplona. His plan was to get there before her on one of those days, tell her she looked familiar, start a conversation. Eventually they'd figure out that they lived in the same apartment building in Boston, and wasn't it funny that they had actually met in Cambridge, and maybe they could get together sometime soon on their side of the river.

But he never got to enact this plan. Everything changed in February. A man had started appearing in Audrey's apartment. A tall jock in a suit, who always showed up with a bottle of wine. Alan knew who he was. His name was Corbin Dell, and he also lived at 101 Bury Street, right down the hall from Audrey.

Chapter 7

Alan had met Corbin Dell shortly after he'd moved to Bury Street. This was before he'd begun watching Audrey Marshall, back when Quinn and he were an amorous young couple sharing their first apartment.

They'd met—Alan and Corbin—in the lobby of the building. Corbin was talking with the doorman named Bob and Alan was checking his mail on his way to play racquetball. The tape-wrapped handle of his racket poked out of his gym bag.

"Squash or racquetball?" Corbin asked Alan, noticing the racket.

"I've played both," Alan said, "but lately I've been playing racquetball. Do you play?"

"I do. Where do you play?" Corbin asked. He was almost impossibly square jawed. In fact, everything about him was square—his wide shoulders, his thick hands, his head, its sharp corners accented by a blond crew cut. Alan knew, just by looking at him, that he would be a far superior player.

"The Y," Alan said.

"Where? On the river?"

"Uh-huh."

"I didn't know they had racquetball courts. We should play some time. You could come to my club."

"I'm not very good," Alan said.

"I don't care about that," Corbin said. "The guy I play with now is so competitive it's stopped being fun."

They introduced themselves. Alan had a business card from the software company he worked at that had his e-mail on it, and he gave it to Corbin.

"You in marketing?" Corbin asked.

"I am. What about you?"

"Financial advisor. At Briar-Crane." Alan recognized the name. Of course he was in finance. Guys who looked like Corbin loved nothing more than currency speculation and talking about rates of exchange. They said goodbye, Corbin telling Alan that he'd be in touch about racquetball. Alan exited through the courtyard on his way to the Y, knowing that Corbin would probably never e-mail, but feeling a strange surge of pleasure that he suddenly lived in a building where men made racquetball dates in the lobby. This was his new life, now that he was with Quinn, who'd always had family money and always would have family money. She'd insisted on moving into 101 Bury Street, even though the rent was four times what Alan had been paying for a two-bedroom in South Boston.

Alan forgot about Corbin Dell, and was surprised when, a week later, he got an e-mail from him that read:

66

Let's play that game of racquetball. I can do
Saturday morning if you can. I got a court for 10
am. Corbin

They'd played, and Alan had been right: Corbin was a far superior player, not just in skill level, but in fitness. After the game, Corbin looked like he didn't need a shower, while Alan, dripping with sweat, worked hard to form complete sentences. Still, after showering and walking back from Corbin's swank club to the apartment building, Corbin said they should play again.

And they did, but just once. It was right before Christmas week, and afterward they got a beer together at the Sevens on Charles Street. The drink at the bar felt to Alan like their racquetball games—Corbin in control and Alan scrambling to catch up. Corbin talked about great restaurants in Boston, mentioned his portfolio, and swiveled his head to watch a beautiful brunette walk across the room. Alan thought Corbin was overcompensating for something, although what that was he didn't know. Maybe it was that stupid, preppy name—Corbin—that he'd been saddled with, or maybe he was secretly gay and trying desperately to hide it. After the beer they walked together down Charles Street. It was just past five but dark already, the store windows festooned and glittery with Christmas lights. "I hate Christmas," Corbin said, almost to himself, then quickly laughed.

"I'm ambivalent. I don't celebrate it," Alan said.

That had been their last time hanging out, except for occasionally running into one another in the building's lobby or courtyard. Alan registered guilt on Corbin's face during those brief run-ins, as though the fact that they no longer played racquetball was a breakup perpetrated by Corbin. Alan wanted to tell him that the breakup was mutual.

Then Audrey entered Alan's life and Alan forgot all about Corbin, all about other people, really. He'd forgotten Corbin so completely that it actually took him a moment to identify him when he first saw him in Audrey's apartment. His blond hair was a little longer, but nothing else had changed. Tall and muscular, dressed in a suit or workout gear. He settled into Audrey's apartment as though he owned it, sprawling on her couch, watching her television. They were always sharing wine. They were rarely physical with one another, although Alan had watched them enter the bedroom together several times and pull the curtains closed. He'd also watched, once, as Corbin lifted Audrey into his arms, her legs around his waist, and kissed her. One of Corbin's massive hands slid under Audrey's skirt and Alan had to look away. Alan told himself that his disgust at seeing Corbin and Audrey together was a good thing, that it might cure him of his need to watch Audrey at all hours. If nothing else, Audrey was not the woman he thought she was, not if she was dating someone like Corbin.

Still, despite these thoughts, Alan found himself

watching Audrey as much as he ever had, cherishing those moments when she was alone in her apartment, reading on her couch like she always had. She'd started a new book, *Gone Girl* by Gillian Flynn, and Alan, on his way home from work, stopped at a Barnes & Noble and bought a copy, just so they could read it at the same time. Days would go by with no appearance by Corbin, and Alan would begin to hope that the relationship was over, but then Corbin would show up on a Friday night, always with a bottle of wine. They rarely seemed to go out together. Alan wondered if they'd come to some kind of sex agreement—neighbors with benefits. The thought bothered him. What did she possibly see in him? Even as someone just for sex.

On one of the nights when Corbin was in Audrey's apartment, Alan, after several beers, decided to send an e-mail to Corbin. It had been nearly a year since they'd last had contact. Alan composed the e-mail, working hard to make it sound dashed off, apologizing for how long it had been, then asking Corbin if he wanted to get together for a quick game followed by another beer at the Sevens. "Or we could skip the racquetball and just grab a drink, if you want," Alan added, thinking that having a conversation with Corbin was his only goal. He hit send as soon as he'd written the e-mail, so as not to give himself time to reconsider. Alan sat back and sighed. If Corbin took the bait, then he'd be able to quiz him about Audrey, maybe find out what was happening in the relationship.

Maybe Corbin and Alan would become friends, this second time around, and that would allow Alan to formally meet Audrey, get to know her. Alan found his mind galloping forward, toward scenarios where Audrey would leave Corbin to be with him. He stopped himself from going too far with these fantasies, got up from the computer, and returned to the window. Corbin was looking at his phone. Alan wondered if he was reading the e-mail he'd just sent. If so, he didn't respond until the following day:

> Hey man. Nice to hear from you. I actually stopped playing racquetball, and only play squash now. But let's get that drink anyway. I'm free Wednesday next week.

Alan replied that he was free as well. As the day neared, he began to wonder if there was any chance that Corbin would bring Audrey along. Because of this slight possibility, Alan dressed in his best pair of jeans and his Rag & Bone blazer. But when he arrived at the Sevens at the appointed time, Corbin wasn't there. And when Corbin finally showed, twenty minutes late, he was alone.

They small-talked through half a beer, Corbin checking his cell phone at two-minute intervals. Realizing he had limited time, Alan asked, trying to sound casual: "Who you seeing these days?"

"Seeing?" Corbin replied. "No one, actually. Well,

there's this girl at work. Married, unfortunately—"

"I thought I heard from someone that you were seeing someone in the building. That girl who lives across from you—I don't know her name . . ."

"Audrey?"

"Yeah, that might be it."

Corbin took a long pull at his Smuttynose beer, a thin line of foam clinging to his upper lip. "I barely know her. Why? Who'd you hear that from?"

"I must have dreamt it, I guess. Or seen you two together."

"Nah, man. I really don't know her. I've seen her, and wouldn't mind knowing her, but nah. How 'bout you? Your girlfriend moved out, didn't she?"

Alan gave Corbin the short-story version of his breakup with Quinn and his plans to either find a new place soon or get a housemate to split the rent. They each finished their beer. The busy bartender swung past, asking them if they wanted another. Alan, not done interrogating Corbin about his love life, was about to say yes when Corbin jumped in and said he had to take off. "Sorry. I've got somewhere to be, unfortunately. Let's do this again, though," he said, unconvincingly.

Corbin left, but Alan stayed, ordering a rye and ginger ale, and wondering why Corbin would deny knowing Audrey. It didn't make any sense. Even if they were trying to keep the relationship a secret for some reason, why would it matter if Alan knew about it?

When Alan returned to his apartment from the Sevens, he went straight to the window. Audrey's apartment was dark.

But the following night she was there, on her couch, reading a *Vanity Fair* and occasionally checking her phone. She seemed jittery, twisting a strand of her short hair around a finger.

Alan went to make himself a drink, something he had learned to do in complete darkness, and when he returned, Corbin was now in Audrey's apartment. They stood talking near her door, and Alan thought it looked like an impromptu visit. There was no bottle of wine, and Audrey was dressed in the black tights and over-sized hoodie that she often wore when she was alone. Alan stood back a little from the window, even though he knew there was no way he could be seen. He watched them talking and knew that something was up. Corbin swung his head in the direction of Audrey's window, and Audrey's gaze followed, a frown creasing her face.

Both of them were staring directly across in Alan's direction.

Alan turned cold. He took another step backward. His binoculars were on the end table next to the couch, and he went and got them, continuing to watch from deep within his apartment.

Corbin and Audrey talked some more. At one point, Audrey shrugged, a smile on her face. Then Alan watched, his skin flushed, as Corbin crossed Audrey's living room and pulled her curtains all the way closed.

Alan lowered the binoculars. He hadn't been spotted, but it was just as bad. He'd been figured out. Corbin had realized that the only way Alan would know that he and Audrey were seeing each other was if Alan had been spying from across the way. Had it occurred to him immediately after the drink? Had he returned to the apartment, checked to see where Alan lived, the location of the apartment, and then realized that it was the exact mirror apartment from across the courtyard? Alan felt physically sick, his stomach clenching. For a brief, horrible moment he wondered if Corbin, and maybe Corbin *and* Audrey, would come over to his apartment to confront him. He instinctively pushed the binoculars down between the sofa's cushions. The lights were out. He wouldn't have to answer the door.

Then Alan told himself to relax, to take a deep breath, to begin to analyze the situation. Even if Corbin had figured out that they'd been spotted through the window, it didn't necessarily mean that they knew that Alan had been obsessively spying on Audrey. What if Corbin did confront him about it? All Alan would have to say would be something casual, like *Oh yeah, maybe that's where I saw you two together. Audrey never pulls her curtains all the way shut.* That thought relaxed him, and he stood again, walked toward the window to look through it. Audrey's curtains were still pulled shut.

Over the next few months, Alan gave up on the fantasy that he could somehow meet Audrey in the flesh.

He knew it would never happen. He also knew that if it did, Audrey would recognize him as the creep from the other side of the building, the one Corbin had accused of spying. She must have taken Corbin seriously that night, because she became a lot more vigilant about pulling her curtains all the way shut, especially in the evenings. She did occasionally leave them open, but Alan had decided to attempt to curb the amount of time he spent looking out of his window. He knew it was unhealthy, and definitely immoral, along with probably being illegal.

He reconnected with some friends he'd lost touch with and accepted invitations from coworkers to get drinks after work. On one of those nights he wound up kissing an intern from Suffolk University. Bella was an avid softball player with long blond hair who photographed everything with her phone. Even though Alan was still in his late twenties, he felt like Bella came from another generation. They went to a movie, and afterward back to Alan's place. He realized she was the only other human who had set foot in his apartment since Quinn had left. The sex was bad, perfunctory and awkward, and Bella talked nonstop out of embarrassment. After she'd fallen asleep—"Is it okay if I spend the night, even though I totally know this is just a hookup?"—Alan, wide awake, had gone into the living room. It had been a few days since he'd checked on Audrey's apartment, but he pulled his curtains apart by an inch and looked across the way. She'd left her curtains slightly open as well. She was on the sofa, curled up asleep, her book facedown on the floor next to her. He'd seen her sleep on the sofa before. Her right hand was curled, palm out, along the center of her chest, her index finger grazing the soft skin under her chin.

Alan went to his own sofa, buried his own face into a pillow, and cried for the first time in years.

No more Audrey, he told himself.

He needed to erase her from his mind. And he'd succeeded lately. For the most part.

Then, on Saturday morning he'd found a stale, brittle cigarette and gone outside to smoke. He'd spoken to the pretty English girl—Kate something, maybe she hadn't told him her last name—and she told him that Audrey was missing. It had been a strange and unsettling conversation. In some ways, Kate had reminded Alan of Audrey. Not the way she looked, although they shared the same pale coloring. Kate—and maybe it was just because he was meeting her face-to-face—had seemed more grounded, while Audrey had always been more ethereal. Pixieish, with her small features, long limbs, and that still quality, as though she'd never move unless it was absolutely necessary. To flip a page of her book, or take a sip of her tea. That was the difference, Alan thought. Kate, almost as pretty as Audrey, with a face that was rounder and hair that was a shade darker, was definitely *not* still. She shifted her weight from leg to leg when they talked. When she pushed a loose strand of hair back behind an ear, Alan noticed that her unvarnished fingernails had been bitten down to the quick.

Then the police had arrived, and Carol, Alan's elderly neighbor from across the hall, had confirmed that a body had been found.

That evening a police officer, a woman who identified herself as Officer Karen Gibson, came to take a statement. He told her the truth. He knew Audrey Marshall by sight, but he didn't *know* her.

That night Alan had slept, but it had been fitful, punctuated by thin dreams in which Audrey was with Alan in his apartment, touching him, speaking with him, whispering in his ear. He'd woken before dawn and gone to look toward Audrey's apartment. It was dark, but he could tell that the curtain was open. He caught a flicker of movement and stared for a long time. The sky was lightening from black to orange, but the interior of Audrey's apartment stayed dark. Still, he watched, scared to even blink too much. Then there was another suggestion of movement, a trace of light as Alan was sure he saw Audrey's door open and shut quickly, a figure leaving the apartment.

Chapter 8

By noon on Sunday, Kate, after beginning but not finishing a lengthy e-mail to her mother, paced the perimeter of the vast apartment. She'd been awake since dawn, when she'd snuck into Audrey Marshall's apartment and seen Alan Cherney through his window. Now, as she paced, she looked out her own windows. The sky was a milky white and the surface of the river was still and glassy. The stretch of Bury Street that she could see from the west-facing windows was quiet. She was hungry, but tired of eating bread and cheese. In the kitchen she opened the door of the massive, stainless steel refrigerator and stared at its meager contents.

Go outside, she told herself.

And before she could change her mind, she was pulling her boots on over her jeans and grabbing her black-and-white polka-dot jacket. A quick walk around the block, maybe find a place to eat lunch, or maybe even buy something to cook back at the apartment.

It was colder than she thought it would be outside, the air raw and damp. Walking across the courtyard, she buttoned her coat up to her throat, wishing she'd brought her gloves.

There was a man pacing on Bury Street, his own hands deep inside his navy pea coat. As she came through the archway, he looked up, expectantly, and their eyes met. He had medium-length reddish hair that was sticking up at the top, and his eyes behind his wire-rimmed glasses were bruised looking, their surfaces wet and shiny. Kate went to cross the road, pausing for a moment to look for oncoming cars, as the man approached her.

"Hi," he said, awkwardly. "Hi, hello there. You live here?"

"I do," she said, her hands instinctively going toward the throat of her jacket, already buttoned up.

"Sorry. I don't mean to frighten you. I was a friend . . . I'm a close friend of Audrey Marshall, and I've talked to the police, and I spoke to your doorman here in the building, and I'm just hoping to get more information."

"I'm sorry. I really don't know anything. I just moved here. I didn't know Audrey."

The man seemed undeterred. His cheeks were mottled and red and she wondered how long he'd been standing out in the cold, waiting for someone to come out of the building. "Have the police talked with you?" he asked.

"They took a statement. I think just because I'm right next door."

"You're right next door? On her floor?"

"I am, but I literally just moved in and don't know anyone. I'm sorry I don't have more information." Kate took a tentative step down the sidewalk in an attempt to escape.

"Do you mind if I walk with you a bit? I need to go get a coffee. I'm Jack, by the way." He removed a glove, and Kate took his dry, warm hand in hers. "Jack Ludovico. I've been friends with Audrey since . . . since—"

Trying to channel her mother, who was always kind, but a master at avoiding unwanted social situations, Kate said: "Jack, nice to meet you, but I'm in a hurry, and I don't think I can help you at all."

"You're not Corbin Dell's cousin, are you? Audrey told me that he was going to London, and you were going to come and live in his apartment."

"I am. I just arrived. Audrey told you that?"

"Yes, I know all about Corbin and Audrey. I don't mean to keep you, but let's walk. I'm cold."

They began to walk together, Kate curious that there had apparently been a "Corbin and Audrey."

"I'm Kate," she said.

Jack introduced himself again, realized he'd already done it, and rapidly shook his head, embarrassed. "I'm a mess."

"You were close?"

"Yes and no. Yes, for me, anyway. We dated in college but it didn't work out, and then, when she moved up here, we got back in touch, just as friends, really, and I can't believe . . ." He stopped walking, put his face in his gloved hands, pushing his glasses up to his forehead, and began to sob, his shoulders hitching up and down.

"It's okay," Kate said, not knowing what to do. She put a hand on his shoulder, and they remained frozen in that tableau for what seemed an eternity. After he removed his hands from his face and wiped his gloves along the thighs of his jeans, he asked: "Who identified her, do you know?"

"No, I have no idea. Let's keep walking, okay?" Kate said, taking his arm and moving him down the street.

"Okay," he said. "Sorry about dumping this on you. You must have just gotten here, and now there's been a murder next door to your new place, and I'm here pestering you." He laughed, an unnerving staccato rattle, his shoulders hitching again like they had when he'd been sobbing.

"It's fine," Kate said. Then asked: "How did you find out . . . How did you find out about what happened?"

"It was in the *Globe* today. I was worried already, because I hadn't heard anything from Audrey for a few days, which was strange, and then I saw a headline that said a woman had been found dead in Beacon Hill, and I knew it was her even before I read the rest of the article."

"What did it say?" Kate asked.

"Just that her body had been found, and that the police were treating it as a suspicious death, and there was a number to call with any information, so I called it. I went into the police station, and they questioned me, but they wouldn't tell me anything, except that she'd been positively identified. Do you know who did that? Do you know who identified her?"

Jack's voice was rising in pitch. Kate, recognizing panic in someone else, felt, as she usually did, comparatively calm. She said, "Jack, I don't know anything. I'm sorry. I just got here. But I'm sure the police can't talk about it because it's an ongoing investigation. Is there someone else you can talk with? One of Audrey's friends? Or her family?"

He nodded. "I will. I don't really know her family, but I can talk with her best friend, Kerry. I know her."

"She might have been the one who alerted the police that Audrey was missing. There was a girl here when I arrived, knocking on Audrey's door."

"Yeah, that was probably Kerry." Something in Jack's voice made Kate think that he wasn't fond of Audrey's best friend.

"You should talk with her," Kate said. "I'm sure she knows more than I know."

"I will." They continued to walk, Kate picking up the pace a little, Jack keeping up. They passed Brimmer and were approaching Charles Street. "So does Corbin know yet?" he asked.

"I gave his e-mail to the police and I think they were going to do it, just in case he had any information. I didn't want to e-mail him myself yet because I didn't know if he'd heard."

"Do you think the police suspect him?"

"I don't. I didn't. They said they didn't. Why, was there something strange between him and Audrey?"

"Well, they had a thing."

"What kind of thing?"

"I don't know exactly. It was an on-and-off thing. Audrey told me that they slept together but that they weren't going out, that he just wanted to keep things between them strictly in the apartment." It was clear from Jack's tone that he hadn't approved of the situation.

"What do you mean in the apartment?"

"In the building. I guess they were hooking up, and Audrey wanted more, more of a relationship, and Corbin didn't. She didn't have particularly nice things to say about him. I'm sorry. I shouldn't be telling you this. I didn't get the sense that she was scared of him or anything. It wasn't like that. Just that he was an asshole."

"I don't really know anything about it," Kate said. They'd reached the corner of Bury and Charles, and were now facing each other again.

Jack's jaw was clenching and unclenching. "I don't think Corbin had anything to do with what happened."

"Well, he was already in London—"

"When did he leave, exactly, do you know?"

"He took a night flight on Thursday, because he got in early on Friday morning. That was the day I left to come here. We almost had time to meet one another, but not really."

Jack said nothing, and Kate watched as he seemed to be calculating whether Corbin could have had something to do with Audrey's death. "When did you last talk with Audrey?" she asked.

His eyes snapped back toward her. "Oh, I'm trying to remember. Sometime Wednesday evening, I think."

"So you think Corbin . . ."

"No, I don't think anything. I guess he could've had something to do with what happened. It's a possibility, right?" He looked almost hopeful.

"I don't know. Maybe someone else heard from her. You should really ask the police about that. I don't know anything."

Jack rapidly shook his head, as though he had water in an ear. "Jesus, I'm sorry. This has nothing to do with you. I'm just freaking out—"

"No, I get it. It's just that I can't help you. I don't know Corbin, and he didn't tell me anything about anyone else who lived here. I hope he had nothing to do with it. What do you know about what happened to her, to Audrey?"

"What do you mean? Like how she was killed?"

"I guess."

"They wouldn't tell me anything. They said they were treating the death as suspicious, which is just what the newspaper said."

A tear bubbled up in one of Jack's puffy eyes, and Kate decided to not ask any more questions about Audrey. She wanted to leave, but Jack looked lost, reminding her of a child suddenly separated from his parents.

"What do you do, Jack?" she asked.

"What do you mean?"

"For work?"

"Oh, I work in hospitality."

"Uh-huh."

"I'm an events coordinator at a conference center. It's not as exciting as it sounds, but I'm busy all the time. The last two weeks . . . I didn't even have time to see Audrey."

The tear slid down his cheek, and he wiped it away with the back of his gloved hand.

Kate, trying again to channel her mother's bluntness, said, "Jack, I really think you should go talk with someone who knew Audrey."

He nodded, and she continued: "Find that friend of hers, or her family. Where was she from?"

"Her family's from New Jersey. I never met them."

"They've probably come up here, don't you think? You should find them and talk with them."

"Yeah, I think you're right." He stayed rooted to his spot on the sidewalk. A family of tourists, the two youngest kids wearing lobster claw hats, maneuvered around him.

"I think I was still in love with her," he said. "I don't think she felt the same way. No, I know she didn't feel the same way. Because of what Corbin did to mess her up, but . . ." He stopped, his eyes settling on some unknown spot in the middle distance.

"It was nice meeting you, Jack," Kate said, and they shook hands again. He kept his gloves on this time. "I'm sorry, but I need to get some shopping done."

She left him on the street corner and walked, at a pace she hoped wasn't too noticeably brisk, toward the small grocery store she'd been to the day before. She felt guilty, but she also knew that she couldn't really do anything to comfort him. He needed to find someone else who knew Audrey. She also wanted to be on her own to think about what she'd learned. Corbin *had* been involved with Audrey. They'd been sleeping together, and it had turned sour, at least in the eyes of Audrey. Maybe in his eyes as well. Kate's mind spun out possibilities. Audrey becoming possessive and Corbin panicking, trying to get away from her. He accepted the job transfer to London. But, then, on his last night in Boston he thought he'd go and say good-bye to Audrey, tell her that he was leaving town. And maybe she freaked out on him, attacked, and Corbin, defending himself . . .

Kate pushed the escalating thoughts out of her mind and opened the glass door of the grocery store. But with a single look at the narrow, crowded aisles, panic flooded over her, hollowing out her insides. She backed away from the fragrant warmth spilling from the inside of the store, and bumped into a couple in running gear, trying to push past her. "Sorry," she said, eyeing an empty bench in front of a store that sold vintage prints.

She sat down and did her breathing exercises.

Face it. Accept it. Float with it. Let time pass.

A plane went by overhead, too low, she thought, and the sound of its engine made Kate's scalp prickle and tighten. She began to tap her finger pads together, then made herself stop, and stood up. She was no longer hungry but knew she had to eat. Across the street was a small, walk-up pizza place called the Upper Crust, where she bought herself a slice of pesto pizza and a cream soda. She went back to the bench to eat. It was cold, but the open air felt better than being inside.

Walking back home, she half expected to see Audrey's lovelorn friend still at the corner where she had left him, but he was gone. He wasn't stalking the front of 101 Bury Street either, and Kate was relieved to make it back up to her apartment without encountering anyone else.

Back inside, she studied the walls around her. Was this the apartment of a killer? If it was, would she be able to tell? There was so little of Corbin here. Besides being luxurious and spacious, it didn't feel like anything. No, that wasn't entirely true. It felt like a dead man's apartment. It felt like Corbin's father's place. The furniture was beautiful but slightly dated; one of the sofas was upholstered in a floral print. And the artwork on the walls—most of it original—was abstract oil paintings, interesting (Kate thought) but dated somehow. No, very few, if any, of the furnishings in the house belonged to Corbin. He'd inherited his father's place and kept it exactly the same, even down to the framed photographs.

Kate, starting to relax a little, sat down and thought about what it meant. What would she have done if she inherited this place? Probably the same. It looked nice—why change it? And maybe Corbin had been particularly fond of his father, and keeping everything the same was a way to honor him. It was a possibility. But it was also a possibility that there was nothing of Corbin's around because he wanted to hide, because he didn't want people to see who he really was. And if that were the case, was there a place where he did express himself? Where was the real Corbin?

Kate went to the window with the best view of Bury Street. It was still quiet. She'd expected to maybe see Audrey's lovelorn friend again, watching the building for any sign of another inhabitant he could grill. Hadn't she read somewhere that criminals liked to return to the scene of their crimes? *No,* she thought. Jack Ludovico had been strange, but one thing he hadn't seemed was guilty of a crime. For once, her mind was not unspooling toward the worst possibility. He was what he seemed. An old boyfriend grappling with disbelief and grief. Easy to read, not like Corbin, who had an apparently complicated relationship with Audrey, plus a key to her apartment.

Thinking about the key made her remember that she needed to call the detective.

She went to the bedroom where she'd left Detective James's card, then thought of her sketchbook under the bed. She was suddenly sitting on the carpet, the sketchbook open to a new page, drawing Jack Ludovico's face, her hand moving automatically and without thought over the page. She drew him with his head cast down

87

slightly, eyes looking up. When she finished, she pulled the charcoal pencil back and knew that she'd got him on the first try. It was a perfect rendering. She dated the picture and put his name under it.

She sat for a moment more, trying to remember why she had come into the bedroom. The detective's card. She was going to call her. She walked to the phone in the living room. The detective picked up after two rings.

"Hi. It's Kate Priddy. You left me your card."

A slight pause, then: "Hi, Kate. What can I do for you?"

"It's about Audrey Marshall. I found a key in my apartment, in Corbin Dell's apartment, really, and it has the initials 'AM' on it."

"You think he might have had a key to Audrey's apartment?"

"That's what I was thinking."

"Did you test it?" the detective asked.

Kate was surprised, not expecting to be asked that, but something about the detective's casual nature caused her to own up to the truth: "Actually, I did. It's the key. It's Audrey's key. I mean, he probably just had it so that he could water her plants when she was gone, or something."

"Yes, I'm sure you're right. We're in contact with your cousin and he's been helpful. I'll ask him about the key."

"Oh, he knows now?"

"He does. He's been helpful but said that he didn't know Audrey particularly well. He sounded most concerned about you."

"He said he didn't know Audrey well?"

"That's what he said. Excuse me a moment . . ."

Kate listened to muffled voices for a moment—the detective speaking with someone else.

"Sorry, Kate, I'm back," Detective James said. "Was there anything else?"

"No, just the key. And I talked with a friend of Audrey's. Jack Ludovico."

"Oh yeah?" She sounded interested. "How did you meet him?"

"He was in front of the building, said he was coming from the police station—that he'd talked with someone there, and he was hoping to get more information."

"What's the name again?"

"Didn't he come to the station?"

"He might have, Kate. I just got here myself and I haven't checked in with all my colleagues yet."

"It's Jack Ludovico. He actually had a different story about Corbin and Audrey. He said they were involved."

"I'd like to follow up with you about this, Kate, if I can. Can I call you back? Is this a good number to reach you?"

"Sure. Yes, I'm calling from the apartment."

"And thank you for letting us know about the key, and don't hesitate to call again with anything, okay? Even if it seems insignificant."

Kate hung up the phone. She sat quietly for a moment, thinking: *Did I make a mistake by not telling her that I'd seen the man from across the courtyard peering into Audrey's apartment?* She decided, swiftly, that not telling the detective about Alan Cherney was *not* a mistake. Of course he was looking across and into the apartment. There'd been a murder. He must have heard about it, and he was curious. Curious and upset, probably. It was natural.

When bad things happened, the world always looked. Kate knew that more than most people.

Chapter 9

Kate finished her long e-mail to her mother, detailing what had happened since she'd arrived in Boston. She knew that as soon as she sent it, her mother would ask her to come home. Not so much for the sake of safety—although that would obviously be part of it—but because of what Kate had gone through with George Daniels.

She'd met George her first year at university. He was in earth sciences, and she was in the arts, but they'd ended up in the same beginning Greek course. Kate struggled in the course and ended up asking George for help. She'd only asked him because he looked studious and trustworthy. He wasn't bad looking, but at eighteen years old he looked like a fully licensed chartered accountant. He was tall and lanky, most of his height coming from his long legs. He wore plain spectacles, always dressed in corduroys and sweater vests, and was beginning to lose his hair. But the hair loss had left George with a prominent widow's peak that she found attractive. After several study sessions, he nervously asked Kate if she'd like to go to dinner sometime; he suggested an Italian place that he'd heard was very good.

She said yes, intrigued about what it would be like to go on such an old-fashioned date instead of just meeting up with some boy at the student union pub. And it *had* felt like an old-fashioned date. George even wore a tie under one of his sweater vests. It should have been awkward, but it wasn't. George and Kate had lots in common; both were secret poetry fans, and both were obsessed with *Twin Peaks*. That weekend they spent all of Saturday and part of Sunday in George's room watching the entire first season on George's laptop in his bed. By Monday they had each lost their virginity, and Kate was certain that she was in love. George, she knew, felt the same way.

They were together for a year, safe in the bubble of their relationship. Kate felt safe, anyway. Her whole life had been colored by her conviction that tragedy was always about to strike. The therapist her parents had brought her to when she was eight had asked her to name the three things she was most frightened of, and Kate had burst into tears, overwhelmed by having to reduce a world of strangers, spiders, gas leaks, bullies, invisible germs, and violent weather into just three simple fears. She was diagnosed with an anxiety disorder—to the surprise of no one—but also with fantasy-prone disorder. She was simply too imaginative.

What was comforting about George was that he planned everything, down to the little details. Kate still worried—her mind one of those rattling filmstrips that only showed lurid safety films from health class—but her worries would never change George's mind, and it took some pressure off her. For summer holiday after that first year of university, he booked a trip around the Greek islands. They were to fly from London to Athens, then take ferries to Santorini, Crete, and, finally, Rhodes. Kate had only flown once, as a thirteen-year-old, to the Azores, and her parents had promised her afterward that they'd never make her do it again. She remembered the feeling well, the plane taking off and her conviction that death was swallowing her whole. The feeling had gone beyond panic and into the cold vacuum of pure terror. Kate told George about it, told him she didn't think she could fly to Athens, but he'd looked at her calmly and told her he'd already planned it. "It's all booked, Kate," he'd said, his voice telling her that there wasn't going to be a conversation.

In a way, it made things easier. The days leading up to the flight Kate felt like she was moving through air that had solidified into something without oxygen. Her chest ached, and she'd begun chewing the insides of her cheeks again, her mouth constantly tainted by the taste of blood. But she knew she couldn't cancel, simply because it had been booked, and George had booked it, and when he made a plan he stuck with it. And in the end, she took the flight, helped along by several gin and tonics. It was bad, but she survived, and once the plane had safely landed and she had been disgorged into the chaos of Athens International, a giddy sense of possibility came over her. That sense carried over into the entirety of the trip. She thought she'd hate the ferries, but she was okay with them, the open sky and long vistas helping her to relax.

It was a happy trip for the first few days, and then George's jealousy and paranoia kicked in.

He'd always been possessive, ever since that first weekend they'd spent together. He'd quiz her regularly on whether she found any of her fellow students attractive. She quickly learned to say no. If they went to a party together—a rare occurrence—Kate learned to talk only to other women, or George would sulk for days. She even learned that if they went to a movie together—something with Brad Pitt, say—that she shouldn't even mention that she found *him* attractive. She learned that the hard way. "He's Brad Pitt. I'd never in a million years meet him, you know."

"And I suppose if you did meet him, you'd just up and fuck him?" George answered.

"Of course not."

"But you find him attractive. Obviously, you want to fuck him, so why wouldn't you if he offered?"

"God, George. I wouldn't be with him because I only want to be with you."

"Then why would you be attracted to him?"

It went on like that for several days, and Kate learned to never mention any man's name—famous or not famous—again.

It got worse in Greece. Maybe it was the beaches, and all that tawny flesh on display. Kate kept her eyes on her book, or off into the blinding distance, but it was impossible to not occasionally glance at the parade of bodies, the men in briefs and the women mostly topless. Kate was self-conscious in her sea-green one-piece, and her pale skin that reddened instead of tanned. One afternoon she found herself watching a teenage girl dart in and out of the Mediterranean. Her bikini bottoms were the color of light brown skin, so that she seemed entirely naked. Even though she was past puberty, she still acted like a young girl, running in and out of the foaming surf. Kate wondered if she'd ever felt that giddy or free, even when she was very young.

That night, at dinner, George, after ten minutes of silence, asked Kate if she was a lesbian. She tried to laugh it off, but George wouldn't let it go, and Kate, for the rest of the trip, tried not to look at anyone.

But the worst incident happened on their last night, in Heraklion, Crete. On the other side of the road from the beach was a long line of competing cafés and restaurants. By late afternoon the restaurants would each send one of their waiters out toward the sidewalk to try to lure the tourists. "Look at the menu," they'd say. "Freshest fish in Heraklion." On the bad night, George and Kate had been coerced into looking at the menu of a pizza place, and then agreed to take a seat outside on the patio. Seating them, the handsome waiter had said: "We'll put the beautiful English lady facing the street so all the men will want to come here." Kate laughed, and to her horror, felt a blush suffuse her cheeks. George got quiet. They ordered a carafe of the terrible Greek wine and a seafood pizza. Halfway through the meal Kate said, "You're not upset about what that waiter said, are you? You know he says that to every woman he seats?"

"So is that why you keep looking at him?" George replied.

"I haven't looked at him once since we sat down, George."

They were silent for the rest of the meal, but continued the conversation later in their inexpensive hotel room three blocks away.

"I would never have brought you to Greece if I'd known what it would do to you," George said. He was so angry that flecks of spit flew from his lips.

"It's not doing anything to me, George. It's doing something to *you*."

"You're honestly telling me that you're not going to lay in bed tonight dreaming of what it would be like to fuck that Greek waiter. I saw the way you looked at him. Why don't you just go back, go be with him . . ."

"Maybe I will," Kate said, and knew immediately she shouldn't have.

George grabbed her by the shoulders and started to push her toward the door. "Go, then," he shouted, his fingers digging into her sunburned flesh. Not knowing what else to do, Kate stopped resisting and dropped to the uncarpeted floor. She began to sob as George repeatedly punched the wall until a crack appeared and his knuckles were bloody.

*

"Does Daddy get jealous?" Kate asked her mother the first time she saw her after returning from Greece.

"Jealous of what?"

"Of you, and other men?"

"God, no. Why?"

"What about when you were first together? When you were dating?"

"Maybe a little, but only because when I started dating your father I was still stepping out with Robert Christie." She took a sip of her wine. Rain slashed against the glass of the conservatory.

"That must have driven him mad?"

"I don't know about it driving him mad, exactly, but it spurred him to action. He asked me to marry him a lot sooner than I think he would have done otherwise. Not that Robert Christie ever would have asked me to marry him."

"And since then?"

"We're married, darling, and your father's not the jealous type. Why are you asking all these questions?"

Kate told her mother about George's jealous streak. She told her pretty much everything, only omitting the night in Heraklion that ended with him cracking the hotel wall with his fist.

"That doesn't sound good, darling."

"It isn't. I love George, but I feel like I'm walking on

eggshells all the time, making sure I don't slip up and mention another man's name."

"That's ludicrous, dear. What does he think, that just because you're together you're not going to find other men attractive?"

"That's exactly what he thinks."

"Good lord, Kate."

"I know, I know. I think I need to end it." It was the first time she'd said these words out loud, and saying them made tears start to roll down her face.

"I think you do, too," her mother said.

*

It wasn't easy. Kate decided to write a long letter to George, explaining her reasons in detail, and trying her hardest to ensure him about how much he had meant to her. She left the letter under his residence door before leaving for summer vacation. A week later she tried to call him and he didn't pick up. She worried, but knew it was for the best. By August she still hadn't heard a word, and that was when she made her mistake. She posted to Facebook that she was spending a week at her uncle's cottage in Windermere. She simply wrote: "Walking holiday. Lake District. Bliss."

George didn't have a Facebook profile, and even though she did, she rarely posted. It never occurred to her that he might read the post. In retrospect, she knew that she'd been stupid, but what she had really been was hopeful.

Hopeful that George was moving on, like she was. But George *did* read her post. He knew the cottage because they'd been there together before, on a minibreak holiday with her family. Years later, Kate wondered how long he'd been in Windermere watching her and following her before he made his appearance. She never sensed him, exactly, although it had been a blustery, dark-skied week, and Kate had had premonitions of death in her troubled sleep. For the first few days of the trip, Kate had shared the cottage with Sadie, her younger cousin, visiting from two villages over. George had probably been watching them, waiting for a moment when Kate was alone. He'd been sleeping rough in a wood nearby. Afterward, after all that had happened, they'd found his tent and a sodden sleeping bag hidden in a copse.

Midway through the week, and the first night that Sadie hadn't slept over in the cottage, Kate woke at just past midnight to find George seated next to her bed, the rifle lying casually across his lap. Kate had opened her mouth to scream and George had leapt on her, his knees on her chest, and pushed the oily barrel of the gun hard against her mouth, splitting her lip and breaking a tooth.

He held her like that on the bed for over an hour, telling her in a strange, flat monotone how she deserved to die for what she'd done to him. The way he spoke, the words he used, felt like they were coming from an entirely different person than the George she had known.

Kate quietly wept the whole time, her mind telling

her that the death she'd always feared was now here, crouched on her chest. She didn't try to bargain or appeal to George's humanity. She submitted, her body going limp like a bird caught in the jaws of a cat. Her bladder released and she didn't even realize it till she smelled the sharp smell of her own urine. Her submission probably kept her alive. If she'd fought back, tried to convince George to not kill her, her words would probably have been enough to allow him to pull the trigger. Instead, he dragged her across the floor and pushed her into the small, cramped closet, shutting the door and jamming it with a wooden chair. Maybe he did it because he knew the dark, tight closet was a fate worse than death for Kate. Maybe he did it because after being unable to kill her, George simply wanted Kate out of his sight. Trapped in the closet, Kate began to scream uncontrollably, violently, till her vocal cords were raw. And then she wept until, finally, she stopped weeping, curled into a tight ball, and felt nothing.

It could have been two hours or twelve hours later when she heard the explosion of the rifle on the other side of the closet door.

Two days later, Kate's cousin returned to find her. The front door of the cottage was unlocked, and George's body was on the floor in front of the barricaded closet. The contents of his skull were spread across the rug.

It was the police who pulled Kate from the closet. She was conscious but unresponsive. Her eyes were squeezed shut, so she didn't see the remains of George Daniels as she was carried from the house. She spent three months in rehab—half of that time unresponsive—before she went home to her parents.

She never returned to university.

*

Five minutes after sending her mother the e-mail about Audrey Marshall, she received a reply:

> Terrible, darling. Your father and I say come home. Has someone told Corbin?

But it has nothing to do with me, Kate began to write back, then stopped herself. Her fingers rested, unmoving, on the keys of her laptop. She deleted the words. She'd reply to her mother later. She'd reply after she figured out what to do, and she hadn't done that yet. She wanted to stay, and begin her course tomorrow, because Audrey's murder (did she even know it was a murder?) really did have nothing to do with her.

You don't believe that, do you? George's voice, but also her own.

Maybe it has something to do with me. Because it has something to do with Corbin, and I'm in his apartment. The police have been here, and Audrey's friend knew something about what might have happened.

Suddenly, the high-ceilinged apartment felt cramped

and too warm. And was it her imagination, or had it turned darker? She turned to the tall windows and saw that an inky cloud had crossed in front of the sun. She watched it continue on its path, till the sun was shining again. Still, the sun was lower in the sky than it should be. She checked the time on her cell phone and discovered it was almost five in the afternoon. How had it gotten so late so fast? She'd been thinking of George, of course, and sometimes when she did that time would slip away. Like it had in the closet when she'd been eaten by the darkness and by time itself. She didn't even think of it as a closet. It had been a room, the smallest room, and she had never left it. It was dark, and all four walls pressed against her.

Go outside, she told herself, and eat a proper meal. And she found herself standing, her head light with lack of food. Before she had too much time to think about it, she grabbed her coat, and an umbrella just in case, and forced herself to leave the apartment.

Chapter 10

Alan had been pacing back and forth across his apartment, steeling himself to go over and talk with Kate, Corbin's cousin who was staying at his place. He wanted to find out what she knew about Audrey and Corbin, even though he knew that the very act of speaking with her was going to reveal his own interest. He'd already told her that he barely knew Audrey. What would he tell her now? The truth? Part of the truth?

He looked out his window, as he'd been doing all day long. The police had not returned. The courtyard was quiet.

He walked to the mirror that Quinn had hung next to the front door. He rubbed at the skin below his eyes as though he could rub away the dark hollows. He wore his favorite vintage blazer and a knotted cashmere scarf. He'd put the scarf on so long ago—preparing himself to leave—that his neck had gotten sweaty. He took it off. Why would he need a scarf just to go across to another apartment?

He paced back to the window and saw Kate crossing the courtyard toward the street. Without thinking, he bolted to his bedroom, grabbed his wallet, then raced out his own door, taking the stairs down to the lobby three at a time.

By the time he reached the courtyard Kate had disappeared, but when he reached Bury Street he spotted her a block and a half away, making her way toward Charles. He began to follow. It was cooler than he thought, and he regretted taking off his scarf. He buttoned all three buttons on his blazer and turned the collar up. The clouds were building up in the sky again and he wondered if it might rain.

When Kate reached Charles, she stopped for a moment. Alan slowed his pace. He was only about half a block away, close enough to see that she held a small orange umbrella in her left hand. She turned left. Alan wondered if she was looking for a place to eat, or if she was just taking a walk. Either way, he'd follow her. It would be easier to approach her in a restaurant, pretend that he was also there for dinner. It might look suspicious, but he *did* live in the neighborhood.

Charles Street was quiet, mostly dog walkers and mothers pushing strollers. A man with a stricken face hustled past carrying a bouquet of expensive-looking flowers. A husband who'd forgotten an anniversary, Alan thought. Kate was walking slowly, pausing to look through the windows of the many small bistros that lined this stretch of Charles. She was clearly looking for a place to eat. Alan forced himself to walk slowly as well, pausing at one point in front of an old carriage house that had been converted into a swank residence. He bent and tied his shoe. The brick sidewalk was still wet from an earlier shower, and he could smell an earthy scent, the smell of spring. Winter, always long in New England, had been particularly brutal this past year, dumping over four feet of snow in a two-week stretch at the end of January.

Alan watched Kate cross the street. She was hesitant, looking to the right and left as though she couldn't remember which way the cars would be coming from. Alan followed her across Charles, then up a narrow gaslit side street where she entered a place called St. Stephen's Tavern that Alan had never been to, even though he'd passed it frequently.

He kept walking, not wanting to look like he was following her. She was probably eating, which meant she'd be there for at least an hour. Alan decided he had time for a quick drink down at the Sevens before showing up at St. Stephen's. He walked fast, down the impossibly steep side street, then back onto Charles, where he pushed through the door into the narrow interior of his favorite bar. He ordered a rye and ginger ale, and drank it standing up, elbow perched on the wooden bar.

He was in a state of nervous excitement, he realized, from following this woman he barely knew. What was wrong with him? Maybe his obsession with Audrey had had nothing to do with Audrey herself and everything to do with the fact that he could watch her from afar.

Not for the first time, an uncomfortable memory resurfaced. He'd been thirteen years old, and his sister, sixteen at the time, had a summer job as a camp counselor in

Maine. His parents had put him on a bus to visit her one weekend, and he'd been given a spare room in the counselors' area, a row of dorm-style rooms on the second floor of the main lodge. On his first night there, he'd discovered a knothole in one of the planks of wood that allowed him to see into the adjacent bedroom. With his own lights off, he'd watched a female counselor, a chubby girl with small breasts, about his sister's age, undress. She put on an oversized T-shirt with the logo from the camp on it, and got in bed to write in her diary. After only about three minutes of writing, she laid the diary on her chest and, with her lamp still on, began to touch herself between her legs. Alan watched, rapt and fascinated. He knew what masturbation was, and had shamefully done it himself, but hadn't known that it was something girls did. The girl began to rub more furiously, then stopped suddenly, closed her diary, slid it under her bed, and turned off the lamp.

Alan lay in the blackness, straining to hear anything through the pine walls. He thought he could hear the rhythmic squeak of cheap bedsprings, but then it stopped. He heard a long sigh, the girl letting her breath out as though she'd been holding it. Then nothing.

The next day he spotted the counselor in the dining hall at a table with some of the younger campers. He'd barely looked at her face the night before, but he studied it now. It was all circles. She had full cheeks and round eyes, and Alan even noticed that her small ears, unpierced, were perfectly round as well. She was laughing uproariously at something one of the campers, a girl with red hair, had just said. The girl flushed, and the counselor put her arm around her, pulling her against her side. She was pretty, the counselor, especially when she smiled, and Alan could hardly believe what he had seen her do the night before. It didn't exactly fit in with the way she was acting now.

"You okay there, little brother?"

Alan was eating at the visitor's table, but Hannah, his sister, had come over to see him. "Fine," he said.

"You looked like you'd been hypnotized. You wanna go on a blueberry-picking trip with cabin five today, or would you rather just hang out by the beach?"

Alan picked the beach, bringing a copy of *Red Dragon* that he'd found in the counselors' quarters. He could swim in the shallow, roped-off section of the lake, but since he hadn't taken his deep-water test, he was banned from swimming off the pier. It was fine with him. He was happy to sit on the beach with his book open in front of him, hoping to see the counselor from the adjacent bedroom. He never saw her by the water, but spotted her later giving tennis lessons to several campers and then at dinner, which was an outdoor barbecue. Each time he spotted her he felt a sickening but addictive rush of adrenaline. He could barely wait for nighttime, when he hoped to see her through the knothole again. He told his sister he had a stomachache and got back to his room early. He turned off his light and waited, feverishly imagining what she might do when she returned to her room.

But when she did show up, she grabbed her robe and a shower caddy and disappeared to the showers. When she returned she was wearing her nightshirt under the robe and slipped immediately into her cot. She was less than a foot away from the wall, and Alan could see the fine blond hairs on the tops of her thighs. She took a deep, yawning breath that turned into a coughing fit, then turned the light out. Alan lay back on his bed and listened to hear if she was touching herself again, but he heard nothing. He thought he could smell the faint, stale odor of cigarettes. She began to breathe deeply. Eventually, he fell asleep.

He never saw her again. If she was at breakfast the following morning he couldn't find her, and after breakfast Hannah drove him to the bus station. Alan still remembered the gutted feeling he'd had as the bus chugged away from the station. He would never see the nameless counselor again. She was gone forever.

He finished his drink, paid, and walked out of the Sevens.

Outside, Alan noticed that the trees, starting to blossom, were newly wet. There must have been a passing shower while he'd been in the bar. The air smelled clean, and all the brick sidewalks had darkened.

He walked up the hill toward St. Stephen's and entered through its frosted glass doors, telling himself to look casual and go straight to the bar, which he did. He ordered another rye and ginger from the pretty bartender in a tight Bruins T-shirt, then leaned back a little on the swivel stool and glanced around. St. Stephen's was not a whole lot bigger than the Sevens. There was room enough for a long wooden bar and about a half-dozen booths. At the bar were two men, each drinking stout and each looking at their cell phones. Alan couldn't tell if they were together or simply seated next to one another.

Most of the booths were empty, but one held a husband and wife with their two kids, and at another was a lone woman looking at a laptop. She had dyed red hair, and was so short that her feet dangled from the booth's wooden seat.

Alan turned as the bartender was placing his drink in front of him. He thanked her and took a sip. He drank from his straw, and the first sip was pure alcohol. He stirred the drink and removed the wedge of desiccated lime. There was no sign of Kate. Maybe she'd just come in for a single drink and then left. Or maybe there was a back dining room that Alan couldn't see. He was about to ask the bartender when the ladies' room door swung open with a harsh metallic screech. Alan turned, and there was Kate.

Chapter 11

After using the dingy toilets, Kate pushed her way back into the restaurant. There, sitting at the bar, was Alan Cherney, looking in her direction. Their eyes met. A warning went off in her head. Had he followed her here? And if so, why?

He swiveled minutely on his bar seat, scrunching his brow as though trying to place her. She stepped forward.

"Hiya," she said.

"Hello," he answered. He wore a beautiful tweed coat, and under it, a shirt with a frayed collar.

"Kate Priddy. I'm in your building. In Corbin Dell's apartment."

"Oh right. Right. I know that. It's Alan."

"Yes, I remember you. You just here for a drink? Is this a place you come to a lot?" Kate inexplicably laughed after asking this question. Whatever ease they had had when they first met had disappeared. Maybe it was because Alan, in the dim light of the tavern, looked like a nervous public speaker facing a massive audience.

"No, no," he said. "I've come here before, maybe once, but not too often. How did you even know about it? I lived here for a year before I found it."

"Corbin recommended it. I'm eating dinner." She indicated with a turn of her head the farthest booth, directly underneath the tavern's lone television, silently showing highlights from a golf match being played somewhere sunny and warm.

"Well, I don't want to interrupt you—"

"No, join me," Kate said, surprising herself. "Unless you have—"

"No, I'd love to."

Alan brought his drink over and sat across from Kate, who was halfway through her second glass of wine. Her bowl of chicken chili had arrived while she'd been in the toilets. It was enormous, on a plate that was festooned with multicolored tortilla chips. "Have you eaten?" Kate asked.

"No, I haven't, but . . ."

"But you took one look at my dinner, and . . ."

Alan laughed. "No, I'm just not that hungry. I keep thinking about Audrey. Remember, we talked about her."

"I know. It's terrible. The police came and talked with me."

"Yeah, me too. Well, they took a statement."

"Did they search your place?"

"No, did they search yours?"

"Briefly."

"Huh." Alan shifted in his seat, crossing his legs under the table and bumping a knee.

Kate then told him about Jack Ludovico, Audrey's

friend, who she'd talked to on the street. Alan listened intently, sipping at his drink.

"What did he look like?" Alan asked when Kate had taken a break from talking to eat her rapidly cooling chili.

Kate hesitated. Alan's rapt attention was unnerving somehow. Maybe she shouldn't have invited him to join her. "Only if you tell me why you're so interested," she finally said. "I know you said you barely knew Audrey, but I don't know if I believe you."

She watched as Alan made up his mind. His expressive face seemed to register everything, and Kate wondered if he knew that about himself, knew how easy it was to read him. "Okay," he said. "I didn't actually know Audrey Marshall. We never met, but I could see her through my window in my apartment. I have the place opposite her and we both look over the courtyard, so sometimes I watched her—I know that sounds incredibly creepy, but it wasn't like that. I couldn't see into her bedroom, or anything, but sometimes I watched her reading in her living room. She just seemed very nice."

"You could tell that from looking through a window?"

"No, I couldn't tell that, obviously, but I *thought* that. I imagined that. Look, I do know it's creepy. It *is* creepy. I guess I became a little obsessed with her."

"In what way?"

"What do you mean?"

"In what way did you become obsessed, like what did you imagine might happen?"

Alan pressed his lips together, hard enough that they became colorless. He ran a finger along the rim of his glass. "I imagined that maybe we could meet and be together. That was it. I actually formed a plan that we could run into one another, but then she started seeing your cousin, Corbin."

"Yeah, I heard that. From the friend."

"He knew?"

"He did. Yeah. He said they were an on-and-off thing, and he sounded suspicious of him. I think he thinks Corbin has something to do with what happened."

"What did this guy look like?"

"Who, Jack?"

"Yeah."

Kate described him. His red, unkempt hair, the wiry frame, his flushed skin.

"I don't know him," Alan said. "I never saw him at Audrey's place."

Kate almost responded by saying that that hardly meant he wasn't there, but she stopped herself. Something about Alan's certainty made her realize that he really had been obsessed with Audrey, and had probably spent an enormous amount of time watching her through the window.

"It's possible he didn't spend time at her place," Kate said.

"Yeah, it's possible. I used to see Corbin there, though."

"At Audrey's place?"

"Yeah, that's how I knew they were seeing each other. He used to be over there a lot."

"How'd you know they weren't just friends?"

"I saw them kissing a few times, I guess," Alan said, clearly embarrassed.

"Did you know Corbin?"

"I did, a little," Alan said. "I used to play racquetball with him. Not a lot, but a few times, and one of those times I asked him about Audrey, about whether he was seeing her, and he denied it. It was strange, at the time, because I'd seen them through the window, and knew that there was something between them. I just didn't understand why he would deny it."

"There could have been many reasons," Kate said, having finally had a few bites of her chili, grown cold in the wide bowl. "Maybe he was seeing someone else at the same time, or maybe Audrey was. Who knows, maybe Corbin just thought you were being a nosy git and didn't want to confide in you."

Alan smiled his beautiful smile, so at odds with the gauntness of his face. "Probably that one," he said.

"Which one? The nosy git?"

"Yeah, that one. I don't know. I think I've just gotten paranoid. It seemed shifty at the time that he wouldn't admit to seeing Audrey even though I knew he was."

"So, you suspect Corbin, too? That's what you're saying?"

"When did he leave for London? Exactly?"

"That's what Jack wanted to know. He took a night flight on Thursday night. I don't know what time exactly, but he got to London early in the morning, so, in theory . . ."

"In theory he could have killed Audrey."

"I suppose so."

"And the police seem interested," Alan said, then tilted his glass to get the last sip of his drink. "They searched your place—his place. What's it like, anyway, his place?"

"Like something from a design magazine, but dated. It was his father's apartment—that's why he's living there."

"I didn't know that."

A waitress swung by to see if they needed anything else. Alan ordered another drink and Kate asked for a water. "My jet lag's been terrible," she said. "I've lost all sense of time since I've been here. I'm exhausted all afternoon and wide awake before dawn."

"Quick. What time is it now?" Alan asked, a slight smile on his face.

"It feels like midnight, but I think it's only around six."

Alan pulled his phone out of his pocket and looked at its screen. "It's just past six." He put his phone down on the scarred wooden table and Kate noticed that his screen image was the purple and black movie poster from *The Exorcist*. It was one of her favorite films, but she didn't say anything. She'd always loved horror movies, despite the traumas of her past and her own fervid imagination. They calmed her, in the same way that genuine apprehension calmed her. And they showed her that nightmares existed for other people, as well, even if those other people were fictional. Alan's screen went to black, and Kate realized she'd been staring at it.

"I'm fading," Kate said. "I think I'll go back soon. I'm not trying to run away from you."

"That's okay if you are," Alan said, and grinned. "I'd understand."

"Why do you say that?"

"Because I just told you how I used to spy on my neighbor through my window and became obsessed with her."

"No. I really am tired. And I wouldn't judge anyone for being obsessive. I've been thinking about Audrey Marshall ever since I got here."

"Because she was murdered in the apartment next to yours."

"No, even before that. When I first heard she was missing, I knew something bad had happened. Well, I always think that—it's my nature—but I was right this time."

The waitress appeared with Alan's drink and asked them if they wanted anything else. Kate asked for a check, then Alan did as well.

"Can I walk back with you?" Alan asked.

Kate pictured the long narrow street that led from the tavern back to the well-lighted busyness of Charles Street. Was Alan a murderer? He'd clearly been obsessed with Audrey. And from afar. But if he was, then why come to her and confess all that he'd confessed? Was it to get information? Find out what she knew?

"It's totally fine if—" Alan started to say, as though reading Kate's mind.

"No, we can walk back together. Sorry, I'm spacing out."

After paying their separate checks, they exited onto the dark street, Alan leaving half his drink behind. The rain had stopped but the trees still dripped, and the sidewalk was covered with fallen magnolia blossoms, the air heavy with their cloying smell.

If we get to the end of this street, and Alan hasn't strangled me, then he never will, Kate told herself. She began to count the steps silently to herself, but Alan said, as though reading her mind, "I had nothing to do with what happened to Audrey."

"I know," Kate said.

"Do you think I should go to the police and tell them what I know?"

"You mean, what you know about Corbin?"

"Yeah."

"You should, probably, unless Corbin already told them. It's not as though you have crucial information. You might just have information they already have. I'll find out for you. I'm definitely e-mailing Corbin tonight. I was putting it off because I didn't know whether he'd heard from the police yet or not."

"You'll let me know?"

"I will," Kate said. They were halfway down the steep side street, Kate walking slowly in her boots because of the slipperiness of the fallen blossoms and the recent rain. She imagined herself falling, sliding onto Charles Street and getting crushed by some huge American SUV. But they made it all the way down and walked the rest of the way back to Bury Street. They talked some of the way, and Kate felt again the same ease with Alan that she'd felt the first time they'd met, as though they'd known each other for years and years. She reminded herself that she'd once felt the same thing for George Daniels.

They parted ways in the lobby of the building, Kate promising to let Alan know what she found out from Corbin.

"Come by my apartment and let me know. You know where I live." He smiled, a little crookedly.

"Is your side the exact same as my side?"

"Exactly." They said goodbye.

Sanders the cat was in the lobby, and he followed Kate up the stairs and down the hall to her door. She opened the door fractionally and placed her foot near the jamb to block him, but he quickly leapt over her foot and into her apartment. She entered and shut the door behind her. The cat was nowhere to be seen, but she decided to not worry about him; it was clear that he belonged to the entire apartment building.

She went straight to her laptop and opened her e-mail account. Corbin had written her:

Just heard about what happened from the police. I'm totally shocked. I didn't know her that well, but I knew her, of course, a little bit. Do you know what happened? The police only told me that she was dead. Was it a suicide? And how are you doing? I'm sorry that your first few days in America have been stressful, and I understand if you want to come back. It must be scary to arrive in a new place and find out that your neighbor has died. Trust me, it's a safe apartment building.

Not that it matters much, but I'm loving my time in London, and your flat is in good hands. Write to me with any news. Sorry, again. Corbin

Kate read it twice. Why would he deny that he had been involved with Audrey Marshall? Why didn't he use her name?

Before writing him back, Kate looked through her other e-mails. Mostly junk, but there was one from Martha Lambert, who lived on the first floor of her building in London. When Kate had first moved in—nearly a year ago—Martha had immediately assigned herself the role of new best friend. Kate hadn't minded, even though Martha's sole interests were going to the pub and landing a man. When Kate moved to London she'd been determined to be a little bit social, and Martha, with her constant invites, had at least made that part easy. Her e-mail, not surprisingly, was about Corbin:

Miss you, Kate, but I am v pleased with your replacement. He's gorgeous, as you know. You should have seen Michael's jaw drop when he saw him down the pudding. He's friendly, too, but I won't go too much into that right now. How is it over there? What's his flat like? Kisses, darling, I really do miss you. Martha

Kate opened up a reply window and stared at it for a minute, not knowing what to write. Should she warn her? Something moved in the periphery of her vision, and her heart stutter-stepped. It was Sanders, returning to the room from his tour of the premises. He sat back on his haunches and looked quizzically at Kate.

"He's not here," she said aloud.

To her surprise, Sanders answered back, a querulous meow.

She got up and went and opened the front door, and Sanders pranced off, brushing his tail against her leg on the way out. She shut the door and pressed her eye against the peephole to see where the cat went, but he was already gone from the hallway.

She returned to the e-mails. Should she tell Martha to be wary of Corbin? She should, of course, but she knew Martha well enough to know that it would totally fall on deaf ears. Instead she wrote:

Don't you dare do anything in my bed, that's all

I ask. Boston is nice, and Corbin's flat is bigger than mine. More later. Still jet-lagged. Kate

She didn't want to say too much more about the flat. If Martha knew how rich Corbin was, her predatory instincts would become even more heightened.

Kate opened up a response box to Corbin, then paused. What should she tell him? She decided to tell him the basic truth, leaving out what she'd heard from Alan, leaving out Alan altogether. So she wrote him back, telling him that the police had asked to search his place and she'd agreed, and she mentioned the key. This information, at least, would give him a chance to let Kate know that he didn't want the police in his apartment without a warrant. She hit send. It would be past midnight in London, and she wondered if Corbin was even up.

Before putting her laptop away, Kate searched for any new information on the death of Audrey Marshall. She found a story that indicated that the body removed from 101 Bury Street had been positively identified as Audrey Helen Marshall, and that her death was being treated as suspicious by the police.

Kate finally put her laptop away after clicking on several other news stories that all had the same, limited information. She went to the bedroom and got her datebook. Even though she knew that her first design class in Cambridge began the following day at one in the afternoon, she double-checked it. She'd already decided to leave early, give herself time to figure out the public transportation, and how to get to the school from the Porter Square T station. She sat on the edge of the bed, exhausted suddenly, but instead of leaning back, tucking herself up under the covers, and going to sleep, she grabbed the Dick Francis she'd started earlier, plus her well-worn copy of *I Capture the Castle,* a book she'd read many times.

She brought both of the books, plus the quilted comforter, across the expanse of the apartment to the leather couch in the den. She stretched out and opened the Dick Francis novel. She read one paragraph, then her eyes closed, the book still propped on her chest.

She was back in Audrey's apartment, and Alan was there, crouched on the floor, his head tilted up and back, and looking at her. *That's not Alan,* Kate thought. *That must be George.* But it *was* Alan. His fingers dug at the floor of Audrey's apartment, as though he was trying to find something buried in the wood. He opened his mouth, and a cat's meow came out. He dug some more, his nails making plucking sounds against the floor. Then he meowed again, louder, almost a keening sound. Kate woke with a jolt, both books sliding with the comforter to the floor.

Sanders was back in the apartment, scratching at the couch's arm.

Chapter 12

Corbin Dell emerged from the taxicab into the cool air of late morning. It wasn't raining but the atmosphere was damp, the sky low and white. Corbin hadn't been to London since the spring semester of his junior year, which he'd spent at the Hutchinson School of Business and Economics, and because of that, he wasn't sure how he'd feel arriving back in this haunted city. But he felt okay. Tired, because he'd only slept for about one hour during the flight from Boston to Dublin. He'd drunk some bad coffee during the lengthy layover and now he was jittery and slightly nauseous, his mouth coated with a bitter taste. The outside air was nice after the long ride from Heathrow.

The driver removed Corbin's matching luggage from the cab and placed it on the sidewalk. Sheepscar Lane was long and gray, the sidewalks lined with pollarded trees. Workmen were fixing a portion of the road, and the air smelled sharply of warm tar. It was that smell, more than anything else, that brought London flooding back. As a student, Corbin had lived in Camden Town, also in North London, and that sticky, slightly sweet smell of tar had always been in the air. He'd forgotten all about it. He felt twenty years old again, walking back in a cold dawn from Claire's flat on the other side of Regent's Park, having finally lost his virginity. He had been happy, exhilarated almost, but the memory of it was painful, for so many reasons. Maybe he shouldn't have come back after all, Corbin thought.

Kate's flat was in a squat stone building with a patch of front garden large enough for one midsized bush. The trim was white, and the front door was painted a deep shade of blue, edged by small panes of glass. There were three mailboxes affixed to the inside of the entryway, and Corbin pulled the envelope from the box for apartment 2. He could feel the contours of the key inside. He slipped it out, opened the outside door, and hauled his giant Victorinox suitcase over the threshold into a narrow, high-ceilinged foyer. When the outside door rattled shut behind him, it was dark inside, even with the multiple small windows. Corbin found a switch; it turned on a hanging lamp that cast a yellow light. The floor of the foyer was covered in black and white linoleum and the walls were thickly painted in a light blue. He carried his luggage up the steep stairwell to the second-floor entrance and walked into the flat.

Kate had described the place in one of her e-mails, but the layout was still surprising. The exterior door opened into the bedroom, then a short stairway led to the bathroom, halfway up the stairs, while the rest of the rooms, a kitchen and a bay-fronted living room, were located at the top of the stairs. There were windows overlooking the street from the living room, and windows down the stairs in the bedroom that looked out over a paved back patio, but that was it, since the building was attached on either side. It should have felt claustrophobic, but it didn't to Corbin. It felt comforting, almost, and it was decorated, not in a feminine way, but in a way that seemed cozy. There were throw rugs in bright colors and large pillows on both the bed and the living room couch. The walls were painted white and hung with graphic prints.

Corbin used the bathroom, then unpacked all his clothes, putting them in an empty drawer that had been marked with a sticky note from Kate, indicating that it had been emptied for him. He thought of showering, but he was too tired. A low, throbbing headache was starting up in his temples, and his shoulders and neck were stiff from the flight. He swallowed four ibuprofens. The tap water was terrible, and he made a mental note to buy a case of bottled water as soon as possible. He stripped out of all his clothes but his boxer briefs and his T-shirt and stretched out on the living room couch with Kate's long, handwritten letter. Annoyance flared up inside of him that she had taken time to write out a comprehensive guide to the neighborhood pubs and restaurants. He was only annoyed, though, because he hadn't done something similar. Well, he could write her an e-mail and suggest some places. And he'd left her that bottle of champagne in the fridge—that would count for something. Besides, wait till she saw his place. She'd be impressed, he was sure of that.

Kate would be on the plane now, pocketed somewhere above the Atlantic. He tried to picture her, but had trouble. He'd only seen a couple of photographs of her before, both from a few years ago. One was a photo that his father had taken during a trip to England a year before he died. He'd gone over for a large family wedding. Corbin remembered that he'd tried to talk both Corbin and his brother, Philip, into coming. Philip never would have come because it would have disappointed their mother, and Philip would never do anything to disappoint her. Corbin hadn't gone because of work. When Richard Dell returned, he'd printed the digital pictures he'd taken and cut them into the size of regular photographs to fit them into an album. Richard showed Corbin the book, pointing out myriad English relatives. That was when Corbin had first seen Kate, bracketed on either side by her father and her mother, Richard's cousin. "My favorite cousin," he told Corbin. "We were more like brother and sister, really, and this girl, this Kate, is the spitting image, the, the . . ."

He trailed off. Richard had retired a few years after the divorce, and since retiring, he'd aged noticeably. Not just physically, although there was that, but mentally. He seemed frail, and even sometimes weepy.

"Maybe I should never have left," Richard said, after they'd looked at every picture.

"Well, then—"

"Well, then, yes, I'd never have had you lovely boys, but your mother . . ."

Corbin didn't need to hear about her. He'd heard plenty already.

The only other picture Corbin had seen of Kate was one that was attached to her e-mail account, a small square color photograph in which Kate's face was three-quarters obscured by a book she was reading. Only her eyes peered at the camera.

There must be pictures here, Corbin thought, and almost got off the couch. There's time, he told himself. I'm here for six whole months, he thought, and the thought scared him a little. He yawned several times, his jaw popping. A spatter of rain hit the pane of glass above him. He fell asleep.

He woke, as he always did, suddenly—his eyes opening on their own, his mind fully conscious, any dreams he might have had already expunged and gone, like blackened matches. He sat up. The headache was gone, but in its place was a ravenous hunger. He checked his phone. It was midafternoon.

He went to the kitchen, found an apple, and devoured it till it was nothing more than a pencil-thin core. He opened drawers looking for something else to eat, but there was very little. Everything in the kitchen was small, including a refrigerator not much bigger than a dorm fridge, a tiny porcelain-topped table pushed into a nook, and what looked like a dishwasher but turned out to be, in fact, a laundry machine. Corbin looked, but couldn't find a dryer. It was something he could ask Kate about in an e-mail. He should check his account, anyway, especially since he hadn't heard yet from the office he was supposed to be reporting to on Monday. He went back to the living room and found the part in Kate's welcome letter where she gave him instructions on how to get onto wireless. He opened his laptop and checked messages, his mind rapidly seeking out Audrey Marshall's name even though he knew that a message from her wasn't a possibility. His brother had written to ask him when he was heading to London, because his mother wanted to know.

Corbin checked the Red Sox box scores from the night before, then jotted off a message to Kate, thanking her for the lengthy letter and mentioning the dryer. Then he shut the laptop down, got dressed again, and went out to find some food.

*

It wasn't even four thirty yet, but the Beef and Pudding, the closest pub and one that Kate had recommended, was filling up. Corbin grabbed an upholstered bench with a low table in front of it, waited for a few minutes for a waitress to appear, then remembered than in England you ordered at the bar. He left his jacket on his seat and shouldered his way into the crowded bar area. He ordered a Guinness Extra Cold, and when he asked about food, was directed to a large blackboard, menu items written out in green chalk. He ordered a spaghetti Bolognese and went back to his seat.

He nursed his Guinness and when the food came he ate it as slowly as he could, even though what he wanted to do was to bolt it like a dog. Done eating, he went back to the bar for more beer, deciding to try cask ales he hadn't tasted before. He sat back down with something called Greene King Abbot Ale, and had finished half of it when a woman in tight jeans and a patterned sweater said hello and asked if he was Kate Priddy's cousin. "I was next to you at the bar and heard your American accent. I live upstairs from you."

They had several drinks together and she introduced him to some of the bartenders, plus a few of her friends. Her name was Martha, and every time she went to the bathroom, she came back with reapplied bright red streaks of lipstick across her mouth. He kept drinking the Abbot Ale and she drank white wine, switching to something with vodka at the end of the night. They walked home together through a light, misty rain, and outside of 684 Sheepscar they wound up pressed up against a temporary Dumpster, kissing and groping at one another. She bit the lobe of his ear and told him she liked his accent. He slid fingers down the back of her jeans and touched the thin floss of her underpants, and that, more than anything else, sobered him up. He could feel that combination of fear and disgust spreading across his body. And even though he knew there was little chance that someone was watching them, it was still in the back of his mind. The way it always was.

It took all his will not to push the drunk girl away. Instead, he stopped kissing her.

"I'm exhausted," he said.

"You must be, poor thing," she answered. Her mouth was ringed with smudged lipstick, and her eyes were slightly out of focus. Corbin could hear the sound of distant laughter carrying through the rain; other drunk people returning from a night out. A drip of cool rain slid underneath his collar and down his back, and he shivered. Then, for one awful moment, he could taste the spaghetti at the back of his throat, and he thought he was going to be sick. It passed, and he told Martha that he really needed to get some sleep. They entered the house together, and Martha kissed him again on his landing. He kept his lips tightly closed even though he could feel the tip of her tongue flicking past her teeth.

Inside, he chugged some of the tepid water in the kitchen and took four more ibuprofens. He actually wasn't tired. He'd slept too much that afternoon, and now, even though it was midnight in London, it wasn't even eight o'clock yet in Boston. Kate would be at his place by now, probably trying to stay awake. He tried to picture her in his apartment in Boston, but couldn't. It felt wrong, somehow.

After doing a hundred push-ups on the orange area rug in the bedroom, Corbin took a shower, carefully stepping over the high lip of the bathtub, then standing under the stream of almost-hot water. He closed his eyes, letting the low-pressure spray hit the back of his neck, and stood so long that the water eventually lost its warmth. He was shivering by the time he pulled on his cotton pajama bottoms and got under the covers of Kate's bed. The sheets were soft flannel, tucked tightly under the corners of the bed, and he kicked his feet out from under them. It was the only way he could sleep, even when he was cold. The bed was softer than he liked. He turned off the bedside lamp, but the room, with the curtains open, was relatively light, and his eyes eventually adjusted so much that he could read the print on the framed poster across from the bed. THE FACE IN THE CORNER: ANIMAL PORTRAITS, NATIONAL PORTRAIT GALLERY, LONDON, 1998. There was a painting of a lady, and in the foreground, a black cat dipping a paw into a goldfish bowl. He thought of Sanders, the cat that was always in his apartment. Thinking of Sanders made him think of everything he'd left behind, but he shut down those thoughts. Instead, he closed his eyes, trying to will himself to sleep. Despite the shower, he could still smell Martha, the girl from the pub, all over him. He thought of her upstairs, now, wondering if she was thinking of him. Of course she was. He could go upstairs right now and fuck her if he wanted to. The thought filled him with sadness, more than anything. He pictured her drunken, excited expression as she opened the door, the way she'd lift her hips to let him take off her tiny underpants, the awful expectant look in her eyes. Then he imagined the look of fear in those eyes.

He turned the thought off as he shifted over onto his stomach. He pressed his face into the unfamiliar pillow that smelled of floral dryer sheets. He hadn't had a thought like that for a while. Maybe it was being in London. Maybe coming here had been a big mistake. He'd thought fifteen years had been enough time, but clearly it wasn't. She'd been on his mind all day. So he allowed himself to think of her, to think of Claire Brennan, the girl who changed everything.

Chapter 13

The Hutchinson School of Business and Economics, where Corbin Dell studied during the second semester of his junior year, was situated in an ugly block of Georgian flats just south of the Mornington Crescent tube station. The school also owned and operated the Three Lambs pub, a wood-paneled drinking hole in the student union. It was there that Corbin met Claire Brennan, who was serving that night at the bar.

"What's good here?" he'd shouted above the overloud Coldplay song coming from the speakers.

She pushed a strand of her raven-black hair behind an ear and leaned across the bar. "Sorry. What'll you have?"

Corbin almost asked her again what was good but her cold blue eyes stopped him. He glanced across the beer pumps, selecting one at random.

"Pint or half?" she asked. Her accent was thick and lilting.

"Half," Corbin said, not knowing what it even meant.

After being served, Corbin sipped at his small glass of malty-tasting liquid. It was his second night in London. He'd gone to an orientation earlier that day with other visiting American students. Most of the orientation had been centered on how to find a flat in the city, and afterward, the other American students, gripping their list of real estate agents, had anxiously formed small groups to hunt for lodging. Corbin already had a place to stay, however, so he walked out of the orientation not having met anyone. His father had set him up in the spare room of a friend's apartment. It was a tiny flat on the third floor of a narrow brick building on a residential street south of the river. The spare bedroom was closer in size to a closet, and judging by the sparse furnishings in the rest of the flat—a stereo system, a loaded bar, a bed with satin sheets in the master bedroom—it was clear that the flat was probably nothing more than a sex hideaway for his father's business colleague. "He's never there," his dad had said. "You'll have your own bachelor pad in London."

Corbin hated the place already, and had gone to the Three Lambs in hopes of meeting other students. After getting his drink he leaned against the bar and surveyed the room, half populated with students, most in groups of three or four. He noticed, with a stab of shame, that the only students with small glasses of beer were female students, and that all the men had full pint glasses. He felt sudden, deep hatred for the bartender for even asking him what size glass he wanted. It should have been obvious he'd wanted a full pint glass.

He turned his back to the room and drank the warm beer down in two gulps. The bartender was now serving three male students, all of whom were getting pint glasses of Foster's. Corbin decided to get one of those as well. He waited patiently for her to serve the other men. She kept dumping the foam off the top of the beer and refilling them. When she was finally done, she turned her attention to Corbin and he ordered a Foster's as well, adding that he'd like a big glass. She'd smiled at that, and Corbin felt the urge to punch her in the teeth.

He took the Foster's—so much better than the other beer—to a high stool along a paneled wall near the bar, and tried to look bored and uncaring. He scanned the room, not recognizing any of the students as Americans. There was a lull at the bar, and the bartender came out to pick up the empty glasses scattered around on tables. Coming back past Corbin, she stopped and asked if he was American.

"I'm a visiting student, yeah," he said.

"D'you know anyone looking for a room in a flat? I have a friend who's looking to sublet out a room."

"Where?"

"Camden. Not far from here."

Corbin told her that he might be interested, that he had a place already but hated it. He told her it was his dad's friend's sex flat, and made up that it was filled with dildos and bowls of condoms. The bartender threw her head back and laughed, exposing her creamy white throat. "You'll look at this other flat, then?" she asked.

Corbin agreed, was given an address, and by the second day of classes had moved into an equally scuzzy apartment that was at least a lot closer to his school. He shared the flat with a morose Irish girl, whose main advantage was that she was never there, and when she was, she was in her bedroom, weeping on the phone. The other advantage was that she was an acquaintance of the dark-haired, blue-eyed bartender, whose name was Claire Brennan, and after the brief conversation at the Three Lambs, Corbin's initial hatred had turned into a deep infatuation.

Before coming to London, Corbin had told himself that there was no way he was going to get romantically involved with anyone while overseas. The previous semester—his first of junior year—he'd been seeing a freshman girl named Sarah Scharfenberg, who lived down the hall in his dorm. She was a rarity at Mather, a midwestern girl who didn't spend freshman orientation week trying to fuck every frat brother she met. She told him she was practically a virgin and wanted to take it slow. It was okay with him. He even drove her to see his mother's home in New Essex on a weekend when he knew none of his family would be there. She'd been impressed. He'd loved seeing the expression on her face as she took in the enormous house, the view of the ocean, his mom's art collection.

Back in his dorm that night, she'd produced a condom and whispered into his ear: "I want to make love with you. Right now." The words sounded rehearsed, and her voice theatrically breathy. They stripped naked, but all Corbin felt was disgust. In the bad dorm lighting she suddenly looked cheap and pudgy, and Corbin noticed a discolored tooth he'd never seen before. He couldn't get hard and told her that he wasn't in the mood. She made it worse by repeatedly telling Corbin that it was okay. She even tried to rub his neck.

He'd stopped seeing her after that, although on the last night of first semester, he'd gotten drunk and pounded on her dorm-room door. He'd decided to give her what she wanted, after all. Her roommate answered, told Corbin that she was probably spending the night at her boyfriend's dorm. The way the roommate looked at him it was pretty clear that she'd heard the whole story. "Fucking whore," Corbin said before going to his own room to pass out.

And now he was in London, where he'd already decided to have nothing to do with girls and sex, and where he'd already fallen for Claire Brennan.

She was easy to find, because she worked most nights at the Three Lambs. Corbin would casually swing by, usually by himself. It turned out that he and Claire were in the same class—Intro to Macroeconomics—and some nights he'd bring a textbook, and they'd talk about it together, Corbin drinking Foster's and Claire drinking wine behind the bar. Even though she was Corbin's age, twenty, she seemed grown-up and sophisticated in a way that American girls didn't. For one, she was working to put herself through school, and she despised most of the

American students, who came over each semester and boozed their way through their three months in London. "Not you, Corbs," she said. "You're one step up from those arseholes, but a very small step." She held two fingers minutely apart, a wide grin on her face.

They rarely saw each other outside of the Three Lambs and the one class they shared, but with the first exam coming up, they wound up studying together at Claire's place in Queen's Park. It was a tiny studio flat, big enough for a bed, a desk, and a chair. They studied on the bed together. "Just sleep here," she'd said, when they'd finally decided to quit. It was past one in the morning, and the Underground was no longer running.

"I can get a taxi," Corbin said.

"Don't be an idiot"—she pronounced it like *eejit*— "just stay here."

"I kind of made a pledge to myself that I wasn't going to get involved with anyone while I was here in London."

She laughed. "Jesus, it's not like that."

They fell asleep without touching each other, but just past dawn, they wordlessly began to kiss, and before Corbin had a chance to tell her that he really meant what he said about becoming involved, they were having sex. It happened so fast that Corbin didn't have time to think about it, didn't have time to panic. Afterward, they kissed more, and Claire fell back asleep. Corbin didn't tell her that it was his first time.

Walking home through the cold, dewy morning, he'd

felt not just elated, but somehow vindicated. It hadn't been *him*. It had been the string of pathetic, inexperienced girl-friends he'd had that had been the real problem. He'd just needed to find a real woman, and he'd finally found one.

He aced the exam—no surprise there—and continued seeing Claire, their relationship completely different from anything Corbin had experienced before. For one, they rarely talked about what was happening between them, not because Corbin didn't want to, but because she didn't. Anytime he'd bring up their situation, she'd make a joke or call him an idiot. Corbin became fixated on what she was thinking, obsessing over the smallest of clues that might indicate her frame of mind. It made him angry with himself, but at the same time, he knew he was in love. He told her once, drunkenly, after returning from a school-sponsored booze cruise on the Thames. It had begun to pour on their walk home, and they'd ducked under the awning of a closed bakery and stood kissing.

"You reek of beer," she said.

"I love you," he responded.

She laughed, not entirely unkindly, then had fero-ciously kissed him. "You're my favorite American," she said, laughing some more.

"Thanks," Corbin said, telling himself to never again let her know how he felt.

He didn't, and the relationship—at least that was what Corbin was calling it in his own head—continued up until the final week of that term. Corbin fretted over the state of their affair, wondering if he should ask her if she wanted to visit him in America during the summer break. But before he'd steeled himself to initiate that conversation, everything changed. It was a Thursday, and Corbin was nursing a pint at a large anonymous pub near where he lived and rereading one of his texts, when Henry Wood, another American student in his program, came up to his table.

"You studying?" Henry asked.

"Yeah." Corbin held up the cover of the book.

"The classes here are ballbusters, eh?"

"Yeah, they are," Corbin said.

Corbin hadn't gotten to know too many fellow students during his time in London, but he'd gotten to know Henry, because everyone knew Henry. He was one of those effortless socializers, someone who remembered everyone's name, someone who always kept the conversation going. Shortly after orientation week he'd thrown a party at his rental, a sprawling ground-floor flat in Hampstead. It was a cold, raw night, but Henry had strung lights in the shared garden and even somehow purchased a keg. It wasn't just Americans at the party but English neighbors as well, sudden lifelong friends that Henry had made during his short time in London.

It had begun to snow that night, small white crystals that melted as soon as they touched a surface, but everyone stayed, huddled in the fenced-in garden till long past midnight. The first two hours of the party were awkward for Corbin, but the beer kicked in, and before he knew it, it was two in the morning and he was talking college football with a girl from the University of Richmond and a beefy student from Baylor who had his bare, tattooed arm draped over the shoulders of the girl. Corbin excused himself, deciding it was time to leave. He wandered back into the flat, looking down a side hall for a bathroom. Henry was in the frame of his bedroom door, an unlit cigarette between his lips. Corbin generally hated long hair on men, but Henry's dark hair—two inches below his shoulders, at least—suited him. He was on the short side, strong looking through the chest and shoulders, and with small facial features. Corbin thought of a fox, anthropomorphized, cocky and handsome.

The bathroom door swung open and a tall redhead in a short skirt emerged. She brushed past Corbin on the way to Henry's bedroom, trailing a hand across Henry's shirt as she entered.

Henry smiled, the cigarette still between his lips, and cocked his head toward the interior of the bedroom, raising an eyebrow. Corbin was confused for a moment, then realized that Henry was asking him to join them. Casually, Corbin held up both hands and shook his head. He could feel the blood rushing to his face and ducked into the bathroom. When he emerged Henry's bedroom door was shut.

Corbin had seen Henry several times since the party, and there was never any indication that Henry remembered the incident in the hallway. Corbin began to doubt what he'd seen. Had he really been asked into the bedroom for a threesome? The details of the night had blurred and now he wasn't so sure. But every time Corbin saw Henry, he felt a click of anxiety in his chest and found himself stumbling over his words. Not that he needed to say much in the presence of Henry, who liked to talk and prided himself on knowing everything about everyone. Corbin tried to convince himself that Henry was a boorish attention seeker, but every time they were together he found himself hoping to please Henry in some way. With a joke, or by telling Henry something he didn't already know. And when that happened, Corbin felt an embarrassing surge of pride. He wondered if other people felt the same way.

Henry, surprisingly, was alone in the pub, and even though Corbin was half panicked in anticipation of his Game Theory exam, he was happy to see him and invited him to sit down.

"You know, I can help you with that exam," Henry said, sprawling on a chair across from Corbin, pint glass in his hand.

"You're not in this class, are you?"

"No, but I got the scoop on it. Same exam every year. Your professor never, ever changes it. Wanna know the questions?"

"Sure."

Henry told Corbin what he'd heard, apparently from a student who'd come to this program the year before. "I memorized all the questions, then ended up not taking the class because it filled up. So that'll help you out, right?"

"You positive about this?"

"Ninety percent sure. Ninety-five percent. Don't worry, dude. Let's have another pint."

Corbin went and bought a round. The questions did sound legit; all of them were around subjects that Professor Hinchliffe—one of those old men with a spiderweb of broken veins on each cheek—had expounded on at length. Corbin decided to trust Henry—it would make his life a lot easier.

Corbin put the book away, and he and Henry had several pints. It was the longest amount of time they'd ever spent in each other's company.

"Where've you been all term?" Henry asked.

Corbin, who didn't think he'd exactly been hiding, said, "I didn't need housing during that first week so I didn't really meet anyone right off the bat. I've been hanging with some of the English students."

"Traitor. You know you're not supposed to meet anyone foreign during your foreign studies program."

"I didn't get that memo."

"No? It's a requirement. Come to Europe as an asshole, make sure you don't meet anyone but other American students, and then return as an even bigger asshole. Spend senior year beginning stories with the words, 'When I was in Europe last summer . . .' Hey, you traveling this summer after classes end?"

"No, I wish," Corbin said. "I have an internship in New York. Starts first week of June."

"Hey, no way. Me too. Where?"

They compared notes on their summer internships. They were at different companies but on the same block in Midtown Manhattan.

"Excellent, dude," Henry said. "We'll be best friends. I already know what bar we should hang out at."

As they discussed the various bars and restaurants they knew in New York City, the phrase *best friends* echoed in Corbin's head. He knew that Henry was just using the words casually, but Corbin, although he'd always had friends, felt he'd never had a best one. He could picture Henry and himself haunting the same bars every night, meeting up without making plans in advance.

"It'll be epic," Henry said. "I mean, I love London, but we need a break, don't you think? Drink in cocktail lounges instead of pubs, meet some tanned women."

They laughed together, then each took a sip of his beer. Henry leaned in, dropped his voice a little.

"You know, Corbs, I think you and I have something in common."

"Oh yeah?"

"Claire Brennan." Henry smiled, lips spreading thinly over his teeth.

"Yeah, I know Claire." Corbin felt like he'd just swallowed a tennis ball.

"Yeah, I know you do. Intimately, I believe."

"Why?" Corbin asked.

"Yeah, I thought that was the case. It seems she's been two-timing the both of us."

"What do you mean?"

"Exactly what you think I mean. Jesus, look at you. Don't have a heart attack, dude."

Chapter 14

"Is that why you came over here to talk with me? Because of Claire?" Corbin asked, some time later.

Henry paused. "No, I just came over to talk. I did think I'd bring up the Claire situation, though. Seemed the right thing to do."

Corbin had regained some composure since Henry had dropped his bombshell about Claire. The sickening gut-wrench of betrayal had been replaced by a mounting feeling of rage. Henry shared the feeling.

"Bitch lied to us both," he said.

They'd gone back over events in their own personal timelines, trying to figure out how she'd gotten away with it exactly. It turned out that Henry and Claire had first hooked up over a month earlier when Corbin had gone for a long weekend to Amsterdam to meet up with two of his Mather friends. Henry, like Corbin, had met Claire at the Three Lambs. He'd asked her out for dinner, and she'd agreed. The dinner had gone well, and Henry had been seeing her off and on for the past few weeks.

"How often do you see her?" Corbin asked.

"We have a standing date on Tuesday nights."

"I have my seminar on Tuesday nights."

"And Sunday afternoons we sometimes go to a pub on the river."

"She told me she always spends Sunday catching up on her studies."

"We got duped, buddy," Henry said, shaking his head. "Did she tell you to not act like her boyfriend in the Three Lambs? That she didn't want people there to know she was dating a customer?"

"Yep. She told me that. Jesus."

Henry finished his current pint in one long sip, then wiped his lips with the back of a hand. His lips curled slightly on one side, as though he were enjoying himself.

"You don't seem as upset as I am," Corbin said.

"I am, trust me. I've just had a lot longer to think about it, and now I'm more pissed than upset."

"How did you find out?"

Henry explained how he'd accidentally spotted Claire the previous Saturday night, coming out of the Camden tube station. He'd waved at her but she hadn't spotted him. She was in a rush, and on a whim, Henry had followed her, along the market stalls and to an Indian restaurant. Corbin was waiting outside, and they had kissed on the street.

"And you didn't tell her?" Corbin asked.

"I gave her a chance to tell me. I saw her the next day and asked if we were exclusive, and she said, yes, that she hoped so. That's when I got angry instead of just disappointed. And I decided I'd just stop seeing her, not give her a reason, and make her stew over it. And then I saw you here tonight. I almost didn't tell you, you know. I mean, you never would have found out, and maybe it wouldn't have made any difference in the big scheme of things. But you seem like a nice guy, and I figured you should know."

"I'm glad you told me. I feel like a fucking idiot."

"You're not an idiot. You just trusted a woman. I'm serious. Don't ever do it again."

"I won't."

"So what are we going to do?" Henry asked.

"What do you mean?"

Henry was playing with his empty pint glass, turning it upside down and making damp rings on the wooden table. "What are we doing to do to get back at her? Ball's in our court. She has no idea that we know."

"That's true."

Henry jumped up. "One more pint, okay, then we'll figure out the best way to fuck her up." He went to the bar before Corbin could answer.

*

They concocted a plan. Henry knew a disused graveyard north of Hampstead Heath called Boddington Cemetery. He'd discovered it in his first week in London on a Sunday afternoon walk. The gravestones were mostly vandalized, and it was completely overgrown with trees and shrubs. Henry had already mentioned it to Claire, telling her that he wanted her to come back there with him before he returned to America, that he wanted to bring his camera and take pictures. She agreed, and they settled on a Wednesday afternoon. Henry hadn't seen anyone there on a sunny Sunday and didn't expect anyone there during the middle of the week. Except for Corbin, who would be waiting in the center of the cemetery, where they'd scare her enough to make her never want to get involved with two men at the same time again. Or one man, for that matter.

Henry gave Corbin a detailed sketch of the park. Near the center, the terrain dipped into a shallow valley. On one of the graves was a moss-covered statue of an angel, the head missing. Henry had written DECAPITATED ANGEL on the sketch, and had designated it as the perfect place.

"What if someone else is there?" Corbin had asked.

"No one will be there. And so what if they are? We're just scaring her."

Wednesday turned out to be typical London weather, the sky filled with low, fast-moving clouds, the cool air peppered with occasional rain. Corbin found the entrance to the cemetery and slid past the broken gate. There was still a discernible path, littered with rotting leaves, and he followed it into the heart of the cemetery. Henry had been right. There wasn't going to be anyone here today. Maybe on a sunny weekend a photographer might turn up, but not on a rainy weekday. He felt confident that he was alone.

Following Henry's sketch, Corbin found the split in the path and turned left, having to push his way past damp branches to reach the hidden clearing. He spotted the decapitated angel right away. She was robed and holding a garland of leaves. The stone was entirely covered in lichen, and she wasn't just missing her head, but both tips of her wings, as though they'd been clipped. A shudder of apprehension passed through Corbin. Were they going too far? But then he pictured Claire going back and forth between his bed and Henry's, and the anger flared up again. Maybe they weren't going far enough.

He took off his backpack, placed the retractable shovel on the damp ground next to the statue, then took out the water bottle that was now filled with the fake blood that Henry had mixed up. "It's awfully brown, isn't it?" Corbin had asked when he'd first seen it.

"Yeah, it's perfect. Blood turns brown after it's been exposed to the air. We don't want you to look like you've just been offed twenty minutes ago."

"I guess not."

Corbin checked his watch. He had half an hour until Henry was supposed to show up with Claire. He sat on the ground in front of the angel, leaning against its base, and smeared the fake blood across his neck and down his T-shirt, pooling the blood in the shirt's folds. He took the knife from the backpack and smeared that with the blood as well; it was Henry's knife, a folding buck, and it was incredibly sharp. He ran its edge along the pad of his finger and it sliced through a single, translucent layer of skin, not drawing any blood. He dropped the knife onto his lap.

He put the water bottle back into the backpack, nestled among the change of clothes he'd brought, then he tucked the backpack behind his lower back and out of sight. When Claire arrived, she'd see his dead body, laid out in front of the statue like a ritual killing. He began to giggle at the thought, couldn't stop himself from giggling, and he was soon laughing out loud, his shoulders shaking uncontrollably. *Jesus, get a grip,* he thought, then decided to let it out of his system. He let out a yelp of laughter that sounded strangely animalistic in his own ears. He stopped laughing, worried that someone might hear him. What if some stranger did come along, wanting to photograph the statue? He laughed some more, nervously, then told himself that no, it would be Henry arriving with Claire, promising that he wanted to show her something that she'd like to see. How would she react? Would she faint? Or scream? The thought made him giddy again, the way he'd felt years ago when he'd shown his brother the photographs he'd found hidden in the attic, the ones with naked girls being whipped and spanked by men in leather hoods. His brother had gone running to their mother, of course, and she'd punished Corbin by not letting him shower for over two weeks. He'd been a fastidious kid and hated the idea of not being clean. Being told he couldn't shower had been torture. "You can shower when your outsides look as dirty as your insides," his mother had told him. He'd asked her every day when that would be, and she'd told him every day that he wasn't dirty enough on the outside yet. She eventually let him take a shower only after his teacher sent him home with a note suggesting that he wasn't properly washing himself. Where had Corbin's father been during all this? His parents weren't divorced yet, but they were, for all practical purposes, separated, his father primarily staying at his apartment in the city. Corbin had wondered if it was because of the photographs; maybe his father was being punished as well for looking at them. It never occurred to Corbin, until much later, that the pictures might have belonged to his mother.

Wind shook the trees, and drops of rain pattered down on Corbin. It was almost time for Henry to show up with Claire. Thinking about the incident with the pictures and his mother had taken some of the giddiness out of him, but that was fine. It was time to get serious. He channeled his nervousness and his anger until he felt only a sense of detachment, the way he used to feel during an at-bat when he played high school baseball, as though he was floating at a slight remove from himself. He began to focus.

He heard a rustling from the undergrowth and watched as a large pigeon with a ring around its neck stepped out into the clearing, then flew away. More rain pattered down, this time from the sky. Corbin stared straight up at the mass of cloud cover, and at the one swollen, ink-colored cloud in the middle that looked like it was about to unleash a deluge. Where was Henry? Maybe Claire had refused to come into the cemetery with him when it looked like it was about to rain? Corbin shifted his position, sitting a little more upright, so that he could watch the path where they would emerge, if they came at all.

He heard them before he saw them, Claire emitting a surprised yelp followed by laughter. She'd probably slipped coming down the incline. The laughter felt like sharp pricks against Corbin's skin. He hadn't seen her, or talked to her, since finding out who she really was; they'd only e-mailed, Corbin claiming he was suffering from a vicious flu and that he was unable to see her.

Henry came first into the clearing, and Corbin caught him glancing in his direction before turning back toward Claire, who was moving gingerly down the slippery path, her eyes angled down.

Corbin closed his lids, pulled in a deep breath of the damp, earthy air, and tried to be as still as possible. The rain was coming down harder, and it made listening difficult. They must be looking at him now. He heard a voice—Henry's—saying something like: *I brought you here to help me.* Then it was quiet for a moment, just the sound of the rain on the leaves, then he heard Claire's voice: "What have you done?"

"I did it for you, Claire," Henry said back. They were closer now. Corbin desperately wanted to open his eyes, to see the pained shock on Claire's face, but he kept them closed. Rain was pooling under his collar, and he could smell the dye from the fake blood.

"What have you done, Henry?" Her voice pitched right on the edge of hysteria.

"I brought you here for two reasons, Claire. I wanted you to see what happens to your other boyfriends. And I need you to help me bury the body." Henry's voice was calm, almost placid, and Corbin was amazed at the performance. He could only imagine the look on Claire's face, the panic in her eyes. He heard her say something but couldn't make it out. It was one word.

"No, Claire. You stay right here," Henry said, and Corbin heard the sound of movement. He opened his eyes a fraction, rain obscuring his vision, and saw Henry gripping Claire by the shoulders. Her face was down, chin burrowing into her chest, head shaking back and forth. Corbin sat up, rain streaming from his hair.

Look up, Claire, he thought. *Look up and see me.*

She didn't look up, but Henry took hold of her face in his hands, pushing her head back up. "Shhh," he said. "Calm down, Claire."

With her face in Henry's hands, her eyes found Corbin. He was sitting fully up now, looking back at her. Her eyes went wide, and what remaining color she had in her face disappeared. Her scream was high-pitched, birdlike. Henry turned to Corbin, then let go of Claire and burst into laughter, putting his hands on his knees. Corbin just stared. He couldn't take his eyes off Claire, who was stumbling backward like a boxer who has just been punched in the jaw.

Henry, done laughing, said to Claire: "Payback's a bitch, eh?"

She turned to leave, took a step on the slippery ground, and went down on one knee.

Corbin stood, the knife slipping from his lap. Henry turned back toward him, grinning wildly, as Corbin stepped forward. Henry reached out the palm of his hand, and Corbin took it. Their eyes met over the handshake. Henry seemed like he'd just won a trophy. "Fucking A, man," he said to Corbin. "Fucking A." Accenting every syllable equally.

"Assholes!" Claire yelled. She was back on her feet, looking at them. "You assholes!"

Henry and Corbin released their hands.

"No, Claire, *you're* the asshole," Henry said.

"Whore!" Corbin yelled.

Her eyes jumped to him, her head shaking. "Jesus, Cor. How'd you get talked into this? You're a decent guy."

She wore a scoop-necked white shirt, and the rain was pulling it down, the edges of her beige bra showing. The exposed skin of her chest was wet and pale. "Yeah, I am a decent guy, and you're a fucking whore," Corbin said, his voice gone shrill.

Claire took a breath and hitched her shoulders back. "Okay," she said quietly. She pushed her wet hair back off her forehead, then tugged her shirt back in place.

"Nice knowing you, Claire," Henry said, and Corbin envied his normal voice, how calm he sounded.

Claire looked at Henry, then back at Corbin, and shook her head. Corbin watched as a slight, sad smile appeared on her face. *She* pities *me,* he thought, *she fucking* pities *me.* As she turned to leave, Corbin ran and shoved her as hard as he could in the center of her back. She jerked forward, feet stumbling, then hit the ground, her head bouncing. Corbin was on her, spinning her onto her back. Her head had hit the edge of a sharp rock, and bright-red blood was running from a flap of skin, mixing with the rain. "How's it feel?" Corbin said, and shook her. She groaned and pressed a hand to the wound. She wore a Claddagh ring—she always had—and the heart was pointing toward her. Corbin had thought she'd done that for him. A surge went through his body, like a ripple going through a whip. He shook her harder, her head repeatedly hitting the ground.

"Hey, hey. My turn." It was Henry, touching Corbin on the shoulder. He was holding the knife.

Chapter 15

They dug a grave in the clearing. The rain had turned the ground soft, the shovel making sucking sounds as they pulled out black clods of earth. When Claire's body was in the hole, but before they covered it, Henry said, in his calm, measured voice: "I think we should take a picture. One of you with her body, and one of me."

"What do you mean?" Corbin asked.

"We need to memorialize this moment."

"Are you crazy?"

"No, listen. It will be a symbol of our trust. We'll each hold proof on the other, and then we'll know that we're forever in this together. Think about it."

Corbin was still in shock, trying hard to comprehend what had just happened. They had actually murdered Claire. The two of them, together, had ended her life. He'd started it, hadn't he, by hitting the back of her head against the ground as hard as he had? He remembered how furious he'd felt, the adrenaline pumping through him, how good it felt to cause her pain. He'd wanted her to die, hadn't he? Or had he just wanted her to feel pain and fear? Had he wanted her to feel the hurt that she'd caused him? He didn't know now. But then Henry had come in with the knife, cut Claire's throat, and when Corbin saw the spray of blood arcing high above her body, a sense of unreality had come over him, like he was suddenly watching everything through a distorted lens. It was a dream. But it wasn't. It was real, all of it. The rain, the blood, the body twisted awkwardly on the ground, water pooling in her eye sockets, the eyes still open.

Henry pulled a Polaroid camera from the backpack he was wearing.

"Why do you have that?" Corbin asked.

"I told Claire I wanted to come here to take photographs. I needed a camera, didn't I?"

It bothered Corbin that it was a Polaroid camera, somehow. Such a perfect camera for taking pictures of a murder. Still, he posed, and Henry took a picture of him standing over the grave, and then they changed positions, Corbin taking a picture of Henry. The plastic camera was yellow and black. It spit the picture out and Corbin watched the image develop. Henry's shoulders were back, a toothy grin on his face. He looked proud.

Corbin handed the camera back to Henry, holding onto the picture. His hands were trembling, the tips of his fingers white as bone and starting to prune. He almost asked to see the picture that Corbin had taken of him, but decided he didn't want that image in his mind.

Henry folded the camera back into its closed position and put it in his backpack, then they covered her, smoothing the dirt down and adding a layer of wet leaves. It looked untouched, like no one had ever been there. It was a relief that the body was no longer visible, that all traces of Claire had disappeared.

"Like no one was ever here," Henry said, echoing Corbin's thoughts. "Let's go."

They walked in single file along the path, each carrying his things. Corbin felt a little better now that they were moving, and talking about what to do next. The rain had even lessened, the clouded sky lighter than it had been. At the cemetery gate they stood for a moment before going their separate ways. "No contact," Henry said. "Unless it's absolutely necessary."

"I agree," Corbin said.

Henry smiled. "I can't believe we did that, dude," he said, and there was true joy on his face, like they'd just won the big game. Corbin smiled back, wanting to let Henry know he felt the same way.

Once Corbin was on his own, walking among the normal pedestrians—returning home from work or heading to early dinner dates—the enormity of what he had done filled him with mounting panic and disbelief. Claire was dead. This morning she'd been alive, going about her life, and now she was buried in the ground. Corbin stopped walking, and a man with an open umbrella bumped into him from behind. "Sorry," Corbin said, ducking into an alley, where he put his hands on his knees. He was nauseous, and his heart fluttered in his chest. He took deep breaths, trying to fill his lungs with the sooty city air.

After a minute he began to feel better. He thought back to what Claire had done, trying to conjure up the rage he'd felt. It began to work, especially when he remembered the pitying look she'd given him in the cemetery, as though he were the asshole. He kept those thoughts in his head as he walked home. He needed to shower.

It was two days later when Corbin first heard about Claire.

"You knew Claire Brennan, didn't you?" one of his fellow students, a girl from UCLA, asked.

"Yeah. I *did*. Why?"

"I heard she was missing."

"Seriously?" Corbin had been terrified of being asked questions about Claire, but now that it was happening, he felt okay. His voice sounded natural.

"Yeah. She didn't show up at the Lambs, and someone went to her place and she wasn't there."

"Maybe she went home early."

Corbin braced himself for a visit from the police, but it never came. A few days later he was on a plane going home, drinking beer after beer in first class, and feeling the muscles in his chest and stomach finally unclench. He hadn't realized how tense he'd been those last few days in London. He'd barely slept, and when he had, it was in that thin realm where dreams and memories overlapped. He'd wake, sweat filmed and guilty, unsure whether what had happened in the cemetery was real or imagined. When

160

he realized it was real, a dread would settle over him, far worse than what his nightmares had conjured. Being on the plane, leaving England, was an overwhelming relief. Was he free now? Had they gotten away with it? Eventually, the body would be found, of course, and then there would be a murder inquiry. Would they come looking for him, and for Henry as well? It depended on what Claire had told her friends about her life, how much she had shared. Did she keep a diary? Corbin and Claire had e-mailed, but only a few times, and nothing that personal. Most of their dates had been arranged face-to-face at the pub. It was entirely possible that no one but she knew about her love life. She'd been secretive, obviously, hiding one boy-friend from another. Maybe there'd been other boyfriends. Maybe she'd been secretive with everyone in her life.

Back in Boston, Corbin stayed with his father in Bea-con Hill for a week. His mother came and took him out to lunch; he hadn't seen her in so long, and it was clear that she'd had more work done to her face. Her lips were fuller, her forehead unlined. She asked him, as she always did, for information about his father. He declined to tell her anything, except that he thought his father was happy, the opposite of what his mother was hoping to hear.

He moved to New York City and began his intern-ship at Briar-Crane. He was sleeping better, the images from that cemetery in London receding slightly. He kept a constant eye out for Henry Wood, knowing that he was also in New York for an internship. They'd agreed to have no further contact after parting ways. In fact, they'd agreed to say they barely knew each other if questioned by the police, that they'd chatted once or twice at a pub. Corbin was eager to know whether Henry had been questioned by the police. He didn't think so. If they hadn't known enough to question him, then chances were they hadn't gone to Henry either.

And it wasn't just that he wanted to find out if Henry had been questioned. Corbin desperately wanted to see Henry again. He didn't know exactly why. Part of it was that they had shared something so transgressive and intimate that Corbin needed to know what effect it had had on Henry. Was he haunted by the image of Claire's lifeless body? Was he sleeping? Was he regretful at all about what they had done?

Corbin had Internet at his sublet in Manhattan, but he never searched for stories about Claire online, telling himself that search histories were evidence. Instead, every day he went to a newsstand near his apartment that sold foreign newspapers, and he bought the *Times* and scanned it for anything on Claire. On June 15, her body was discovered, dug up by an Irish wolfhound that was being walked through the cemetery. It was big news. There were pictures of Claire, looking rosy-cheeked and beautiful, plus a published shot of Claire's parents arriving in London to identify the body. There was no mention of suspects, no mention of Claire having dated an American student. Done reading, he threw the *Times* out in a public trashcan as he always did.

In early July, drinking with coworkers at Jimmy's Corner, Corbin spotted Henry, sitting in a booth with an older woman in corporate clothing. Henry was wearing a light gray suit, his maroon tie loosened, and his hair had been cut short. Corbin had been midsentence with Barry, a fellow intern, but stopped speaking the moment he saw Henry.

"You okay?" Barry asked, casting a look back toward where Corbin was looking.

"Yeah, yeah. I thought I saw someone I know. What was I saying?"

For the rest of the conversation, Corbin kept an eye on Henry, not sure what to do. Should they still pretend they didn't know each other? When his coworkers decided to move on to another bar, Corbin stayed, still unsure about whether he should approach Henry, but desperate to find out how he was doing. He finished his old-fashioned and ordered another. He took one sip, and felt a hand clap onto his shoulder.

"Dude. I've been wondering when I'd run into you."

"Hi, Henry. I saw you, I just didn't know if I—"

"You should've come over. Met Anna. She had to leave, and I was all set to go myself when I saw you, lurking here." He laughed, and Corbin smiled. "This seat taken? Look at you, drinking—what is that?—an old-fashioned. Dude, a few weeks in the city . . ."

Henry ordered the same, and they clinked glasses. "To

us," he said, then he lowered his voiced and added: "And to getting away with it." He touched a knuckle to the wooden bar.

*

They spent the summer in each other's company, developing a routine, meeting every evening after work for a cocktail at Jimmy's Corner. Sometimes there were other people there—coworkers, college friends—but more often than not, they were alone. They usually had a martini, altering the ingredients on a nightly basis in a quest to discover the perfect concoction. After that initial cocktail they'd move on to other venues, other drinks. Henry had rules. "Always head downtown as the night progresses." "Never have more than two drinks at any given bar." "Don't waste everyone's time talking to girls before midnight."

They'd break these rules, but not often.

Their nights together blurred into one long shimmering party. Henry made friends at every bar they frequented, yet he never abandoned Corbin. They'd always find one another toward the end of the night. Sometimes, of course, Henry would wind up going home with someone. But it was always a one-night stand, and never turned into anything serious. On one sweltering night in July, at a bar called Balcony, Henry left with a couple he'd met, an older man with a younger woman, and Corbin remembered the party in London when

Henry had beckoned him into the bedroom. He wondered if there'd be another similar invitation, a night that would end with Henry and Corbin in bed together with the same woman. Corbin hadn't been with anyone since Claire, and the thought of any kind of sex made his stomach buckle with a combination of anxiety and lust. But it never happened. Henry, for all his success with women, seemed, conversationally at least, uninterested in sex. He was, however, always interested in talking about murder.

When they were alone, they often recounted the story of what had happened with Claire, telling it in the same way that new lovers tell each other the story of how they met, going back and forth, remembering every detail.

"And then there was that look she gave you, dude, like you were some little boy who got talked into doing something he shouldn't have done," Henry would say.

"I remember that look very well."

"She read you wrong, that's for sure."

The conversations made Corbin feel infinitely better, more at ease with what they had done. He still thought back with horror about what had transpired in that cemetery, but talking about it, especially in the way that Henry talked about it, well, it normalized it a little. They had been wronged, and they got their revenge. And now they'd gotten away with it. And that was the whole story.

"Think of all the men we've saved from Claire Brennan," Henry liked to say.

"A lifetime's worth. God knows how many."

Toward the end of the summer, just before their senior years began, Corbin took Henry to his mother's house in New Essex while his mother and his brother were touring Europe. They had the house to themselves for three warm days, punctuated by bouts of rain. They watched movies—thrillers, mostly, from the 1960s and '70s—and because of the rain, had the beach to themselves, swimming in any weather, including a thunderstorm at dusk during a slack tide, the water frothing around them from the torrential downpour.

On their last night they watched *Knife in the Water*, then sat on the deck, drinking a bottle of Corbin's mother's expensive Bordeaux and sharing a joint. Henry said: "We should do it again."

"Do what? Come back here? Sure, man, anytime."

"No. I'm talking about Claire, and what we did to her. We should do it again someday."

It was sunset, and the house cast a long, narrow shadow across the dunes and onto the flat of the beach. "The right person, though," Corbin finally said, when he'd realized what exactly Henry was proposing.

"Fuck yeah, the right person." Henry slid forward in his chair, pulling a Parliament from his pack and lighting it. "Someone like Claire. Someone who would get involved with two guys, with both of us, and think she was getting away with it. I was thinking about it with Anna this summer till I realized I couldn't spend another moment with her. You could've hit on her some night, see what she would do—well, we know what she would do—and then we'd punish her, the way we punished Claire."

Corbin's stomach had tightened, but there was something about Henry's excitement that was contagious. And the longer he'd known Henry, the more he wanted to please him. "We'd have to be careful. We lucked out with Claire."

"I know that. I think about that all the time. But don't forget—we have each other. We could always be each other's alibis. We'll always have each other's backs."

Below, on the beach, a middle-aged woman was speed-walking near the surf and for one terrible moment Corbin thought that his mom was back at the house. His eyes adjusted and he realized that it didn't look remotely like her. He plucked the lit cigarette from the ashtray and took a long drag before realizing it was Henry's. "Sorry, man. I just took a drag off your cigarette." He put it back next to the stub of the joint they'd smoked.

"Don't worry about it. It's not my cigarette, it's our cigarette."

"I don't even smoke. I think I'm just stoned."

"Dude, I know," Henry said and started to laugh. Corbin joined him, their laughter mixing with the perpetual squawk of gulls.

*

It was ten months later when they found a candidate. Her name was Linda Alcheri, and Henry had met her in

Hartford when he moved there after graduation from Aurelius College. Corbin was back in New York City, where he'd been offered an entry-level job at Briar-Crane.

"Thing about her," Henry said on the phone, "was that she started telling me how much she loved me about a week after we started seeing each other. It's bullshit, though, I know it. For one, she started saying it the night I took her to a really expensive restaurant. Not a coincidence, I'd say."

"Doesn't mean she's being unfaithful."

"Oh, I think she'd hook up with anyone if she thought there was something in it for her. I think she'd take one look at the way you wear a Brooks Brothers shirt and drop me like a hot potato."

So, Corbin came up during a weekend when Linda Alcheri was throwing herself a birthday party at her apartment. Linda lived in a complex in West Hartford, and the party was taking place on a shared roof deck. Henry begged off early, but Corbin stayed late into the night, until only he and Linda were left. "How are you getting back to Hank's house?" she asked Corbin. She had to put one of her hands against the railing of the roof deck in order to stay standing.

"You call him Hank?"

"Don't you?"

"No, I call him Henry."

"Henry. Hank. Whatever. Where is he, anyhow?" She looked around as though he might still be somewhere on the roof.

Corbin walked her to the bedroom, Linda leaning heavily against him. "Thank you, Corbin," she said, and gave him a sloppy kiss on the side of his mouth. She entered the room and shut the door behind her. Corbin called Henry on his cell.

"So?" Henry asked.

"She kissed me good night, and now she's passed out in her bedroom."

"What kind of kiss?"

"Pretty innocent."

"You should go crawl into bed with her, see what happens."

"She's pretty drunk."

"Exactly."

"Nah, man. Come and get me."

"I'll come early in the morning. Sleep on her couch."

Corbin stripped to his boxers and lay on the couch under a fleece blanket. He never slept particularly well, and drinking too much made it worse instead of better. He lay awake, staring at the ceiling of the old apartment. There was glitter in the textured stucco. He worried a little about Henry's plan to kill again, but he worried more about losing Henry's friendship. The few times he'd expressed reservations about their plan Henry had looked so disappointed.

"It's who we are, Corbs," Henry had said. That was during the winter break, when they'd spent a long weekend skiing at Sunday River. "Besides, how much time do you spend worrying about what happened to Claire Brennan?"

"I don't," Corbin said. It wasn't true. He did think of Claire, but not as often as he used to, and when he did think of her, he reminded himself that Claire had brought him together with Henry. Claire had given him that one thing. A best friend.

"Exactly," Henry said. "We'll pick someone else like Claire, someone the world will hardly miss. It'll be like stepping on a bug."

Just as the sky outside was getting light, Corbin felt his eyes grow heavy. He closed them, twisting onto his side, and was about to slide into sleep when the sound of bare footsteps on the parquet floor woke him up. Linda was standing above him, wearing an old Whalers jersey that hung halfway to her hips and nothing else. She took Corbin by the hand and led him back into her bedroom. "You're shivering," she said, when they were under the sheets together.

"Why don't you warm me up?" Corbin answered, knowing that her fate was now sealed.

Two weeks later, Henry lured Linda to an abandoned Boy Scout camp on a swampy pond forty-five minutes west of Hartford, telling her he was bringing her to a friend's luxurious cabin. Corbin was waiting there, posed as before, like he'd been stabbed to death. It felt so similar to being in the cemetery in London, but it also felt completely different. Lying there, the dampness of the ground spreading through his clothes, the fake blood drying along his collarbone, Corbin knew what they were planning, knew that Linda was about to die a painful, scary death, and something close to terror swept through him. It was a cold, paralyzing terror, the kind he used to get as a small child when the lights were turned off, but he couldn't sleep, and the monsters that hid in the walls began to whisper. He felt light-headed—he hadn't slept or eaten in the last eighteen hours—and sat up to take a deep breath of the piney air.

Henry and Linda were ten yards away, Henry's hand on Linda's arm.

When she saw Corbin sitting up, blood-splattered, she tore away from Henry's grip and ran, screaming, into the woods. Henry took off after her. And Corbin, once he stood on his weak legs, followed. Maybe it wasn't too late to tell her it was just an awful joke? But when he caught up to them, Henry had already killed her, using a large sharp-edged stone. "Sorry, man, I think she's dead," he said, smiling, looking down at her caved-in skull. Corbin's skin broke out all over in cool sweat, and for a moment he thought he was going to faint. Henry snapped his fingers. "Dude, you okay?"

"Yeah, man," he said back. It was done. Linda was dead.

Together, they dragged her body back out of the woods, and Henry sent Corbin back to his SUV to grab the shovel he'd brought.

It was a quarter-mile hike to where Henry had left his vehicle—Corbin telling himself that what they'd done was what made them special, better than the rest of the world—and when he got back to the camp, shovel in hand, he was ready to embrace the ritual act of burying the body. But he was stopped by the sight of Henry standing over Linda's body, grinning, his hands palms out as though he were presenting a gift. Corbin looked down. Henry had sliced Linda with his knife, a deep cut from her hairline down the center of her face, that continued down her torso, her clothes and skin split open.

Corbin turned, dropped to his knees, and emptied his stomach onto the weed-choked gravel.

"Sorry, man," Henry said. "I thought you'd like it. Half for you, and half for me. We split everything right down the middle."

"It's just . . ." Corbin began but couldn't finish.

"A little theatrical?" Henry said and laughed.

Corbin looked up. Henry was holding out a pair of rubber gloves, the same flesh-colored style that he was wearing himself. Corbin noticed that he was also wearing a thin ski cap that he hadn't worn before.

"Let's bury her and get the fuck out of here," Corbin said as he took the gloves.

Corbin tried as hard as he could to not look at her while they dug her grave, then rolled her body into it, but that single glance, her skin pulling away from the center of her face, black flies beginning to gather in the bright

July sunshine, stayed with him after Henry and he cleared the crime scene and went their separate ways. It stayed with him—permanently burned onto the undersides of his lids—for weeks after that afternoon. Every time he shut his eyes, every time he blinked, there she was. His insomnia got worse, and so did his paranoia. He kept waiting for the police to show up at his door, especially since he'd learned from Henry that Linda Alcheri never knew Henry's real name. He'd told her it was Hank Bowman, and lied about where he worked and where he was from.

"I gave her my *real* fucking name at the party," Corbin said over the phone.

"Dude, she's not going to tell anyone."

"She could've told one of her friends, written it down somewhere, Jesus . . ."

"Sorry. I should have told you to use a false name. But you just told her 'Corbin,' right? Not your last name? You have got to relax."

"She had friends there who met me."

"Same with me. We're in the same boat, but it's not a bad boat, man. Not at all. They haven't even found the body yet. It's going to be like last time. They'll never connect her to us."

It turned out that Henry was right.

Like Claire Brennan in London, Linda Alcheri became a well-covered missing-persons case. Her body was discovered in early August, when a group of teenagers caused a small brush fire on Eel River Pond that needed to be put out. But in all the articles and reports that Corbin read, none mentioned Henry Wood, or Hank Bowman, for that matter. And no detective showed up at Corbin's door in New York. They'd gotten away with it again, even though that fact did little to alleviate the fist-sized knot in Corbin's stomach. It had been different with Linda—so different from when they killed Claire. With Claire, Corbin had been propelled by her wrongdoing and his enormous rage. She knew how much he'd been in love with her, and she let him believe she might feel the same way. And they hadn't even planned on killing her. It had just happened, and it only happened because Claire had smiled at him. That half smile of pity directed toward Corbin.

No, with Linda it had been something else. Premeditated, for one. And more like a sick, twisted game. Corbin began to wonder if Henry had ever really been that involved with Linda in the first place. He'd said they were, but maybe he had lied.

Corbin kept thinking back to the night of the party, to the way that Linda had acted toward Henry before he'd left the roof deck. She'd seemed glad to see him, giving him a kiss when he arrived, but she hadn't acted clingy, or even particularly affectionate toward him. She'd flitted around with her other guests. Maybe Henry was just someone she was hooking up with, a casual thing. And if that were the case, then what she did with Corbin that night wasn't straight-out cheating. Henry had rigged it, lying to Corbin about the extent of his relationship. Or had he?

With obsessive regularity, Corbin struggled to remember all the details that had led to Linda's death. He tried to remember what had happened after she woke him from the couch, then pulled him with her into the bedroom.

"I hate sleeping alone," she'd said. "Does that make me a slut?"

Corbin remembered the strong smell of alcohol coming from her pores, how she'd reached down and touched him, then told him maybe they could just cuddle.

"What about Henry? Hank, I mean."

"Oh," she'd said, sounding a little surprised to be asked the question. "He'll be okay."

"She was the life of the party, that's for sure" was what a lot of her friends said about Linda Alcheri after the body had been found. That was the most common quote. There was never any mention of a boyfriend.

The more Corbin thought about it, the more he realized that Henry had desperately wanted them to kill again, to replay the events in London, and he'd made it happen, lying to Corbin, making sure he spent the night with a girl who probably slept with everyone. It had been an entirely different situation than what had happened with Claire.

He'd planned everything, even knowing ahead what he was going to do to Linda's face after she was dead.

Maybe Henry had planned the murder of Claire in London, as well?

He suggested they bring the knife and the shovel to the cemetery?

But the knife and shovel were there for a reason, Corbin told himself. They were there to fool Claire into thinking that Henry had killed Corbin.

Why had that knife been so sharp?

No, Corbin thought. Henry hadn't planned on it all, because it was Corbin who had started it, who shoved Claire, then banged her head against the ground.

Still, in midsummer, after a night of drinking, Corbin called Henry on his cell phone.

"Hey, man. Great to hear from you," Henry said.

"We're done," Corbin said. "It's done. I don't want to do it anymore."

"Okay. Relax. What are we talking about?"

"You know what we're talking about."

There was a pause. The air-conditioning in Corbin's Midtown one-bedroom clicked on and began to hum. "Dude, let's not have this conversation over the phone, okay?" Henry said.

"The conversation's over. You know what I'm talking about, and I don't want to be part of it anymore."

"Fine. I hear you. We'll, uh, not find any more girls to play with."

"And I don't think we should hang out together anymore. It's risky, and . . ."

Henry was quiet.

"You there?" Corbin asked.

"Yeah, I'm here. I'm trying to understand what it is that you just said."

"I think . . . I think, for now, at least, we are no longer friends. I don't want to be your friend."

"Whatever the fuck you want, man. I hear you, but keep your head, buddy. Don't forget about the Polaroids." Henry's voice was different. Calm, almost.

Corbin ended the call. His palms were sweaty and he wiped them on his shirt.

He hoped he'd never hear from Henry again.

And he didn't, not for a long time. Not until after he'd met Rachael Chess.

Chapter 16

Corbin would never have met Rachael if he hadn't decided, shortly after his father died, that he needed to have a better relationship with his mother and his brother. They were both planning on spending the months of July and August at the New Essex house on the North Shore of Massachusetts, and Corbin, now living in his father's apartment in Boston, asked if he could join them for two weeks.

His brother Philip's response: "Dibs on the front bedroom, Corbin. I always stay there now."

His mother's: "I thought you hated the New Essex house. There's greenheads on the beach, remember?"

He'd gone anyway. The day he arrived he knew it had been a mistake. Philip had taken the boat out—in a transparent attempt to avoid Corbin's arrival—and while his mother had made an attempt at civility, he caught her looking at him in a mirror while she mixed gin and tonics. She wore an expression of visible disgust, her wrinkled mouth turned down at the corners, translucent nostrils slightly flared. She'd never loved him. He'd known this from a very young age, and accepted it the way that children will always accept the rules of their universe. As he got older, he realized that his mother despised him because he reminded her of her husband, and that she loved Philip because he reminded her of herself. One of the reasons that Corbin wanted to visit his mother after the death of his father was to see if she'd softened at all, if her attitude had changed. It hadn't. He felt it immediately, and in a strange way it comforted him. If his mother had become affectionate, the way she was with Philip, well, the thought of that almost made him physically sick.

He stayed for the two weeks, anyway, determined to enjoy the house, with its views of the Atlantic, and spend as little time with his family as possible. On his second night in New Essex, he ate dinner at the Rusty Scupper—a bar and grill walking distance from his mother's house—and that was where he met Rachael Chess. She was escaping from her family as well, having just begun her annual two-week stay at their year-round house just off the town beach in the southern part of town. He walked her home, and they sat talking on her front porch for hours. He told her about the recent death of his father and the awful members of his remaining family, and she told him how she'd been sleeping with one of her teachers, a married man, at the nursing school she was attending.

By sunrise, they were kissing, and they'd agreed to a two-week fling, no strings attached. He walked home along the beach in the milky light of dawn and felt a strange sense of calm, as though the world were shifting in his favor.

He and Rachael had made plans to meet for lunch the next day, and when she was late, he wondered if he'd dreamt her. But she showed up, and they spent almost every moment of the next two weeks together. Rachael was an open book, telling Corbin intimate details from her complicated life. Corbin, in turn, told her about the way his mother had paraded her sexual affairs in front of his father, and Philip and him, for years before his father finally left. He even told her about some of his own sexual problems during college; she was sympathetic without being pitying, and Corbin found himself desperately wanting to tell her what had happened with Claire in London, and then with Linda Alcheri in Connecticut. He knew that he couldn't, of course, but it was the first time he had ever wanted to talk about those events with another person. And because Claire and Linda were on his mind, he suddenly found himself plagued with terrible dreams, conflations of the two murders he'd committed, mixed in with images of chasing Rachael along the beach, a buck knife in his hand. At the end of the two weeks, when both Rachael and he returned to their normal lives, he felt heartsick but relieved.

Two months later, Rachael texted Corbin to tell him she was going to be back at her parents' house over Columbus Day weekend, and did he want to come up. He told her he'd be away for work—the truth, since he was going on a company retreat to the Cayman Islands. But even if he wasn't going to be away, he wasn't sure he wanted to see Rachael again. He remembered the dreams.

When Corbin returned from the retreat, he found out, while watching the local news, that Rachael Chess had been murdered, her body discovered in the dune grass by a beachcomber on Monday morning.

Corbin called in sick to work for a week, not leaving the apartment in Beacon Hill that his father had left to him. His boss had joked that the Caymans had done him in. Corbin didn't let on that he'd known the girl on the North Shore who'd been killed, even though the police had taken a statement, having found out from one of Rachael's friends that she and Corbin had been involved. An officer had interviewed him over the phone, then presumably checked his alibi through the Briar-Crane offices. Corbin said they'd had a casual fling and that they'd had minimal contact since.

He didn't tell them that he knew who had killed Rachael Chess. She'd been killed by Henry, of course, sending Corbin a clear message. He knew this with a certainty, even before the police released the information that Rachael Chess had postmortem wounds. They didn't specify what they were, but Corbin knew: Rachael had a single, deep cut down her middle, same as Linda Alcheri.

How had Henry even known about Rachael, about Corbin's relationship with her? Had he been up in New Essex watching Corbin in August? The thought terrified him. He googled Henry Wood and found nothing. The most recent mention he was able to locate was some cross-country track times when Henry had been at Aurelius. He tried Hank Bowman, the name that Henry had used when he'd been dating Linda Alcheri, and found nothing under that name either. He considered, for the first time ever, going to the police and confessing everything, showing them the Polaroid he still had of Henry standing over the body of Claire Brennan in the London graveyard. But what would happen to him? Even if he lied and said he'd only ever been an accomplice in the murders, he'd still go to jail for a long time. He'd still become a public figure, known for his atrocities, and also for his cowardice.

No, he could never confess. Corbin realized that Henry, by killing Rachael Chess, by making himself known to Corbin, had trapped him. He was being watched and he couldn't see his watcher. He felt a hatred toward Henry deeper than any hatred he'd felt before. Corbin decided on the only option he felt was available to him. He would lay low, and he would never become involved with a woman again. If Henry Wood ever showed himself, or if Corbin was ever able to track him down, he would kill him himself. He'd done it before and he could do it again.

Chapter 17

Soon after the death of Rachael Chess, Audrey Marshall moved into a vacant apartment on Corbin's hall. 101 Bury Street was mostly occupied by older couples, and it was a shock when he first saw Audrey carrying boxes into Apartment 3C. She was not the type of woman he was naturally attracted to; she was a wispy blonde, fragile looking, with milk-white skin, but seeing her wrestle with her door, her thin arms straining to hold on to the box, Corbin felt a jolt of longing. He offered to carry up some of her things from the moving van parked on the street, and to his surprise she'd happily accepted. It was box after box of books. She told him she'd been working as a literary agent in New York, but had moved to start a job in editing at Boston's biggest publishing house. After emptying the van, she'd said: "Now I owe you. As soon as I get settled let me make you dinner. I can't wait to use the kitchen in this place."

"You don't owe me anything," Corbin had said, and returned to his own apartment. He hoped that his coldness would eliminate any further contact.

It did, for a time. He passed Audrey in the hall and in the courtyard, and they were always civil, if not overly friendly. Whenever he saw her, she was alone, usually carrying a manuscript or a book. He began to imagine her life, alone in a new city, and felt a little bad for his aloof behavior on the day she'd moved in.

The second winter after Audrey's arrival was one of the worst in Boston's history, snow piling up and day after day of subzero temperatures. The largest of the storms began on a Thursday night in January and paralyzed the city all through the weekend plus most of Monday. It was during that weekend that Audrey, after saying hello to Corbin in the front lobby, showed up twenty minutes later at his door.

"I'm so stir crazy that I made enough chili to feed the entire building. Please come over and have some."

"I . . ."

"I'm not taking no for an answer—unless you have other plans—*and* I'm not hitting on you, I promise. You don't have to stay long."

Corbin agreed to come over at six. He found a good bottle of red wine and changed out of his workout clothes into jeans and a flannel shirt. He knocked on Audrey's door at five minutes past six and she let him into her place, considerably smaller than Corbin's massive end apartment. NPR was playing through her speakers, and Corbin wondered if that was a deliberate choice, so that their eating dinner together would seem less romantic. If it was, it backfired. Something about Audrey tending to the chili while Corbin made a salad, the news of the day prattling on in the background, made them seem like an instant couple, comfortable with each other and comfortable in their own skins. Corbin stayed till midnight. They finished his wine and drank another bottle that belonged to Audrey. She admitted that she'd been lonely in Boston, but not unhappy. He told her that he loved his solitary lifestyle. Back in his apartment, while brushing his teeth, Corbin felt a sharp pain in his chest. He thought it was heartburn and pressed a hand against his pectorals. To his shame, tears filled his eyes. The night with Audrey had made him realize how lonely he'd become.

They didn't see each other for over a week, not till Corbin was opening his door to let Sanders, who'd been scratching for at least ten minutes, into his apartment. Audrey was walking down the hall, stripping off a long, padded jacket that was damp with the latest snowfall.

"Hey, stranger," she said.

He'd invited her in, since she hadn't seen his apartment yet, and they ended up drinking wine and ordering a pizza.

"I like you," she said to him at the end of the night. "Even though I can't read you at all. You're a complete mystery."

"I'm not, really," Corbin said.

"No, you are. Are you going to kiss me?"

He did, and Audrey stayed the night. After she fell asleep, Corbin went to the bathroom on the distant side of the apartment, sat on the toilet lid, and cried again; his chest felt like there was a knife in it. Several knives.

"Do you mind if we talk a little bit?" Corbin asked Audrey as she was getting dressed the next morning. He hadn't slept at all.

"That was soon," she said. "You have a girlfriend? You're gay? You just got out of a really damaging relationship?"

"None of those," Corbin said. "But I have a strange request, and I will completely understand if you want nothing to do with me after I request it."

"Okay," she said, her voice wary. Audrey stood in just her jeans and a thin pink bra that she hadn't clipped at the back yet. Corbin noticed the faint scar from an appendectomy above her right hip.

"I'd really like to continue seeing you, but I think we should only see each here in this apartment building. At my place or your place, but not in public. I know that sounds horrible, but I have a reason, and it's a reason I can't tell you."

"Obviously, you have a girlfriend," Audrey said.

"I don't. I know you won't believe me, but I really don't. It's something else that I can't tell you about it. The closest I can say is that I've had girlfriends in the past and things went wrong, and I swore I wouldn't become romantically involved again. But this feels right, but only if it's here, just here, in this building."

She hooked her bra and took a deep breath. "Okay,"

she said. "I guess it's convenient." She laughed, but Corbin thought it seemed a little forced.

The arrangement actually worked for a while. Most of the time Corbin would go to Audrey's apartment. He'd bring wine, and they'd watch a movie on television, or they'd cook together. There were so many elements of Audrey that attracted him. She was matter-of-fact, not duplicitous at all, always telling him how she felt. In the bedroom she was responsive but not overly eager. She never said dirty things, and she preferred the lights off, like he did. Periodically, however, she would bring up the arrangement. Sometimes as a joke: "So which one of us is going to walk down to the 7-Eleven for ice cream, since we can't walk together?" Sometimes not: "My sister is coming to visit, and it's ridiculous that I can't introduce you to her. You realize that?"

Corbin always responded the same way. He said that it was unconditional that they never be seen in public together, and that it had everything to do with him and nothing to do with her. But every time he was forced to say those words to Audrey, his anger and resentment at Henry grew. Henry had made Corbin a murderer, and as though that weren't enough, he was now out to destroy Corbin's life, to destroy any possibility of happiness. Because why? Because they were no longer friends?

In his spare time, Corbin hunted for Henry Wood across the Internet, even contacting some fellow classmates from the semester in London to see if any of them knew what had happened to Henry. One of them said he'd run into him in New York City, but that was two years ago. The thought of finding Henry, and making him pay for what he'd done, consumed Corbin, especially now that he was with Audrey. If Henry were dead, then he could be with her without the constant fear of being seen together. And that was what it was: a constant fear. As much as he wanted to be with Audrey, he wondered all the time if he would come home some day to find out she'd been killed, that Henry, the invisible monster, had found out about them and made Audrey pay for it with her life. It was nonstop paranoia.

The worst moment came when Corbin was having drinks with the only other young resident of the building, a guy named Alan Cherney with whom he'd played racquetball a few times. Alan point-blank asked him if he was seeing Audrey—he'd heard rumors, he said, although he didn't say where he'd heard those rumors from. Corbin had played it cool, but the conversation kept replaying in his head over the next twenty-four hours. If Alan knew they were seeing each other, then other people could know. And if other people knew, then Henry, wherever he might be, might know, and he would come for Audrey the way he had come for Rachael Chess.

Even though they didn't have plans, Corbin barged in on Audrey the following night and accused her of letting someone in the building know about their relationship.

Audrey's eyes went large in disbelief. "Jesus, Corbin," she said, shaking her head.

"It's not funny. I was out having a drink with a guy from across the way and he asked me about the two of us. He knew."

"So what?"

Corbin made himself wait two seconds while he unclenched his jaw. "I know that you don't care because I haven't told you my reasons, but you *do* know how important it is to me that no one knows we're together. Don't pretend it's no big deal."

"No, trust me. I know it's a big deal. What do you want me to say? I haven't told anyone. We don't go out in public together, so I have no idea how he knows about us."

"Well, he knew."

"Who is he? Do I know him?"

"Alan something. He lives on the other side of the building."

Audrey looked out her window. "He lives across from me. I've seen into his apartment. He's probably seen into here, and seen you. That's all."

Corbin looked through Audrey's living room window and across at the dark windows on the other side of the courtyard. "You think?" he said.

Audrey smiled, for the first time since Corbin had entered her apartment. It wasn't much of a smile, but it was a smile. "Yeah. What else could it be? He probably watches me and he's seen you come over. Big deal."

"You don't care that he's watching you?"

"I don't know. Maybe it's exciting. Maybe I should be going out with him instead of you." She was still smiling. Corbin went and pulled the curtain across Audrey's window.

That night, that conversation, was the beginning of the end.

It wasn't surprising to Corbin. He knew it was never going to last. They spent a few more nights together, but Audrey kept pressing him about his reasons for keeping the relationship private. He couldn't answer her, except to say, "It's to keep you safe, you have to believe me on that."

"Do you have any idea how creepy that sounds?" she said.

When it was officially over, Corbin, in a way, was relieved. He went back to a solitary existence, working long hours, going to the gym every day, but at least it was an existence in which Audrey wouldn't be hurt. He occasionally fantasized about opening a newspaper and seeing an obituary for Henry Wood. He pictured himself finding Audrey on the street in broad daylight and kissing her there in front of everyone. It would be like one of those films he hated, but he wouldn't care. He couldn't get the image out of his mind.

When the opportunity to transfer to London came up, he jumped at it. Six months away from Bury Street, from living next to Audrey, would be good for him, and good for Audrey, as well. It made him nervous to return to the city where he had fallen in love with Claire Brennan and first encountered Henry Wood, but it was also the city his father was from. Maybe he'd reconnect with that side of his family. He remembered the pictures his father had shown him from that trip he took to England the year before he died. There'd been several of his cousin Lucy and her husband and daughter. Something had happened to that daughter since those pictures had been taken; she'd been stalked and nearly killed by an ex-boyfriend. At least that's what Corbin's mother had told him, although how she found out he didn't know. Corbin wrote to his father's cousin, Lucy, and told her he was probably coming to London, and said that maybe they could meet. She was the one who suggested a possible switch of apartments with Kate. She said that an adventure would do her daughter good. It had all been arranged so easily. The thought of Kate moving into his place made Corbin somehow feel comforted. Maybe she'd become friends with Audrey and report back. It would be a connection, even the tiniest one.

For his first full day in Kate's cozy flat, Corbin only left once, walking to the nearest grocer for food and bottled water and wine. During this excursion, he was enormously relieved to not run into his new upstairs neighbor Martha. It had been a mistake getting drunk and making out with her the night before. She'd be hard to avoid but not impossible.

The rain came and went all day, battering at the large bay windows at the front of Kate's flat. He watched

English television while doing push-ups and squats, then cooked the chicken breasts he'd bought. He checked his e-mails. Audrey still hadn't responded to the last one he'd sent her, the one in which he said he hoped things were easier now that he was out of the country, and he hoped she met someone who was worthy of her. He wrote an e-mail back to Kate thanking her for recommending the pub down the street, and he even mentioned meeting Martha, curious to see if she'd have anything to say about her. Martha had claimed that Kate and she were best friends, but somehow Corbin doubted it.

By Sunday afternoon he still hadn't heard back from Kate in Boston. For some reason it worried him. He took a long run, even though it was still raining, and wound up at a park called Primrose Hill with a hazy, distant view of central London. The wet soil in the park sucked at his running shoes, and he thought of that day in the cemetery with Henry, digging a grave. He ran home, showered, then checked his e-mails again.

Still nothing from Kate, but someone named Roberta James from the Boston Police Department had written to inform him that his neighbor Audrey Marshall had been found dead under suspicious circumstances, and would he get in touch with them as soon as possible.

Chapter 18

Kate sat up so fast that Sanders, startled, bolted from the room.

How did he get back in? She'd let him out, hadn't she? Her mind scrambled to remember. She'd opened the door for him after he'd meowed at her. She'd watched him leave, hadn't she? But then she remembered that she'd looked for him through the peephole and she hadn't seen him in the hallway. She thought it had been strange at the time, but had just assumed that Sanders had raced down the hallway and out of sight before she'd had time to see him. But maybe he'd never left at all. Maybe that was it. That possibility allowed her to breathe, pulling in several lung-filling intakes of breath.

She stood, walked on tingling legs to the den door, and switched on the recessed lighting that ran along the shelves and cabinets. "Hello, there!" she shouted, trying to make her voice sound rational. She'd still look around the place, make sure no one had opened a door, make sure that no one was inside the apartment. Just in case. She told herself that Sanders must have not actually left.

No, he left. You saw him. It was George's voice in her head. He giggled. It was something the George inside of her sometimes did, even though the real George, the *dead* George, had never giggled.

I didn't see him, she told George's voice. *I just opened the door and thought that he brushed past my leg on the way out. I was wrong.*

She stepped from the den into the hallway and walked toward the living room, turning on lights as she went. Sanders stood at the front door again, staring at it, as though it might magically open of its own volition.

"Sneaky kitty," Kate said to Sanders as she walked toward him. "I thought you'd left."

He meowed back at her, and Kate cracked the door open, watching as he left this time, his tail twitching. She locked the door behind her and pressed her back to it, looking at the living room, trying to sense whether someone was in the apartment. *No,* she told herself. *I'm alone. Sanders must have been here all along.* Still, she walked across the living room to the fireplace, its grate stacked with real wood, and picked up the fire iron that leaned against its brick exterior. She immediately felt better with its weight in her hand. Moving swiftly, she searched the apartment, turning on every light she could find and peering into every room. The place was empty, as far as she could tell. The front door was locked, and so was the door in the kitchen that led to the back stairwell.

She returned the fire iron to its place. Her hand was sweaty where she'd gripped it, and there was a faint line of soot across her palm.

Leaving all the lights on, she returned to the den, telling herself that she was alone in the apartment, that Sanders had not been let back in by some mysterious stalker, that he'd never left. She was overtired. She needed to sleep. She bent and picked up the comforter from the floor in front of the couch. Her copy of *I Capture the Castle* flopped out and banged onto the floor, a photograph sliding out of its pages. She picked it up and looked at it; it was a picture from a holiday she'd taken with her parents and some family friends to Torquay many years ago. The picture was of Kate and her mother, sitting next to their luggage on the steps of the guesthouse they'd stayed in. She couldn't remember if they were coming or going. The sliver of sky that had been captured in the photograph was dark and ominous. Kate remembered it had rained all week. She also remembered that it was during that holiday—Kate was thirteen—that she'd gotten her first period. Her mother had announced this fact over a full English breakfast in the crowded dining room of the guesthouse, and her father had beamed at her like she'd won some kind of prize. It had been a mortifying week.

But she did like the picture of her and her mum. They were shoulder to shoulder on the wooden steps, and they were smiling, but not toward the camera. They'd clearly been talking about something amusing. Kate liked the picture because she didn't look anxious in it (it must have been taken at the *beginning* of the week), and that was probably why she'd kept it and hidden it away in the pages of her favorite book. It was something she often did with photographs that she didn't know what to do with. Put it in a book, and maybe discover it later on. Or maybe not.

Kate had a thought, wondering if Corbin put secret pictures in books to discover later, as she did, or even to hide them. And as soon as this thought passed through Kate's mind, she knew that she would have to look through every book. It was the way she was. Once she fixated on something, she would need to see it through to the end. A year ago, she'd half recalled a quote from an Agatha Christie book, something about how all killers are someone's oldest friend, but couldn't remember what book it came from. Over Christmas, back in her childhood room, she'd scoured obsessively through every Christie book she had till she found it.

Kate stood and went to the television, surrounded by its wall of books. The shelves were filled with airport thrillers and business books. Here and there was a stack of coffee-table books, stacked on top of one another so they'd fit on the narrow shelves. Like the books in the living room, these looked like they belonged to Corbin's father, not to Corbin himself. Still, she wondered what she might find if she looked through the pages. There were a lot of books, but she had a lot of time. She knew she needed sleep, but she wasn't really tired, not since being woken up by Sanders.

She had to stand on an ottoman to reach the first book

on the far left of the top shelf. It was a hardcover copy of John Grisham's *The Firm*. Using her thumb she fanned through the pages, then tipped it upside down and shook it. Nothing. She replaced it and checked the next book.

By the time she'd finished going through all of the books on the den's shelves, she'd found many bookmarks, five receipts, all from at least ten years ago, and one cut-out magazine picture of Ashley Judd in her underwear that was folded up inside a paperback copy of something called *Who Moved My Cheese?*

Kate sat on the leather ottoman. What was she looking for? A picture of Audrey Marshall with the words KILL HER in red ink across her face? No, but maybe something to prove that Corbin had some kind of personal life that he kept hidden, and possibly one to do with Audrey. So far, Kate had three accounts of that particular relationship. Corbin said they barely knew one another. Audrey's friend said that Corbin and Audrey were casual hookups. And then there was the third account, from Alan Cherney, who claimed that Corbin was over at Audrey's place a lot. Why would Alan lie about that? Kate believed him, or at least she believed that he believed it. He'd clearly been obsessed with Audrey Marshall, but she trusted him. And not just because she found him attractive and easy to talk to.

She left the den and walked into the living room, now filled with milky morning light. It was dawn already. She checked her e-mails. Martha had written a long detailed e-mail back about Corbin. They'd met at the Beef and Pudding, then snogged, "just a little," on a walk back to their flats, but Corbin told her he'd been tired and went alone into Kate's flat. Martha hadn't seen him since. "Does he have a girlfriend back there?" Martha wrote. "E-mail him and ask him. Pretty please."

That's what I'm *trying to find out,* Kate thought. She was relieved to hear that Corbin seemed to be avoiding Martha, and that she probably didn't need to warn her friend that the hot American might be a girlfriend murderer.

Kate needed coffee but thought she'd get a start on the books in the living room first. There were many more in here than in the den, and the shelves stretched all the way to the very high ceilings. There was a sturdy-looking desk by one of the windows, and she pulled it over to stand on. Standing on the desk, she was just able to reach the top shelf, and pulled out the first dusty hardcover. As she riffled through its pages, Kate was struck by a wave of déjà vu that felt almost physical. Her knees buckled. She had a clear memory of going through the books on these shelves before. Of standing on this desk, and of the way her bare feet felt against the grain of the desk's wooden surface. A bubble of anxiety formed in her chest. She said her mantra to herself and did her breathing exercise. The déjà vu passed, and in its place, Kate was flooded with the dreams of the night before. In her dreams, she'd searched through these books, as well.

At least, that was what she remembered. Tipping the books upside down, their pages sliding out and covering the floor of the apartment, the pages filling the rooms like snow fills an empty swimming pool.

Did I really dream about searching all these books, and now I'm doing it? Kate thought. And for one terrifying moment, she thought she was still dreaming. Then the feeling passed.

She made herself coffee before going through the rest of the books. She must have checked hundreds before she finally found something of interest.

She had reached a stretch of books on one of the low shelves that felt different, and Kate felt that these books—a lot of Stephen King, *The Wheel of Time* series by Robert Jordan, two Chuck Palahniuk novels—had belonged to Corbin. She went through these books more carefully than she had with the others, and it paid off. In a paperback copy of something called *Ender's Game* by Orson Scott Card, she found three photographs of the same girl. It might have been the same girl from the photograph Kate had found earlier in the closet off the den, although it was hard to tell because these pictures were slightly out of focus, taken on a narrow bed in what looked like a narrow bedroom. The walls were white, and an unframed poster—a Picasso print?—was taped to the wall.

In the first photograph, the girl, laughing, was striking an exaggerated pinup pose, propped up on an elbow, the photographer above her. She was wearing faded jeans and a pink camisole. In the next one she was laying back on the bed in a more natural position, her face now serious. Kate imagined Corbin's—these must be his pictures—instructions: *No, don't be silly, just be natural. You look beautiful.* She did look beautiful, especially in the third and final photograph. It was a close-up, her skin dotted with freckles, her mouth slightly parted. Looking at the pictures, Kate felt as though she was spying on something incredibly private, prying into a shared, and sexual, moment. She placed the pictures back in the book and replaced the book on the shelf, then quickly looked through what remained of Corbin's novels, finding nothing.

She leaned back against the shelf and closed her eyes briefly. She was exhausted, and not sure how much time she'd spent ransacking the apartment. And all she'd found was evidence of an old girlfriend tucked away in a forgotten book. What had she been expecting?

There was a clock on the fireplace mantel, and Kate checked the time. Just past seven. Maybe she should get a quick nap in since she had her class today. She curled up on the nearest sofa in the living room, her head on a satiny, embroidered pillow. She closed her eyes and was almost immediately into a dreamless sleep.

*

There was a knock on the door, three sharp raps, and Kate bolted upright. She stood, still half asleep, and walked toward the door. There was a mirror near the door and Kate looked at herself. Her hair, unwashed for a couple of days, hung lifeless and lank. She pushed it back behind her ears. She looked through the peephole; it was Mrs. Valentine, the older woman who had shown Kate the apartment when she'd arrived on Friday. Kate swung the door open.

"Oh, Kate, did I wake you?"

"No, no. Come on in."

Carol Valentine was swathed in a complex white sweater belted across the middle. "I won't come in, but I wanted to invite you to our apartment for that drink. Any chance you're free tonight?"

Kate's mind quickly ran through a number of excuses, but then she heard herself say: "Tonight's perfect. I'd love to."

They agreed on seven o'clock, and Carol Valentine departed down the hall, leaving behind the scent of Jean Naté. That after-bath smell reminded Kate that she should probably take a shower at some point in the day, then she suddenly remembered that her class was starting that afternoon. She ran to her phone to check the time. It was just eleven. How long had she been sleeping?

She showered quickly, then dressed in her best pair of jeans and her favorite sweater. The only good thing about wasting the entire morning napping was that she now had less time to worry about her first class, and less time to worry about the subway trip. She ate a hunk of untoasted bread with honey and butter, and had a second cup of coffee, even though she knew it was a mistake. Her skin was already rippling with anxiety, and she had begun tapping the pads of her thumb and index finger together in anticipation of the afternoon.

She went to the bedroom and pulled her empty backpack from her larger bag. In her class confirmation e-mail, the instructor had said that there was no need to bring anything, that there were computers on site. Still, Kate wondered if she should bring her laptop. She decided against it, but grabbed her sketchbook from under the bed and put it in her backpack along with her pack of charcoal pencils. If she had time to kill, she could sketch, an activity that always calmed her down.

She had to walk several blocks down Charles Street to get to the station she was looking for on the Red Line. The sky was half filled with fast-moving clouds, and when the sun shone through the day felt warm, like early summer. But when a cloud covered the sun, and the wind picked up, the temperature seemed to drop about twenty degrees.

Charles Street Station was a massive structure made of glass, across a hectic intersection from Kate. She waited for walk signals, even though pedestrians in Boston darted across busy streets when there was any kind of pause in the traffic. Inside the station she bought a CharlieCard and put twenty dollars on it. It was easier than she thought it would be, and as she took the escalator to the outside platform, she was filled with a sudden surge of well-being. Here she was, in Boston, about to attend a class on InDesign. Life was good. And now that she was outside of the apartment, it suddenly seemed ridiculous how much she'd been obsessing about Audrey Marshall's death and Corbin's part in it. If he had been a genuine suspect, the police would have been back to search the apartment again.

A train approached, rumbling to a protracted stop on the tracks. Kate stepped into the car and took an end seat closest to the sliding doors. About half the seats were taken, mostly by lone commuters wearing earbuds and staring at their phones. Two women in baggy, light-blue nurse's uniforms had gotten onto the car with Kate. As the train pulled away from the station, one of them said something to the other and they both broke into a laughing fit. The train went over a bridge and Kate got a good view of the river and the Back Bay. There were sailing boats on the river, circling an inlet. Then, in a flash, the train entered a tunnel, the lights flickering. Kate shivered.

The train stopped at Kendall Station. Three more stops and she'd be at Porter, her destination. Very few of the passengers departed at Kendall, however, and many got on. A man who smelled like fast food settled down next to Kate, his large thigh pressed against hers. She pulled her leg in and squeezed up against the barrier. A woman with graying hair but a relatively young face took hold of one of the grimy-looking bars in front of Kate. How old was she? Kate wondered if she should give up her seat and offer it to this woman, or would that be an insult. She decided to stay put. The doors shut with a hiss and the train rattled forward. She took a deep breath, but the air seemed thin, and she immediately began to tell herself what she always told herself in these situations. Let the panic come. It cannot hurt you or change you. She felt a little better. To do something with her hands, she unzipped the backpack on her lap and pulled out her sketchbook. She wanted to look at the drawings she'd done so far. She cracked the book. There was Alan Cherney, her first impression of him, and she thought she'd done a good enough job. Having spent more time with him the previous night, she now thought that his cheekbones were a little more pronounced, his lips just a little thinner. Later, she'd draw a new picture of him.

She flipped the page and looked at the self-portrait she'd drawn, then quickly flipped the page again to look at Jack Ludovico. She stared. It no longer really looked like him, at least not the way she remembered him in her mind. Close, but the eyes were wrong, and the face had a different shape. How had she drawn him so wrong? Or had this been the way he looked, and she was remembering him wrong?

She really studied the picture, her heart beginning to race in her chest. Now she was sure it was not the picture she had originally drawn. Someone had gotten hold of the book and changed it. *No,* she told herself, *not possible.* And if that wasn't possible, then she'd changed it herself, gone back in and altered the features somehow. But why would she do that? And why couldn't she remember doing that if she had?

The train came to a rasping halt. There was an indiscernible announcement over the loudspeaker that could have been saying something about Porter. Kate stood and looked through the grimy window of the train. They were at Harvard Station, one stop away. Even more people were squeezing their way into the car. Why was no one getting off?

Her heart hammering, Kate pushed her way through the herd of passengers and out onto the platform. Clutching her sketchbook, she gulped at the air as the doors shut and the train moved away.

Chapter 19

Kate made it to her class with five minutes to spare. After leaving Harvard Station, she was able to navigate down Massachusetts Avenue toward the Graphics Institute, housed in several rooms of a gray Victorian mansion. It wasn't too far to walk, less than a mile. Walking briskly in the open air cleared her head a little, and she decided she'd overreacted to the drawing of Jack Ludovico. So she'd got his face a little wrong, after meeting him briefly. That was all. She'd just come to a new country, and she was jet-lagged.

The class was easier than she'd predicted. She was worried that the instructor would have the students go around the room and introduce themselves, but as soon as she walked into the second-floor classroom filled with twelve stations, each with its own Mac, she was simply told to take a seat. The instructor, who had a southern twang and a large ginger beard, jumped right into an explanation of the tools of InDesign. Kate was slightly familiar with the program, having been shown the ropes by the art teacher from the hospital she'd been held at after George Daniels's death. Kate had always been artistic. Her first great love had been coloring books, and she sometimes wondered if that would be how she'd spend her declining years as well, an old lady doing paint-by-numbers morning to night. Even from a young age, she realized that being lost in an art project, or even simply doodling in the margins of a notebook, was the one sure way she could relax. It turned out to be the same with computer graphics, once she got past her initial fear of not understanding the programs. She had become very good at Photoshop, and picked up some freelance jobs through a graphic design temp agency in South London. She'd decided that, for better or for worse, she'd make it her career. It was a far better option than becoming a portrait artist, which is what her mother had been pushing her to do. Doing someone's portrait was inherently intimate, in a way that made Kate nervous just to think about. Plus, the chances of disappointing a client were somehow much higher when doing their portrait.

After class, the girl sitting next to Kate, who was so tiny that Kate initially thought she was a child, introduced herself.

"My mother's English, too," said the girl after hearing Kate's accent. "English by way of Pakistan."

They walked from the classroom to the street together, then stood for a while, talking. Kate told the girl, named Sumera, about the apartment swap and the plan to live in Boston for six months.

"Do you have friends here?"

"No," Kate said.

"Oh my God. You are so brave. I'd never do something like that."

Kate laughed. "That's the first time, and probably the last time, anyone's called me brave."

"No, you really are," Sumera said. "I mean it."

"Okay. I'll accept it."

"Where's your apartment?"

Kate told her that she was living just off Charles Street near the river, and Sumera said: "Did you hear about that murder over there? Some girl was killed in her apartment."

"It happened in my building," Kate said, deciding to not add that it happened in the apartment next to hers.

Sumera covered her mouth. "Oh my God. That's terrible."

"How did you know she was killed? I thought the papers only reported that she'd been found dead."

"It was on Reddit," Sumera said. "Check it out. It's awful. Someone said she'd been split open."

"What do you mean?"

"I don't know if it's true, but they said she'd been cut open down the middle, like maybe it was some kind of surgery thing. It's obviously some kind of serial killer thing. I mean it's Reddit, so who really knows—"

"I don't know what Reddit is," Kate said.

As Sumera explained, Kate tried to shake the image of Audrey Marshall cut open. Until this moment, she'd not imagined the specific details of Audrey's death for the simple reason that there were too many possibilities.

But now that she knew what had happened, her mind was picturing it, and she wondered why she'd seen nothing—no bloodstains at all—when she'd snuck into Audrey Marshall's apartment. Had that been a dream?

"Look, I don't know if you should stay there. In the same building."

"I think it will be fine," Kate said. She suddenly wanted to leave. Sumera's face, ever since they'd started talking about the murder, had been wide-eyed in alarm, and it was starting to make Kate nervous. "It was nice meeting you, Sumera. My neighbors invited me to their apartment tonight, so I should probably get going."

"Maybe they'll know more about what happened."

"Maybe. I'll see you back in class on Wednesday."

"Okay. Are you walking to Porter T?"

She'd been planning on it, but Kate said, "I'll probably walk to Harvard. I have some things . . ."

Sumera, finally sensing Kate's discomfort, let her go, and Kate began the walk back along Massachusetts Avenue. The wind had lessened, but the sky was now entirely filled with clouds, so that the light seemed to blur. She wondered if she could walk the entire distance home; she was pretty sure that the wide, busy avenue that she was currently on extended all the way into Boston. But as she approached Harvard Square and spotted the T station, she decided that it was important she rode the subway again. It was only a few stops. Her panic earlier had had more to do with the sketchbook than with the claustrophobia of the train. And she'd be heading home this time, back to the relative safety of her apartment.

Without hesitating, she entered the subway station, weaved through a disembarking crowd, and got onto a nearly empty car. It was a much easier ride on the way back. She was anxious to get back and see what she could find out on the Internet about Audrey Marshall. She wondered if Sumera had even known what she was talking about. Was there genuine information out there about the nature of Audrey's death? Before she knew it, she'd made it to Charles Street Station. On her walk home, she stopped for more provisions. Her next class was not until Wednesday, and she wanted to at least give herself the opportunity of spending all of Tuesday inside.

Back at the apartment, Kate climbed onto her bed and pulled her sketchbook from her backpack to take one more look at the sketch she'd done of Audrey's friend. Maybe she'd overreacted on the subway earlier. But, no, looking at the drawing again it seemed significantly wrong, maybe even more so in the better light of the apartment. The eyes had completely changed.

Someone else drew those eyes. George's voice again.

She tried to ignore him, flipped a page, removed a charcoal pencil from the pack, and quickly sketched Sumera, her round face and thick, unplucked brows, hair parted in the middle. She didn't know how to spell *Sumera,* so under the picture she wrote, GIRL IN GRAPHIC DESIGN CLASS, CAMBRIDGE, MA, and then the date. She flipped to another page and started to draw a new sketch of Jack Ludovico, but it wasn't coming out right. She had lost confidence in what he looked like. She did something she rarely did, and sliced that page out with the razor blade she kept with her art supplies. She crumpled the page into a tight ball and threw it out.

She got off the bed and went to the computer, searching for any new information on the murder, but could find nothing. She even went to Reddit and tried to find out something there, but she could barely comprehend the Web site, let alone figure out how to navigate it.

She checked her e-mails. No response from Corbin, even after telling him that the police had searched his apartment.

At seven o'clock, after changing into a summery dress and a cardigan, Kate walked out of her apartment, down the stairs to the lobby, then up the stairs to the other side of the building. She wondered if maybe Carol Valentine or her husband would know something about the Audrey Marshall investigation. She assumed it would be part of the evening's conversation.

As she rounded the corner onto the Valentines' hallway—decorated on this side in a wallpaper of black and silver—Alan Cherney was coming out of his apartment, locking the door behind him. He turned, and Kate noticed he was holding a bottle of wine. She wondered briefly where he was going before realizing that he was probably invited to the Valentines' apartment as well.

"I'm crashing your welcome party," he said as she approached him.

"I didn't bring anything," Kate said, her eyes on the wine bottle. "I didn't even think of it."

"Here." Alan held the bottle out toward Kate. "I've already blown my first impression on them, months ago. You bring it."

"No, no," Kate said.

"They only invited me because I ran into Carol in the lobby this afternoon, and I told her that I'd gotten to know you a little."

"Is it going to be a big party? I thought it was just me having one or two drinks."

"No, it'll just be you, and maybe Mrs. Anderby who lives downstairs. And now me. I think it's kind of a Bury Street tradition. All new tenants get invited to the Valentines'. I'm only bringing wine so I don't come empty-handed, but they'll serve martinis, and you'll be expected to drink one."

"Really?"

"They did when Quinn and I were invited over."

"We should go in, don't you think?"

"We should."

Alan knocked and the door was opened by Mr. Valentine. He was a short man with beautiful white hair. Whether he'd always been short, or it was a function of his extreme old age, was hard to tell. He wore suit pants and a pale blue cashmere V-neck, and he beckoned them in with a long, thin silver spoon. "Olive or a twist?" he asked.

Kate, confused, thinking he'd said "Oliver Twist," turned toward Alan.

"I'll have a twist, please," he said to Mr. Valentine, then turned to Kate, and asked, "Do you want an olive or a twist of lemon in your martini?"

"Oh, an olive, please," Kate said, as Mr. Valentine turned and departed, just as Carol appeared. She was still wearing the wraparound white sweater she'd been wearing that morning, but her gray hair, which Kate had only ever seen up, was down, swept back off her forehead, and stiffly held in place by some sort of hair product.

"Come in, you two. Kate, what a lovely dress. Please excuse Bill. He doesn't talk until he's had his first martini of the night, and then you can never shut him up."

They followed Carol into the elegant living room, the furniture mostly white and the walls papered in pale gold. Alan, as they followed, whispered to Kate: "She said the exact same words last time I was here." As he whispered, their bodies bumped together, and Kate found herself glad that he had come as well.

In the living room, Bill Valentine was at a sidebar stirring a pitcher of martinis with the long spoon he'd held when he greeted them. Weaving between his legs was Sanders the cat, who stopped and stared at the new guests.

"Oh, Sanders," Kate said.

"Is he in here?" Carol said, spotting him. "I'm sure he's already tried to get into your apartment. You don't have to let him, you know, if you don't want to. He thinks the entire building is his house, and everyone's his staff."

"I haven't met the woman who owns him," Kate said.

Alan and Carol both said "Florence Halperin" at the same time.

"No one sees her," Carol continued. "As far as I know, she doesn't leave her apartment. Her groceries are delivered."

"I've never seen her," Alan said.

There was another knock on the door, and Carol said, "That must be Mrs. Anderby. Please excuse me."

Left alone, Alan walked toward the bar to see if Bill Valentine needed any help, and Kate wandered farther into the opulent room. There was the sharp, unpleasant smell of lilacs, and Kate turned and spotted a large bouquet on a waist-high, marble-topped table. Above the table was a tall oil painting, a portrait of Bill and Carol that looked like it had been painted about twenty-five years ago. Bill was seated, and Carol stood behind him, a hand on his shoulder. They looked the same except for their hair, Bill's dark and just beginning to be streaked with gray, Carol's fully blond. Alan appeared beside her holding two martinis, one with a lemon twist and one with an olive. He handed Kate her drink. Her hand shook a little, and the surface of the drink, poured right up to the lip of the glass, spilled over. Kate dipped her head and took a slurping sip of the ice-cold gin, some of which dribbled down her chin.

"God. I'm glad you were the only one to see that."

Alan laughed, then turned as Carol came in with Mrs. Anderby, older than either Bill or Carol. She was short, with a slight dowager's hump and hair that was thinning on the top, revealing her pink scalp. Carol introduced her to Kate, who was surprised by the firm grip of Mrs. Anderby's plump hand.

"Yes, she is pretty," Mrs. Anderby said.

"No," Kate said. "It's my name. It's Kate Priddy. P-R-I-D-D-Y." It was something she was used to having to explain.

"Oh, I see. Well, you're also pretty, dear."

"Thank you."

It took a while, but eventually all the guests were settled in various seats around a white lacquered coffee table that held several small bowls filled with nuts and olives. Kate had finished half her martini, just to keep it from spilling, and she already felt the effects. She'd had plenty of gin, but never without tonic in it, and she decided that she liked this concoction, despite the little shivers she got every time she took a sip.

Bill Valentine was halfway through his martini as well, and explaining to Kate the history of the building they were in. "It's the Italian courtyard that really sets this building apart from other similar buildings in the Flat of the Hill."

"What's the Flat of the Hill?" Kate asked.

"That's our neighborhood—"

"Beacon Hill, really," Carol said.

"No, not really. People say we live in Beacon Hill, but we're not on a hill, are we? What we're actually on is landfill that pushed the river back so they could create more housing. That's why it's flat."

"Whatever it's called, it's the most beautiful neighborhood I've ever lived in," Kate said.

Bill continued to tell Kate about the local history, including a long list of famous residents, none of whose names Kate recognized. Carol, meanwhile, grabbed Alan's attention and began to talk with him and Mrs. Anderby. As Bill monologued on, Kate could hear snippets of the other conversation and realized they were talking about Audrey Marshall. She tried hard to stay interested in what her host was saying, but she kept straining to hear what Carol was saying—something about the incompetence of the police. There was about a half ounce of gin left in Kate's glass, and she drank it down—it had warmed and now tasted harsher—and then ate her olive, hoping Bill would notice her empty glass and offer her a refill. His eyes flicked to her empty glass, and he swiftly finished his own. Kate asked him if he wanted another and began to rise, but he quickly stopped her and said he'd make them. He pushed himself with some effort up off the couch, and took both empty glasses back to the bar. Kate felt a pang of guilt, but she really wanted to hear what the others were saying. She slid along the couch so that she was closer to them.

Carol turned to Kate and said, "We're talking about Audrey Marshall. I hope that doesn't upset you. Nothing like arriving in America and finding out your next-door neighbor's been murdered."

"It's officially a murder, then?"

"Oh yes, I think so." Carol's eyes darted from guest to guest for confirmation.

Mrs. Anderby, speaking in a deep, masculine voice, said, "Oh, it was murder. Sex crime, probably. It's just not safe in the city anymore, even with a doorman. I told my son that I'll have to hire a full-time dog walker for Scout because I don't know if I can safely walk the streets. I don't even recognize my own neighborhood anymore."

"Lila, I don't think these streets are any more dangerous now than they've ever been," Carol said.

"Well, I just don't know."

"Has anyone heard anything about how Audrey Marshall was killed?" Kate asked. She was hoping to get some confirmation of what she'd heard earlier from the girl in her class.

"No, even Bob said he wasn't sure, and if Bob doesn't know . . ."

"With a knife, and she was mutilated," Alan said, as casually as though he'd just revealed that the five-day weather forecast was looking good. All eyes turned to him.

Chapter 20

Mrs. Anderby actually placed a hand against her chest and gasped a little after what Alan had said. "Well, that's what I read," Alan continued. "Online."

"Was it on Reddit?" Kate asked.

"No, it was in the comments section of a *Globe* article. I realize that doesn't sound very reliable, and it probably isn't, but one of the commenters said he knew the ambulance driver who took her to the morgue. He said it was the worst crime scene he'd ever seen."

"Good lord," Carol said.

"I heard the same thing today," Kate said. "Not from online but from this girl in my class. She said she read it on Reddit. I don't even know what that is."

"Well, let's hope that it's not true," Carol said. "If that gets out we'll be absolutely swarmed with gawkers and reporters. It'll be just like what happened over in Charlestown after the, after the . . ."

"Have they arrested anyone yet?" Mrs. Anderby asked, directing the question midway between Kate and Alan.

"No," Alan said. "At least not that I read about. I really don't know much of anything."

"Did you know her?" Carol asked.

"Um . . ." Alan glanced in Kate's direction. "I didn't really. I mean, I saw her around like everyone else, but no, I didn't know her."

"We had her over here, right after she moved in, didn't we, Bill?"

Bill Valentine was settling back into his seat after handing Kate her fresh drink. "She was very pretty," Carol continued, "but I can't say that I came away from the evening with any real sense of what she was like. What was it she even did, Bill, was it publishing, or something like that?"

Bill shrugged and shook his head.

"I got the feeling that she was—"

"I don't understand what he means by mutilated," Mrs. Anderby, her voice a deep croak, interrupted Carol.

"Honestly, it's just a rumor," Alan said. "I'm sure it's actually not true."

"They did spend an awfully long time at the crime scene," Carol said.

"Have the police come and spoken with you yet?" Kate asked.

"They came and took a statement. They took a statement from everyone in the building."

Kate told the group how her place had been searched immediately after the police had first arrived on the scene.

"Did they have a warrant?" Bill asked.

"They didn't. I didn't know what to do. I'd just arrived here, and I wasn't sure—"

"Oh, I'm sure Corbin has nothing to hide," Carol interjected. "He wasn't even here when it happened, was he? But I wonder why they searched his place and no one else's."

"It was probably just because he was the direct neighbor," Alan said.

"I'm sure that was it. Did they know one another, Kate? Audrey and your cousin?"

Kate glanced at Alan. "They did know one another. I don't know exactly how well, but the police e-mailed Corbin to let him know what had happened. I don't think they've asked him to come back to Boston, or anything." Kate took another sip of her second martini and told herself to slow down, even though it tasted far more delicious than the first.

"I still don't understand about this mutilation," Mrs. Anderby said.

"No one does, Lila," Carol quickly said. "We don't even know if it happened. But maybe we should change the subject to something else. Kate, tell us all about yourself."

All eyes turned to Kate, and she felt her cheeks flush red. She put her martini down on the coffee table and opened her mouth to say something, although she didn't know what. Carol prompted her further, asking what part of England she was from.

"Braintree, Essex," Kate said, "but don't hold that against me." Judging from the blank stares, she didn't think any of the guests had any opinion whatsoever of

Essex. Kate talked a little about her upbringing, and how she'd done some portrait painting and now wanted to get into graphic design. As usual, when talking about herself, Kate was overly aware of the blank years in her biography, the time after university, after what had happened with George Daniels, when she was either hospitalized or home with her parents, unable to leave their house.

"And is this your first time in America?" Mrs. Anderby asked.

"It is."

"We should make Kate a list of things she has to do while she's here." This was from Alan, and Kate immediately recognized the suggestion as a tactic to remove the focus from her. It worked. Everyone started speaking all at once, throwing out suggestions as to what Kate absolutely *must* do during her time in Boston. Kate glanced toward Alan, hoping to thank him with a look, but he wasn't looking at her. She studied his profile for a moment, noticing for the first time how full his lower lip was. She felt a surge of affection that he'd sought to protect her. They'd met three times and she felt as though she'd known him her entire life. Self-conscious suddenly, she stopped looking at him and picked up her martini again from the table to take another sip. She was drunk, she realized, her fingertips numb against the still-cold glass. She scooped a number of cashews from the small dish on the table and began to eat them, one by one.

After about twenty minutes, the guests, orchestrated by Alan, had assembled a definitive list of things Kate had to see or do during her time in Boston. They included the Isabella Stewart Gardner Museum, a Red Sox game at Fenway Park, the lobster roll from Neptune Oyster, taking the ferry to Provincetown, and visiting the Athenaeum, a private library, on the other end of the Common. The latter suggestion was Alan's, and after he'd made it, he told Kate that he'd be happy to take her there himself.

Bill stood, asked, "Who here wants one more for the road?"

Mrs. Anderby raised her hand, as Carol said: "Bill, I'm sure the young people have dinner plans."

Alan turned to Kate, a question in his eyes. Kate, who hadn't spoken for a while, said to the room: "I think two martinis is my martini limit." Everyone laughed, and she wondered if she'd slurred her words.

Carol walked Alan and Kate to the front door as Bill made another drink for Mrs. Anderby. "I'm sorry we had to cut short the conversation about Audrey Marshall, but Lila won't sleep for days," she said. "Kate, I've spoken to the building manager, and individually with both Bob and Sanibel and, who's the new one . . . ?"

"Oscar," Alan said.

"And Oscar, and all three are going to be *extra* on-their-guard in the coming months."

When Alan and Kate were left alone in the hall—Carol having insisted that they come back soon, maybe even for dinner—they stood for a moment, quietly, each looking at the other. The pause in conversation made Kate all the more aware of how drunk the two martinis had made her, the walls of the hallway shimmering as though they were underwater.

"I think I need to eat something," she said.

"Those were big martinis," Alan said.

"How many did you have?"

"I had two, but I'm a professional."

"Yeah, I think I'm an amateur."

"I'm not much of a cook," Alan said, "but I'm good at breakfast food. I can make you an omelet."

"That sounds lovely."

Alan's kitchen, like Kate's, had a large granite-topped island. She sat and watched him make the omelet. He'd offered her a glass of wine, but she asked for water instead. He'd already whisked the eggs, and was now shredding a block of Jarlsberg cheese. "I'm sorry I don't have any vegetables," he said.

"Please. I'd be happy eating that block of cheese."

"I can make you some toast, too, if you'd like?"

"Yes, please. And I can make it if you point me toward the bread."

As Kate made the whole wheat toast, Alan went to the living room and started playing music, some sort of jazz that was vaguely familiar to Kate. Tenor saxophone, piano, drums. He came back and started the omelets, sliding a large pat of butter onto the hot surface of the pan.

He had a look of intense concentration on his face, and Kate instantly saw what he would have looked like as a small boy, hovering over a spelling test at school. It was then that she decided to definitely sleep with him.

She hadn't been with anyone since George Daniels. Over five years. The thought of being intimate with someone again terrified her, although she'd known for a while that it was something she needed to do. She had no intention of exiting this realm having only ever had sex with a man who'd tried to kill her. But the timing had to be right. She was worried about picking the wrong person and the wrong moment, and winding up traumatized again. But now—right this very moment—the conditions were perfect. She was drunk, and in another country. If she needed to suddenly escape, her own apartment was in the same building. And she was attracted to Alan, and he seemed to be attracted to her. And even though there was something a little off about him—his obsession with Audrey, for one—he seemed kind. And it was time, she told herself.

Knowing what was probably going to happen next, Kate lost her appetite. Still, she ate her omelet and the buttered toast, while they talked about Carol and Bill. Alan told her that Bill had run a major airline once upon a time, and that they spent their winters in Palm Beach. They'd had one son, who had committed suicide nearly twenty years earlier.

"How do you know all this?" Kate asked.

"Quinn, my ex-girlfriend, found out. We'd had drinks

with them—an exact replica of tonight's evening, by the way—and Quinn had apparently passed the test, and I did not, because Carol and Quinn became sort of friends. Well, they had lunch on one of Bill's golfing days, and I wasn't invited to play golf."

"Do you play golf?"

"No."

"So what makes you think you made this bad impression?"

"I made a comment about how unnecessary a door-man was in a building in Beacon Hill. Something like that. I got a lecture. And I'm not sure they liked the shape of my nose."

"Seriously? Really?" Kate said.

"No, not really. I mean, because I'm Jewish."

"Oh."

"Did you know I was Jewish?"

"No, I never even thought about it."

"Maybe I was being paranoid, but the whole night I was sitting there, I kept thinking that all they were seeing was this ugly Jew with a beautiful shiksa, and wondering how I'd made it into their building. They were probably thinking it again, tonight."

"I think you sound paranoid."

Alan laughed. "No, I'm definitely paranoid. Doesn't mean they didn't think it, though."

"And I don't think you're ugly," Kate said. "Not at all."

They cleaned the dishes, and Kate accepted a glass of

white wine. The food had sobered her up, and she wanted to regain a little bit of the feeling she'd had earlier. After the kitchen was clean, Alan went into the living room to put on a new record, Kate following him. The music started—jazz again, but with a female vocalist—and Kate put her glass down on a wooden side table. Alan put his glass down next to it, and with only a little hesitation took Kate into his arms and kissed her. Kate froze a little, then relaxed and parted her lips. The tips of their tongues touched, and Kate's legs weakened. She pulled away a little.

"You okay?" Alan asked.

"It's been a very long time since I've done this."

"Okay."

"And there's a reason for that. I have baggage."

"Okay. We can talk about it if you like."

"No, I don't want to talk about it. I just wanted you to know in advance in case it got weird."

Alan smiled. "Thanks for letting me know." His voice sounded a little hoarse. "Forewarned, forearmed."

They kissed some more, standing next to the record player. Kate recognized one of the songs: "Bewitched, Bothered, and Bewildered." It was an old song, and it made her feel as though they were kissing in a different era. Years earlier. It helped Kate pretend she was someone else, someone who wasn't scared all the time, someone who slipped in and out of passionate affairs on a weekly basis.

"Do you want to . . . ?" Alan began to ask.

"Stay?"

"Yes."

"Okay."

They moved to the bedroom, which was as neat as the rest of the house, the double bed tightly made, no clothes lying on the floor. Above the bed was a framed print that Kate recognized as a Chagall. She wondered if it was Alan's or a memento from his failed relationship. Alan used the bathroom first, then Kate did, and when she returned Alan was already in bed. She now felt entirely sober, and nervous, but she wasn't panicking. She felt ready. George Daniels crept around in the back of her mind, of course, watching them, but Kate could handle it. He was always there, and she was used to him.

Kate noticed a T-shirt and what looked like a pair of pajama bottoms neatly folded at the foot of the bed. Alan said: "In case you wanted something to wear." She realized that Alan, ever since she'd confessed to him that she hadn't done this in a while, had been overly careful with her. She pulled her dress over her head, unhooked and took off her bra, and slid next to him. The sheets were crisp and cool, and Alan pulled her in close to his thin, warm body. His hand slipped around one of her breasts. His mouth still tasted like wine.

*

She woke at dawn, the bedroom's only window suffused in a pearly gray light. Alan was snoring lightly, one of his hands resting on her hip. Standing over them was George

Daniels. He was holding his hunting rifle in one hand. With his other he was unzipping his pants. He smiled at her, his mouth a gaping hole, without teeth. Kate wondered where his teeth were, then realized they were in her own mouth, a pile of them, rattling around like little sharp-edged marbles, choking her.

*

She woke again. The window looked the same, glowing dimly in the dawn, but there was no George, and Alan's hand was no longer on her hip. Her heart was skipping a little too fast, and her skin was damp with sweat. It was just George, in her dreams again, the only place he could reach her. She slid out of the bed and walked naked to the bathroom. She flipped the switch, and a harsh, bright light—four oversized bulbs above the vanity— flooded the bathroom. She closed her eyes, then opened them slightly to allow them time to adjust. Her mouth was dry, and she drank cool, tinny water directly from the faucet. Then she looked at herself in the full-length mirror, her nakedness making her acutely aware of what had just happened. It had been good. More than good, really. They'd kissed for a while, touching each other shyly under the sheets. It was very clear that Alan was taking things slow, and she'd started to regret telling him she had baggage, but after she removed her own underwear and asked him if he had a condom, he took charge, slowly at first, then, after he was inside of her, with a sense of purpose that George, awkward and needy, had never had. She'd enjoyed it, even though she'd felt at a remove, watching the proceedings, desperately happy that it was happening, but never entirely in the moment. Afterward, Alan had buried his head in the space between her neck and shoulder and let the full weight of his body press against hers. She could feel the breath moving in and out of his lungs, and the sticky warmth between their skin. It had been her favorite moment. She'd touched the tip of her tongue against the side of his neck just to taste him. Thinking of it now, she still felt relief that she had finally been with someone besides George Daniels, but she was also anxious. Despite the way that Alan made her feel, she barely knew him.

She turned the light off, and the bathroom went black. She found the doorknob and stepped into the dimly lit hallway. Back in the bedroom, Alan still slept, his face planted into a pillow, one leg kicked out from under the comforter.

Quietly, Kate collected her clothes and left to dress in the bathroom. Seeing him lying there—innocently asleep—had caused a flutter of fear in her stomach. It was the way George Daniels had always slept, flipped onto his stomach, a hand tucked under his chin.

It's just the way Alan sleeps, she told herself. *He's not George.*

But she could feel the good feelings she'd just felt about Alan evaporating away. It was like a rapid change in the weather.

She dressed and left his apartment, walked to her side of the building. She didn't see anyone, but the sound of her shoes on the tiled floor made her feel as though the entire apartment building knew where she had been.

Back behind her closed door, she felt her mind starting to race out of her control. She barely knew Alan. He'd been obsessed with a woman in the building who was now dead. After meeting her once in the courtyard, he'd showed up at the restaurant where she was eating dinner. He'd probably followed her there, and he'd probably also made sure to get himself invited to Bill and Carol Valentine's apartment for drinks. At best, he had decided to seduce her—and succeeded, almost instantly. At worst, he was a psychotic murderer. She caught herself rapidly touching the pad of her thumb to each fingertip, three times on each finger, then made herself stop.

There was a knock on the door, light, almost hesitant. There was no need to look through the peephole. *It's Alan,* came George's voice. *He's chased you down.* Still, Kate looked. And there was Alan's face, serious, almost haunted. And was there something else? A little bit of anger, maybe.

Kate slid the shoes off her feet and backed away from the door, as quietly as she could, George still whispering in her ear.

Chapter 21

Kate tried to sleep some more, and when that didn't work, she showered and got dressed, even though she had no intention of leaving her apartment that day.

She opened up her e-mail account, saw that Martha was also online, and sent her a message: Hiya.

Five minutes passed, during which Kate read an e-mail from her father telling her that he hoped she wasn't becoming too stressed. She knew that the e-mail had been dictated to her father, or flat-out written, by her mother, who didn't want to write the same message herself. She was about to google Alan Cherney when Martha wrote back: Hi.

> **Kate:** How's life? Haven't snogged with my cousin again, have you?
> **Martha:** I wish. he scampered
> **Kate:** What do you mean?
> **Martha:** Haven't seen him, or heard him. Not that I've been trying to (complete lie), but he's not around
> **Kate:** Since when?
> **Martha:** Since the last time I saw him. I don't

know. Heard him Saturday, I think.

Kate: Strange.

Martha: He ask you about me? Did you tell him to run for the hills?

Kate: I recommended he get as far away as possible.

Martha: You probably did, you dirty bitch

Kate: He probably rented some glamorous flat to get out of mine. If you see him, let me know, though.

Martha: What's going on?

Kate: Nothing. Just being nosy. Gotta run.

Kate logged out of her e-mail account. Where did Corbin go? Was he on his way back here? And if so, why hadn't he let her know?

Kate went back to googling Alan Cherney, finding very little. It looked as though he'd been a fencer, and his name showed up on tournament results, plus one photograph from the Tufts varsity squad, a picture that was ten years old. She remembered what he'd said the night before at the cocktail party about how he'd found out Audrey Marshall had been mutilated from a *Boston Globe* article. No, not from an article, but from the comments section of an article. Kate went to the *Globe*'s Website and found an article on Audrey Marshall. There were a few comments, but nothing mentioned how she'd been killed. She checked every article she could find, and all the comments. Nothing. Either it had been deleted—pretty likely, if you thought about it—or else Alan knew what had happened to Audrey for some other reason.

Kate slid the computer off her lap and stood quickly, felt light-headed, then sat again. Her mouth was still dry from the night before and all that gin. She stood again, slower this time, and went to the kitchen. She drank orange juice straight from the carton. Once she began, she felt as though she couldn't stop, chugging it till it ran down her chin. Then she ate a vanilla yogurt. She started to feel a little better.

She went back into the living room and looked out the window at the day. It was bright and clear, not a cloud in sight, the first day she'd seen like that since coming to Boston. The part of the river she could see, however, rippled with wind, and a nearby tree, filled with new leaves, was bending and unbending. She pressed the palm of her hand against the glass of the window; it was cool to the touch, and she could feel the wind's vibration through her hand.

Maybe she would take a walk today, she thought, then dismissed it. She felt okay behind the locked door of the apartment, and out there in the world—out there somewhere—was Audrey's murderer. And maybe that murderer was now interested in Kate.

She tried to tell herself she was being paranoid, but it wasn't working. What had happened to Audrey had something to do with her. Maybe not at first, but now it did. Corbin had been involved with Audrey and was now lying about it. And here she was, in Corbin's apartment. Even the police were interested in Corbin.

And there was Alan. What had she been thinking, sleeping with Alan? Even if he had nothing to do with what had happened to Audrey, he'd spied on her for months and months, obsessed with her, plotting a way to get to know her. *Normal people don't do that,* Kate thought. But maybe Kate just wasn't attracted to normal people. Maybe she was attracted to psychopaths. George Daniels hadn't gotten her psychopath attraction out of her system. She needed to go to an entirely different country and find another one. She pictured Alan's distorted face through the peephole just a few hours earlier, and she was scared. He was probably at work now, but he'd be back at her door later that evening. She was sure of it.

The phone in the living room rang, a sharp jangling sound. Kate walked toward it, her heart speeding up a little. Would Alan have this phone number? It was possible. Maybe it was even listed. She let it go till it stopped ringing. A few seconds passed and it started again. It was definitely Alan, Kate thought, and told herself to pick up. If she was going to have to speak with him—and she'd slept with him, so, yes, she needed to speak with him—it would be easier to do that on the phone than in person.

She cleared her throat, picked up the handset, and said, "Hello?"

"Is this Kate Priddy?" It was a woman's voice.

234

"Uh-huh."

"It's Detective James calling. I was wondering if we could come by this morning and take another look at your apartment?"

"I guess so. Do you, uh, have a warrant?"

"I don't, although we can get one if you'd prefer."

"I think it will be okay."

"I'm bringing Audrey Marshall's parents to Audrey's apartment so they can collect what they want. I thought it would be good to leave them alone for a little while. It would give us an opportunity to talk, and for one of my officers to take a better look around Corbin's apartment. Your apartment, now, of course."

"Oh. Okay. Is Corbin a suspect? Have you talked with him?"

"I can answer your questions when I get there, Kate, okay?"

"Okay."

Kate hung up the phone. She wondered if they were coming back with an enormous team, with men in rubber gloves with little baggies to collect evidence. It didn't sound like it, if they hadn't gotten a warrant. Still, they clearly knew that Corbin had been in some sort of relationship with Audrey. As before, the imminent arrival of the police was making Kate want to search the apartment again herself. But she also wondered if she should be careful about touching things. She stood frozen by the phone. They'd want to see the key to Audrey's apartment, she imagined. Where was that key? Kate, for a moment, couldn't remember, then had a vague recollection of putting it back in the drawer where she had found it. She walked to the kitchen to check. It wasn't there. There were several unmarked keys, and then the few that were labeled, although she couldn't find the one that was labeled AM. Kate thought hard. Maybe it was still in the pocket of the jeans she'd been wearing the night she went to Audrey's apartment. She raced to the bedroom, searched through her clothes, and couldn't find the key. She returned to the kitchen and searched the drawer again, lifting out the cutlery tray to make sure that the key hadn't slid beneath it. She racked her brain but came up with nothing. The last time she remembered having the key was when she returned from looking at Audrey's apartment. She'd watched Alan across the way. She shivered a little, then pushed him out of her mind.

She looked through the labeled keys again, picking up the one that was marked STORAGE. She'd seen that key before, and assumed at the time that it was for some storage unit that either Corbin or his father had rented, but what if it wasn't? What if it was for a storage unit in the basement of the apartment building? It didn't seem likely that with apartments so large there'd be extra space for storage, but the more she thought about it, the more she realized that of course there would be. She gripped the key tightly between her fingers. Maybe that was why she'd found so little evidence of Corbin's personal life in his apartment; it was all in his storage unit. Detective James had said that she'd be at the apartment in about an hour. Kate decided she had time to quickly check the basement and see what was down there. As soon as the idea entered her head, she knew she had to do it. It was a compulsion she was familiar with: if she didn't look, then there was something terrible in the storage unit. She needed to look to make that terrible thing go away. And what was that terrible thing? The halved remains of endless murdered girls?

Kate tapped her fingertips together, dropping the key. It hit the slate floor with a snapping sound.

She picked it up and unlocked the kitchen door. Mrs. Valentine had told her, when she'd first given Kate the tour of the apartment, that the door in the kitchen led to the basement. Kate swung the door open, then found the switch, and a dim yellow light flooded the narrow, steep stairwell. Testing first to make sure that the door wouldn't swing closed behind her of its own accord, Kate took the stairs down the three levels, the air cooling as she descended. At the bottom of the stairwell was an unlocked door. She pushed through and into the basement. She was expecting dim lighting and damp walls, but it wasn't like that at all. It was a wide, uncluttered, well-lit space. The floor was spotless poured concrete, and the finished walls were painted an industrial gray. Along one wall was a row of water heaters, and opposite them was a series of wooden doors constructed from particleboard. The doors all had stenciled letters on them and were padlocked. Storage units. Kate found the door marked 3D and tried the key. It slid into the padlock. Kate turned it and the lock snapped open.

This is it, Kate thought, her mind careening down its path of atrocities. She touched her upper lip with a dry tongue.

She swung the door open on its well-oiled hinges. It was dark inside but not so dark that she couldn't see what was in front of her. There wasn't a shrine to Audrey, splattered in blood. There wasn't a corpse, or even a pool of blood. There were stacked boxes, plastic crates of sporting equipment and CDs. Kate stepped into the space, let her eyes adjust. A barbecue with a bubbled metal lid gave the space the smell of dusty charcoal. Stacked along one wall were half a dozen cheaply framed posters. She flipped through them. One was a crude picture she recognized as an album cover for a band called Ween. It was a photograph of a woman's torso. She was wearing a plastic belt with the band's logo, and a shirt that just barely covered her breasts. Kate stared at it, transfixed but not knowing why. The other posters were primarily of Italian sports cars, the types of posters that would seem pretty cheesy even on the walls of a university dorm room. There was also a poster for *Fight Club,* and a poster that listed the Twelve Reasons Beer Is Better Than a Woman.

Kate opened the nearest box. It was filled with comic books in plastic sleeves. She pulled one out—*The*

Fantastic Four—and put it back. The rest of the boxes contained comic books, as well, all preserved in plastic sleeves. One box also contained a stack of sports car magazines, and hidden within them, a well-thumbed issue of *Penthouse*. Kate had a moment of guilt, prying through Corbin's things. She thought of her own closet in her flat, the box that contained all her old sketchbooks, including one that was dedicated to drawings of boy bands and unicorns. She hoped he wasn't looking through those. Then again, Kate wasn't looking just to satisfy a prurient interest; she was looking for evidence. And suddenly, having that thought, she felt ridiculous. The police would be here soon, also looking for evidence, and they actually knew what they were doing. And there was nothing here in the storage unit to see. It was just items that Corbin wasn't quite ready to throw out yet. Everyone's storage unit looked like that.

She left the unit and swung the door shut behind her, and felt a splinter from the cheap wood slide into her thumb. She immediately put her thumb in her mouth, then took a look. The dark splinter was visible under her translucent skin. She felt for its bottom ridge with her index finger and tried to push it out, but it was in deep. I'll deal with it upstairs, she thought, and was about to relock the padlock, when she felt a sudden compulsion to look again at the posters. There had been something odd about the one of the girl with the large breasts. She opened the door and went to the posters, pulling it out.

The frame was incredibly light. There was a darkish line that ran down the center of the poster. That was what had brought Kate back. The sides of the posters were held by thin plastic frames—Kate pulled the top one off, and the sides fell away. The thin transparent plastic covering the poster slid away as well, and Kate saw that the poster had been sliced down the middle. The line she'd seen had been a cut, and half the poster fluttered to the floor, landing face up so that Kate was looking at half a woman, severed down the middle.

The blood rushed from Kate's head and she felt cold all over. She crouched, instinctively, to pick up the poster half and try to put it all back together, then abandoned the idea and decided to get out of the storage unit, out of the basement.

She backed away, shutting the door, and locking it this time.

She turned to go, but a flash of movement from the shadows behind one of the water heaters caught her eye. She stopped and listened, heard scratching noises, then crouched and saw Sanders emerge, something in his jaws. He turned toward her, his eyes two buttons of reflective yellow. She tried to make out what he had caught. It was either a small rat or a large mouse. He dropped it to the floor and it moved sluggishly away. Sanders leapt and pinned it under his paws. Then Sanders looked directly at Kate and hissed loudly.

Kate left the basement on hollow legs. What did the

mutilated poster mean? Was it possible that the poster had been folded and had, over time, separated at the crease? No, not really possible. The poster wasn't torn, it was deliberately cut. Deliberately cut, then reframed. Did Corbin have some kind of sick fantasy about mutilating a woman? A fantasy that he had finally enacted with Audrey Marshall? Kate reentered the apartment and stood for a moment, thinking, tapping her fingertips together in a deliberate pattern.

Back in her living room, Kate heard a commotion in the hallway. She looked through the peephole, just in time to see Detective James removing the police tape from Audrey Marshall's door while a middle-aged couple—Audrey's parents—waited quietly. They looked older than Kate would have imagined. The woman used one of those canes with a large four-pronged base. Maybe they'd had Audrey late, or maybe these were grandparents. With the tape clear and the door open, the detective led the couple into the apartment while two uniformed officers remained in the hall. Kate stopped watching, went to the kitchen to get a drink of water.

A knock came at the door, sooner than she expected, and she let in Detective James, plus one of the uniformed officers.

"I need to talk with you," Kate said to the detective as she crossed the threshold.

"Okay. Let's sit."

The uniformed officer—a young black man with a

shaved head—seemed to know what to do without being told. He went toward the kitchen, pulling on gloves. Kate tried hard to not look at the holstered gun on his belt.

The detective sat on the edge of the couch, smoothed out the legs of her black pantsuit, and said, "Are you okay? You look a little upset."

"Was Audrey Marshall mutilated?"

The detective's face didn't change, but Kate thought she saw an alteration in her eyes. A look of interest, and also concern. "Where did you hear that?"

"I met a woman in a class I'm taking, and she told me that she'd read it on the Internet. And then I heard from someone else that he'd also seen it online, in the comments section of an article that he'd read." Kate was aware that she hadn't mentioned that one of the sources of her information was Alan Cherney, but if the detective asked, she'd tell her. She'd decided to tell her everything.

Detective James nodded slowly at the information. She seemed to be considering her options. "Without going into too much detail, Kate, yes, Audrey Marshall, after she was dead, was cut in several places. I'm going to ask you to keep that information to yourself since we haven't released it to the press yet. Although clearly someone has."

"Okay, I promise," Kate said. "How was she cut? I mean, where was she cut?"

"Why do you want to know that?"

"I'm pretty sure that Corbin, that my cousin Corbin, had something to do with Audrey's death. I went down to the storage units in the basement—"

"In the basement here in this building?"

"Yes."

"When did you do this?"

"Just this morning. Just now, before you got here."

Kate told her what she'd found, describing the poster of the sexy girl, and the way it had been sliced down the middle, and then reframed. As she explained it, she wondered if she sounded paranoid, but the detective was interested, noticeably sitting a little taller on the edge of her seat. When Kate was done, the detective thanked her, then said she wanted to make a quick phone call. She stood, pulled out her cell phone, and walked over to the window. Whoever she called, they talked for less than a minute, the detective pocketing the phone as she walked back toward Kate.

"Audrey Marshall's cause of death was a knife wound to the throat, but, there were also postmortem wounds, a slice from her head down the length of her body." The detective ran her finger down her own center.

"Oh," Kate said, her mind immediately picturing the skin folded back, a skull revealed. She tasted bile at the back of her throat.

"Why did you go to the storage unit in the first place?" Detective James asked. "Are there other reasons you suspect your cousin?"

Kate filled her lungs with one long, deep breath, then let it out. She knew she had to tell this detective everything. She began, first telling her about what she had learned from Alan Cherney, how he was able to see into Audrey Marshall's apartment, and how he had become convinced that Corbin was dating Audrey. How he'd seen them kiss.

Kate thought the detective would want to know why Alan Cherney was spying on Audrey Marshall, but, instead, she asked: "Even if Corbin was romantically involved with Audrey, why would that make you so suspicious? There must have been something else."

"Well, it was because he denied it. And Alan says they were involved, and so does Audrey's friend, Jack—he seemed to think that Corbin had something to do with what happened, as well."

"I definitely want to get back to Jack Ludovico, and hear more about that conversation, but first, is there anything else that has caused you to suspect your cousin? Obviously, you've been looking around . . ."

"I told you about the key that he had to Audrey Marshall's apartment."

"Yes."

"There's that. Although that could mean anything, of course. He was her neighbor, after all. And, then, there was what I found in the storage unit. The cut picture."

"Do you have the storage unit key with you now?"

"Yes, here," Kate said, reaching into the front pocket of her jeans, but not finding the key. She stood, searched her other pockets. Nothing.

"Did you put it back in the drawer?" Detective James asked.

"God, I must have," Kate said, and turned to walk to the kitchen.

"That's okay," the detective quickly said. "We'll find it."

Kate sat back down. Yes, now she remembered: she'd put the key back in the drawer of the kitchen. "I'm sorry," she said. "I haven't been sleeping, and I've been freaking out about what happened in this building."

"Totally understandable," Detective James said. She reached out and briefly placed two fingers on Kate's knee to reassure her. Kate recognized the gesture, and the detective's half smile, from the dozens of psychiatrists and counselors she'd had contact with in the course of her short life. She wasn't crazy, though. Not right now. The police presence proved that. There had been a murder next door. And Corbin was somehow involved.

"Tell me more about Ludovico. Do you know how he spells his name?"

"I don't know. The way it sounds, I guess," Kate said. "Why?"

"Because after I talked with you last, and you told me that you'd talked with him, I tried to look him up, and didn't find anything."

"Didn't he come by the police station?"

"He didn't. Did he tell you that he had?"

Kate tried to remember. She was still frazzled by not

remembering where she'd put the key, and suddenly all of her memories felt unreal to her. "He did," she said at last. "I'm sure of it. He came here to the building to get information. He said that he'd been to the police but that they'd told him nothing. He said he'd been questioned, I think."

"Did you tell me everything about your conversation?"

Kate thought back. "I did. He was a friend but he clearly had a thing for Audrey. He said he worked in the hotel business."

The detective was rapidly writing in her notebook. She looked up, and asked, "Can you describe him for me? What he looked like?"

Kate thought hard. She kept picturing the sketch she'd done that had changed somehow. She almost went to get it, then said, "I can draw him for you, if you'd like," she said. "I'm better at drawing than describing."

"Sure," Detective James said, and passed Kate her notebook and pencil.

She quickly sketched Jack Ludovico, his smallish features that made him look more like a boy than a man, the hair that stuck up. The strange picture from her sketchbook kept jumping into her mind as she drew, getting in the way of her memory, so that his eyes came out wrong somehow, in a way she didn't quite understand. Still, she handed the notebook back to the detective.

"His hair is red. I should have indicated that."

"I'll remember. You're a good artist. This is helpful," the detective said.

"It's not perfect. I only met him the once."

"It's good. Thanks. Can I ask you one more thing? When did you and Corbin make the decision to swap apartments? Do you know when he first contacted you?"

Kate thought back. She remembered her mother broaching the idea of the swap after dinner on a Sunday. It was late February, she thought, or early March, the days still short.

"Sometime in late February," she told the detective.

"Any chance you can be more specific than that?"

"Oh. I would say either the last Sunday in February or the first Sunday in March. I can ask my mum. She'll remember, and if she doesn't, she's probably written it down somewhere."

"That would be great." Detective James closed her notebook, rocked backward a little in preparation for getting up. Kate noticed how perfect the detective's posture was, her back straight, her wide shoulders back, and sat up a little straighter herself.

Before the detective had a chance to get up, Kate asked, "So Corbin was involved with Audrey Marshall? That's why you're here, right?"

"He was. Audrey kept a diary, and he's mentioned in it. And we've confirmed from one of Audrey's friends that they were involved for a period of time over the past couple of months."

"Oh." Even though she'd suspected it—known it, really—the blunt fact still surprised her. "So they were definitely involved. So he's a definite suspect."

The detective smiled and scratched at her wrist, underneath the strap of a chunky watch. "He is a definite person of interest, Kate. We'd very much like to talk with him."

"I thought you had."

"There was an e-mail exchange, but a London police officer went to question him at your flat and he wasn't there."

"No. He's gone missing from there, I think."

"How do you know that?"

Kate told the detective about her friend Martha, and how she hadn't seen him around.

"If you communicate with Martha again, please ask if she's seen him come and go."

"I will. Are you going to arrest him?"

"We just really want to speak with him. Sooner rather than later."

The detective's phone rang, and she pulled it from her pocket. "Good, you're here. Just come straight up. It's one down from Audrey Marshall's, the door at the end of the hall." She ended the conversation but kept the phone in her hand as she said to Kate, "My colleague from the FBI will be coming up, as well."

"Why the FBI?"

"There's a chance, Kate, that this crime is connected with two previous crimes, one of which occurred in Connecticut, and that was when the FBI became involved. We're following every lead, and I am very interested in seeing what you found in the storage unit downstairs."

There was a knock on the door, and the detective jumped up to answer it. An Asian woman wearing a black leather jacket over a white top entered. She didn't look a whole lot older than Kate. The detective introduced her to Kate as Abigail Tan, then asked, "Kate, can you come with us to the storage unit, show us what you found?"

Chapter 22

When Alan woke to find Kate gone he knew that something was wrong. She'd obviously had a change of heart, otherwise she'd have at least said goodbye. Alan went to his phone to text her before realizing that he didn't have her number. He got out of bed, pulled on a pair of jeans and a T-shirt, then walked through the quiet apartment building to her side and knocked on her door. She was there, he knew it, on the other side. He couldn't hear her, but he sensed her. The dark peephole stared at him, and he was suddenly angry at himself for chasing her down. He returned to his apartment, shucked off his shoes, and tried to decide what to do next. He was up hours earlier than he usually was, but he was far too wired to consider going back to bed. His stomach had a queasy hollowness, and there was a dull thudding somewhere in his head. He drank two glasses of water and swallowed some aspirin.

If he was slightly hungover, Kate was probably hungover as well, maybe worse than he was. Maybe she'd woken up, felt sick, and returned to her own place. Or maybe she'd woken up and felt ashamed of what they'd done. She'd told him that she had baggage, and that she hadn't been with anyone for a long time. He'd been sensitive to that fact, going slow, even though he'd been overcome with not just intense physical longing, but something emotional as well. Afterward, with their chests pressed together, their breathing synced, he felt healed of an injury he hadn't known he had.

And now she'd run away.

For something to do, he made a pot of coffee, then nuked some instant oatmeal even though he wasn't hungry. He went to his computer, opened his work e-mail account, and sent a message to his boss that he'd woken up with some sort of stomach ailment and planned on staying home. He drank a cup of coffee, sitting by the window, with its view of the courtyard. It was strange to sit there and not be fixated by Audrey Marshall's window. She'd been dead less than a week, and her importance in Alan's life was already diminishing.

The day was bright but windy. A plastic bag spun in circles around the apartment building's courtyard. At just after seven the lobby's doors swung open and a man in a business suit emerged, a newspaper tucked under one of his arms. Alan recognized him but couldn't remember his name. A financial analyst, he thought, who lived on the first floor with a wife who never appeared. The plastic bag snagged on the man's right shoe as he traversed the courtyard. He bent and pulled it off, holding it at a distance as though it were toxic. He hesitated in that pose for a moment, and Alan knew he was weighing his options. Should I drop it back into the courtyard for someone else to deal with, or should I throw it out myself? He dropped it, wiped his fingers on his suit pants, and continued on his way.

Alan kept watching. If Kate emerged from the apartment that day—and it was definitely an *if,* not a *when*—then Alan could race down and confront her. She'd have to talk with him. She'd have to tell him what had happened to make her run from his apartment. He knew how it would look, him tracking her down, but he didn't care. Besides, it would be better than returning to knock at her apartment and knowing that she was on the other side, not answering the door. Was it just shame on her part? Or had he done something wrong? He scoured his memories from the night before, looking for clues, but finding nothing.

He only left the window once during the morning, to quickly race to the bathroom, wash up a little, brush his teeth, and pull on clean clothes. On his way back he stopped in the kitchen, peered at the uneaten oatmeal congealing in a bowl, then rolled a piece of turkey up with a piece of Swiss cheese and brought it back to his post by the window. He watched the mailman arrive, trudging across the courtyard while pulling out a large parcel of mail from his saddlebag. Several other inhabitants from the building passed by, all on their way out into the brightness of Tuesday morning. He watched as Mrs. Anderby stepped into the courtyard with her pug, letting him off his leash to go sniff around the shrubbery for a place to urinate.

There was a large burst of wind, and Mrs. Anderby stutter-stepped a little, so she wouldn't fall over.

At around eleven, Alan watched as two gray sedans pulled up on Bury Street, parking side by side at an angle, both cars jutting into the street. He knew it was police, even before he watched a tall woman in a dark suit emerge from one of the vehicles and two uniformed cops from the other. The three conferred briefly, then crossed the courtyard and entered the lobby. Alan recognized the female detective from before. He assumed that they were returning to Audrey Marshall's apartment for whatever reason. His eyes went to her windows, the interiors dark. Even so, he caught a flutter of movement, as though someone had just let go of the curtain in the bedroom window. He sat up straighter and stared hard at where he thought he'd seen the curtain move. He could make out a reflection of the enormous rustling maple that loomed behind the apartment building. Was that what he had seen? The movement of a reflected tree?

He shifted his eyes back to the living room window that was directly across from him, the curtains partway pulled. He waited for the police to enter. If there was already someone in there, then they'd find him or her. Most likely, if there was someone in there, then it was probably another police officer. Alan told himself to be rational, even though he wasn't feeling particularly rational.

After a few minutes, it became clear that the police had not arrived to re-search Audrey's apartment. So where were they? Were they back at Kate's place, maybe searching it again?

Alan was so fixated on Audrey's windows that he almost missed the man coming out from the lobby and walking briskly across the courtyard. Alan didn't recognize him as someone who lived in the building. His hair was red, and he was wiry and small. He fit the description of Jack something-or-other that Kate had given him. The man who claimed he'd been Audrey's ex-boyfriend. Had he been the one in the apartment? Still, he'd been moving too fast for Alan to catch up with him, even if he'd wanted to. He turned his attention back to Audrey's windows. Still no activity. Alan looked out toward the street, where the police vehicles had left just barely enough space for a passing car. Near the vehicles was the man he'd just seen coming out of the apartment building. He was standing on the sidewalk and staring up at the building, staring up at exactly where one of Kate's windows would be.

Alan pulled his shoes on, grabbed his keys and his leather messenger bag, and went out the door. Even though he hadn't decided yet exactly what he planned on saying to this guy, it felt better than just sitting by a window waiting for something to happen. He bolted down the steps but walked casually through the lobby and courtyard, not wanting to look insane. On Bury Street he turned right, but Jack had disappeared. He looked toward Charles Street and spotted him loping along the sidewalk. Alan followed.

Jack—if it was Jack—turned left onto Brimmer Street instead of continuing all the way down to Charles. Alan sped up a little so as not to lose him, but when he turned left on Brimmer there was no sign of anybody. Alan continued to walk, looking left and right in case he'd ducked between one of the buildings, but Brimmer was almost entirely lined by redbrick apartment buildings. There was nowhere to hide.

"Are you looking for me?"

Alan turned at the sound of the voice. Jack was behind him, and Alan scanned the street to see where he might have been hiding. There was one large tree—a ginkgo—and maybe Jack had been behind it.

"I am," Alan said, and was embarrassed to hear that his voice quavered a little. "Can I ask your name?"

"You can ask me, but I don't know if I'll tell you." He smiled, showing off prominent canines. His short messy hair moved in the wind.

"It's Jack, right?" Alan asked. "You were Audrey Marshall's friend."

"How did you know that?" Jack asked, still smiling, but now with a perplexed look in his eyes.

"I guessed. I saw you leaving the apartment building. I live there, too, and I'd heard about you. You've come to the building before, right?"

He hesitated a fraction. "Yeah. A couple times."

"Right. I'm Alan."

Jack held out his hand, and Alan took it.

"Did you know Audrey, then? I don't remember her mentioning you."

"I didn't, no. I know Corbin a little bit, and I'm friends with Kate, Corbin's cousin, who's now living in his place. She told me she'd met you. How long did you know Audrey?"

"Since college, but we fell out of touch. We reconnected when she moved here. When she moved to Boston." Jack blinked several times, as though the wind had blown something into one of his eyes.

A car pulled around the corner, moving slowly, as though the driver were looking for a specific address. Jack watched the car as it departed down the street, then turned his dark, questioning eyes back to Alan. "So are you going to tell me what you want? You did follow me from the building, didn't you?"

"What were you doing there?"

"Doing where? At Audrey's apartment? That's not really any of your business."

"So you *were* in Audrey's apartment?"

"Again, that's not really your business." Jack's words were aggressive, but his manner really wasn't. He still had that frozen, wolflike grin on his face. Alan felt himself struggling to remember his reasons for following Jack.

"Fine," Alan said eventually. "Then you won't mind if I report that I saw you to the police."

"Please, go right ahead. I'll tell them myself, if you want. I have nothing to hide."

Alan, his embarrassment growing, said, "Look, I'm not accusing you of anything. But there's been a murder in my building, and then I saw you lurking around . . ."

"No, I understand. Sorry to give you a hard time. Feel free to tell the police you saw me there. I was just going, because . . ." He trailed off, and Alan watched as his eyes turned glassy and wet.

"Sorry, man," Alan said.

Jack turned his head away, into the wind, and rubbed at one eye with a knuckle. They stood quietly for a moment, Alan trying to conjure up something to say that would end the conversation.

Jack finally said, "Have you heard anything from the police? Are they bringing Corbin back from England?"

"No, I haven't heard anything. You think Corbin had something to do with this?"

The puzzled expression returned to Jack's face, as though Alan had just asked a simplistic, obvious question. "Yeah, he did it. Audrey told me all about their relationship, how he wouldn't let them go out in public, how he was always lying."

"You told the police this?"

"Yeah, I told the police this, and I told that girl living in his apartment now. She better get out of there before he comes back, because when he does . . ."

"You think he'll come back."

"I guess not," Jack said. "I mean, yes, he'll be back because the police will bring him back, but I doubt he'll come back on his own. I wouldn't. If he does, I'll be waiting for him. I don't really care who knows, but if he comes back I'm going to kill him myself. I'm not even joking."

The odd, humorless grin was back, and Alan thought that Jack looked more like a young suburban dad telling a mildly dirty joke at a cookout than someone in a murderous rage.

Chapter 23

It was late afternoon by the time Kate was alone again in the apartment. After she'd shown Detective James and the FBI agent the storage unit, and the slashed poster she'd found, they'd sent her back up to the apartment. She'd waited in the living room, looking at her laptop while the two officers upstairs had thoroughly searched each and every room.

"Is it okay if I continue to stay here?" Kate had asked Detective James before she left.

The detective looked Kate directly in the eyes and said, "Like I said before, Corbin Dell is a serious person of interest. According to Audrey's diary they had a relationship that didn't end particularly well. When we spoke with Corbin he told us that he barely knew her. Obviously, that's rung some bells around here, and since we don't have another suspect, he moved up on the list. That said, Kate, there is nothing else—no real evidence—to link your cousin to what happened next door. If Corbin were on his way back here, and he's not, then I would be the first to let you know. He can't use his passport without us knowing it. So I would say it's okay for you to stay here, as long as you don't mind staying in the apartment of a murder suspect." Detective James smiled, just enough to show a small portion of her very white teeth.

"Why do you think he's claiming he didn't know Audrey?"

"That's what we're trying to figure out."

"It doesn't make sense. It makes him look guilty, so, if he is guilty, why would he lie? He'd just be caught out."

"Welcome to my world," the detective said, then added, "Look. I won't leave you in the dark. If anything happens with Corbin you'll be the first to know, or one of the first, I promise."

"Thank you."

"Do you have a phone number for the woman who lives in your apartment building, Martha . . ."

"Martha Lambert, yes."

Kate got her cell phone and gave the detective Martha's number.

After the detective left, Kate wandered the apartment, looking to see what had been disturbed. But everything, except for maybe the looted den closet, looked the same. She stared through the window out onto Bury Street and caught the detective's car pulling away toward the river. The day was darker, and the wind had picked up, buffeting and rattling the window. Kate stood frozen for what seemed like several minutes, unable to decide what to do next. The longer she stood, the more anxious she felt. She knew that she needed to do something, but still didn't move. She could make herself lunch, or do the assignment she'd gotten from her class, or go sketch for a while. Maybe do a portrait of the detective—what was her full name, Roberta James?—while her face was fresh in her mind. And what about Alan? What was she going to do when he came back from work and tried to see her again? He would, wouldn't he? She couldn't just hide from him in her apartment. She couldn't hide forever, could she?

Finally, she willed her feet to move and went and got her laptop. Maybe Martha would be online, and she could ask her again if Corbin had made an appearance at her flat.

She took her computer to the bedroom. She was cold, and got under a blanket on the bed.

She opened her e-mail account, looked for Martha's name on her list of contacts, but she wasn't online. Instead, Kate sent her a short e-mail: Any sign of Corbin, or has he totally disappeared? She looked through some of her other e-mails, mostly junk, and considered sending another one to Corbin, when she noticed that his name, down the left bar, had a green dot next to it. That meant he used the same e-mail service as she did, and was currently online. She opened a chat box to him, wrote: Hello there.

And waited. Minutes passed.

She opened another browser page and googled *woman cut down middle*. Most of what came up had to do with middle-aged women's haircuts, for some reason. She tried *woman cut in half*, and there were links to several videos—none that Kate watched—of train and elevator accidents. There were a few links to stories about magicians. Kate tried *postmortem mutilation* and looked through news stories. There were too many, but she kept scrolling, eventually finding a newspaper article from three years earlier titled "Mutilated Body Identified as Rachael Chess, Nursing Student from Portland, Maine." Kate clicked on it. It was a local story, from a Gloucester newspaper. The body had been found on a New Essex beach by an early-morning shell collector. Police had not released all details, except to say that they had found postmortem wounds. Kate's mind immediately flashed to the picture she'd found in Corbin's box when she'd first searched the apartment. A brunette woman on a beach. Her name, written on the back of the photograph, had been Rachael.

Kate wrestled the blanket off her and got off the bed. She ran across the apartment to the closet in the den, pulling open the door. The boxes were gone, including the one with the photograph. She'd suspected this, having seen a bunch of boxes being toted off as evidence. If the woman in Corbin's photograph was really the murdered Rachael Chess, then the police would figure that out, as well. She walked back through the living room, then remembered the other photographs she'd found, the ones in the copy of *Ender's Game.* She found the book again, took the photos from it, and fanned them out in her hand, the pretty woman with the freckles staring into the camera as it got closer. She carried the photographs back past the kitchen, and heard a scratching sound that made her stop. She went to the kitchen door that led to the basement and listened. Another scratching sound, plus an audible meow. She opened the door about two inches, and Sanders squeezed through, making a beeline to toward the living room. Kate shut the door and locked it. She was happy that Sanders didn't still have that dying mouse in his jaws.

Back in the bedroom, she read more about the case of Rachael Chess. No one had ever been arrested, even though it had been discovered that she was having an affair with one of her married instructors at nursing college. But that instructor, Gregory Chapel, had a solid alibi for the night that Rachael had been murdered. There was no mention anywhere of a Corbin Dell. There was also a notable lack of good pictures of the murder victim. Most of the news stories used the same one, a highly pixelated black-and-white picture of a girl in a graduation gown and mortarboard, smiling widely into the camera. It was probably the picture that Rachael's parents had provided. Kate studied it, comparing it to the pictures from the book. She didn't think it was the same girl. Same dark hair, but the faces were different. She tried to remember the picture of the girl on the beach. All she could remember was wind-blown dark hair, jeans, and a sweater. The beach had been named on the back of the picture, as well, Kate thought, but she couldn't remember it. But that picture must have been of Rachael Chess. It was the same unusual spelling of her first name. And the beach, a cold New England beach, connected them as well. Didn't it?

A loud beep emanated from her laptop, and Kate toggled back to her e-mail page. She'd gotten a response in the chat box from Corbin. Hi, he'd written back. Her heart fluttered a little, as though he'd suddenly shown up at the door, not just on her computer screen. She took a moment, then wrote: **Did you kill Audrey Marshall?**

Then deleted it.

Then wrote it again, and pressed send. There was a lengthy pause, a series of dots flashing next to Corbin's name, indicating that he was composing his answer.

> **Corbin:** I didn't. I promise you. Do the police think I did?
> **Kate:** They've been back here. They say you were in a relationship with her. Were you?
> **Corbin:** I was.
> **Kate:** Why did you lie about it?

Another pause. Then: Habit, I guess. When we were seeing each other, it was a secret, so I just got used to not talking about it. I didn't kill her.

> **Kate:** Do you know who did?
> **Corbin:** No. I wish I did.
> **Kate:** Where are you now?
> **Corbin:** Home. Your home, in London. It's rainy

here. What's it like there?

Kate: Nice. Windy and nice. The police are going
to send someone to talk with you.

Corbin: That's okay. I'll talk to them.

Another chat box suddenly appeared. It was Martha.
You there?

Kate wrote back to Martha: **Yes. Do me a big favor. Are
you home?**

> **Martha:** yes
> **Kate:** Can you go knock on my door and find out if
> Corbin's there? Don't say anything about me.
> **Martha:** okay, but I don't think he's there, haven't
> heard anything from your flat for days
> **Kate:** Please check.

Kate turned her attention back to Corbin's chat box.
He'd written: **Everything ok with you?**

> **Kate:** Everything's fine. Sanders says hello.
> **Corbin:** Ha!

Kate almost asked a question about Rachael Chess,
but stopped herself. He'd know that she'd been snooping
around his place, trying to discover if he was a murderer.

Instead she wrote: **What was Audrey Marshall like?**

Corbin: She was great. It's awful what happened. I can't stop thinking about it.

Kate: Did you know her friend Jack?

Corbin: No, I didn't. Who's that?

Kate: A friend from college. He knows about you.

Corbin: Jack what?

Kate: Jack Ludovico.

Corbin: What did he look like?

Kate: Pretty ordinary. Short, reddish hair. Glasses.

Corbin: And you talked with him?

Kate: He came here, looking to find out what had happened. He stopped me on the street and asked me all these questions.

Corbin: Did you tell the police about him?

Kate: I did, but I don't think they've talked with him yet.

Martha was back in the other chat box, and she wrote: not there.

Kate responded to Martha: You sure?

Martha: I pounded on the door. maybe he's hiding, but no, he's not there. I'd have heard him come in and out

Kate: Thanks. How's the weather?

Martha: sun's out this morning for the first time since you left. didn't even know what it was at first

Kate: Martha, I have to run. Kisses.

Corbin had written: I should go.

Kate: Say hi to Martha for me.
Corbin: Have you talked with her?
Kate: A little. She said you were an upgrade from me.
Corbin: She seemed nice.

Kate didn't write anything back, not immediately. Neither did Corbin, and it felt like an awkward silence, if you could have an awkward silence during an e-chat.

Kate finally wrote: I'll let you know if anything happens here.

Corbin: Okay. Bye.

Kate logged out of her e-mail browser. She was still cold, despite the blanket, and shut the laptop, pressing its warm plastic against her chest. Why had Corbin lied about being in her flat in London? Unless he was hiding in there, the blinds pulled, refusing to answer the door. It was possible, of course. Martha could be a little aggressive.

Sanders came into the bedroom, jumped up onto the bed, and meowed. Kate sat up, and Sanders leapt to the floor, racing toward the front door. She followed him and let him out, then went to the kitchen for a drink of water. The digital clock on the microwave read 6:25. It seemed late. Had she fallen asleep on the bed?

After drinking two glasses of water, she realized she was hungry, made herself a piece of toast from the stale sourdough bread, then slathered it with butter and honey. She carried the toast with her across the apartment, turning on lamps and pulling curtains halfway closed. The door to one of the spare bedrooms was open wider than she'd remembered, and she went inside. It was that time of night when the fading light outside made the inside seem darker than it was. She turned on a bedside lamp and finished her toast, having to lick honey from her fingers. This bedroom was vaguely feminine, with flower prints hung on the wall and a cream-colored blanket on the bed. She noticed a slight indentation on the blanket, and looked closer. There were white hairs—Sanders's hairs— and Kate pressed her hand on the bed; it was still a little warm from where he'd had his afternoon nap. That was why the door was ajar. She breathed a little deeper and left the room, leaving the light on.

She peered into the dark, windowless cave of the den, considering trying to watch some television, but she felt too jumpy. Instead, she decided to sketch, getting the sketchbook and pencils from the bedroom and bringing them to the living room. She stretched out along the couch and opened the book. She was prepared for the picture of Alan that she'd drawn on her first full day in Boston. It was less than a week ago, but felt like a year. She studied it. She'd caught his likeness, she thought, except for the eyes. They were vague, a little glazed, instead of intent. She stared at them, her scalp prickling. Had his eyes been changed, maybe a little? No, she told herself, but they seemed smudged. Maybe it just happened on its own.

Yeah, his eyes got smudged but the rest of his face didn't.

Did I do it? she thought. *Of course not,* George said, but she ignored him. Her days and nights since she'd arrived in Boston had been so fuzzy that it was hard to remember. It wasn't unheard of that she went back over drawings she'd done and altered them slightly, usually with a fingertip. Cleaning up lines, adding texture. She flipped past it, determined not to make herself insane, and found a fresh, unmarked page. She quickly sketched Alan again, trying to get the eyes right this time. When she was finished, she held the book at arm's length and looked. It was Alan, but she'd tried so hard to get the intensity of the eyes right that he looked pissed off, a little bit scary. Then she realized that that was exactly how he'd looked when she'd peered through the peephole earlier in the morning, when she hadn't let him in. Had she made a mistake? He'd probably just been worried that she'd left without saying goodbye. But, no, the sketch was accurate—he'd been upset. She'd made a *big* mistake, not just in sleeping with someone she barely knew, but in sleeping with someone who, at the very least, was a voyeuristic creep, and maybe a whole lot more. She turned to the next page, and quickly drew Detective Roberta James's face. She did a pretty good job, nailing the high cheekbones, the dark eyes. It was the mouth that wasn't perfect. Too severe, the lips not full enough. She smudged it out and gave the detective a half smile. Satisfied, she labeled the sketch and dated it, and then started another drawing.

It was fully dark outside by the time Kate had finished sketching Mrs. Valentine, Mr. Valentine, the other woman at the drinks party (she'd forgotten her name), and, finally, a picture of George Daniels. She'd never stopped drawing him. A number of counselors had suggested that it wasn't healthy to dwell on his likeness, but she couldn't help herself. He was always somewhere in her head, and it felt good to pull him from inside of her and put him on the page. In today's picture, she drew him as she'd seen him in her recent dream, his mouth toothless and grinning.

It was a good drawing, the best she'd done that day. She used the flat of her thumb to smudge the forehead lines, and felt a sharp prick where she still had the splinter from the storage unit door. She'd forgotten all about it, and took a look, the swollen skin around the splinter now a pinkish red. She went to the kitchen and washed the charcoal off her hands, then searched through drawers until she found a safety pin and a book of matches. She burned the sharp tip of the pin, then returned to the living room, where the light was better. There, she picked at the opening in her thumb, widening the ragged skin so that she could see the splinter and prod at it with the pin. It was pretty deep. She sucked on it, tasting her own blood, but it didn't budge. She'd have to look for tweezers, but the thought exhausted her. What would happen if you left a splinter in your thumb? Would it eventually work its way out on its own, or would it stay there forever and become a part of you?

A scratching sound from the kitchen startled her. She'd let Sanders out, hadn't she? She put the safety pin down on her sketchbook, got up, and returned to the kitchen. She heard the sound again. It was coming from the door that led to the basement—Sanders again, having looped around through the basement. She opened the door, and there was Alan, holding his palms toward her, his eyes bleary and wild looking. "Please let me in," he slurred, taking a step into the kitchen before Kate could slam the door.

Chapter 24

Alan wasn't exactly sure how he'd gotten so drunk, but it had happened, almost accidentally, and now he was walking back through the darkness, determined to see Kate, even if she didn't want to see him.

After encountering Jack on Brimmer Street earlier in the day and hearing from him that he thought Corbin Dell had murdered Audrey Marshall, Jack had become chatty, suggesting they go somewhere and talk more. Alan, more than anything, wanted to turn around and go home, in hopes that he'd spot Kate in the courtyard, but decided instead to spend some time hearing what Jack had to say. Alan suggested St. Stephen's. When they got there, settling into one of the high-backed booths, Alan ordered a large Coke and Jack ordered a bottle of Heineken. The waitress spun on her heels to get their drinks, and Jack immediately started talking about a woman named Rachael Chess, who had been found murdered on a beach in New Essex a few years earlier.

"She was mutilated," Jack said, "just like Audrey was." His voice cracked every time he said Audrey's name.

"How did you hear that Audrey was mutilated?" Alan asked.

"It's all over the Web, and so I started to search other cases, other cases where someone had been cut down the middle, sliced open, and I found Rachael Chess."

"And what does she have to do with Corbin Dell?" Alan was interested in what Jack had to say, but also a little wary. Jack was becoming increasingly animated, almost manic, in the way he was talking. The waitress returned with their drinks. Jack took a long pull from his bottle of beer.

"Get this," he said, setting down the beer hard enough that foam spilled over its lip and rolled down its side. "Corbin Dell used to live in New Essex, and his mother still does. She has a place right on the beach—"

"How do you know all this?"

"Audrey told me some, and some of it I just looked up online. That's not the point, though. The point is that Rachael Chess's parents also lived in New Essex, not right on the beach, but close. It's how Corbin and Rachael met, obviously. He's a psychopath. Audrey told me that when they were together he was paranoid about being seen in public with her, that he always wanted to stay in. It's because he didn't want to be associated with her, because he knew he was going to kill her. But then she started to see me, and wanted nothing to do with Corbin anymore, and that was why he killed her. It's him. I know it." Jack scratched at some raised welts on a reddened arm.

"You okay?" Alan asked.

"Hives, I think. I hate the spring."

"Have you gone to the police with all this?" Alan asked.

"I will. I promise. But I want to get all my ducks in a row. He's not getting away with this."

Alan knew that he hadn't gone to the police because he was playing amateur detective, maybe even hoping to get revenge on his own.

"I think you should go to the police. They'll probably know if there was ever a link between Corbin and this Rachael person."

"Another thing that he always told Audrey was that he wasn't any good for her, almost like he knew what he was going to do. You want to get something to eat? It's lunchtime."

Alan had already finished his Coke, and agreed to get lunch. Jack waved the waitress over and they both ordered cheeseburgers. Jack asked for another beer, and Alan decided to have one as well.

"Jack, how often did you see Audrey?" Alan asked, after they gave their orders. He was hoping to get some information on why he'd never seen him before through Audrey's windows.

"About once a week," Jack said. "We'd get together for coffee or for drinks. I think at first she thought I was trying to date her again."

"But you weren't?" Alan asked.

"I don't know. Yes. No."

"I never saw you at the apartment building. Were you ever there, or . . . ?"

"A couple times."

Alan thought he was lying about being in Audrey's apartment. He guessed that in Jack's mind, the friendship with Audrey—maybe a couple of coffees, a few text messages—was much more important than it had been to her. The beers came and Alan took a sip. It was so cold it made his teeth hurt.

"Just this one beer and then I should go to the office," Alan said. "It *is* a Tuesday."

"Thanks, man," Jack said. "Thanks for spending time with me. It's nice to talk with someone who doesn't think I'm crazy. You don't think I'm off the rails about Corbin, do you?"

"I don't."

"So you agree with me?"

"I agree that Corbin had a motive, and he probably had a key to Audrey's place, and he left town right after she was murdered."

"Why do you think he had a key?" Jack asked.

"Just thought it was probably likely. They went out. They lived next to one another." He didn't want to mention what he'd learned from Kate. He wasn't exactly sure why, but somehow he wanted to keep her out of it.

"I can see that," Jack said.

The food came and Alan listened as Jack explained, again, the reasons he was sure that Corbin had killed before. Everything he was saying made sense.

Alan and Jack stayed at St. Stephen's till late afternoon,

each drinking several more beers. It had been a strange few hours. Alan found himself telling this man all about his relationship with Quinn. He almost found himself telling him about the previous night with Kate, but stopped himself just in time. Why was he talking so much? He went to the bathroom, stared at himself in the mirror, and didn't like what he saw. Why was he drunk in a bar with a stranger on a Tuesday afternoon? He decided he needed to leave.

As they stood outside the bar, saying goodbye, Jack's eyes filled with tears. "Thank you, thank you, for hanging out with me. I know . . . I know it wasn't . . ."

"It was nice," Alan said, and put a hand on Jack's shoulder.

Jack removed his gloves and wiped at both eyes, then held out his hand to shake Alan's. Alan was relieved that there had been no hug; the handshake, long and aggressive, had been enough. "Which way you headed?" Jack asked, and Alan, suddenly desperate to escape, tilted his head east, since Alan was already taking a step down the hill back toward Charles Street. They parted ways, and Alan walked through a residential neighborhood he had never walked through before. The wind had died down a little, but the tops of the trees still rustled, and Alan's T-shirt flattened out against his body as he walked aimlessly. He was hungry again, and needed to pee. He spotted the State House and walked toward it, knowing there'd be bars nearby. The first one he passed was a faux-Irish pub on the corner called Rosie McClean's that was empty except for a table of Japanese tourists eating an early dinner. Alan sat at the bar and ordered fish and chips and a large Coke. After drinking the Coke, he asked for another, but with Old Overholt in it. He knew enough about day drinking to know that if he quit now, he'd wind up with a splitting headache for the rest of the night. The fish and chips came and the food made him feel better, less drunk, and he ordered another rye and Coke and thought about his conversation with Jack.

Alan's phone rang. He pulled it out of his bag and checked the screen. His sister. He was all set to hit Ignore, but then decided to answer, just in case she had a real reason to call and wasn't just checking up on him.

"Just checking in," Hannah said after they'd said hello.

"I'm fine."

"You sound funny. Have you been drinking?"

"A little bit. I'm eating, too. My mouth was full."

"Don't forget to call Mom on her birthday."

"Uh-huh. That's why you called?" Alan was annoyed, even though he probably would have forgotten.

"No. I'm worried about you. I had this crazy dream."

Alan listened while Hannah described, in detail, the dream she'd had where she found Alan dead in his apartment, a rotting corpse, after not hearing from him for years. During the description, Alan finished his drink and ordered another one by catching the bartender's eye and pointing at his empty glass.

"Hey," Alan said after Hannah stopped talking about

the dream, "do you remember that time you were a camp counselor and I came up for the weekend?"

There was a pause. Alan could hear one of her kids—it sounded like Izzie—laughing in the background. "I guess so. I think so. Oh yeah, Mom and Dad made me take you so they could go to the Cape alone."

Alan didn't remember that part. He said, "You know, that was the first time I saw a naked girl. I spied on her through a hole in the wall."

"What? A counselor?"

"Uh-huh."

"Ha. Do you remember who it was?"

"I don't know if I ever knew her name. She was kind of chubby."

"Was it Allie something?"

"I never knew her name, but I think she turned me into a pervert."

"What are you talking about?"

"Because I was spying on her, without her knowing I was doing it."

"Oh God. You and everyone else at that pervy camp. All the walls had knotholes in them. She probably knew she was being watched. Look, as much as I'd love to hear more creepy stories from my drunk brother, I've gotta go. Call Mom, and don't be a fucking stranger."

When Alan finally left the pub, it was filled with after-work drinkers. The darkness outside somehow shocked him. It was colder, too, and Alan, wearing only a T-shirt, was nearly shivering by the time he reached 101 Bury.

Maybe because he was drunk, or maybe because of the peculiar light that night, the apartment building seemed taller than usual, towering behind its gate. Moonlight reflected on the slate roof of the next building over, and across the street, a homeless man was trying to keep warm in a doorway. Low lights were on in Kate's apartment. During the walk, he'd decided that he needed to see her no matter what. He needed to find out why she'd left his apartment without saying goodbye. He needed to tell her what he'd learned from Jack, and he even wanted to tell her how his sister had called, and he'd finally told her the big secret about what he'd done at her summer camp, and she'd barely cared. He walked across the courtyard and through the lobby, nodding toward Sanibel, and wondering if the doorman even noticed that he was taking the stairs toward the north wing and not the south. He walked down the hallway, aware, peripherally, of Audrey's door and of what had happened in that apartment, but focusing on Kate's door. He was about to knock, but stopped himself. What if she didn't answer? In fact, why would she answer? She hadn't earlier in the morning, when he'd known she was just on the other side, probably looking at him through the peephole. Alan formed a different plan.

He went back to the stairwell and walked all the way down to the basement level. He passed through the fluorescent-lit basement, thankful that it was empty, then found the back stairwell that would lead to the kitchen entrance to Kate's apartment. At least, he thought it would. He was always leaving that entrance unlocked in his own place and was hopeful that Kate had as well. At the very least, he could talk with her through the door without having to stand in the hallway. He could say his piece.

He climbed to the top of the steep, narrow stairwell and quietly tried the knob. It was locked. He was about to knock when he had an idea. Sanders the cat was always scratching at his own back door, trying to get into his apartment. He wondered if he'd done the same here. Knowing it was a terrible idea, but deciding to do it anyway, Alan half knocked, half scratched at the door. And waited.

He heard faint footsteps in the kitchen, and then the door was being opened, and he was looking at Kate's horrified face. He quickly put his hands up, stepping across the threshold with one foot. "Please let me in," he said, willing his voice to sound harmless.

Kate pressed a hand against her chest. She was pale, as though all the blood had drained from her face.

"I need to talk with you. I can do it from here, but we need to talk. I don't think you should be in this apartment. You should be in my apartment." The words weren't coming out the way he'd planned.

"You're really drunk," Kate said.

"I know. I know. I met Jack, and he told me all about Corbin and he got me drunk."

"Who's Jack?"

"Jack. *Jack*. That guy who was friends with Audrey that you told me about. On the street. You met him on the street."

Before answering, Alan began to move farther into the kitchen. Kate jumped back, said, "No, no. Stay there."

Alan took a step back. "You're not scared of me? Oh no, you're scared of me." He felt terrible, and kept apologizing.

Kate said, "It's okay. I know you're sorry. Tell me about Jack."

"I saw him this morning coming out of the building—"

"Coming out of where? Out of here?"

"Yes. Right after the police arrived. I didn't recognize him, but he was looking up at your window, so I followed him and he caught me and then we were talking. We went to that bar you and I . . . St. Stephen's, and he told me about his theory, how Corbin's a serial killer."

"What do you mean a serial killer?"

"He said that there was this other girl that Corbin murdered. She was also mutilated, and he's sure that Corbin killed Audrey, and I just don't think it's safe for you to be in this apartment all by yourself."

"If Corbin killed Audrey, then he's not going to come back here, is he? That wouldn't make any sense."

"Then you're going to stay here? Tonight?"

"Alan, I'm sorry. I think we rushed into things last night, and it was . . . for me, it was a mistake. No, let me talk. Let's meet tomorrow, okay? For coffee or something in the morning, and we can talk about all of this. But not now. Not while you're like this. Okay?"

It was the expression on Kate's face as she said *okay* that made Alan realize he needed to leave. She looked like she was about to cry. Alan, without saying anything, turned and walked back down the stairwell, pressing his palms against the walls to keep himself steady.

Back in his apartment he lay on his bed, shoes kicked off, jeans and T-shirt still on. When he closed his eyes, the room tilted. When he opened them, the world stood still. He kept them open as long as possible, trying to reassemble in his mind everything that had happened that day, everything that had happened recently. He closed his eyes. The room tilted again, but backward, and Alan slid into a deep, troubled sleep.

Chapter 25

It's time to go home, Kate thought, after Alan had finally left. Back to England. She placed a hand on the kitchen countertop to steady herself.

She felt George's voice rising in her head, his words starting to form, and she managed to stop him from speaking to her by pacing the kitchen floor.

I should never have left the country. I should never have left my parents' house. Not to go to university, not to go on holiday in the Lake District, not to go to London, and *definitely* not to travel to Boston. Bad things happen to me.

Bad people happen to me.

Kate poured wine into a water glass. She carried it from room to room in the apartment, checking window locks and looking into closets. Her hands shook with adrenaline, and her heart tripped along in her chest, but she was okay. One more night in this cavernous apartment filled with shadows, and she could head home—back to her parents' house—never to leave again. She checked the front door lock and looked out into the quiet hallway. A murderer had stood outside Audrey Marshall's door with the intention to kill her. And then he'd gone inside and done it. Killed her with his knife. Mutilated her.

She looked for a long time out into the hall, con-torted by the peephole into a tunnel with curved walls. She expected someone to turn the corner and make an appearance at any moment. Sanders the cat. George Dan-iels back from the dead. Corbin Dell back from England. Alan stalking her from the front door instead of from the back. But nothing happened. The well-lit, carpeted hall remained empty.

She went online and looked at airfares for returning to London. She began an e-mail to her parents telling them she was coming home, but didn't finish it. She could do it tomorrow, after she booked something, when it was all finalized.

She looked at the Rachael Chess articles again online. That must have been who Alan was talking about when he mentioned the other woman who had been killed. So Jack had been doing his research as well.

She went back to the kitchen to get more wine, but the bottle was empty, and she poured herself a glass of milk instead. She brought it to the den and turned on the television. The old movie channel was playing a film that she knew pretty well, because it was one of her father's favorites. *I Know Where I'm Going!* starring Wendy Hiller and Roger Livesey. She curled up on the couch, rested her head on two oversized pillows, and attempted to let the black-and-white images soothe her. She kept thinking of Alan, though, behind the door in the kitchen.

Seeing him, visibly drunk, standing there, Kate thought she was about to die. It was George Daniels all over again—another man come to kill her. Although George, for all his rage and craziness, had never been a drinker. In fact, whenever Kate had more than a couple of glasses of wine, he'd start to get mad at her, asking her repeatedly why she needed to drink so much.

In the film, the woman played by Wendy Hiller was desperately trying to get to the Scottish island where her fiancé was, but a storm had trapped her on the coast, where she'd fallen in love with another man. She was trying anyway, in a small boat, and a whirlpool was pulling her to her death. Kate pulled the comforter on top of her. The movie ended, and another immediately started up. *Pygmalion*. Another Wendy Hiller. She thought of her father, who would love this movie channel that only showed old films. She started watching the film, but she had to pee, and her jeans were uncomfortably tight. She forced herself to get up and walk through the living room and past the kitchen to the bedroom, where she changed into pajamas, peed in the en suite bathroom, and brushed her teeth. She passed back through the bedroom, where the strong moonlight through the window cast strange shadows in the twisted sheets of the bed. This apartment is haunted, she thought, and walked briskly back toward the den, lit in flickering black and white from the massive television.

Leslie Howard was standing in the rain, secretly

listening to Wendy Hiller's cockney accent as she was selling flowers.

Kate didn't remember falling asleep. It felt as though one minute she was watching the television, wondering if any of the actors were still alive, and then her eyes must have shut, and she was suddenly in the world of the film, the voices part of her dream. The couch was swallowing her, and she was on the brink of sliding into the true blackness of sleep when the dream shifted, and there was a hand pressed against her face, and she felt herself rising back up from the depths, jerking awake, but the hand was still there, pressed hard against her mouth, another hand gripping her shoulder.

This is real, she thought and began to struggle, fully awake.

The room was dark, the television still on, and the man who held her was making shushing sounds. It wasn't Alan. She could see razor-cut blondish hair and the line of a square jaw, and she could smell his sweat, stale and powdery. Her heart was beating so fast that her chest hurt, and tears sprang to her eyes. The man about to kill her was a stranger, although he was vaguely familiar, as though she'd passed him on the street or seen him in a dream.

He was speaking in a low whisper. "Kate, please listen to me. It's Corbin. It's your cousin. I am not going to hurt you. I need you to be very quiet. There's a man in this apartment and he's a very bad man. Shhhh. If you scream, or make a noise, he's going to come in here. I need you to hide, and then I can go deal with him. Nod if you understand."

Kate shook her head. Only half the words had made any sense to her. Was it really Corbin, or was he lying? How was he here, in the apartment? She thought of trying to bite his hand, but it was pressed hard against her mouth, her lips flattened against her teeth. She could see the man's eyes, darting furiously over the edge of the couch toward the dark interior of the rest of the apartment. He looked scared. *It is Corbin,* she thought, recognizing him from pictures she'd seen.

"Shhh," he said again. "You *have* to trust me, or we are both going to die. Do you understand?" His voice had become more urgent, cracking almost, and Kate nodded this time, deciding that she needed to do what he said. He'd either kill her or he wouldn't. It was happening again—not with Alan, the way she'd thought earlier—but with some man she had never met.

After feeling Kate nod, Corbin looked her in the eyes. He loosened the hand around her mouth, but didn't remove it. "Do you believe me? You have to believe me."

She nodded more, and took a deep breath.

"Everything's going to be all right," Corbin said, but his eyes were still darting toward the hallway. "Do you know about the closet in here?"

"No," Kate said in a cracked whisper through his hand.

"There's a false back in it. It's where my dad kept val uable things. Press your hand all the way to the right and push. You'll hear a click and it will swing open. There's enough room for you to hide there."

Kate, not even realizing it, was shaking her head again, saying "no" into Corbin's hand. He continued:

"Just stay there until I come back to get you. If I don't come back, then just stay there longer. He won't find you, and eventually he'll give up. You have to trust me, okay?"

"I can't," Kate said. She felt tears sliding down her face. She breathed in deeply through her nose, her chest swelling. She thought for a moment she might start laughing.

"You have to," Corbin said. "You'll be safe. I promise."

She looked at him and for the first time they made eye contact. It was like finding a handhold on a sheer cliff. Making a decision, she nodded, calmly, and Corbin took his hand all the way off her face.

"Who is it?" she asked. "Who's here?"

"It doesn't matter. We don't have a lot of time."

She followed him to the closet, her numb legs somehow operating independent of the rest of her body. He gently pushed her into its interior, filled with dry-cleaned suits hanging in plastic. "Just push, all the way to the right. You'll hear the click," he repeated.

"Okay," she said, the sound of her voice coming from far away.

Before shutting the door, he whispered: "I am going to save you." And then she was enveloped in darkness. She did as he said and pressed her hand against the back wall. It gave a little, clicked, and swung open. She stepped inside and felt around. There was a small metal handle and she pulled the door back in toward her, but not all the way. The small enclosure smelled of untreated wood and musty paperbacks. She felt as though she'd stepped back through time, into that other closet in another country, another madman on the other side, only this time she was calmer. No, it wasn't exactly a sense of calm. It was resignation. It was over. The world had been trying to kill her in the worst way possible, and now it was finally going to do it. She gave in, the calmness spreading through her. She even pulled the false door all the way closed; the handle turned and she knew she could get out again, but maybe it didn't matter. She slid her hands along the wood. The space was the width of the closet, wider than her outstretched arms, but it couldn't have been more than a foot deep. With her back pressed tight against the rear wall, her breasts grazed the false door. A wave of unreality passed over, and she welcomed it. And she waited.

She listened. She could hear her own breathing and her heart in her chest, but nothing else.

How had Corbin gotten back to America? Or had he never left? No, he had left and gone to London, because Martha had seen him, hadn't she?

He'd come back because he'd killed Audrey and now he was going to kill her, and this hiding in the closet, this other man, was all part of some elaborate game he was playing.

Or could there really be someone else in the apartment?

Was it Alan, still drunk, who'd found another way to sneak in?

Or was it finally George Daniels? Kate felt the laugh again, rising up through her lungs, and she held it down by tensing her jaw, her neck muscles almost seizing up. George Daniels back from the dead, and in another country. In some ways, she wouldn't be surprised. As she always said to herself: he was always with her, always along for the ride.

His voice in her head: *You are going to die in a closet, Kate*. Giggling.

She closed her eyes, and nothing changed. The world was still black.

She tried not to think of her parents and how they would feel when they heard she'd been murdered.

She thought of Alan. Twenty-four hours earlier she'd been in his bed, allowing herself to feel something. She'd been happy, celebratory almost, that she was finally with another man. Maybe that was what George Daniels had been waiting for all along, waiting for her to finally cheat on him, so that he could finally give her what she deserved. Maybe he really was alive, and the police, and her parents, and everyone else had lied to her. For a horrible instant, she believed it.

And then she heard something. A human sound, like a grunt. Or maybe it was a scream that had suddenly been cut off. She waited, barely breathing, but there was nothing else, just the sound of the building humming and sighing around her. And suddenly she wondered if she'd heard anything at all. She allowed herself to take a breath, sipping at the thin air in the closet. She cracked the false door open a little, relieved that it hadn't locked her in. She tapped her fingertips together, felt a sharp pain when she tapped her swollen thumb, the splinter still embedded deep in the pad. She put the thumb in her mouth and tore at the skin with her teeth, eventually sucking the splinter out. She wiped the blood down her shirt. Removing the splinter had made her feel sane for a brief moment, but now she wondered how much longer she could stay in this closet. What was happening out there?

She formed a plan, just to see how it would feel in her head. She would push her way out of the closet and move as swiftly and quietly as possible from the den to the hallway, then from the hallway to the living room and foyer, then she'd go through the door and run as fast as she could to the front desk. It was a big apartment. Corbin, or whoever else was in here, might be somewhere else. She might get free. And if she didn't? Then at least she wasn't cowering in this closet anymore.

Her thumb continued to drip blood, and she sucked at it some more, actually savoring the taste in her mouth.

She'd often wondered about the night that George Daniels had tracked her down in the Lake District and sealed her in the closet. She wondered whether, even if the door hadn't been blocked, she'd have been able to leave. Not while he was still out there, but after she heard the gun go off. She'd been trapped, and there was nothing for her to do but wait, but even if the door had been open, Kate sometimes thought that she'd have stayed there forever. She'd crouched into a ball, like an injured animal, and hadn't moved, not even when the frightened copper had opened the door and reached in to take her out. But now she had a chance to run, and she knew she needed to take it, for better or for worse.

She swung the false back door all the way open and stepped into the main space of the closet, pressing her ear to the door. She listened for a minute but heard nothing. She put her hand on the knob. She breathed in through her nose and blew out through her mouth.

She tried to remember a prayer from childhood, but all she could remember was what she learned from her grandmother to say at bedtime. She said it now, to herself, her eyes closed:

> *From ghoulies and ghosties*
> *And long-leggedy beasties*
> *And other things that go bump in the night,*
> *Good Lord, deliver us*

Calmed by the words, her grandmother's voice in her head, she swung the door open and stepped out of the closet into the still-flickering light of the den.

Chapter 26

On Monday morning, after calling the London office and letting them know he was deathly sick, and asking if he could start the following week, Corbin Dell took out fifteen thousand pounds in cash from the local branch of the Royal Bank of Scotland. He'd opened an account online before his departure to avoid having to pay transaction fees on all his withdrawals. The teller, an Indian woman wearing a head scarf, registered almost no reaction to the request, but she did spend close to fifteen minutes making calls and typing into her computer before finally handing over the money in twenty-pound notes.

With the hefty packet of money in the inside pocket of his raincoat, Corbin took a taxi to Camden Market and began to wander the stalls, looking for a candidate. He wasn't going to rush it; he had all day, and knew his chances were best when the pubs opened. But he had a plan. He was going to find Henry Wood and he was going to kill him. And this was the best opportunity he was going to have.

It was almost two in the afternoon when Corbin spotted the first promising match. It was in a dingy pub several blocks from the market area. The man had a beard and longish, greasy hair, but other than that, he looked a lot like Corbin. Same coloring, similar features, prominent jawline. And he looked mildly down and out, drinking a pint glass of cider over ice in the middle of a rainy Monday afternoon.

Corbin ordered himself a pint of Stella and another cider, and brought both over to where the man was seated, at a table near the grimy windows. There was just enough light coming through for the man to read his Charles Bukowski novel.

Corbin sat and pushed the cider over to the man, who looked alarmed as he lowered the well-thumbed paperback. He really did look like him, enough anyway.

"Can I ask you something?" Corbin said. "Do you have a passport?"

"The fuck you want?" the man answered. The words were clear, but Corbin didn't recognize the accent.

"I have a proposition for you, but I need to know if you have a passport first."

"Yeah, I've got a passport." Maybe it was a German accent.

"I'd like to borrow it, plus any other identification you have. It will be no more than a week, I promise. I can give you eight thousand pounds in cash right now, and I'll give you another two when I return everything. There'd be no risk for you, at all."

The man laughed. "Go away."

"I'm telling you. It's ten thousand pounds and no risk."

"No risk? It's my fucking passport you'd be using."

Corbin took a sip of his beer. He'd sold enough financial opportunities over the years to know that this guy was already hooked. Getting his passport was not going to be a problem. "How tall are you?" Corbin asked. "Do you mind standing up?"

The man didn't answer the question. Instead, he said: "What if you don't come back?"

"Then report your passport stolen. It happens all the time. Where are you from, anyway? I don't recognize your accent."

"I'm from Rotterdam. I'm Dutch."

"What's your name?"

"It's Bram. I haven't decided to do this, you know."

"Listen, Bram. It's ten thousand pounds. In cash. All you have to do is hand over the passport, and help me book an airline ticket with your credit card. I'll pay you in cash for that as well. I need to take a trip but don't want someone to know where I'm going. That's all there is to this. In one week I return everything. If something goes wrong, you just have to say that your passport and credit card were stolen and you didn't notice right away. There's no downside to this."

Bram thought for a moment, then said, "I'll do it for fifteen thousand pounds."

Corbin stood up. "I'll keep looking. There'll be someone else 'round here that looks like me."

Corbin returned his empty pint glass to the bar and

exited the pub. Bram caught up with him on the street. "Okay, okay," he said. "I'll do it."

Bram Heymans was squatting in a large nearby flat that was under construction, sleeping on a rollout and living out of a backpack. Despite this, he had an Apple laptop and a portable wireless router. Corbin studied Bram's maroon passport. In the picture Bram was clean-shaven, his hair swept back off his forehead. Corbin had been hoping that the picture would have the bearded version of Bram, but the clean-shaven picture was good enough. Corbin would pass as Bram, so long as he didn't draw too much attention to himself. There were no flights going to Logan for the remainder of that day, so Corbin, using Bram's Visa card, booked an early morning flight for the following day. He gave Bram the eight thousand pounds, plus an extra eight hundred for the ticket, and took possession of the passport.

"You'll still be here in a week?" Corbin asked Bram, who was flicking through the bills with a nicotine-stained thumb.

"What, here? In this flat?"

"Yeah."

"Yeah, I'm not going anywhere."

"So one week from today I'll be back here with your passport and ID. At noon. You'll be here?"

"I'll be here," Bram said, still looking at the bills.

*

296

The line at the Gatwick security gate was at least a hundred travelers long, but Corbin was early. He was happy to see the crowd; it would hopefully mean that whoever looked at his passport might rush the job, not studying the picture too hard. Corbin had been anxiously analyzing the small photo all through the night and into the morning, trying to decide if it was going to work. He thought it would, especially since the picture was seven years old. He had been trying to decide whether it would be better to keep his current style or to imitate the hairstyle in the photograph, and decided to keep his current style. If the hairstyles were perfect then the security agent, or the customs agent in Boston, might look too closely at the facial features, realize that the eyes weren't quite right, the ears entirely different.

The hungover-looking agent at the end of the line barely looked at the passport after placing it on the scanner, just perfunctorily moving his eyes from the picture to Corbin's face, then ushering him through toward security.

It was a little rockier in Boston, where they'd recently installed Automated Passport Control. Corbin stood in front of a computer screen, scanned his passport, then stood still and stared at a camera, waiting to have his photograph taken. He hadn't been prepared for this, and his heart sped up as he waited for the camera to flash. Instead, words appeared on the screen—the machine had failed to capture a recognizable face—and Corbin thought he was finished, that some software program was figuring out that the face in front of them didn't match the face on the passport. Corbin tried the picture again and got the same message. A customs agent drifted over, adjusted the height of the machine, and it worked. A light flashed, and a slip of curled paper slid from the machine—a black-and-white image of Corbin's alarmed face. He brought the slip of paper and his passport to another agent, a young acne-ridden man with a military-looking mustache, who grilled Corbin about his trip to the United States, asking him where he was staying and how long he planned to stay, and studying the passport, although paying relatively little attention to the picture. Finally, the customs agent stamped Bram Heymans's passport and Corbin, armpits damp but otherwise okay, walked through the double doors into Logan airport. He could see through the terminal, and the large sliding doors, to the taxis idling on the curb outside; he was free, unmoored. He was in America and no one could ever prove it. As long as he wasn't caught, he had a perfect alibi. He had tremendous power, he realized, so long as he could find Henry.

He was suddenly nervous that someone would recognize him now that he was back in his hometown. Should he disguise himself? Where was he going to stay? He hadn't thought everything through since he'd been so concerned with whether he could return to America without using his own passport. Now that he'd done it, what was next?

He took a taxicab to a boutique hotel on Beacon Street and checked in using Bram's passport and cash, claiming, with a terrible Dutch accent, that his credit card had been recently stolen. The clerk said they needed a credit card for incidentals, but Corbin offered a cash deposit of two thousand dollars (he'd traded in nearly five thousand pounds at the cash exchange at Logan, using Bram's ID), and the hotel manager finally agreed. Alone in the room, Corbin stripped off his clothes and stood under the shower for nearly half an hour, trying to will his body to relax. Ever since he'd received the e-mail from the police, Corbin had felt like a man possessed, finally knowing what he had to do. What he hadn't yet allowed himself to feel was the pain of what had happened to Audrey, the sadness that she was gone forever. But now the thoughts came anyway, along with uncontrollable tearless sobs, Corbin's jaw clenched so tight that he worried his teeth might shatter. The only thing that calmed him was the thought of getting to Henry and crushing him in his hands, making him pay for what he'd done. Henry had been in Boston less than a week ago. *There's a chance I can find him,* Corbin told himself. As soon as it got dark he would walk to his apartment building and wait in the bushes, to see if anything happened, if Henry, for whatever reason, made an appearance.

It was almost noon. He had barely slept or eaten since hearing about Audrey, but now his stomach was growling loudly, and his head was light with lack of food. He pulled on jeans, a T-shirt, and the hooded Jack Wills sweatshirt he'd bought at Gatwick. He pulled the hood tight around his head, tightening the strings so that it wouldn't come loose, and left the hotel, turning right and walking toward the hospitals. He passed a barbershop he'd never really noticed before, doubled back, and pushed through the doors. There were two barbers, one old and bald, and the other young and bald, clearly the son. The dark interior was about as wide as a train car and smelled of pomade. The young barber was free, and after being seated, Corbin asked for a buzz cut.

"How short?" the barber asked.

"As short as you can go."

The barber set his clipper to the lowest setting and began taking off almost all of Corbin's hair. Sports talk radio was playing from an old boom box high up on a shelf, and Corbin was able to turn his mind off for a moment, listening to callers complain about the lousy relievers the Red Sox had this season.

"You want a shave as well?" the barber asked after finishing.

Corbin ran his hand across his chin. He hadn't shaved in over a week, and his beard was thicker than it had ever been. "Sure," he said. "Shave everything but the mustache." He'd read or heard somewhere that if a man wanted to change his appearance he should shave his head and grow a mustache. It was one of those things that had stuck in his head for years, even though he'd always wondered if it were true. But when the barber was done, and Corbin stared at his nearly bald head and the beginnings of his reddish mustache, he did think he looked different enough to possibly fool someone who happened to glance at him. It was enough.

After leaving the barbers, Corbin walked down toward Mass General Hospital and found a Greek pizzeria he'd never been to; he ate a large meatball sub and drank two Cokes. Then he got a turkey sub to go and brought it back to the hotel. Who knew when he'd get a chance to eat again? Back in his room, he cracked the window that looked out over slate roofs toward the Common. It was a windy day, and it felt good to let some of the blustery, cool air into the stuffy room. He opened his laptop, keyed in the wireless code, and checked his e-mails. He'd left his phone behind. Even with GPS turned off, it would still make him nervous, but he felt okay with using the laptop, fairly certain it wouldn't give his location away. There was nothing new from his cousin Kate, just the e-mail she'd sent him on Sunday night that the police had asked to search his apartment. He was still wondering about that. There must have been some way they'd connected him with Audrey, although he didn't know how. Maybe they'd interviewed other residents in the apartment and Alan had said something. It didn't really matter. They weren't going to find anything in his apartment.

Corbin opened a browser window and, for the thousandth time, searched for anything related to a "Henry

Wood," or "Hank Bowman," or "Hank Wood." There was nothing. He lay back on the bed and stared at the high ceiling, the ornate molding. The wind whistled through the room, fluttering the curtains, and Corbin closed his eyes, pretended he was a kid again, lying on Annisquam Beach, the salt air moving over him. He fell asleep and dreamed that he was innocent, that the murderers were coming for him, and that he wasn't one of them.

Chapter 27

A beep from his computer woke Corbin. The hotel room was cold, and he was shivering. He sat up and looked at his computer screen. He had left his e-mail account open, and Kate Priddy had sent him a message in a chat box. Hello there, it said. He stared at it for a long time, his teeth now starting to chatter from the cold. It felt as though she could see him through the computer screen, see where he was. He got up and shut the window, pulled his hoodie back on. Hi, he wrote back.

Did you kill Audrey Marshall?

Corbin, barely breathing, put his fingers on the keyboard. He wanted to write that he knew who killed her, but he wasn't brave enough. Instead, he wrote to Kate that he hadn't killed Audrey, and asked if the police thought he had. They say you were in a relationship with her, Kate wrote, and Corbin admitted that he was. He told her their relationship had been secret and that's why he hadn't brought it up. He knew how lame it sounded, of course. Why *hadn't* he just opened up about his relationship with Audrey as soon as he'd found out she was dead? It wasn't to protect her anymore.

He promised Kate he hadn't killed Audrey. It seemed to work, since they were now chatting about the weather and Sanders, the cat. She asked what Audrey was like, then mentioned a friend of Audrey's who she had met.

Corbin's skin prickled. He asked her who the friend was.

Jack Ludovico.

Corbin asked what he looked like and she told him he had reddish hair and glasses. It didn't sound like Henry, but he could have easily dyed his hair.

Corbin quickly googled the name. Nothing. Then googled the name with *Henry Wood*. Still nothing. They chatted a little more and said goodbye. He felt nauseous at the thought that Henry had possibly met Kate. Corbin had to find him.

Why Ludovico? It sounded familiar to Corbin, and he googled it. The first item that came up was the Ludovico Technique, the aversion therapy from the scene in *A Clockwork Orange* in which they pry Alex's eyes open and make him watch violent pornography. It had been Henry's favorite film, or one of them. He loved all of Stanley Kubrick's films, and Corbin and Henry had watched many together that summer in New York City when they had been so close. It felt like decades ago. Henry obviously had gotten that particular pseudonym from the film; what about his other false name—Hank Bowman—that he'd used when he lived in Hartford?

Corbin punched *Kubrick* and *Bowman* into the search engine, and the film *2001* immediately came up. Corbin's heart began to race, and a flush of excitement went across his skin. He looked at the list of all of Kubrick's films. They'd watched *The Shining* together several times. What was Jack Nicholson's character's name? Corbin looked it up. It was Jack Torrance. He punched in *Henry Torrance*. There were a few hits. An actor who'd been in a bunch of B movies. Corbin added Boston, and a mediation consultant came up. There was a Web site, and even though there was no picture of Henry Torrance, Corbin somehow knew right away that he had finally, after all this time, found him. The biography listed Aurelius College and Columbia University for a master's degree in conflict resolution. It was definitely Henry. There was a phone number and an office address in Newton.

He'd found him.

Even though it was nearly five, and the chances of Henry's still being at work were slim, Corbin hailed a taxicab on Charles Street and gave the address of Henry's office in Newton. It took forty-five minutes to get there through stop-and-go Boston rush hour traffic. The office was in the village of Newtonville, above a bakery on a tree-lined street that ran parallel to the turnpike.

There was a bench across the street, and Corbin sat there, keeping an eye on the building. He needed a moment to think. He couldn't quite believe how close he'd finally gotten to Henry. It was entirely possible he was up in his office right at this moment. The thought filled Corbin with equal amounts of hope and fear. If Henry actually was up there, he had no doubt that he could kill him with his bare hands, choke the life out of him. But what if there was someone with him? Or someone on the same hall who heard the commotion? What if Henry had a gun?

Corbin stood, the seat of his jeans now slightly damp from the wooden bench, and looked up and down the commercial block. There was a tavern, a sub shop, two banks, a jewelry store, and down at the far corner, what looked like a mom-and-pop hardware store. It was exactly what he was looking for. He walked briskly to its entrance, pushing through the door, jumping a little as it set off a bell to let the owners know they had a customer. The place was dark and narrow, its aisles just wide enough for one person.

"Can I help you?"

Corbin didn't immediately know where the voice was coming from. He swiveled his head and spotted a woman with tightly curled gray hair behind the register. He thought for a moment that she was kneeling, because her head barely rose above the countertop, but then watched as she scooted up onto a tall chair. She was incredibly short, possibly with some dwarfism.

"No, thanks," Corbin said. "Just looking around." His voice, to his own ears, sounded nervous and disingenuous.

"Just holler if you can't find something you're looking for."

He entered a random aisle that turned out to have plumbing supplies, shelf after shelf of plastic pipes and fittings. *What am I looking for?* Corbin thought. He found another aisle filled with hand tools—hammers and screwdrivers and wrenches. There was a smallish hammer, its rubber handle only about five inches long. It fit nicely in his hand. He could easily knock Henry out with it, then either strangle him or hit him till he was dead. But even though it was small for a hammer, it would be awkward to carry, too noticeable in his jacket pocket. He kept browsing, considered a chisel that really wasn't sharp enough, then found what he was looking for, a heavy-duty box cutter with a rubber grip. It was small enough to fit in his pocket with the blade retracted. He could even carry it in his fist without its being too visible.

He was about to take it up to the register, but paused. If Henry was in his office, and Corbin killed him with the box cutter, then wouldn't the woman working at the neighboring hardware store remember the shady man who bought the cutter just before the murder occurred? He glanced at the ceilings, looking for mounted cameras, but saw none. He slid the box cutter into his sweatshirt pocket, wandered over to the next aisle, picked up a cheap bottle of rubber cement, and brought that up to the register.

The woman put down her Dean Koontz paperback

and rang up the rubber cement on a cash register that looked as old as she did.

"Found something you couldn't live without, I see," she said and smiled.

"Can never have too much glue," Corbin responded, trying not to make eye contact. Maybe he should have just walked out of the store with the box cutter in his pocket. Now this woman would definitely remember him.

Back outside, carrying the small plastic bag with the rubber cement, Corbin walked with purpose down the street toward the sub shop. There was a large garbage bin on the corner, and he dropped the rubber cement into it, then stripped the box cutter of its flimsy paper packaging and threw that out as well. There were people around, mostly commuters, a few preteens on skateboards, but no one was paying any attention to Corbin. If Henry was in his office—and that was a big if—then Corbin needed to take advantage of that fact. It didn't matter that the woman from the hardware store might remember him. The only thing that mattered was getting to Henry.

He crossed at the crosswalk and made his way through the glass door into a small vestibule with water-stained walls and linoleum floor. The cramped space smelled of fresh bread and industrial cleaner. On the largest wall were three buttons, and three businesses listed. Corbin pressed the buzzer next to HENRY TORRANCE, MEDIATION SPECIALIST, and waited. What would he say if Henry's voice came through the speaker on the wall? Corbin could feel the adrenaline in his blood. He decided to say nothing. If Henry was here, he'd simply bolt up the stairs, break down his door if necessary, and slit his throat with the box cutter. His fingers twitched at the thought.

But there was no answer to the buzzer. He pressed it again, held it longer. No one was there.

Corbin went up the narrow stairwell anyway. Off the landing was a short, poorly lit corridor with three closed doors. MELANIE GELLAR, LICENSED THERAPIST. JOSEPH HAHN, CPA. And then simply HENRY TORRANCE. That door was locked, but the knob felt flimsy in Corbin's hand, like a tin can that he could crush. He considered busting through into the office for a lead on where Henry lived, but then he heard a phone ring in one of the other offices and a man's voice answer it. Corbin took his hand off the doorknob. No, now he knew where Henry worked, and if he broke into his office, then Henry would be alerted. It was better to leave now and come back early the next day, stake out across the street, wait for Henry to show up.

Back outside, Corbin realized he didn't have a way to get back to his hotel. Newton, although just on the outskirts of Boston, was still a suburb, and not an easy place to flag a cab. He spotted a bar across the street called Edmands Tavern. Inside, a small after-work crowd was filling up the padded leather seats around the horseshoe bar. Corbin leaned against the bar, ordered a Lagunitas Pils, and asked the bartender if she'd call a cab for him. She was young—college age at the most—with an arcane symbol tattooed onto the back of her long neck, and she looked at Corbin as if he'd just asked her if he could tie his horse out back for the night.

"I lost my cell phone," Corbin explained.

She pulled out hers, and with rapidly moving thumbs, located a cab company and called them, handing the phone over to Corbin. He named the bar he was in and was told to wait ten minutes.

"You should get Uber," the bartender said when he handed the phone back to her.

"I have it, but it's on my phone."

"Oh right." She laughed, sliding down the bar toward a pair of bearded men in polo shirts who had just arrived and were studying the beer list.

Instead of having the cabdriver take him back to the hotel, Corbin gave 75 Bury Street as his address, then he leaned back on the worn vinyl of the backseat and closed his eyes for a moment, willing himself to relax. He started with his face, forcing his jaw muscles to slacken, then worked his way down his body. He was so close to getting to Henry, and because of that, he allowed himself the briefest of fantasies, one that he'd had a few times. If he could kill Henry and get away with it, then he'd have his life back. Some semblance of a life, anyway. Maybe over time he could learn to forgive himself for what they'd done to Claire and to Linda, and the part that he'd played in Rachael's and Audrey's deaths. No, he could never truly forgive himself. But maybe he could atone. He didn't know exactly how he would do that, but the image that sometimes came to his mind was an image of himself with a family, daughters of his own that he would protect. As soon as that image came into his mind, he pushed it away, knowing it was far too optimistic. No, if he could kill Henry, then the most he could expect from the rest of his life was to not hurt anyone else, to get through the days and years unscathed. That would be enough.

*

The taxi let him out a block away from his apartment building. It was now dark, the wind lessening but the temperatures dropping. He pulled his hood up over his head and tightened the strings. With his hands pushed into his jean pockets, he walked toward 101, but before he reached the gated entryway, he crossed the street, not wanting to bump into a resident face-to-face. He moved slowly, looking for a place where he could hunker down and keep an eye on the building. If Henry had visited Kate already, he might visit again. He'd feel better watching his apartment building than he would in his hotel room, waiting for morning to arrive.

Bury Street was primarily redbrick and residential, the entryways well lit, but 106 Bury Street had retained its old stable doors, slightly recessed so that Corbin could sit on a low stone riser. It wasn't a hidden spot, but he was halfway between streetlamps and relatively in the dark. More important, he could see the entryway to his building and also the living room windows of his own apartment. They glowed with lamplight, the curtains halfway pulled. Corbin pulled his legs up tight, pressing his back against the wooden stable doors, and tried to make himself as unnoticeable as possible.

Over the next two hours, Corbin watched several people come and go from the building. Most of them he recognized. There was the old woman who was friends with the Valentines, out walking her small asthmatic pug. She took the dog just beyond the gates, toward the short hedge that bordered the neighboring property. The pug snooped around and eventually peed on the sidewalk. The woman cast a glance in Corbin's direction. He raised his head slightly, hoping she'd see that he was Caucasian. Otherwise, she just might call the police. A short time later, Corbin watched Mrs. Heathcote get out of a taxi-cab in front of the building, the driver carrying her two bags of groceries across the courtyard for her. A few other people Corbin didn't recognize came and went, but none of them was either his cousin Kate or Henry Wood.

As the night darkened, the streetlamps seemed to cast brighter, wider circles of light, and Corbin wondered how long it would be before some paranoid neighbor called the police to report a loiterer. If the police did come, he could simply say he was resting. He could use a Dutch accent and provide Bram's ID. They'd move him along, but they wouldn't take him in. At least, he hoped not.

Corbin heard loud, irregular footsteps and watched

as a man who looked about his age stopped in front of the courtyard. He swayed slightly, as though drunk, then looked up, directly at the windows of Corbin's—now Kate's—apartment. Was it Henry? It didn't look like him from behind—too tall and solid—but maybe it was. Then the man turned his head, and in the light from the moon and the streetlamp, Corbin recognized Alan, the guy from the other side of the building who had asked Corbin once if he was seeing Audrey Marshall. Why was he looking up at Kate's windows? Maybe that was just his thing—a weirdo who liked to look into windows. Hadn't he decided that that was how Alan had found out about his relationship with Audrey? Corbin pulled his legs in tighter and lowered his head, as though he was trying to keep warm. Alan lurched through the gates into the courtyard; with each step he looked as though he was about to fall, just managing to get a foot down before it happened.

The street was quiet again, and Corbin started to stand, wanting to stretch his legs, when he saw another figure rounding onto Bury from Brimmer Street. He quickly sat back down, pressed against the door into the shadows.

It was Henry.

Corbin was almost sure of it. His whole body was pulsing in time with his heartbeat. Even though he couldn't see the man's features, the way he was walking—fast clip, shoulders back—was so familiar. He was so sure it was Henry that he was baffled when the man walked straight past the entryway to 101, not even turning his head, and kept walking toward the river. Corbin stood and watched. The man—now he was unsure whether it was Henry or not—walked past the next building, then suddenly cut right and out of sight. Corbin crossed the street, breaking into a jog, holding onto the box cutter that was still in his sweatshirt pocket. He slowed when he got to the place where the man had disappeared. There was a narrow, almost impassable alley between two buildings, and just enough moonlight to see that the alleyway was now empty. Corbin stepped into it, each side brushing a shoulder. The pavement below his feet was slippery, and a smell like spoiled milk reached his nostrils. Without thinking too much about it, Corbin turned his body slightly and briskly walked the length of the buildings, coming out on another alley, much wider, that ran behind the backs of Bury Street residences. There was no sign of the man he was following, but he must have turned right, since the alley dead-ended to the left. Corbin walked slowly and carefully toward the back of his apartment building. He'd never seen the rear of 101 Bury, and was surprised to find a wide metal door built into the brick wall, a door that more than likely led to the apartment building's basement. There was a security camera bracketed to the wall above the door, but it was angled toward the entrance to the alleyway.

Now there was no doubt: that had to have been Henry he was following, and Henry had come back here to enter the building. But why? And how did he get in?

Corbin's apartment keys were in his hotel room. Now was his chance. If Henry was still in the basement he could kill him there. If Henry wasn't in the basement, then where was he? No matter where he was, Corbin would find him.

Back at the hotel room, a little breathless from the speed with which he'd walked, Corbin got the apartment keys from the zippered pocket on the outside of his carry-on luggage. There were three on the metal ring: one for the apartment, one for the storage unit, and one that opened the front doors, even though he'd never used that key, since a doorman was always present and the front doors were never locked. Still, he wondered if that same key also opened the back door that led to the basement. It was worth checking.

Before leaving, Corbin chugged three short glasses of water in the bathroom. He looked in the mirror. The short hair and the half-grown-in mustache *had* changed his appearance, but only superficially. He stared into his own eyes. He was scared but also certain. Henry needed to die, and he was going to kill him.

Chapter 28

Back at 101 Bury, Corbin tried his key in the rear door's lock. It stuck at first, then turned after he jiggled it for a while. He swung the heavy door open. He'd been right; concrete steps led down into the storage area of the building. He hesitated at the top of the steps, listening to hear if anyone was in the basement. The worst thing would be for some other resident to see his face, especially before he had a chance to find Henry. After listening for a minute, he tightened the hood around his head and stepped down into the harsh white fluorescence. There were very few places to hide in the main room of the basement area; locked storage units dominated one wall, boilers and water tanks the other. Corbin, hugging the wall, crept toward where he could see behind the water tanks. There was no one there.

He crossed the room toward the corridor that led to the back stairwells. His shoes tapped on the poured-concrete floor and he wished he'd changed into the sneakers he'd brought. He opened the door and peered into the empty corridor. Henry, if he had entered the building, must have gone up toward one of the back entrances to an apartment. It was possible he had gone to Audrey's apartment, revisiting the scene of the crime. But it was also possible he had gone up to Corbin's own apartment, that he was stalking Kate, for whatever reason.

He walked the length of the corridor to the stairwell that led to his apartment. He'd gone up and down the narrow stairs toward his place many times, but he'd never been so aware of how the low-wattage bulbs on each landing barely illuminated the steps. He felt almost blind, his hands on either banister. When he reached the back entrance to his apartment, he pressed an ear against the door, straining to hear anything, but there was no sound. He honestly did not know what to do. Henry had disappeared. If only he'd had his keys on him earlier, then he'd have been able to follow Henry into the basement. Henry could be anywhere now.

Corbin decided that the best course of action would be to return to the basement, hide behind the water tanks, and hope that Henry reappeared.

He was about to start down the steps when he heard something, a sound from below. He stood perfectly still. It was footsteps, quiet but steady. Someone was coming up the stairs.

In a panic, Corbin fumbled for his keys, feeling for the one that opened the doors to his apartment. He slid the key into the knob and, quietly as he could, opened the door, stepped into the dark kitchen, and closed the door behind him.

He stood, still as possible, listening for sounds from

the stairwell, but also listening for any sounds coming from within the apartment. His eyes adjusted until he could see the kitchen in the moonlight streaming in through the window. For a moment, there was pure silence, then he heard the approaching footsteps, slow and careful, on the other side of the door. They stopped on the landing. Corbin gripped the box cutter, using his thumb to slide out the blade. Suddenly, the weapon felt inadequate, the blade sharp enough but too small. He'd have to take a perfect shot at Henry to do any damage. Moving slowly, his eyes on the glint of the doorknob, he backed toward the nearest counter, pressing up against it. He slid his left hand along the granite countertop and found the block where the knives were kept. He felt with his fingers for the largest handle and removed the knife. He put the box cutter back in his pocket and switched the knife to his right hand.

What was happening on the other side of the door?

If it was Henry, and he was waiting, for whatever reason, to enter the apartment, Corbin would wait as well. With his free hand on the edge of the countertop, he slowly and quietly moved farther back so that he was partially hidden in the alcove next to the refrigerator. He concentrated on his breathing, making sure it was steady and silent.

He heard something, not from behind the door, but from the interior of the apartment. The rustle of clothes, bare feet on the wooden floors, and Kate was suddenly walking past the kitchen toward the bedroom. If she'd entered the kitchen, or even just turned to look in, she would have seen him. He remained perfectly still, listening. The toilet flushed, and he heard the familiar clunk in the plumbing, the tap being turned on. Moving quickly, Corbin left the kitchen and entered the large living room, lit by a single lamp; he crossed to the darkest part of the room and hid behind the curtain. A few minutes passed and Kate crossed back through the living room. He only heard her steps, and not the rustle of her jeans. She must have changed into whatever she slept in.

After five minutes, he stepped halfway out from behind the curtains. He could hear the faint sounds of the television in the den. At least now he knew where Kate was; it was only a matter of waiting to see if Henry appeared. He stayed where he was, listening intently. An hour, or what felt like an hour, passed. Corbin began to wonder what he was doing there, what he hoped might happen. He even began to wonder whether he'd really heard anything on the stairwell below him. Maybe he'd imagined it. These were the thoughts that were going through his head when Henry Wood, casually, as though he lived there, walked into the living room. Corbin, frozen, watched him, his fingers numb where they held the knife. It was definitely Henry, his hair cut short and dyed, wearing a dark midlength coat with an upturned collar. He was headed toward the den.

Corbin dropped to one knee and yanked his shoes off,

one by one. Why hadn't he done that earlier?

In his socks, being careful not to slip, he moved down the hall and entered the den. A black-and-white movie filled the screen. Kate was under a blanket on the leather couch, clearly asleep. There was no sign of Henry. He spun, looking back down the hall that culminated in the living room. Henry was in one of the two spare bedrooms, the second bathroom, or the laundry room. Kate shifted on the couch behind him, emitting a tiny snort. Corbin thought of the hideaway in the closet in the den, the secret place that his father had had built in when he'd first bought the apartment. He needed to wake Kate and tell her to hide there. That way, if he couldn't find and kill Henry, or if Henry killed him, at least Kate would be safe. It would be all over for him no matter what happened, but he could accept that.

Keeping Kate alive was all that mattered now.

He dropped to her side, put the knife on the floor, pushed the hood off his head, and pressed his hand against her mouth. She woke, struggling, and he put his other hand on her shoulder to hold her in place. He told her—using what he hoped was a reassuring voice—who he was.

"You *have* to trust me," he whispered, "or we are both going to die. Do you understand?"

Kate finally nodded, and Corbin felt like maybe she'd begun to listen to him. He told her about the hidden back in the closet—the one his father had put in to hide gold after the collapse of the technology bubble—and how she'd need to go in there and stay in there until he came to get her. She seemed to get frantic again, but she was struggling less. He kept telling her that she needed to do this, and finally he felt her body relax. She nodded, and he took his hand away from her mouth. Strands of hair, wet with tears and saliva, fanned across one of her cheeks.

"Who is it?" she asked. "Who's here?"

Corbin told her it didn't matter, that she needed to go to the closet. Obediently, she followed him. He felt as though her will had been broken. He desperately wanted to pull her close to him, to hug her. They were family, after all, even if they didn't know one another. He resisted, but right before she stepped toward the back of the closet, he said, "I am going to save you." For that moment, he believed it.

With the closet door shut behind him, he went to the foot of the sofa and picked up the kitchen knife. The film still played behind him, something in black and white, with English accents. A man and a woman at a fancy ball. He was glad for the sound of the television; hopefully, Henry still had no idea that there was someone else in the apartment besides Kate and himself.

Corbin looked down the hall. The doors to the bathroom and the laundry room were closed, but both of the doors to the guest bedrooms were slightly ajar, one more than the other. It was more than likely that Henry had gone into one of the bedrooms. Corbin crept along the hallway's Persian runner and was about to peer into the first bedroom, when movement from the living room caught his eye. He turned and looked. And there was Henry, looking back at him. The light from the single lamp was enough so that Corbin could read his expression. Surprise, mostly. Maybe even some amusement.

Corbin pressed the flat edge of the knife along his jeans to hide it and walked toward Henry.

"You came," Henry said, and smiled, his upper lip pulling back to reveal the large white canines.

"What are you doing here, Henry?" Corbin asked, his voice sounding calmer than he was.

"I'm here because of you, dude. You didn't think . . ."

Knowing he couldn't get into a conversation with Henry—knowing he needed to act—Corbin took two large strides and lunged with the knife, but he wasn't quick enough. Henry pulled his stomach in, hunching his shoulders, like a kid trying to avoid getting tagged in the playground. Then, with Corbin off balance, Henry tackled him, bringing them both crashing down onto the floor, the air punched from Corbin's lungs. Henry pinned Corbin's hand that still held the kitchen knife, and with his other hand tried to twist the knife, slicing open his palm. He hissed in pain, and Corbin, his lungs beginning to work again, managed to hold on to the handle of the knife while toppling Henry off his body and onto his back on the floor. Corbin took a wild shot at Henry's head, stabbing the knife's tip into the floor next to Henry's cheek. Henry's eyes were wide with adrenaline and what Corbin hoped was fear. Corbin began to pull the knife out of the hardwood plank, but his hand, slippery with sweat, slid off the handle. The motion caused him to rock backward a little, landing off-balance on the palm of his left hand. The knife vibrated like a tuning fork. Corbin watched as Henry quickly got to his feet, grabbed the handle of the knife, twisted it out of the floor, and lunged. All Corbin could do was put up his right forearm for protection and kick out with his legs. It wasn't enough. The knife found his throat.

Corbin rolled onto his back, both of his hands instinctively grabbing at the wound, warm blood oozing out between his fingers. He heard scrabbling along the floor, but couldn't raise his head to look for Henry. Instead, he stared up at the coffered ceiling, all feeling from his body beginning to dissolve. He was ready to close his eyes when he saw Kate crouched above him. *You look a little like my father,* Corbin said, but all that came out was the sound of his own blood gurgling in his throat. *You have his eyes.*

Chapter 29

Alan woke, the alarm clock rattling in his ear. He gingerly turned his head toward the digital numbers. They were telling him it was ten thirty. For a moment he didn't know if it was day or night, then he realized it was dark outside. He thumped at the clock and closed his eyes again. His temples throbbed as though his skull were pinched in a vise.

The alarm went off again. He sat up this time and looked around. It wasn't his clock. It was the door buzzer. He jumped off the bed, surprised that he was still dressed, and walked sloppily across the living room to the intercom. *Kate,* he thought. Fragments of the evening came flooding back to him. There was Jack, and the long, rambling monologue about Corbin having killed before. There was the walk back across Boston, and the Irish pub, and then it started to get hazy. Still, he remembered seeing Kate. They were arguing and she looked scared. It was in a kitchen, he thought, but he didn't remember how he'd gotten there, or how he'd gotten back to his own apartment.

He pressed the button that answered the intercom.

"They're on their way up," the doorman said.

"Who?"

"The police. They showed me a warrant."

There was a loud rap on the door. Alan felt a wave of nausea but went and opened the door.

"Alan Cherney?" It was the woman cop he'd seen before. Behind her were two uniformed officers, both male, both shorter than she was, plus another woman in plain clothes, who looked like an intern along for the ride.

"Yes."

"I'm Detective Roberta James, and this is Agent Abigail Tan from the Federal Bureau of Investigation, and we have a warrant to search your premises." She handed Alan a piece of paper that looked as though it had been folded and unfolded many times.

"Okay," Alan said, and took a step backward to allow all four into his apartment. "Does this have something to do with Audrey Marshall?"

"It does, actually," the agent said, her voice sounding as young as she looked. She removed two pairs of latex gloves from her jacket pocket and handed them to the uniformed officers. "Is there anything you'd like to tell me about your relationship with the deceased?"

Alan rapidly shook his head, aware that he was having trouble meeting her stare. He felt another sharp wave of nausea. "Excuse me," he said, and bolted for the bathroom.

He managed to get the door shut behind him before kneeling on the hard tile, vomiting until there was nothing left but bile. Then he splashed cold water on his face and brushed his teeth. He studied himself in the mirror. His eyes were bloodshot, the lower lids wet with tears from throwing up. His skin was the color of chalk. Wiping away the tears, he felt a terrible sense of dread, not just because the police were searching his apartment, but because he knew something was very wrong.

He heard a police radio out in his living room. What were they looking for? Before heading back out, he opened his medicine cabinet to look for ibuprofen, grabbed his allergy medicine by accident, and putting it back on his shelf, got a sudden, jarring flash of Jack scratching at his forearm in the bar the day before. Hives, he'd said, something about springtime. Only they hadn't looked like allergic hives to him, and Alan suddenly realized what they were, and what that meant. A dizziness coursed through his body at the thought, and he felt an alarm go off that Kate was in terrible danger. He didn't know why, exactly. It was just a feeling, but a feeling as real as anything he'd ever felt.

He exited the bathroom, turning into the living room just as the young agent was crossing the room toward him. She was removing her gloves. Behind her, in the alcove kitchen, he could see the other cop bagging one of his kitchen knives. Alan began to speak, although he was not entirely sure what he was going to say. He stopped when he saw the agent remove her handcuffs from under her jacket. "Alan Cherney," she said, her eyes expressionless,

"I'm arresting you on suspicion of the murder of Audrey Marshall . . ."

She read him his rights as she cuffed his hands behind his back.

PART II

AN EVEN SPLIT

Chapter 30

The friendship—or whatever you wanted to call it—with Corbin Dell had been special. Henry Wood, for the first time in his life, imagined that he felt what normal people felt when they fell in love, or looked at a parent, or brought a new puppy home to live with them. Then the friendship ended—Henry getting the call from Corbin after they'd *both* murdered the insignificance that was Linda Alcheri—and Henry felt deeply hurt, another new emotional experience. Not just hurt, but shocked. After all, Henry had introduced Corbin to a new and better world. He'd taken him from Kansas to Oz, and now Corbin, for some reason, wanted to go back to Kansas.

Had Corbin not realized that what had happened in the Boddington Cemetery was something beautiful? And that what had happened on Eel River Pond could have been even more beautiful?

That was how Henry thought of it, especially their shared moment in London with Claire Brennan. Some of it was probably the heightened nostalgia of college memories, but, no, he had felt the incredible beauty at the time, as well. For the short time after the murder that Henry was in London, and then all during that incredible summer in New York, the world was composed of new colors. Henry, every night as he fell asleep, replayed every detail of what had happened between Corbin and Claire and him on that wet Wednesday afternoon. It had been a spontaneous dance in which each participant knew their dance moves without having practiced them before. That was how he remembered it. Claire's death was the climax, and her spilled blood was shared, in perfect equal measures, by Corbin and him. Even the rain, coming when it did, had added to the beauty, washing the blood away, cleaning the air.

Occasionally, Henry altered what had happened, tweaked it to make it a little bit better. For instance, he always took away that awkward moment when he'd slipped on the slick ground and fallen to one knee, the knife slipping from his fingers. He also always reduced the amount of time it had taken to dig the grave, Corbin beginning to panic that someone would come along. And sometimes he allowed himself to add a scene, one in which they'd slice Claire's body down the middle before burying it. *One half for Corbin, and one half for me,* Henry thought. *An even split.* It would have been a way to memorialize why Claire had died; that she'd foolishly shared her love and paid the price. But it would also have memorialized what had happened between Henry and Corbin.

Of course, Henry found out, after Linda Alcheri, that Corbin didn't really understand, and never would really understand. Cutting Linda had been a present that Corbin didn't appreciate.

Still, when the phone call came—Corbin telling him that their friendship was over—Henry was shocked.

And then he got angry.

What did Corbin think? Did he think that after what they'd done together, he could just somehow stop? Did he think he was going to go back to a normal life? Did he want to get married? Have children? Did he actually think he'd be happy back in Kansas, living in a world drained of all color? And Henry decided that, if nothing else, he would make sure that none of that ever happened. That was not how the world worked. Corbin was like him. He could pretend he wasn't, but that wasn't going to change facts, and Henry would make sure that Corbin never forgot it.

Henry Wood became Henry "Hank" Torrance, mediator specializing in business disputes in St. Louis, Missouri. It was easy work. There were so many simple ways to manipulate people, especially people weakened by grievances. Especially stupid people. He met a woman named Kaylee Buecher who reminded him of Claire, the way she looked and moved, and the smuttiness behind her eyes. He took her to dinner and listened as she told him, in that ugly midwestern accent, how she was the first one in her family to go to college, and her parents didn't appreciate her, just wondered why she hadn't gotten married yet. He never called her back but stalked her for half a year.

She lived in a single-family in Webster Groves, a rental. He followed her, learned her schedule. He bought a set of picklocks, taught himself how to use them, and broke into her house whenever he felt like it. He liked to rearrange her things, spit in her leftovers, read her pathetic diary ("Hi Future Me!"). One afternoon, she came home early from work with a man from her office. Henry hid in the bedroom closet and listened to them have sex. Afterward, the man cried, moaning that he was married and he'd never cheated on his wife before. Or that's what he said, anyway. After he left, Kaylee got on the phone and told some friend of hers all about it, then she called her office to tell them she'd be at home the rest of the day with a migraine. Henry stayed in the house all that evening and through half the night, leaving at three in the morning after standing over Kaylee's bed and watching her sleep.

Being alone in the house with Kaylee was the best feeling he'd had since spending time with Corbin.

He visited as much as possible. He learned every hiding place in Kaylee's Dutch Colonial, memorized every creaking floorboard and unoiled hinge. He found he could move around the house at ease with Kaylee in it. He was nearly caught only once. He was in the downstairs bathroom, the one Kaylee never used, when she came home from a night out, bolting into the bathroom to pee. Henry had time to step into the shower stall but not to pull the curtain all the way across. Kaylee sat on the toilet, ferociously emptying her bladder, and if she'd looked up and into the mirror she would have seen Henry's face from behind the shower curtain. But she never looked up, never taking her eyes off her phone. It was what had saved her, some text she was reading that was making her laugh and cry at the same time.

Eventually, the owners of Kaylee's house put it on the market because of the real estate boom, and Kaylee decided to move back into the city with a girlfriend. On Henry's last night with Kaylee in the house, he cut a deck of cards in the living room while Kaylee slept upstairs. Red and he'd kill her in her bed, black and he'd let her live. It was a seven of clubs. Before leaving, Henry got a pair of scissors and cut every picture of Kaylee Buecher that he could find in half, replacing the two pieces back into the frame, or taping them together and putting them back up on the fridge. Then he stole a hand-signed screen print of Andy Warhol's portrait of Mao that was probably worth tens of thousands.

Being with Kaylee had been fun, but also somehow lonely. Even though he'd left her the photographs he'd improved, she would never know it was he that had done it. It would just be a mystery in her life.

Henry decided it was time to find Corbin. Time to get revenge.

It wasn't hard. According to LinkedIn, after a few years in New York City, Corbin had moved back home to Boston to work at the headquarters of Briar-Crane. During his summer vacation, Henry flew to Boston to look for

Corbin. He shadowed Briar-Crane's small South End offices; it was clear that Corbin was away. Henry left a fake business card with the chatty Briar-Crane receptionist and learned that Corbin was on the North Shore with family for most of August. Henry rented a car, drove north, and checked into the New Essex Motor Court, the only hotel with a vacancy at the height of the summer season. He tailed Corbin and his beautiful, dark-haired girlfriend for the week. Corbin was tan and muscled. He ran on the beach every morning. And he seemed genuinely happy in the presence of the townie he'd picked up. Henry learned her name. Rachael Chess. She had long, dark hair like Claire Brennan had, and she was always smiling in the presence of Corbin, or draping an arm around his shoulders, or wrapping her legs around him when they were in the ocean together. Wrapping those legs around him every night, as well, Henry imagined. And never suspecting that her golden god had once pounded a woman's head into the ground till she was unconscious. Henry's rage almost made him want to just take Corbin out, sneak into his bedroom some night and slit his throat, stare him in the eyes as he bled out. But, no, that was too good for Corbin. He decided to have some fun first.

Rachael Chess had an active Facebook account, and when Henry learned that she was returning to New Essex over Columbus Day weekend, he flew back. Corbin was not around—surprising, but it made things easier. He managed to meet Rachael at a beachside bar called the

Rusty Scupper. Not surprisingly, she was an uppity bitch who refused his offer to buy her a drink. He left the bar to wait in his car. She left at closing time. Some guy kept trying to kiss her in the parking lot, and she kept pushing him away until he stalked off, driving away in a pickup truck that needed a new muffler. She walked toward the beach. Henry removed his backpack from the trunk of his rental car. It contained the new filleting knife he'd bought at Walmart the day before, sharp enough not just to kill her, but to carve her body in a way that would leave no doubt in Corbin's mind as to who had killed his girlfriend.

A year later, more out of boredom than anything else, Henry moved to Boston, opening a walk-up office in Newtonville and renting a furnished apartment downtown. There was a coffee shop across the street from where Corbin worked, and sometimes Henry would wait for Corbin to appear, almost always at six thirty in the morning. Usually, he would go to the nearby gym after work; sometimes home. But he never met anyone, certainly not a woman. By now, he knew the consequences. He knew what had happened to Rachael Chess.

Henry wondered what Corbin thought of him now. Was it pure hatred and fear, or was there some admiration, as well? Was there jealousy? Regret?

When Corbin was at work, Henry would sometimes break into his apartment building, picking the lock at the rear entrance and going through the basement and up a back stairwell that led to Corbin's massive apartment.

He didn't do it too often; he was scared of being spotted coming through the back entrance, although he never saw anyone in the basement at all. It contained storage space and not much else. Sometimes there was a cat down there that would follow Henry up the dark, narrow stairwell, meowing plaintively. He wondered if it was Corbin's, but doubted it, since there was nothing in Corbin's apartment—no litter box, no food bowl—that would indicate he had a cat. Sometimes Henry imagined how easy it would be to snap the cat's neck, then spread its guts all over Corbin's Oriental carpets. He didn't do it, though. He wasn't ready for him to know how close he was, and he enjoyed his time in Corbin's apartment far too much.

It was a Thursday afternoon when he discovered that Corbin was hiding a girlfriend. He'd been lounging on the sofa, drinking some of Corbin's Belvedere vodka, when there was a knock on the door. Henry moved quickly and silently to the door, pressing his eye against the peephole. There was a blonde who looked somewhat familiar. He heard a key in the lock and fled toward the master bedroom, just entering the hallway as the door swung open. He didn't panic; he'd had so much experience spending time with Kaylee in her house without her knowing he was there. He ducked into the kitchen and hid in the nook on the far side of the refrigerator, listening for any noise. Henry didn't hear a thing till the front door opened and shut again. He slowly emerged back into the hallway, then back into the living room. There was a note on the coffee table, pinned under his glass of vodka. She had confident, looping script:

Dear Cor,

Used my key and broke into your apartment because I have a migraine coming on and that stuff you have is the best. Didn't snoop, I promise. Don't come by tonight because I might be under a sheet with my earplugs in, but maybe I'll come over if the headache's gone?? It's been too long.

Audrey

Corbin had a girlfriend. A fuck buddy, anyway. And now Henry remembered where he'd seen this girl. She lived in the building, a cold-looking blonde with a man's haircut, always carrying a bag that looked full of books. Always coming and going. She didn't seem Corbin's type. Both Claire and Rachael had been dark-haired girls with soft, curvy bodies. This one was hipless, all legs, looked like she'd be knocked over by a warm breeze. But still, they were involved. And it would be so easy to find out her name, what apartment she lived in, how seriously she and Corbin were involved.

Henry felt a great unloosening in his chest, an anticipation of all that was to come. Corbin might be done sharing with him, but Henry wasn't done sharing with Corbin.

Chapter 31

Her name was Audrey Marshall. She worked in publishing. She'd moved to Boston from New York City. And she lived in the apartment right next to Corbin Dell's.

Henry got all this information off a simple Google search, preceded by one trip to the lobby of the apartment building with a fistful of leaflets advertising handyman services. The doorman took the leaflets, promising to add them to the residents' mail, although Henry doubted it. "You don't need to add one to Audrey . . . Audrey . . ." He snapped his fingers rapidly, as though trying to remember.

"Audrey Marshall," the sleepy-eyed doorman said.

"That's her. She has my info. I painted her walls a little while ago."

The doorman looked a little confused. "When was that?"

"Few months ago, I think," Henry said as he ducked out the door.

He began to follow Audrey on occasion. She worked strange hours, sometimes not going into the office until midmorning, often not coming back till nearly midnight. And occasionally, on a weekday, she'd stay home. Because of her erratic schedule, it made Henry nervous about breaking into her apartment, something he very badly wanted to do. It wasn't until he saw her leave one morning with a large piece of hand luggage, a taxi idling at the side of the curb, that Henry felt like the opportunity had arisen. He broke in that night, moving through the empty basement and up a different stairwell. Her back-door lock was a five-pin tumbler, and it took him a while to pick it, but eventually he got in. He kept the lights off, letting his eyes adjust to the dark, then moved through the sparsely furnished space, a lot smaller than Corbin's but still big for city living. There were books everywhere in the living room, stacks on the floor that formed a cityscape. The living room curtains were open, so Henry moved into the bedroom, where the curtains were drawn. He brought out his penlight and searched through her things. In the drawer next to her bed, he found what he was looking for, a red leather notebook with a rubber band around its middle. He removed the band and opened the book; it was a diary, page after page of the cursive that Henry had seen on the note she'd left for Corbin. He sat on the edge of the bed and began to read; she dated the entries, which were rarely longer than two or three sentences. It was boring mostly—books she'd read, phone calls with a needy sister—but then the mentions of Corbin began and it got a little more interesting. The first mention he found was from a few months earlier, in January:

Hot Neighbor came for dinner. I can't read him at all. It's like staring at a blank page, a very hot blank page. We drank two bottles of wine and I thought he was going to make a move but then he was out the door like I'd hit him with a cattle prod.

After that the mentions were more frequent, every few days:

Spent the night with Hot Neighbor in his ginormous place. Slightly weird, but nice. Gave me the Not Looking For Relationship speech.

Finally told Kerry about Hot Neighbor. She asked a ton of questions, natch, and I didn't have answers. I said I thought he just wanted to be with someone but didn't want a girlfriend. Because he already has one, Kerry said. I laughed, but it's not as though I haven't thought that a hundred times. Thing is, I don't think he does. I think it's more complicated than that.

For better or worse, HN and I are now definitely a thing. I just don't know what that thing is. The sex is nice, and I have feelings for him and he has feelings for me, or pretends to, and for the life of me I can't figure out why we're not even allowed to take a walk around the block together.

Need to break up with HN, sooner rather than later. If I thought we were just sex buddies, then that would be one thing, but I know that we are more and he still won't tell me what is happening inside of that big, thick skull. I need to get out before I get hurt. We exchanged keys the other day, more of a neighborly thing, but still, it seemed like something. Corbin, if you're in my apartment and reading this, then fuck you, and stop doing that thing with your tongue in my ear. It's gross.

HN is broken. Something is seriously wrong with him. If he won't talk to me, then it needs to end.

It's over. He came over and accused me of—I don't actually know what he accused me of. Telling someone about us. One of our neighbors! I'm beginning to think there is something really wrong with him, and now I want out.

Cor is moving to London for six months, and his cousin is moving into his place. I'm happy. Why wouldn't I be? If only he hadn't looked so sad when he told me.

That was the last entry that mentioned him. It was dated a week before. Henry was shocked. Corbin was

343

moving to London. When was that happening? Something about it pissed him off. London was their place, and now he was returning as though nothing of importance had happened there. As though it were just another city.

The next day, Henry broke into Corbin's apartment and found a folder on his desk that contained travel documents and copies of the work visa for his time in London. He was leaving in a week, a Thursday night flight. Henry made an easy decision—that same Thursday night he would break into Audrey's apartment again, and if she was there, he'd kill her.

It was time to fuck over Corbin for real, and let him know who had done it to him.

Henry stayed away from Beacon Hill and Bury Street for the next week. He knew he'd been pushing his luck by spending so much time in that neighborhood. Someone was going to notice. That week, he finished a job at a Cambridge nonprofit in which one of its internal groups was considering becoming its own nonprofit entity. He also booked a new client, a small law firm in Waltham with a personnel dispute, and over the weekend took the executive assistant from the nonprofit out to dinner. It was a boring date, and an awful restaurant, so Henry amused himself by telling her a long, improvised story about an affair he'd had with a famous television star. Watching the woman's eyes light up with utter belief as he made up stories of the actress's pathetic behavior almost salvaged the evening.

When Thursday night arrived he filled his backpack with his favorite tools, pulled a tight synthetic ski hat over his hair, donned gloves, and walked all the way to Bury Street. It was a beautiful spring night, the air rain-washed and smelling of crushed blossoms, and Henry felt as if the muscles of his body were singing in unison. He felt as though he could kill Audrey Marshall and tear her in two with just his hands.

It hadn't worked that way.

After he entered through the kitchen, Audrey must have heard him.

"Corbin?" she said nervously as she stepped into the kitchen. Henry grabbed her from behind and stuck the knife in her neck before she could say another word. The spray from the artery went from the counter across the cabinets to the ceiling as she crumpled to the floor.

It was early morning before he left her apartment the same way he had entered it. He left her body arranged the way he'd wanted it. Split down the middle. *Half of her for Corbin, and half of her for me.* But it had been messy, hard work, and midway through the job, Henry had been stung with a surge of loneliness that almost took his breath away.

He felt better when the job was done, when he was walking home in the early hours. There was no doubt that Corbin would become a suspect, and if they pinned it on him, well, they wouldn't be wrong, would they? Corbin was as guilty of Audrey Marshall's death as

Henry was. Just as he'd been guilty of what happened to Rachael Chess. It was half and half. Always and forever.

Henry got home just as the emerging sun was beginning to lighten the sky. There were fragments of mist on the roads and sidewalks. It would be light in London by now, midday. How long would it be before Corbin heard what had happened with Audrey, before he knew that Henry was still in his life, that Henry would always be in his life?

*

It wasn't until Saturday afternoon that Henry first read about the murder, an item appearing on the *Globe*'s Web site.

He'd done some thinking since then. Even though he was pretty sure that Corbin would become a suspect—the police would read Audrey's diary, for one thing—Henry wanted to make sure that it happened. He wanted Corbin's name dragged into it, and, ideally, he wanted him arrested. Corbin's pretty face would be splashed across the Internet; preppy, blond killer of innocent young girls.

The question was: Would the diary be enough to land Corbin squarely on the suspect list? It would, of course, but there needed to be more. And if Henry was going to play this game, he really wanted to play it. He needed to plant the idea that there was something suspicious about Corbin Dell, and he thought of a way he could do that.

The next day at noon he went to 101 Bury Street,

346

waiting around outside on the street to see if anyone might come out of the building. It felt good being there and being untouchable. In his mind, he was a friend of Audrey's who had come to grieve. Maybe he was a friend who was secretly in love with her, although he couldn't admit it to himself. A man came out of the building in a fleece jacket and poorly fitting jeans. He stopped in the courtyard to find the song he wanted to hear through his headphones, then double-knotted both shoelaces before setting off on what looked like a habitual walk. He didn't glance in Henry's direction.

The next person to exit the building was a woman in a stylish black-and-white jacket, walking anxiously as though she were trying to escape from someone. As she neared, Henry felt a click in his chest. She looked like Corbin, not a lot, but enough to make him think she might be the cousin. At the street crossing, she instinctively looked right instead of left, then corrected herself. It had to be the English cousin. He stopped her, told her the story about being a friend and trying to get information. She kept trying to end the conversation, but he wasn't going to let that happen. For one, she had nervous, haunted eyes. Something had happened to her. She was damaged goods, and that was more beautiful to Henry than her lovely bone structure and her plump mouth.

He walked with her to Charles Street, telling lies. It was gratifying playing the bereaved friend. He wore his reading glasses, the ones that made him look sensitive and vulnerable, and even managed to squeeze out some tears. Before they parted ways, he made sure to tell Kate that Audrey had told him how weird Corbin had been. He then purposefully asked Kate exactly what time Corbin's flight to London had been. He'd done enough, he knew. He caught her tapping the fingertips of her right hand against her thumb, back and forth in succession. Kate would probably do one of two things. She'd either contact the police and tell them what she'd heard, or she would contact Corbin and tell him about the visit. Either way, Henry had alerted her that something was amiss. She was just an ordinary prey animal and she'd start to get nervous.

He returned to his apartment. He kept thinking of Kate, and how much he'd enjoyed talking with her, and how much he'd like to spend time in the apartment with her, especially if she didn't know he was there. He retrieved the hollowed-out copy of *The Monetary History of the United States* from the bedroom bookshelf. It contained his birth certificate, his certificate of name change when he legally became Henry Torrance, a lock of hair from Jenny Gulli, the first girl to really disappoint him, all the way back in high school, and the Polaroid he had of Corbin standing over the corpse of Claire Brennan. It was their insurance, of course, since Corbin owned a similar photograph of Henry, but Henry had always thought it was something more. A pact. A promise. He wondered where Corbin kept his Polaroid.

Probably in a safe-deposit box somewhere. Henry knew that he should do the same, but he liked looking at it too much; he liked to have it close.

He paced the apartment with the photo in his hand. He hated being alone in his place; he'd hated it ever since his exciting visit with Audrey Marshall. Knowing suddenly what he was going to do, he logged onto his business e-mail account and canceled his meetings for the following day with the family law firm in Waltham. He packed his backpack with everything he needed. He was going to move in with Kate.

Chapter 32

Henry walked across the park in the dusk light. It had rained earlier, and there were puddles on the walkways and rain dripping from the trees. He crossed Beacon Street and then walked the one block of Charles that took him to Bury. He turned, and there was Kate, coming directly toward him. He lowered his head and kept walking. She never looked at him. Her eyes had that glazed emptiness of someone deep in thought. He almost followed her, just out of curiosity, but decided instead to take the perfect opportunity that had been given to him. He continued to walk toward the apartment, nearly bumping into a man about his age, hurrying along as though he was late for something. They each apologized at the same time, Henry catching a glimpse of a gaunt face, dark eyes.

He walked past the apartment building and through the two alleys that brought him to the back entrance. No one was in the basement, as usual. Henry's feet were wet and muddy, and left tracks on the floor. He found an old stiffened rag behind one of the water tanks and cleaned his shoes off, then wiped away the tracks. He took his time, confident at this point that the residents in this building rarely visited their storage units. Why did they need these units when their apartments were so massive? Some didn't even have locks on them since they were probably unused. Corbin's unit—the door stenciled with 3D—had a stainless steel padlock on its flimsy door. Could that possibly be where Corbin kept the photograph of Henry with the body of Claire? He decided to visit the unit when he got a chance. The lock would be easy to pick.

Henry entered Corbin's dark apartment, or Kate's apartment, since it was now hers. He removed his shoes in the kitchen, wrapped them in one of the plastic bags he'd brought, and put them in his backpack. He knew the apartment well, and had already decided that the best place for him to hide would be in the north-facing guest room, the larger of the two guest rooms. There was a relatively deep closet; one side had shelving that held linens and towels, but the other side was recessed slightly, and empty. Two suits, in plastic garment bags, hung on the closet rod, and if he positioned them carefully he'd be able to stand in the recess and be hidden, so long as no one moved the suits.

The guest bedroom was mostly covered by a large pile rug, beige and with a fleur-de-lis pattern. The bed was a four-poster with about two feet of clearance underneath. Henry thought he could comfortably sleep under the bed. He stashed his backpack in the closet and walked through the entire apartment, automatically picking out quick hiding places—behind curtains, a walk-in pantry—that he could use if he had to. He wasn't too worried about it.

He went into Corbin's obscenely large bedroom. He studied the framed pictures on top of the low bureau, even though he'd looked at them before. There were many of Corbin when he'd been young, and some of him when he was college age, the age when Henry had first met him. The pictures were almost humorously upper class; most were on boats, and the blond, tanned inhabitants were all holding gin and tonics and wearing the half-amused expressions of people so rich that they could hardly be bothered to smile completely for a picture.

After looking at the pictures, Henry searched the bedroom for signs of Kate; she'd barely unpacked. Her toiletries were spread around the bathroom, but a large duffel on the carpeted floor was still filled with clothes, some spilling out. The bed had been slept in, then half made again, the sheets and duvet pulled up, but not tucked in or smoothed. Henry pressed his face against the sheets and breathed in deeply through his nostrils. They smelled of detergent and not much else. He dropped to the floor to look under the bed; there was only about a foot and a half of space, enough to get under if he needed to, but not very comfortably.

There was a book under the bed with a black faux-leather cover. Henry opened it. There was a charcoal sketch of a man's face, a perfect rendering of the man that Henry had nearly bumped into on Bury Street earlier. Who was that man, and why had Kate—this had to be Kate's sketchbook—drawn him? He flipped over a page and there was a sketch of Kate herself, stunningly real, her wary eyes staring out at Henry as though she could see him. On the next page was Henry's own face, his name under it—JACK LUDOVICO (she'd spelled it right)—and today's date. It wasn't a bad drawing, and Henry found himself mesmerized, as though he was looking at himself through someone else's eyes. She'd drawn him with his head angled down, his eyes with a touch of sadness behind the lenses of his glasses. It was exactly what he'd been trying to convey, and she'd gotten it perfectly. He felt proud of himself, as he always did when someone entirely believed the mask that he was wearing.

He wondered if Kate tried to sketch everyone she met or just those people that she was interested in, people who affected her in some way. If that was the case, then who was this neighbor on the first page—ALAN CHERNEY, she'd written—and why was he walking behind her this evening? Had he been following her?

Almost unconsciously, Henry touched his tongue to the tip of his index finger and brought it down within an inch of the charcoal sketch. He very badly wanted to smudge the man's eyes, alter him somehow, maybe just enough to freak Kate out when she looked back at the sketchbook. What he really wanted to do was smudge the eyes entirely. He thought back to his sister's *Tiger Beat* magazines and how he used to meticulously go through them, whiting out the eyes of all her favorite boy bands, making the Hanson brothers look like eyeless zombies. Sometimes he'd get a red pen and draw blood coming from their eyes and mouths. After he'd done it to his sister's middle school yearbook, his mother made him go see a therapist—the only therapist in Stark, New York, a fat middle-aged woman who was so stupid that Henry was able to convince her that his sister had been the one tormenting him, and that he was only defending himself. He was eight years old at the time. His sister was twelve. The therapist must have gone to his mother and suggested that Mary was the problem, because all Henry knew was that he didn't have to go see Nancy the therapist anymore, and that his sister had started to go. Henry stopped mutilating Mary's things, but he did find ways to torture her that were never tracked back to him. Easy ways. He started rumors about her that wrecked her friendships. He got her fired from her first job at the pharmacy by making it look like she was stealing. For a time he added tiny amounts of antifreeze to her Gatorade, till she was hospitalized for over a week. She dropped out of high school junior year and left town with the local drug dealer. They had one postcard from Mary five years later—Greetings from San Diego—and that had been it.

It had been so long since he'd thought of his family, and as always, it filled him with a combination of amusement and shame in their mediocrity. His parents were still together, living in the same ranch house in Stark. On the few occasions when he spoke with them, he sometimes lied and told them that he'd hired a private detective to track down his sister, and they'd thanked him, and prayed that wherever she was she'd found peace. He could hear in their voices that they actually didn't want to find her, that they'd already accepted a life without their children. They didn't want him back. He knew that much. He hadn't laid eyes on them for ten years.

Henry refocused on the sketch in front of him. He decided not to smudge the eyes, as temping as it was. It would probably be too much; Kate would call the police, probably leave the apartment. Instead, he turned to the picture she'd drawn of him and used his finger to smooth out some of the lines that defined his face, then he allowed himself to dab at the charcoal eyes with a moistened finger, altering them just enough so that they looked out of focus. Satisfied, he shut the book and slid it back under the bed, wondering how long he'd been sitting there. Disoriented suddenly, he stood, the room swimming a little in his vision. He was hungry, and he went to the kitchen to see if there was enough food that he could take some. If not, his backpack was filled with granola bars.

Kate came home around eight that night. Henry was in the guest room, sitting in the dark. He didn't bother to hide. If she came looking, he'd have enough time to duck into the closet while she was turning on the light. And if he didn't, and she spotted him, well, Kate would have to die. Henry wondered how Corbin would react to that. Would it be more personal because she was family, his blood, or less personal because he'd never fucked her?

Either way, it would flush Corbin out from his hiding place in London. He'd *have* to return to Boston. Henry was pondering this when the white cat he'd seen in the basement trotted into the bedroom and stared at him, eyes glowing yellow in the dark. Henry hissed and the cat cocked its head, then turned and left the room.

He waited and listened. He heard the front door open and close, and wondered if Kate had left, but somehow he doubted it, and he stayed where he was. Fifteen minutes later, she came padding down the hall, heading for the media room, or whatever Corbin called that dark-paneled man cave with the overstuffed leather sofa. Henry let five minutes pass, then stepped out into the hall. The lamp by the leather sofa was on, and even though its back was to Henry, he could see the crown of her head and hear the dry flicking sound of a page being turned. She was reading. Henry stayed where he was, still as he could be, waiting for another page to turn. She must be a slow reader, he thought, then he heard the book clunk to the floor and Kate shift on the sofa. She'd fallen asleep.

He stood behind the sofa. She was half covered by a lumpy duvet, one of her hands turned so that the palm faced outward and the knuckles rested on her cheek. He watched her for a while, amazed that people were held together by something as fragile as skin. Even in the dull light from the lamp, he could see the blood moving beneath it. Her jaw moved, and with it, the delicate tendons of her neck. She began to snore, then shifted, her eyes squeezing shut as though trying not to see whatever it was that her dreams were showing her. Henry backed away, then turned and walked to the kitchen, where he drank milk directly from the bottle. Just to amuse himself, he thought of sleeping in Corbin's bed. There was a good chance Kate was going to stay all night on the sofa. No, he thought. He was having too much fun and didn't want it to end. He'd sleep under the bed in the guest room. It was the safest place.

He put the milk back in the refrigerator, then heard a soft scratching sound on the door that led to the basement. He opened the door and let in that idiotic cat. It actually rubbed up against his leg. He bent and picked it up, turning it over and holding its skull, not quite the size of a tennis ball, in his hand. The cat purred. Could he crush its head with just his hand? He thought he probably could. He began to squeeze, then decided against it and dropped the cat to the floor, where it scampered off toward the living room, unaware how close it had been to death. It would be more fun for Kate to find the cat in the house again and have her wonder how it got back in.

Henry returned to the guest room, slid under the bed, and closed his eyes. He wasn't tired, but long ago he'd figured out how to get himself to fall asleep at almost any moment. He imagined himself floating down an enormous river. In front of him were all the people he knew who'd been born before he was, growing older as they floated, and sinking one by one below the surface as time, or disease, or just bad luck, caught up with them. Around him were the people his age, the sheep he'd gone to high school with in Stark, the entitled kids from college who acted like they'd live forever, his workmates and clients, all of them treading water hard in the middle of their lives, just trying to stay afloat. And behind him were those younger than him, the ones being born, new bodies trying to enter the slipstream, growing more multitudinous as the people in front of him thinned in their ranks. Once the image was clearly in his mind—a phalanx of human bodies with Henry in the middle, moving constantly toward the front—he allowed himself to sink below the surface of the water so that all he saw were the legs churning in the froth of the moving river. And like a snapping turtle that pulls a baby duck down underneath the surface of a pond, Henry knew that he could take hold of someone's legs and bring them down to the dark, cold river bottom, where he could breathe but they could not.

Thinking this, he'd fall asleep. And never dream.

Chapter 33

Henry stayed under the bed until Kate left the apartment. It was around noon.

Kate had gotten up early, before dawn. The reappearance of the cat had clearly freaked her out. She'd yelled "Hello, there!" into the apartment; then, a little later, she'd turned the lights on in the guest room for ten seconds. He had held his breath, wondering if he was going to see her head dip down below the bedspread, but it hadn't happened. She turned the light back off, and for a few hours Henry could hear her moving through the apartment.

Then it was quiet for a while, and Henry wondered if she'd gone back to sleep, or maybe even left. Then voices—someone was at the door. Kate's distinctive, accented speech, and another woman's. An older woman with a raspy bark. He worried briefly that it was a detective, that Kate had called to have the place searched, but then the voices stopped, and shortly afterward, he heard the front door close. He was pretty sure Kate had left. Sure enough to slide out from under the bed.

He stood, knees popping, then swung his arms around to get the joints working properly. He rolled his head on his shoulders, then slipped from the room. He was fine. Kate was gone. He could sense it in the air of the apartment.

He washed his face in the guest bathroom, then changed his shirt, making sure to apply an extra amount of odor-free antiperspirant. If he was going to live here with Kate for a while, it was important that he smelled as neutral as possible. In the kitchen, on one of the top shelves, Henry found a half-filled box of Rice Chex. He filled a bowl, then covered them with the small amount of Kate's skim milk that he felt he could get away with stealing. The cereal was stale, but reminded him of Corbin. The last time he'd had Rice Chex had probably been their weekend together in New Essex, years and years ago. He hadn't had any since.

He washed out the bowl and returned it to its place, then wandered the apartment, forming a plan. He went to look at Kate's sketchbook, wanting to study the picture she'd drawn of him again, but it wasn't under the bed. She'd taken it with her.

He remembered the storage unit down in the basement. Even though he had his lockpicks, he went to the kitchen drawer where he knew Corbin kept spare keys. He grabbed the one with the label that said STORAGE and went down to the basement. He entered Corbin's unit, pulling the door shut behind him, and used his penlight to search the small space. There was box after box of comic books, neatly organized. There was a barbecue grill, and there were several framed posters, the type of posters someone in their early twenties might hang on a dorm-room wall or a first apartment. Car posters. Girlie posters. He wondered why Corbin had kept them. One of the posters was a large framed album cover: Ween's *Chocolate and Cheese*. A woman's torso, the bottoms of her meaty breasts hanging below a cutoff top. Henry felt for his pocketknife. He decided to do some surgery on the poster.

Kate was back for some of the afternoon, Henry hiding in the guest room, but she left again. He went to the bedroom, where her shucked jeans were on the floor, still a little warm. He sniffed at them, detecting almost nothing of her scent, just a faraway whiff of baby powder. Where had she gone that she needed to change out of her jeans? He looked in the bathroom; her toothbrush was recently used, still wet, and he put it in his mouth, sucked the minty taste out of the bristles.

Ever since cutting the poster, Henry, instead of feeling pleased, was agitated and anxious. He wanted something to happen, for Corbin to return or for the police to come, or even for Kate to discover him hiding in her closet, the pocketknife conveniently held between his fingers. He did his stretching exercises, then found a fresh bottle of vodka and cracked its seal, pouring half a tumbler's worth over crushed ice. Hours later, Kate was still gone, and Henry, his face numb and tingling from drinking the vodka, was pacing the apartment, hungry and annoyed.

He decided to leave, stashing his backpack in the guest room closet and heading out into the night through 101's back entrance. Before he left, he returned the storage key to the drawer, but pocketed one of the other unlabeled keys, assuming it was a spare for the apartment, plus a key that was labeled AM—Audrey Marshall's apartment, probably. He had the picks, but they took time, and it was always better to have actual keys. He walked across the Commons to a dark bar he liked called the Proposition, ate two orders of wings, and drank several Heinekens.

"You've been away," the bartender said.

He looked at her, and it took him a moment to realize they'd talked before, but then it all came back. Samantha. Bay State College undergrad. She had to take a semester off from school because her grandmother had been paying her tuition but now her grandmother was in an expensive nursing home, and she hadn't squared away her financial aid package yet. Henry also remembered the things he knew about Samantha that she hadn't told him. The bulimia she'd been fighting on and off for years, evident by the puffiness of her face and the loss of enamel on her teeth. The way she'd sleep with any guy who was halfway nice to her, and plenty who weren't. How bad she felt about herself most of the time.

"Not away, just trying to eat better," Henry said.

"I hear you," Samantha said, and ended the conversation. Henry wondered if she sensed he didn't want to talk, and found himself annoyed that she probably had.

He hated being read by anyone, even by stupid female bartenders. He cracked a chicken bone between his teeth and sucked at the marrow.

Henry returned to Bury Street, studied Corbin's windows from the sidewalk, and decided that Kate wasn't back. Or if she was back, she'd gone straight to sleep. He'd risk it, either way. He entered the basement, which was empty except for the cat that was always around. "Here, kitty, kitty," he said, pushing his fingers underneath its chin. The words sounded a little slurred in his own ears, and he wondered if he'd had too much to drink, if maybe he should just head home to the South End and sleep it off. He rubbed the cat's twig-like jawbone. It didn't purr, and when he pulled his hand away, it latched onto his forearm with both paws, its claws sinking into his flesh. Henry, shocked, pulled back, feeling his skin tear, and the cat hissed viciously, then turned and bolted before he had a chance to stamp it to death. He looked at the wound, the skin already beginning to puff up and little pinpricks of blood appearing, like condensation on a glass. He sucked at the wound, tasting his own salty blood. It was beginning to itch.

Instead of going up to Corbin's apartment, Henry went up the stairs that led to Audrey Marshall's place. He hadn't been there since the night he'd killed her. He picked the lock of the door and entered. The curtains of the apartment were open and the night was light enough that he could maneuver through the apartment. There were marks on the floor from the crime scene investigators, taped areas on the kitchen tile where he'd left Audrey's body. Had they noticed how her hand had been positioned, pointing with an index finger toward Corbin's apartment? Henry smiled at the memory. Arranging Audrey had been the most fun he'd had in years, the most fun he'd had since Corbin and he had killed Claire in the cemetery. After Audrey was dead, and he was free to arrange her as he wanted to, he'd contemplated trying to actually cut her in half, find a way to saw through her spine, but decided against it. Still, the image of it, the thought of her actually in two pieces—a perfect half of her for each of them—almost made him giddy. One day he could do it, but he didn't think he could do it alone.

He wandered the apartment. In the bedroom, some of Audrey's things—clothes, books—had been boxed up and left. Maybe the family had begun the process, then got overwhelmed and quit. Henry wondered what would happen if he died. Would his parents come to reclaim his things? Of course they wouldn't. They were never going to leave Stark, except maybe if Mary reared her ugly head, but not for him. They were a little scared of him, he knew that. He could hear it in their voices on the few occasions when he called home, that slight vocal hitch in the "Hello, Henry" after they'd picked up the phone, expecting nothing more than a call from their church deacon to let them know that the bake sale was going to be understaffed this year, and could they help.

In the living room, Henry stared down at the empty courtyard, then across into the opposite apartment. There was movement, a light on in an alcove kitchen. Henry watched. It was a man and a woman, the man crossing the dimly lit living room toward a woman with dark blond hair in the kitchen. Henry stared, and began to think that it was Kate that he was looking at, although he couldn't be sure. The man was in the kitchen again, a tall man with messy black hair who could have been the man that Henry had bumped into on the street, the man Kate had drawn in her sketchbook. That would make sense. Somehow they had met, and now Kate was fucking this guy. When had she got here? Three days ago? She'd wasted no time.

He watched for about twenty minutes. He couldn't see all the way into the kitchen, but it looked like they were eating around an island. The man came into the living room again, crouched in a corner—getting more alcohol, maybe—then returned to the kitchen. The light caught his profile, the blade of his nose. Jewish, Henry thought. He started to get bored, and the boredom made him a little angry. He wanted Kate back in their apartment, curled up and asleep in her nest of blankets on the couch. He wanted to watch her twitching face, and listen to her breathe, and know that somehow, some part of her, the animal part, would know she was being watched. They always do.

But at least now he had the place to himself for the night. He returned to Corbin's apartment, going straight to

Kate's bedroom to look for the sketchbook. It was under the bed again, and he opened it to that first picture, confirming that it was the same man across the courtyard. He took his index finger and pressed hard against both of the eyes in the picture, trying not to overly smudge them. It felt good, and he liked the effect. The eyes looked different, but subtly different, just enough to make Kate wonder.

He used the bathroom, then went to his bedroom. He stared out the window, toward the river. The night sky was clear, a scattering of stars visible, a rarity for the city. He lay down on top of the bed, on top of the covers, folding his hands across his stomach, and let himself sink into a river of sleep.

Kate returned in the early morning. Henry thought of hiding beneath the bed, but decided not to bother. It was easier to listen from where he was. She answered a phone call midmorning, and he heard her asking whoever was on the other end if they had a warrant. If the police were coming then it was time to leave. It got quiet again for a while, and he hoped she was either napping or had left. He put his shoes on, gathered his backpack, and decided to go. He could come back that night and see Kate again. Or maybe he could come back and visit as Jack Ludovico, the bereft friend, see if he could get her to sleep with him. He thought it would be pretty easy.

He moved silently across the apartment, rubbing his arm where the cat had scratched him, but when he got to the kitchen he saw that the door to the basement was open. She must have gone down there, herself. He made a sudden decision to leave out the front of the building. It would be safe enough, especially since Kate was in the basement. He exited through the front door and walked down the hallway, then heard footsteps coming up the stairwell, plus the identifiable squawk of a police radio. His mind furiously considered his options. Walk casually past the police. Reenter Kate's apartment. Then he remembered the key that said AM on it and dug it from his pocket. He opened Audrey's door, ducked under the police tape, and was inside, breathing rapidly. He listened to the police lumbering down the hall. A woman's voice was giving instructions—he heard her say that they were looking for a thin knife. A man's voice came back: "Like a filleting knife?" He didn't hear the woman respond. They were knocking on Kate's door. *Yes, like a filleting knife,* Henry said to himself. He counted to thirty, then let himself out of Audrey's apartment and took the stairs down to the lobby, and he was outside in the bright, windy day. He filled his lungs, almost laughed out loud at how close he'd come to being caught by the police. Still, what would have happened? He'd have told them the same story that he'd told Kate. He used to date Audrey Marshall and had been coming to her apartment in order to grieve. Walking down Bury Street toward the park, he imagined the conversation with the police officers in his mind, how he'd make them believe he was some loser who'd lost the girl he loved, while Corbin was the creep next door.

The fantasy conversation was so enjoyable that he almost didn't notice that he was being followed. But he did notice. He could feel it, the way you could feel warmth on your skin when your eyes were closed and know that the sun had come out from behind a cloud. He took a sudden left turn onto another residential street. There was a tree half a block down the brick sidewalk. He briskly walked, then leaned against its trunk where he wouldn't be seen by someone coming from Bury Street.

Fifteen seconds later he heard the hurried footsteps coming his way, then watched as Kate's boyfriend—Alan was the name—raced past like a man who'd lost his dog.

"Are you looking for me?" Henry asked, and the man jerked around, like a fish that's been hooked.

Chapter 34

Henry spent a very pleasant afternoon with Alan Cherney. He remembered his surname from Kate's drawing. They went together to a small neighborhood bar about three blocks from Bury Street. Henry did the grieving friend act and told Alan all about his theories that Corbin was a serial killer who liked to mutilate his victims.

He told Alan about Rachael Chess, found murdered on a beach in New Essex, the same place Corbin's mother lived. Alan was riveted, but slightly uncomfortable. Henry talked him into having a couple of beers, and that began to loosen him up. Color came back to his face. As they talked, Henry tried to get a read on this Alan character. He was about the same age as he was, successful enough, or rich enough, to live where he did on Beacon Hill. He was that typical Jewish intellectual who thought he was smarter than everyone in the room, but acted neurotic so no one would know it. He'd known the type well at Aurelius. But there was something else that he couldn't read, like a blurry line of text in an otherwise simple book. Alan cared too much about Audrey, for one thing, or maybe he cared for Kate. Either way, he cared about what Henry had to say, was hanging on every word. So

Henry led him directly to Corbin, in the same way he'd led Kate to Corbin. He painted him as a psychopathic killer, and he painted himself as the unhinged boyfriend who was out for revenge.

Alan drank several beers, becoming more and more animated. Henry matched him, not just beer for beer, but also in his exuberance. They were like two college freshmen arguing philosophy in a dorm room. Alan kept sliding forward in the booth, one knee vibrating like a tuning fork. He *feels* too much, Henry thought, fascinated. And while they talked on, Henry formed an organized fantasy in his mind. He pictured Alan and himself killing a woman together, maybe Kate, maybe someone neither of them had met yet. And they were taking their time in killing her and arranging her. And they were splitting her down the middle. And no one ever would know why except the two of them. Corbin would know, though. Corbin would know exactly what was happening. Then the fantasy passed, and Henry felt a strange, unfamiliar sense of shame, as though those thoughts constituted not infidelity, exactly, but something like desperation. The need to take a singular experience and try and replay it with someone else.

"You okay?" Alan said.

"I am. Sorry," Henry replied. "I get these moments when everything seems normal, the world exactly as it should be, then I realize that she's not in it anymore. Audrey's dead. And the world hasn't stopped with her."

Alan's lips were pursed. He nodded his head in understanding. Henry straightened up, felt as though he was seeing Alan for the first time properly. He wasn't another playmate. He was a patsy. The perfect patsy. "Sorry, man," Henry said. "I keep talking about myself, and Audrey. What about you? You must have a girlfriend."

Alan hesitated. Henry wondered if he was about to mention what he had done with Kate the night before. Instead, he said, "Nothing much to tell. I had a girlfriend. We lived together, and she moved out. But you don't need to hear about that."

"No, please. I want to hear about it. I want to just stop thinking about my situation for a moment. Please, tell me."

Alan spoke while Henry thought. *Maybe this guy really should be the patsy.* All along, Henry had thought that he wanted Corbin arrested for the crime of murdering Audrey Marshall. Maybe not arrested, but suspected. It was all part of the game they were playing. But maybe he didn't really want Corbin arrested. And it wasn't just because Corbin would try and finger him for his part in the crimes. He could handle that. It wouldn't be easy to track down Henry Wood these days. Not impossible, but not easy, not since he'd legally changed his name. It would sound as though Corbin were making up a bogeyman. But, no, Corbin in prison was not really what Henry wanted. It was more fun to play with something when it wasn't in a cage.

Henry formed a plan, then turned his attention back to Alan, who was sputtering along about someone named Quinn. Their eyes met, and Alan suddenly stopped talking, as though embarrassed. He excused himself to go to the bathroom.

Henry moved fast. The bar was empty except for two men, both in button-down shirts, sitting at the bar and watching sports highlights on the television. He removed the knife, still in its plastic bag, from his backpack. It had been reckless to hold on to the murder weapon for so long, but now it was going to come in handy. He pulled it from the plastic bag, pinching the blade between the sides of his fingers so as not to leave prints. Alan had brought a leather bag with him, about the size of a briefcase. Henry opened it. Inside was a computer tablet, a book—*The Wind-Up Bird Chronicle*—and a thick wad of unopened envelopes, mail he hadn't dealt with yet. Henry dug toward the bottom of the bag. A small, black umbrella nestled there, and Henry slid the knife underneath it, returning the bag back to the way it had been, just as Alan came back into the bar. "I should go," he was saying.

"Sure. I understand," Henry said. They paid the bill at the bar, each contributing cash, then walked out together, Alan slinging his bag over his shoulder.

*

Henry made the call to the Boston Police Department Tips Line from a pay phone near the Tufts Medical Center.

He wore gloves to touch the phone, just in case.

"I know who killed Audrey Marshall," he said to the man who answered the phone.

"Can I get your name, please, sir?"

"I'd rather not say. I'm calling from a pay phone because I'm scared." Henry let his voice, pitched a little higher than usual, noticeably tremble.

"Can I ask you what you're scared of?"

"I'm scared of Alan Cherney. He lives in the same building that Audrey Marshall lived in, and I'm pretty sure he killed her."

"Can you tell me his apartment number?"

"I can't. I don't know it. But he lives right across from where she lived. It's not hard to find out. All you need—"

"Okay, of course. We'll look it up. It will be easy to find out. Can you tell me why you think Alan Cherney was involved in Audrey Marshall's murder?"

"Because he has the knife that killed her. It's in his bag."

Henry hung up and, keeping his head down, walked away from the phone. He hadn't seen any surveillance cameras around, but he couldn't be sure.

Chapter 35

When he got back to his apartment, Henry put on New Order's *Brotherhood* as loud as he thought he could without getting a complaint. He'd known, as soon as he hung up the phone, that he'd made the right decision. It was time to take some of the heat off Corbin. Even if Alan wasn't convicted, Henry had muddied the waters. It was going to be fun to follow it from afar. His work was done, for now.

He took a long, stinging shower, then dressed, replayed the album, and lay down on his made-up bed. He was going to miss Kate. When he'd left the apartment that morning he'd only thought of it as a temporary absence. Still, it was best that he stayed away. He closed his eyes, flexing one foot in time to the music. He floated on his river, cool and refreshing, and fell asleep while he was still on the surface, bobbing along, contented, maybe even happy.

He woke in a dark apartment, cold and shivering. He'd slept too long, and when he sat up the air felt liquid and he nearly lay back down again. He was plagued with doubts. Had he gone too far with the call to the police? Alan Cherney didn't know his real name—he'd just said

"Jack," hadn't he?—but he could describe him. And so could Kate. She could draw him, as he knew. Henry decided that his involvement with Kate and Corbin and Alan was now done. He'd set his traps, and it was time to walk away. He'd been extraordinarily lucky so far—the near miss with the police this morning—and for the next few weeks he wouldn't leave his apartment except to go to his office in Newtonville.

He made himself a cheese sandwich and drank a glass of milk, then went to unpack his backpack. He carefully laid out everything he'd brought to Kate's house. His extra shirts, the gloves, his outdoor hat, his antiperspirant, his granola bars, the empty bottle in case he ever needed to empty his bladder while hiding, his antislip socks with the rubber grips, his night vision goggles with the head strap, and his sheathed filleting knife, brand new. It was all accounted for except for the Lycra ski mask he slept in so as not to leave hairs behind. He searched the pockets of his backpack, then the pockets of his pants and his jacket. It was nowhere. He remembered pulling it on the night before when he'd been sleeping under the guest room bed. It had gotten warm in the night and he'd pushed it up to his hairline. That was his last memory of the ski mask. It must have slipped off his head in the night, and was probably still under the bed. Where else could it be?

He headed back out into the night.

Before returning to Kate's apartment to look for his ski

mask, Henry visited Audrey Marshall's place one more time. He knew it was his last chance.

He stood in the dark kitchen, breathing the air, remembering . . .

Not the work of cutting her—no, that had been hard—but the way she had looked when she was done, cut open, an arm outstretched to point toward Corbin's apartment. There was so much spilled blood on the floor that the floor simply looked red, a shining pedestal for a girl who got involved with the wrong man. Henry closed his eyes and stood absolutely still for a moment, savoring the moment. With his eyes closed, he felt invisible, the way a child thinks they're invisible because they can't see anything themselves. Except that children were wrong, and Henry was right. He was invisible. Almost, anyway. No one could see him but Corbin. And Corbin could do nothing about it.

He went back down the stairs to the basement corridor, then up toward Corbin's apartment. As he neared the top, he felt a tiny ripple in the air, and thought he heard the click of a door closing. He paused and listened for a while. Nothing. Then he climbed the remaining stairs and paused outside the door that led into the apartment. He listened for a long time. Just as he felt confident enough to open the door, there was the sound of movement, the pad of steps. Henry sat on the top step and waited. He could be patient. All he needed to do was enter the apartment, go to the guest room for his ski mask, and then leave.

He heard a flush, the sound of water moving through the building's walls. He thought he heard steps again, then it was quiet. He waited for what felt like twenty minutes before folding his hand around the doorknob and turning it. The door was unlocked. He was pleased, but wary. It was the first time he'd found it that way. Had Kate simply forgotten? He swung the door open and stepped into the moonlit kitchen. The apartment was quiet. He shut the door behind him and walked toward the living room, turning into the hallway that led to the guest room. Muffled sounds plus a flickering light at the end of the hall told him the television was on, which meant Kate was probably asleep on the couch in front of it. Henry ducked into the bedroom, lay down on the plush carpet next to the bed, and felt with his outstretched fingers along the spongy fibers for his lost ski mask. Shifting himself farther under the bed, he found the bunched-up hat. Relief swept over him. Once he was standing, he shoved it into his jacket pocket. He was about to leave the bedroom when he sensed movement in the hallway. Kate must have gotten up. But, no, it was coming the other way. Henry stepped back, watching shadows move along the doorframe. Whoever it was entered the room with the television. Henry, feeling trapped in the bedroom, moved rapidly the other way down the hallway toward the living room, where he stopped and turned. He felt better in the cavernous dark. There was a large armoire near the front door and he stood next to it, waiting in its shadow.

Who else was in here? He guessed it was Alan, coming over for a repeat of the night before. Still, he waited to find out what would happen, listening intently, but all he could hear was the muffled sound of the television.

And then Corbin appeared, unmistakable, even with short hair. He was in the hallway, coming forward, and something dropped down the center of Henry, like a rock sinking through water. It was fear, but it was also excitement.

"You came," Henry said to Corbin. It was something he'd said to him a hundred times in fantasies, wanting Corbin to know that he had summoned him, that he was the one pulling on his strings. It was all worth it, Henry thought, no matter what happens next.

"What are you doing here, Henry?" Corbin asked, sounding like a stern teacher disciplining a student.

Henry began to speak, to explain, when he realized that Corbin had a knife and was coming toward him. A surge of adrenalized joy went through Henry as he jumped back and avoided Corbin's lunge. Then he leapt, riding Corbin's body down to the wooden floor, pinning him and wrestling for the knife. He nearly had it when it sliced across the palm of his hand, and he instinctively jerked backward. Corbin came after him again, nearly stabbing him in the face, but the knife stuck in the floor, and Henry was able to get to it with his good hand, leaping onto Corbin, slicing with the knife at his throat, the skin parting the way skin does. So easily. Corbin fell to the floor. In the dim light the blood that came from his neck was an inky black.

Henry stood, stumbling backward. His hand thrummed, and he looked at it. Blood was oozing its way down into his sleeve, and his thumb hung loose, the tendon severed. He quickly looked around the room for something to stanch the bleeding, then remembered the ski mask in his pocket. He set the knife down, pulled the hat out with his good hand, and crouched down to dress his hand. He gingerly slid his dangling thumb through an opening in the slick material, then wrapped his hand, tucking the excess material so that it held. It would have to do for now. Corbin was still making sounds, soft, bubbling gurgles, and Henry turned his attention to him.

They were no longer alone. Kate had entered the living room and was now crouched over Corbin's crumpled body. She hadn't noticed Henry. He took the knife from the floor and stood. He watched for a moment, the world slowing down into this one frozen tableau. Corbin dying, and an angel in white already at his side.

Then Corbin's gaze shifted, and for a brief moment, his eyes made contact with Henry's, the two of them looking directly at one another after so many years. Corbin was gesturing with his blood-slicked hand, moving a finger, and trying to say something to Kate. It caused her to turn, and that was when Henry leapt, landing on her back. He heard the air leave her lungs, her head thunk as it hit the floor. He pushed the knife into her back, encountering a shoulder blade, pulled it out again, and stuck the entire blade into the softness high up next to her spine. Henry rolled off her and into a sitting position. Corbin's hand still clutched at his throat. Henry moved closer, looked at his eyes, open but unfocused now, blood bubbling from his mouth.

There was a loud knock at the door, followed by a woman's voice: "POLICE. OPEN UP."

Henry, in the seconds he had, began to calculate. Should he run for the basement? Then he watched, in amazement, as Kate, knife still protruding, stood up and wobbled toward the front door, opening it up as though a cocktail party guest had arrived. Henry pulled his small pocketknife from his jacket pocket, flicked out the blade, then took Corbin by the shoulders and yanked him toward him to act as a shield. The policewoman entered, gun drawn. Henry watched her eyes scan the scene, from Kate to Corbin and then to Henry, who was now dragging Corbin's body back onto his, holding the pocketknife to Corbin's damaged neck, the smell of blood thick in the air.

She took a step into the room, gun pointed at Henry. "Let him go, and let me see your hands." She took her left hand off her gun and fumbled for the radio at her belt.

Henry paused, holding on to the knife. He was grateful, in a way, that it had come to this.

Chapter 36

Detective Roberta James took careful aim, exhaled, and fired her Glock at a living target for the first time in her life. The .40-caliber bullet hit the smiling man in the upper lip, and his smiled collapsed inward as he fell backward and hit the floor. The knife that he'd been pushing into the neck of the bleeding man clattered to the floor.

While radioing in for immediate backup, she dropped to a knee and took a look at the man with the neck wound. The blood was coming fast, although it wasn't spurting. She turned to Kate and calmly asked for clean towels.

"Is he dead?" Kate asked. Her voice sounded too casual, as though she wasn't comprehending what was happening.

"I don't know. I need to get some towels and stop this bleeding." She stood, and that was when she noticed the handle of the knife that was jutting at a ninety-degree angle from the top of Kate's back, just behind a shoulder. "I'll get them, Kate. You just stay there. Where are they?"

"There's a bathroom right down there," Kate said. She swiveled, made a funny expression, and asked: "Is there something on my back?" She reached back with a hand and Detective James stopped her, gripping her forearms and bringing them down to her side. Kate's eyes were bright. The detective knew she was in shock. "I need you to have a seat, right here, and not touch your back. The ambulance is on the way."

She left Kate where she was and moved as fast as she could, located a bathroom, and pulled a towel from a rack. Returning, she was relieved to see that Kate had stayed where she was, her hands primly on her knees. "It's Corbin," she said to the passing detective.

"Who is?" Detective James asked while pressing the towel against the blood flow from the neck.

"He is. That's my cousin, Corbin Dell. He was trying to save me." Her voice was far too calm, the voice of someone speaking in their sleep.

James held the towel in place as it turned dark and damp from the blood. At least the knife hadn't severed the carotid artery, or he'd be dead already. Still, he had lost a lot of blood. She looked at his face; it did look like the pictures she'd seen of Corbin. His eyes were glassy, and she said, "Corbin, hang in there."

She thought she saw some comprehension in his eyes.

"Is he dead?" Kate asked.

"No, he's still alive. The ambulance will be here any moment. Tell me what happened."

"Corbin woke me up and made me hide in a closet. He was trying to save me. I should have stayed in the closet."

James heard a distant siren and silently prayed that it was the ambulance coming for them. She pressed two fingers underneath Corbin's chin. If there was a pulse, it was very, very faint.

"You saved her, Corbin," she said, in case he was listening.

"Hi, Sanders," Kate was saying, and James spun her head. A white cat went up to Kate and rubbed against her leg. Kate stroked its back, leaving a streak of blood on its pristine white fur. The siren got louder.

*

Six hours earlier, Detective James had entered her condo in Watertown, a little bit relieved that the FBI was officially taking over the Audrey Marshall homicide. She calculated that she'd slept a total of maybe twelve hours since the body had been discovered on Saturday. It was now Tuesday evening. She poured herself a Famous Grouse on the rocks and changed into the tank top she liked to sleep in and the Celtics pajama shorts she'd gotten for Christmas from her parents. She liked them, not so much because they were emblazoned with the Celtics logo, but because they were comfortable, and even in the coldest stretch of a Boston winter, she hated to sleep in full-length pajama bottoms. She lay down on her sofa and held the lowball glass on her stomach. The pajama bottoms weren't the only Celtics-related item she'd received this past Christmas. She'd gotten a mug, as well, from her niece who always got her a gift, and a pink long-sleeved T-shirt from her sister with the Celtics logo on it.

It was clear what she was becoming—that relative who was only associated with one thing. *She's a Celtics fan, so get her something Celtics if you can't think of anything else.* She was like that old uncle who liked golf, so all he got was golf stuff. And the message from her sister was also very clear; the fitted pink shirt was suggesting that it wasn't too late to snag a man.

She sat up a little and took a sip of her scotch. Why was she thinking about this stuff? *Because I'm exhausted,* she told herself.

She closed her eyes. The image of Audrey Marshall on the kitchen floor, butchered like a piece of meat, swam immediately into her mind, as it had been doing, regularly and without mercy, for the past three days. She sat up on the sofa, had another sip of her drink, and stretched her back out, listening with satisfaction to the small popping sounds coming from her spine.

Her cell phone rang, and she knew instinctively that it was her captain before she even saw his name on the screen.

"Thought you'd like to know that we got an anonymous call right after you left. It came from a pay phone in the South End, from a man who claimed to be one of Audrey Marshall's friends, but he wouldn't give us a name. He said that Alan Cherney is the killer, and that Alan has a bloody knife in his possession."

"Jesus. How did he know that?"

"He didn't say."

"Probably knew because he planted it on him."

Mark laughed, and as usual, laughing made him cough. "Thought you'd like to know, even though I know you were going home to get some sleep."

"Strike that off the agenda. Tan's been told?" Abigail Tan was the FBI agent now assigned as lead in the case.

"Yes. She's off to get a search warrant."

"What did she think?" James asked.

"She didn't tell me, but she wanted me to tell you. What do *you* think?"

"It's our Jack, I'm sure of it. He's setting up Alan Cherney, I guess. I don't know why, exactly."

"Probably what Tan thinks, too."

"But let's execute the warrant, and if we find a knife, arrest Cherney. We can find out more about Jack, at least, and get something, anything—"

"Oh, gotta run, Roberta. I'll call you right back."

He'd rung off. James took a sip of her scotch but it was gone, and the ice tapped against her teeth. She paced the room, thinking.

Jack was getting bold, which meant he was probably about to screw up. Or that's what she was hoping for, anyway. He was now their principal suspect, despite the fact that Corbin Dell had gone missing from his borrowed apartment in London. Corbin was involved somehow, but James did not believe he had killed Audrey Marshall. The timeline made it a very remote possibility. She believed the killer was the man who was calling himself Jack

Ludovico, and she believed that he'd killed at least two women before, one on the North Shore of Massachusetts named Rachael Chess, and one in Connecticut named Linda Alcheri nearly fourteen years earlier. Both women, like Audrey Marshall, had been cut down the middle after they'd been killed. Rachael Chess had been found on a beach in New Essex, not far from where Corbin Dell's mother had a house. James had studied the file, and Corbin's name had come up as someone who knew the deceased, but he'd been eliminated from the inquiry since he'd been out of the country when the murder had been committed. There was no connection that James could find between Linda Alcheri, the dead girl from Connect-icut, and Corbin Dell. She'd been found dead at an old Boy Scout camp outside of the city. Cause of death had been a blow to the head from a rock, but before she'd been buried she'd been cut down the face, and her clothes and some of the skin on her torso was cut away. Why had no one made a connection with the second murder in New Essex? Cause of death had been different, but the postmortem wounds were the same, or at least they were extremely similar. Now that there'd been a third murder—another woman with the exact same wounds—the FBI had arrived. James heard that some of the police were now calling the murderer the Failed Magician. *He tries to cut his women in half.*

Abigail Tan, despite her age (she didn't look much older than twenty-five), seemed competent. Earlier that day, James told her what she'd found in the Alcheri files. "Two of Linda's friends mentioned in interviews that Linda had briefly been seeing someone named Hank. They both remembered a first name, but not a second. They never found this Hank."

"And you think this Hank is . . . ?"

"I think the person who called himself Hank back then might be calling himself Jack Ludovico now."

"What makes you think he's not just who he says he is, a friend trying to get some answers?"

"Then why didn't he come to us? And why doesn't Audrey Marshall mention him in her diary?" What James didn't say was that she just somehow knew. Both murders involved a shadowy figure who never came forward, and she knew that that person, probably not named Hank or Jack, was the same person.

"Okay, then, if he's the killer, then why is he hanging around? Why did he go and talk with Kate Priddy?"

"I think he's trying to pin this murder on Corbin Dell. Audrey Marshall's arm was bent back over her head, pointing toward Dell's apartment. The coroner said her arm was placed in that position after death. He wants us to think it's Corbin, so that's why he's hanging around. Maybe killing Rachael Chess was his first attempt at framing him, and it didn't work."

"Should we publish the sketch that Kate Priddy did?"

James had thought of that. "Not yet. I don't think he lives locally, and if the sketch shows up on the front page, he'll leave town. He's being reckless right now, returning to the scene of the crime to talk with a neighbor. Let's wait him out and see if he pops up again."

And now he had, trying to frame Alan Cherney for some inexplicable reason.

James picked her phone back up to call the captain, but before she could call him, the phone was vibrating in her hand. Abigail.

"Did you get a warrant?" James asked.

"Not yet, but I talked with Dietrichson. He agreed to stay late."

"Want company?"

"That's why I'm calling."

They met at the courthouse, and got Judge Albert Dietrichson's fairly reluctant signature on the search warrant for Alan Cherney's apartment at 101 Bury Street. James had to convince him that the anonymous call that had been recorded that afternoon was not the sole reason for the search warrant.

"Did you get a statement from Alan Cherney after the body was discovered?" the judge asked, as he was packing his briefcase to go home for the day.

"We did. I didn't take it, myself, but Officer Karen Gibson did. She said he reported that he didn't personally know Audrey Marshall, but that he knew her from sight. She reported that he was acting strange."

The judge raised one eyebrow and looked at James. "Did she specify what she meant by strange?"

"She reported that he seemed visibly shaken by the death in his apartment building. She didn't know whether it was because of the proximity of the crime, or because he knew the victim more intimately than he was indicating. And one more thing, Kate Priddy, the cousin who is currently occupying Corbin Dell's apartment, has gotten to know Alan Cherney, and she indicated to us that he used to watch Audrey Marshall through her window."

"From where? The street?"

"No. From his own apartment. Their windows face one another above the courtyard of the building. It's shaped like a U."

"Got it," the judge said. His expression didn't change as he signed the warrant.

An hour later, James met up with Abigail Tan at 101 Bury Street, and together, along with Mike Gaetano and Andre Damour from the department, entered Alan Cherney's apartment and served the warrant. He had been sleeping, and he was extremely drunk, blurry eyed and slurring his speech. He'd gone to his bathroom to be sick; they'd located the leather courier bag that the anonymous caller had identified, and found and bagged the knife. Abigail made the arrest.

Back at the station, James got Alan, who had declined the offer of legal representation, a cup of coffee and brought him to an interrogation room. He was alternating between docility and panic. "I didn't kill Audrey

Marshall," he said, as she walked him into the room. "You know that, right?"

"Agent Tan's going to be questioning you in just a few minutes, and you can tell everything to her."

Before leaving the room, leaving Alan alone to stew for a few minutes, he blurted out, almost near tears, "It wasn't hives." It was something he'd said earlier, when she'd first cuffed him.

James paused. She knew she should leave him alone, let him answer questions once the official interrogation began, but she turned back toward him anyway. "You need to go and check on Kate Priddy," he said. "He said he had hives on his arm, but it wasn't. It was Sanders who scratched him, but Sanders only scratches anyone when he's in the basement. He's a different Sanders down there, and that's where Jack got scratched. He's coming and going through the basement. I think he's after Kate. I have a bad feeling. It's a really bad feeling."

"Sanders?" James asked.

"He's the cat that's always around. He's friendly, but if you try and pet him when he's in the basement, he scratches you. Jack is coming through the basement. That's how he's getting in."

James said, "Someone'll be right here, Alan, okay?"

An hour later, James watched the beginning of the interrogation, watched as Alan, who seemed to be sobering up, said the exact same thing about the cat to Abigail Tan. Hearing the words again made James's scalp tingle.

She left the station and drove back to 101 Bury Street. She sat in her car for a moment, staring up at the blank windows of the apartment building. It wouldn't hurt to just check on the apartment. She'd knock gently on the door. She'd listen, and if she heard nothing, then she'd return to her own apartment.

"Hey there, Sanibel," she said to the doorman, no longer needing to show him her badge. "Just checking in on Kate Priddy in 3D. She's expecting me."

She'd only just reached the door when she heard scuffling sounds from inside, then what sounded like a bag of sand being dropped onto a concrete floor. She unholstered her gun and banged on the door. She should have gotten backup, but it was too late now.

Chapter 37

The man Detective Roberta James had shot in the face was pronounced dead at the scene by the EMTs.

Kate Priddy was taken by ambulance to Mass General Hospital, where on-call surgeons removed the five-inch knife that was buried high up in her back. Somehow, the blade had missed her spinal cord, plus all major arteries. There was bone damage, and she had a concussion, but the doctors and nurses who were present at the surgery would have a story to tell for many years about the girl who survived a knife wound that should have been fatal.

Corbin Dell was strapped to a gurney and taken to a separate ambulance. The EMTs managed to stop the bleeding, but he'd already lost too much blood. He was pronounced dead en route to Mass General.

Alan Cherney, his interrogation interrupted when Agent Tan was told what was happening at Bury Street, sat for several hours in the interrogation room, eventually putting his head down on the table and going to sleep. His interrogation was completed early the next morning, then all charges were dropped and he was released.

*

The first face Kate Priddy saw upon opening her eyes at midday on Wednesday was Detective James's.

"I'm alive," Kate said.

"You are."

James put her hand on Kate's shoulder and watched the young woman close her eyes and go back to sleep.

*

When Kate woke again, a nurse was checking her vitals. "Hi, there," Vicky Wilson said, when she saw Kate's half-opened eyes. Vicky was secretly thrilled to be in charge of the celebrity patient, but tried to conceal it as she asked: "How are we doing this afternoon?"

"Thirsty."

"I can probably get you some ice chips, sweetheart. What else can I get for you?"

"The detective." Kate's voice was a faint croak.

"A detective?"

"No. Detective James. Roberta." Kate had to swallow after saying the words. Her throat ached.

"When I'm done here, sweetheart, I'll go find Detective James, okay?"

Kate closed her eyes again.

When she opened them, Roberta James was there, and Kate said: "Tell me everything."

James smiled. "I'll tell you what we know, okay?"

"Is Corbin dead?"

"Yes, Corbin Dell is dead."

"What about Jack Ludovico?"

James paused, enough so that Kate had one awful moment where she thought he'd somehow gotten away. "The man you knew as Jack Ludovico is dead as well. He went by a lot of names, and we're still trying to figure out what the real one is. Does the name Henry Wood mean anything to you?"

Kate shook her head, causing small detonations of pain in her neck and shoulder. She must have grimaced, because Detective James said, "We'll talk more about this later. You'll be glad to know your parents are en route from England."

"That's nice."

"And there's a man, Alan Cherney, who very much wants to see you. He's here, now, in the hospital."

"Not right now, okay," Kate said, closing her eyes.

"Of course. I'll let you sleep."

James was standing up when Kate opened her eyes again and asked, "How did Corbin Dell get back into America? I thought you said—"

"That we were monitoring his passport. We were. He used someone else's, a Dutch passport."

"Why?"

"We don't know everything yet, Kate. We think that the man you knew as Jack Ludovico, who also went by Henry Wood, had been targeting Corbin Dell, maybe trying to set him up, frame him for a murder."

"So Corbin's not a killer?"

"There's a lot for us to unravel, Kate. We just don't know the whole situation."

"They were both in the apartment. How did . . . ?"

"How did they get in? Corbin had a key, and we found lockpicks on Jack. We think he was coming in and out of Bury Street through a back entrance that led to the basement."

"How long had he been coming into the apartment?" Kate's mouth was getting drier the more she talked.

"We don't know that, but there's evidence—forensic evidence—that he'd been all over the apartment. I'm going to tell you everything as we learn it, Kate, but right now, I think you need some more rest."

"Okay," Kate said, and let her lids close. There was pain in her upper back and at the base of her skull, and that pain was spreading and joining, and becoming stronger. She heard the detective's chair scrape along the linoleum floor, then she knew she was alone. She tried to open her eyes, found she couldn't, and was asleep again.

*

James returned to the waiting area where Alan Cherney sat, an unread book on his lap, a hopeful expression on his face.

"She's not ready to see you yet," she said to him.

"Okay," he said. "I'll wait a little longer."

"She didn't recoil in horror when I mentioned your name," James said, wanting to reassure him for some reason. She supposed she liked him, and not just because he had probably saved Kate Priddy's life by convincing James to return to Bury Street. He'd been right about the scratch on Henry's arm; the coroner said it had come from a cat.

Alan smiled. "That's something."

James moved out of earshot of Alan and called in to the station. The Bureau had descended in force, Abigail Tan replaced by a senior agent named Colin Unger, who looked like a model from a military recruitment catalog. James got through to her captain and reported on Kate's condition.

"I'll let them know she's awake and ready to be questioned."

"Let them know in a little while. She's going to be overwhelmed."

"You think she knows anything?"

"About what? Henry Wood? No, nothing. She knows what happened the night she was nearly killed, but that's it. She told us all about it while she still had a knife stuck in her back. Oh, she wanted to know if Corbin was innocent."

"What did you tell her?"

"Told her we'd talk later. She's still pretty fragile."

After hanging up with her captain, she thought of the Polaroid picture they'd found in the apartment that belonged to Henry Wood. It was of Corbin Dell, standing in the rain, above an open grave that contained the body of what looked to be a brunette woman. There was an old gravestone in one corner of the picture, suggesting that he was in a cemetery. Corbin, to James's eye, looked about eighteen years old. It was hard to read the expression on his face; his eyes were maybe a little shocked, but he looked relaxed, his mouth parted slightly. It was that image that had been haunting James for the past thirty-six hours, even more than what she'd seen in Kate's apartment, the bloodbath that was stopped when James took a man's life with a single bullet. It hadn't saved Corbin Dell, but her being there had probably saved Kate Priddy.

It was something.

Four hours later, Agents Unger and Tan arrived at the hospital to question Kate.

"You want me in there, as well?" James asked.

"We do," Unger said. He had a slight southern accent. North Carolina was James's guess.

"Okay. Happy to. We can't wake her, but we can wait till she wakes up on her own."

They didn't have to wait too long. In half an hour a nurse came to tell them that Kate had woken and that she'd asked for Detective James again. In that half an hour, Abigail Tan filled James in on what they'd learned. Corbin Dell and Henry Wood had studied at the same program in London fifteen years earlier. Not only that, but there was an unsolved homicide from the time, an English student at the same business school they'd both attended by the name of Claire Brennan. She'd gone missing at the time when Corbin and Henry had both been in London, and her body had eventually been found, buried in an old graveyard in North London. No one had ever been arrested for the crime.

"Was she mutilated postmortem?" James asked.

"She wasn't, no," Tan said.

"Still."

"Right, still."

"What are you thinking right now? They killed women together?"

"That's what it looks like," Tan said. "Henry and Corbin meet in London and kill Claire Brennan together. They take pictures, then maybe do it again here in America. First Linda Alcheri, and then Rachael Chess."

"Corbin Dell was out of the country when Rachael Chess was killed," James said.

"Corbin Dell is supposed to be out of the country at this very moment, according to flight records."

"Okay. Point taken. Then what? They kill Audrey Marshall together, and then Corbin Dell returns here so that they can kill his cousin? It doesn't make a lot of sense."

"No, I know. It doesn't," Tan said. "We're hoping Kate Priddy can help out."

"She told me what happened on that night. According to her, Corbin was suddenly in her apartment. He woke her up and told her to hide in a closet, that a bad man was there. Those were his words. When she came out, Corbin was bleeding out on the floor and she was attacked from behind."

"Then you showed up," Tan said.

"Yes, then I showed up."

After Kate woke, Agent Unger, with some assistance from Agent Tan, questioned Kate Priddy for about twenty-five minutes. She told them exactly what she'd told James before. Nothing more, nothing less. At the end of the conversation, when Kate's eyes were starting to close, she said: "It's me, I guess."

"What's you?" Agent Unger said.

"It's my fault. They come to me, psychopaths. I'm like a magnet."

"I don't know everything right now, Kate, but I do know that none of this is your fault. None of this." James decided that she liked Agent Unger, despite the flat-top haircut and what had to be a pretty serious gym addiction.

Back outside in the hall, Unger asked James what Kate had been talking about.

"She was attacked about five years ago by an ex-boyfriend. This was in England. He locked her in a closet and committed suicide, leaving her there."

"Goodness." Unger drew the word out, made it sound like a curse.

"Yeah."

"But there's no connection?"

"Not that we could find," James said. "I think it's just random, or maybe she is a psycho magnet, like she said."

399

She'd said it as a joke, but Unger frowned, as though he was considering it. "Either way, poor thing," he said, then added: "Are you going to tell her that it looks like Henry Wood had been hiding in her apartment for at least two days?"

James had already thought about this. The crime scene officers had found fingerprint evidence from Henry Wood all over the apartment: on food in the kitchen, in most of the rooms, on Kate's possessions. They'd also found hair and DNA evidence that suggested he'd been sleeping underneath one of the beds in a guest room.

James, remembering Kate's request that she be told everything, said, "Yeah, I'll tell her."

*

When Kate's parents finally reached the hospital, it was just past visiting hours, but James escorted them past a uniformed officer into a private room, where Kate lay sleeping.

They watched her sleep for half an hour, not willing to wake her. "Let's go check into the hotel, then come back," Patrick Priddy said in a whisper to his wife.

"You check us in, darling, and I'll stay here."

But before Kate's father had left, Kate opened her eyes, saw both her parents, and for the first time since she'd been admitted to the hospital, began to cry.

*

Corbin Dell was officially identified by his brother, Philip Dell, who had driven down from New Essex to make the identification. Detective James hadn't met him, but she heard from the grief counselor who'd been present that he displayed no emotion whatsoever and kept insisting that he needed to return to his mother, who was not used to being left alone.

Philip Dell was questioned by the FBI. Abigail Tan told James that he'd never heard of a Henry Wood. When asked about his brother's semester abroad in London, Philip Dell said that he hadn't remembered his brother going to London at all. When asked about Rachael Chess, and Corbin Dell's relationship with her, Philip said that Corbin's sex life was no concern of his.

*

On the day that Kate Priddy was released from the hospital, she agreed to see Alan Cherney, who'd shown up that morning at the hospital the way he'd shown up every morning since Kate had been admitted. He entered Kate's room, pale and nervous and holding a bouquet of paperwhites. Kate was sitting up in bed, drawing in a new sketchbook that her parents had brought to her the day before. She'd already sketched four nurses and two doctors.

"Thank you for the flowers," Kate said as Alan handed them over. They were strong smelling, and Kate couldn't stop herself from making a face as she placed the vase on her side table.

"They smell terrible," Alan said. "Sorry."

"No, they don't. They smell better than this hospital room, anyway."

"I heard you were getting out today."

"That's what they tell me, but I'll believe it when it happens."

"What are you going to do?"

"My parents have a suite at a hotel around the corner, so I'll stay there tonight, I guess. Then I'll go home."

"You're not going to stay and finish your courses?"

Kate laughed. "No, I don't think so. Where would I even stay?"

"Well, you could stay with me, of course. It wouldn't be a problem. I'd like it . . ."

"Thanks, Alan, but I don't—"

"I totally understand. I just wanted you to know that there was an offer on the table. A real offer. I didn't expect you to say yes."

"What's it like there?"

"Where? At Bury Street?"

Kate nodded.

"It's insanity. For the first twenty-four hours they cordoned off the whole building because there were so many reporters. Now, it's just your whole wing, but there have been nonstop police officers coming in and out, and news vans parked outside almost all the time. You know I was arrested, right?"

"I know all about it. Roberta—Detective James—has

told me everything. Or at least she's told me that she's told me everything. She said that after you were arrested she came back to the apartment because of you—because of what you said."

"Honestly, that whole night is pretty blurry for me. I remember going to your apartment—sorry, again, about that—but I don't really remember what we talked about. Then I went home and fell asleep and next thing I knew the police were there, arresting me, and all I could think about was that you were in danger. I was sure of it."

"He'd been hiding in my apartment. When I was there."

"I know. That's what the papers are saying. It's terrifying."

"What else are the papers saying?"

"You heard about the unsolved murder in London?"

"Detective James told me about it. Was it them?"

"It looks like it. There was preserved DNA evidence at the crime site, so if it was them, then I guess the police will find out for sure. This is a massive story, you know that? There's bound to be a TV movie ramping up in production right now."

"I'm getting that feeling."

"Reporters have been contacting me with requests for exclusive interviews. I've been offered money."

"Oh yeah?" Kate said. "What are you going to do?"

"Nothing. I don't care about that. I'm worried about you."

"I think I'm going to be okay, honestly. Maybe I'm still in shock, but for some reason I'm not as traumatized or frightened as I should be. I should have died—I should have died twice, really—and here I am still alive. I know this sounds strange, but I feel lucky. Tell me more about what you're reading in the papers."

They talked for a while more, Alan filling her in on everything that had happened since the night that Corbin Dell and Henry Wood had both died. He even told her how his ex-girlfriend Quinn had gotten in touch, wanting to know if he wanted to get a drink.

"You think she wants to get back together with you, now that you're famous?"

"I think she just wants to hear the details."

"You should take advantage of your fame. It's fleeting." Kate smiled, weakly.

The smile was enough to allow Alan to say what he wanted to say. He shifted forward a little on the molded plastic chair. "I have a speech," he said. "I apologize in advance."

"You don't have to make a speech," Kate said, but she was still smiling.

"I'm only going to make it once, then I'm done. It's short. I promise."

After the speech, Kate nodded and said she'd consider it. Alan thanked her and left the hospital room. At least he'd had his say. He'd told the truth, or close enough. Saying how much their night together had meant, how bad he felt about crashing into her apartment through the basement, and how he genuinely believed she should stay for a while in America and give their relationship a shot, was just a long way of saying what he really wanted to say. That even though they'd only just met, he knew he was in love with her.

*

Jim and Lina Wood drove eight hours from Stark, in upstate New York, to help identify their son. They were both surprised that they weren't brought into a basement morgue, Henry's body under a sheet, his face revealed. It was the way they'd seen it done on countless television shows, and they assumed it was the way it was done in real life. Instead, they were brought to a sterile, well-lit office, where they were shown photographs of Henry's face, surrounded by what looked like a blue sheet. It was their son, of course. Neither was surprised.

Jim had wanted to turn around and drive all the way back to Stark, but Lina talked her husband into spending the night. They found a Super 8 just west of the city. It was across the street from a diner that looked like it might be okay for dinner. Jim wouldn't admit it, but his driving skills, especially at night, were not what they used to be.

After dinner, they returned to the motel. Jim found a baseball game on the television. They hadn't talked about Henry. They'd talked about him plenty when he'd been younger. They'd prayed about him, too. That it had ended as it did was neither a shock nor a comfort to either of them. It was just a fact. Something had been wrong with him, and now he was in God's hands. It was terrible that they were saying he had killed those women, but at least now he couldn't kill anyone else.

Jim fell asleep with the game still on, and Lina turned the television off. Jim's breathing was labored and raspy. She was worried, but figured he'd be okay for one night without his apnea mask.

Before falling asleep herself, she allowed herself one selfish moment, one moment of remembering Henry when he had been an infant, just five or six months old. She used to put him on her thighs while she sat on the couch, hold his tiny chest in her hand, and gently shake it, and Henry would laugh and laugh, staring up into her eyes.

Then she let the memory go, and told herself she could never think of it again.

Chapter 38

"I've decided I want to stay here, just for a short while." Kate said these words on her second night at the large hotel near to the hospital. She was eating dinner with her parents at the restaurant called Foliage, the one restaurant of the three in the hotel that wasn't squarely aimed at the business traveler with a hefty expense account.

"Why?" her mother said, a quivering spoonful of crème brûlée halfway to her lips.

"Where?" her father asked.

"Just for a little while. I can't explain it. I might take the ferry over to Provincetown and spend a couple of nights alone. I haven't been—"

"We could all go, darling," her mother said.

"No, I want to do this alone. I think if I go straight back to England, and back with you to your house, that I'll never leave again. It's just for a few days."

To Kate's surprise, her parents agreed without putting up too much of a fight. They went with Kate to the concierge and found information on taking the ferry directly from Boston Harbor to Provincetown, on the tip of Cape Cod. The concierge offered to book Kate a hotel room for when she got there, but she insisted that she'd find her own place to stay. Kate's parents offered to book a return ticket to London, but Kate told them she'd book it herself when she was ready to come home.

"Not too long, okay, darling?" her mother said.

"Your grandparents are not going to believe we've let you stay here after what happened," her father said.

"Tell them I'm a grown woman, and I'll be back soon."

Kate's parents put her on the ferry on the afternoon of their return flight to England. Before leaving, Kate called Detective James from the hotel and told her where she was going to be, in case they needed to further question her. She doubted it, though. And there wasn't going to be a trial. Corbin Dell and Henry Wood had died together.

"Provincetown is nice," the detective said.

"I heard it was."

"Take care of yourself, Kate. You've been through a significant trauma."

"Story of my life," Kate said.

The midsized ferry chugged out of Boston Harbor toward the expanse of the Atlantic Ocean, sparkling under a cloudless sky. Kate stood on the front deck for the entire ninety minutes, her face tilted toward the sun, occasionally closing her eyes. She didn't really know what she was doing. She only knew that she didn't want to return home to the coddling of her parents, to questions from relatives and friends, or worse, silence. And she couldn't return to the apartment on Bury Street. And she still hadn't made a decision about Alan Cherney, even though he'd been right when he told her in the hospital that there was something special about their one night together. There had been. She had felt it. But she had also felt that enormous fear upon waking, the terror of putting your life and happiness in someone else's hands.

Kate spotted the long spit of Cape Cod, shimmering along the horizon. Then she could make out a tall stone monument and a water tower looming above a town packed tightly with houses. The ferry moved through Provincetown Harbor, studded with moored boats, and tied up at a concrete pier. She walked down the rickety gangway and onto solid ground, slightly nauseous from the boat trip but happy, suddenly, to be somewhere new. To be a stranger.

She got a fried clam roll at the first place she hit coming off the ferry, sitting outside at a wooden picnic table even though the air was cool. It was before the season, she knew, the calendar having just flipped from April to May, but there were lots of people about. She knew Provincetown was famous for its heavily gay population, but the residents and visitors who walked past Kate during her lunch seemed as varied as any place she had ever been to. There were heavily muscled young men in couples and groups, families of tourists, two old women still dressed in their winter coats, both pushing bicycles, a fat man in a business suit smoking a cigar, a group of twenty-year-old women in rugby jerseys. After lunch, Kate wandered, finally checking into a guesthouse up Howland Street.

The Spartan room was perfect: painted wooden floors, four-poster bed, no television, and a narrow window with a view toward the water.

She stayed three days, taking long walks, reading several Barbara Pym novels that she'd found in a used bookstore in town, and eating most of her meals at the long curving bar of a Portuguese restaurant on the east side of town. The fear was still there. Walking home after dark, all the footsteps she heard were following her, and the shadows between houses were filled with murderers and rapists. During the day, Kate waited for some drunk driver to veer onto the narrow sidewalks of Commercial Street and crush the pedestrians. She watched the skies for storms that would rip the roofs off the salt-weathered houses. And she even watched for George Daniels, seeing him as she always did in the long-legged strides of distant strangers and in the haircuts of waiters. It was funny that it was still George who haunted her, now that he'd been joined by Corbin Dell and Henry Wood. She knew that Henry, or Jack, as she still thought of him, would show up in her dreams eventually with his twitchy body and his white teeth. It would be okay when he did. He couldn't hurt her anymore.

She wondered if Corbin would ever enter her nightmares. Even though she'd found out that there was strong evidence he was involved in at least two murders, the college girl in London and the woman from Hartford, Connecticut, Detective James had told her that they were now positive Corbin had not been involved in Audrey Marshall's death.

He had come back from London to save her. Whatever he once had been, he'd changed, hadn't he?

Packing up to leave Provincetown, a slip of paper fell out from between two sweaters that Kate hadn't worn on her trip. It was a note from her mom:

> Darling, letting you out of our sights and not bringing you back home with us has been the hardest thing I've had to do, but Daddy insists you're okay, and I tend to agree. I want you to know how proud we are of you. We know that life isn't easy for you at the best of times, and you've weathered the worst. Twice. I've always been a little fretful myself, but I'm not worried about you now. You are going to be fine. We'll see you at home soon. Love you, darling, Mummy

Kate read the note several times, then placed it within the pages of the book she was reading.

It was early evening when she got back to Boston. It was warmer in the city than it had been on the Cape, but the skies were half filled with clouds, the air heavy with the possibility of rain. She took a taxi from the harbor to Bury Street, expecting the driver to make some comment about what had happened in the building, but he didn't. He merely helped her with her bag and left her on the sidewalk in the approaching dusk. The apartment building looked unchanged. There was no police tape, no news vans. The only thing she noticed was a young couple slowing down as they passed the building, the woman pointing toward the windows of Corbin Dell's apartment.

Kate entered the lobby, surprised to see the doorman named Bob at the station, since he didn't usually work evenings. He was more surprised to see her.

"Hello, miss," he said. "Nice to see you."

"Hi, Bob. I'm actually here to visit Alan Cherney. Do you know if he's in?"

"I'll check for you." He picked up his handset, and after a brief conversation, sent Kate up the stairs toward Alan's wing.

She had no plans, beyond wanting to see him again. Heart beating, Kate Priddy walked to Alan Cherney's door. It was open and he was standing there, a nervous grin on his face. She put down her luggage and stepped into the small circle of his waiting arms.

also by Peter Swanson

The Kind Worth Killing

'Nerve-shredding.' *Sunday Mirror*

'*Gone Girl* on speed.' Daisy Goodwin

THE *SUNDAY TIMES* TOP TEN BESTSELLER

When his flight gets delayed, Ted Severson meets Lily, a magnetic stranger, in the airport bar. In the netherworld of international travel and too many martinis, he confesses his darkest secrets, about his wife's infidelity and how he wishes her dead. Without missing a beat she offers to help him carry out the task . . .

'Extremely hard to put down.' Sophie Hannah

'Chilling and hypnotically suspenseful . . . an instant classic.' Lee Child

ff

The Girl With A Clock For A Heart

'Impossible not to read in one sitting.' *Observer*

'Takes your breath away . . . A plot that twists like a corkscrew.' *Daily Mail*

FIRST LOVE IS DEADLY . . .

What if your college sweetheart, the girl of your dreams, suddenly disappeared?

Twenty years later she's back, she's in trouble and she says you are the only one who can help her . . .

'A twisty, sexy, electric thrill ride.' Dennis Lehane

'A well-plotted, enjoyably twisty debut.' *Sunday Times*